Also by Stephen King from Warner Books

CUJO
DANSE MACABRE
THE DEAD ZONE
DIFFERENT SEASONS
FIRESTARTER
SKELETON CREW

KT-377-515

The Eyes of the Dragon

A STORY BY

Stephen King

WITH ILLUSTRATIONS BY

David Palladini

WARNER BOOKS

A *Warner* Book

First published in Great Britain in 1988
by Macdonald & Co (Publishers)
Published by Futura Publications in 1988
Reprinted 1991 (twice)
This edition published by Warner Books in 1992
Reprinted 1993 (twice), 1997

A CIP catalogue record for this book is
available from the British Library.

ISBN 0 7515 0457 2

Printed in England by Clays Ltd, St Ives plc

Warner Books
A Division of
Little, Brown and Company (UK)
Brettenham House
Lancaster Place
London WC2E 7EN

This story is for my great friend BEN STRAUB, and for my daughter, NAOMI KING.

nce, in a kingdom called Delain, there was a King with two sons. Delain was a very old kingdom and it had had hundreds of Kings, perhaps even thousands; when time goes on long enough, not even historians can remember everything. Roland the Good was neither the best nor the worst King ever to rule the land. He tried very hard not to do anyone great evil and mostly succeeded. He also tried very hard to do great works, but, unfortunately, he didn't succeed so well at that. The result was a very mediocre King; he doubted if he would be remembered long after he was dead. And his death might come at any time now, because he had grown old, and his heart was failing. He had perhaps one year left, perhaps three. Everyone who knew him, and everyone who observed his grey face and shaking hands when he held court, agreed that in five years at the very most a new King would be crowned in the great plaza at the foot of the Needle . . . and it would only be five years with God's grace. So everyone in the Kingdom, from the richest baron and the most foppishly dressed courtier to the poorest serf and his ragged wife, thought and talked about the King in waiting, Roland's elder son, Peter.

And one man thought and planned and brooded on something else: how to make sure that Roland's younger son, Thomas, should be crowned King instead. This man was Flagg, the King's magician.

Although Roland the King was old – he admitted to seventy years but was surely older than that – his sons were young. He had been allowed to marry late because he had met no woman who pleased his fancy, and because his mother, the great Dowager Queen of Delain, had seemed immortal to Roland and to everyone else – and that included her. She had ruled the Kingdom for almost fifty years when, one day at tea, she put a freshly cut lemon in her mouth to ease a troublesome cough that had been plaguing her for a week or better. At that particular teatime, a juggler had been performing for the amusement of the Dowager Queen and her court. He was juggling five cunningly made crystal balls. Just as the Queen put the slice of lemon into her mouth, the juggler dropped one of his glass spheres. It shattered on the tiled floor of the great East Courtroom with a loud report. The Dowager Queen gasped at the sound. When she gasped, she pulled the lemon slice down her throat and choked to death very quickly. Four days later, the coronation of Roland was held in the Plaza of the Needle. The juggler did not see it: he had been beheaded on the executioner's block behind the Needle three days before that.

A King without heirs makes everybody nervous, especially when the King is fifty and balding. It was thus in Roland's best interest to marry soon, and to make an heir soon. His close advisor, Flagg, made Roland very aware of this. He also pointed out that at fifty, the years left to him in which he could hope to create a child in a woman's belly were only a few. Flagg advised him to take a wife soon, and never mind waiting for a lady of noble birth who would take his fancy. If such a lady had not come into view by the time a man was fifty, Flagg pointed out, she probably never would.

Roland saw the wisdom of this and agreed, never knowing that Flagg, with his lank hair and his white face that was almost always hidden behind a hood, understood his deepest secret: that he had never met the woman of his fancy because he had never really fancied women at all. Women worried him. And he had never fancied the act that puts babies in the bellies of women. That act worried him, too.

But he saw the wisdom of the magician's advice, and six months after the Dowager Queen's funeral, there was a much happier event in the Kingdom –

the marriage of King Roland to Sasha, who would become the mother of Peter and Thomas.

Roland was neither loved nor hated in Delain. Sasha, however, was loved by all. When she died giving birth to the second son, the Kingdom was plunged into darkest mourning that lasted a year and a day. She had been one of six women Flagg had suggested to his King as possible brides. Roland had known none of these women, who were all similar in birth and station. They were all of noble blood but none of royal blood; all were meek and pleasant and quiet. Flagg suggested no one who might take his place as the mouth closest to the King's ear. Roland chose Sasha because she seemed the quietest and meekest of the half-dozen, and the least likely to frighten him. So they were wed. Sasha of the Western Barony (a very small barony indeed) was then seventeen years old, thirty-three years younger than her husband. She had never seen a man with his drawers off before her wedding night. When, on that occasion, she observed his flaccid penis, she asked with great interest: 'What's that, Husband?' If she had said anything else, or if she had said what she said in a slightly different tone of voice, the events of that night – and this entire history – might have taken another course; in spite of the special drink Flagg had given him an hour before, at the end of the wedding feast, Roland might simply have slunk away. But he saw her then exactly as she was – a very young girl who knew even less about the baby-making act that he did – and observed her mouth was kind, and began to love her, as everyone in Delain would grow to love her.

'It is King's Iron,' he said.

'It doesn't look like iron,' said Sasha, doubt-fully.

'It is before the forge,' he said.

'Ah!' said she. 'And where is the forge?'

'If you will trust me,' said he, getting into bed with her, 'I will show you, for you have brought it from the Western Barony with you but did not know it.'

3

The people of Delain loved her because she was kind and good. It was Queen Sasha who created the Great Hospital, Queen Sasha who wept so over the cruelty of the bearbaiting in the Plaza that King Roland finally outlawed the practice, Queen Sasha who pleaded for a Remission of King's Taxes in the year of the great drought, when even the leaves of the Great Old Tree went grey. Did Flagg plot against her, you might ask? Not at first. These were relatively small things in his view, because he was a real magician, and lived hundreds and hundreds of years.

He even allowed the Remission of Taxes to pass, because the year before, Delain's navy had smashed the Anduan pirates, who had plagued the Kingdom's southern coast for over a hundred years. The skull of the Anduan pirate-king grinned from a spike outside the palace walls and Delain's treasury was rich with recovered plunder. In larger matters, matter of state, it was still Flagg's mouth which was closest to King Roland's ear, and so Flagg was at first content.

Although Roland grew to love his wife, he never grew to love the activity which most men consider sweet, the act which produces both the lowliest cook's 'prentice and the heir to the highest throne. He and Sasha slept in separate bedrooms, and he did not visit her often. These visits would happen no more than five or six times in a year, and on some of those occasions no iron could be made at the forge, in spite of Flagg's ever more potent drinks and Sasha's unfailing sweetness.

But, four years after the marriage, Peter was made in her bed. And on the one night, Roland had no need of Flagg's drink which was green and foaming and which always made him feel a little strange in his head, as if he had gone crazy. He had been hunting that day in the Preserves with twelve of his men. Hunting was the thing that Roland had always loved most of all – the smell of the forest, the crisp tang of the air, the sound of the horn, and the feel of the bow as an arrow left on a true, hard course. Gunpowder was known but rare in Delain, and to hunt game with an iron tube was considered low and contemptible in any case.

Sasha was reading in bed when he came to her, his ruddy, bearded face alight, but she laid her book on her bosom and listened raptly to his story as he told it, his hands moving. Near the end, he drew back to show her how he had drawn back the bow and had let Foe-Hammer, his father's great arrow, fly across the little glen. When he did this, she laughed and clapped and won his heart.

The King's Preserves had almost been hunted out. In these modern days it was rare to find so much as a good-sized deer in them, and no one had seen a dragon since time out of mind. Most men would have laughed if you had suggested there might still be such a mythy creature left in that tame forest. But an hour before sundown on that day, as Roland and his party were about to turn back, that was just what they found . . . or what found them.

The dragon came crashing and blundering out of the underbrush, its scales glowing a greenish copper colour, its soot-caked nostrils venting smoke. It had not been a small dragon, either, but a male just before its first moulting. Most of the party were thunderstruck, unable to draw an arrow or even to move.

It stared at the hunting party, its normally green eyes went yellow, and it fluttered its wings. There was no danger that it could fly away from them – its wings would not be well developed enough to support it in the air for at least another fifty years and two more moultings – but the baby-webbing which holds the wings against a dragon's body until its tenth or twelfth year had fallen away, and a single flutter stirred enough wind to topple the head huntsman backward out of his saddle, his horn flying from his hand.

Roland was the only one not stunned to utter movelessness, and although he was too modest to say so to Sasha, there was real heroism in his next few actions, as well as a sportsman's zest for the kill. The dragon might well have roasted most of the surprised party alive, if not for Roland's prompt action. He gigged his horse forward five steps, and nocked his great arrow. He drew and fired. The arrow went straight to the mark — that one gill-like soft spot under the dragon's throat, where it takes in air to create fire. The worm fell dead with a final fiery gust, which set all the bushes around it alight. The squires put this out quickly, some with water, some with beer, and not a few with piss – and, now that I think of it, most of the piss was really beer, because when Roland went a-hunting, he took a great lot of beer with him, and he was not stingy with it, either.

The fire was out in five minutes, the dragon gutted in fifteen. You still could have boiled a kettle over its steaming nostrils when its tripes were let out upon the ground. The dripping nine-chambered heart was carried to Roland with great ceremony. He ate it raw, as was the custom, and found it delicious. He only regretted the sad knowledge that he would almost certainly never have another.

Perhaps it was the dragon's heart that made him so strong that night. Perhaps it was only his joy in the hunt, and in knowing he had acted quickly and coolheadedly when all the others were sitting

stunned in their saddles (except, of course, for the head huntsman, who had been lying stunned on his back). For whatever reason, when Sasha clapped her hands and cried, 'Well done, my brave Husband!,' he fairly leaped into her bed. Sasha greeted him with open eyes and a smile that reflected his own triumph. That night was the first and only time Roland enjoyed his wife's embrace in sobriety. Nine months later – one month for each chamber of the dragon's heart – Peter was born in that same bed, and the Kingdom rejoiced – there was an heir to the throne.

5

You probably think – if you have bothered to think about it at all – that Roland must have stopped taking Flagg's strange green drink after the birth of Peter. Not so. He still took it occasionally. This was because he loved Sasha, and wanted to please her. In some places, people assume that only men enjoy sex, and that a woman would be grateful to be left alone. The people of Delain, however, held no such peculiar ideas – they assumed that a woman took normal pleasure in that act which produced earth's most pleasurable creatures. Roland knew he was not properly attentive to his wife in this matter, but he resolved to be as attentive as he could, even if this meant taking Flagg's drink. Only Flagg himself knew how rarely the King went to his Queen's bed.

Some four years after the birth of Peter, on New Year's Day a great blizzard visited Delain. It was the greatest, save one, in living memory – the other I'll tell you of later.

Heeding an impulse he could not explain even to himself, Flagg mixed the King a draught of double strength – perhaps it was something in the wind that urged him to do it. Ordinarily, Roland would have made a grimace at the awful taste and perhaps put it aside, but the excitement of the storm had caused the annual New Year's Day party to be especially gay, and Roland had become very drunk. The blazing fire on the hearth reminded him of the dragon's final explosive breath, and he had toasted the head, which was mounted on the wall, many times. So he drank the green potion off at a single gulp, and an evil lust fell upon him. He left the dining hall at once and visited Sasha. In the course of trying to love her, he hurt her.

'Please, Husband,' she cried, sobbing.

'I'm sorry,' he mumbled. 'Huzzz . . .' He fell heavily asleep beside her and remained insensible for the next twenty hours. She never forgot the strange smell that had been on his breath that night. It had been a smell like rotten meat, a smell like death. Whatever, she wondered, had he been eating . . . or drinking?

Roland never touched Flagg's drink again, but Flagg was well satisfied, nevertheless. Nine months later, Sasha gave birth to Thomas, her second son. She died bringing him forth. Such things happened, of course, and while everyone was saddened, no one was really surprised. They believed they knew what had happened. But the only people in the Kingdom who really knew the circumstances of Sasha's death were Anna Crookbrows, the midwife, and Flagg, the King's magician. Flagg's patience with Sasha's meddling had finally run out.

Peter was only five when his mother died, but he remembered her dearly. He thought her sweet, tender, loving, full of mercy. But five is a young age, and most of his memories were not very specific. There was one clear memory which he held in his mind, however – it was of a reproach she had made to him. Much later, the memory of this reproach became vital to him. It had to do with his napkin.

Every first of Five-month, a feast was held at court to celebrate the spring plantings. In his fifth year, Peter was allowed to attend for the first time. Custom decreed that Roland should sit at the head of the table, the heir to the throne at his right hand, the Queen at the foot of the table. The practical result of this was that Peter would be out of her reach during the meal, and so Sasha coached him carefully beforehand on how he should behave. She wanted him to show up well, and to be mannerly. And, of course, she knew that during the meal he would be on his own, because his father had no idea of manners at all.

Some of you may wonder why the task of instructing Peter on his manners fell to Sasha. Did the boy not have a governess? (Yes, as a matter of fact he had two.) Were there no servants whose service was dedicated wholly to the little prince? (Battalions of them.) The trick was not to get these people to take care of Peter but to keep them away. Sasha wanted to raise him herself, at least as much as she could. She had very definite ideas about how her son should be raised. She loved him dearly and wanted to be with him for her own selfish reasons. But she also realized that she had a deep and solemn responsibility in the matter of Peter's nurture. This little boy would be King someday, and above all else, Sasha wanted him to be good. A good boy, she thought, would be a good King.

Great banquets in the King's Hall were not very neat affairs, and most nannies wouldn't have been very concerned about the little boy's table manners. *Why, he is to be the King!* they would have said, a little shocked at the idea that they should correct him in such piddling matters. *Who cares if he spills the gravy boat? Who cares if he dribbles on his ruff, or even wipes his hands on it? Did not King Alan in the old days sometimes vomit into his plate and then command his court jester to come nigh and 'drink this nice hot soup'? Did not King John often bite the heads of live trout and then put the flopping bodies into the bodices of the serving girl's dresses? Will not this banquet end up, as most banquets do, with the participants' throwing food across the table at each other?*

Undoubtedly it would, but by the time things degenerated to the food-throwing stage, she and Peter would long since have retired. What concerned

Sasha was that attitude of *who cares*. She thought it was the worst idea anyone could ever plant in the head of a little boy destined to be King.

So Sasha instructed Peter carefully, and she observed him carefully on the night of the banquet. And later, as he lay sleepy in his bed, she talked to him.

Because she was a good mother, she first complimented him lovingly on his behaviour and manners – and this was right, because for the most part they had been exemplary. But she knew that no one would correct him where he went wrong unless she did it herself, and she knew she must do it now, in these few years when he idolized her. So when she was finished complimenting him, she said:

'You did one thing wrong, Pete, and I never want to see you do it again.'

Peter lay in his bed, his dark blue eyes looking at her solemnly. 'What was that, Mother?'

'You didn't use your napkin,' said she. 'You left it folded by your plate, and it made me sorry to see it. You ate the roast chicken with your fingers, and that was fine, because that is how men do it. But when you put the chicken down again, you wiped your fingers on your shirt, and that is not right.'

'But Father . . . and Mr. Flagg . . . and the other nobles . . .'

'Bother Flagg, and bother all the nobles in Delain!' she cried with such force that Peter cringed back in his bed a little. He was afraid and ashamed for having made those roses bloom in her cheeks. 'What your father does is right, for he is the King, and what you do when you are King will always be right. But Flagg is not King, no matter how much he would like to be, and the nobles are not Kings, and you are not King yet, but only a little boy who forgot his manners.'

She saw he was afraid, and smiled. She laid her hand on his brow.

'Be calm, Peter,' she said. 'It is a small thing, but still important – because you'll be King in your own time. Now run and fetch your slate.'

'But it's bedtime –'

'Bother bedtime, too. Bedtime can wait. Bring your slate.'

Peter ran for his slate.

Sasha took the chalk tied to the side and carefully printed three letters. 'Can you read this word, Peter?'

Peter nodded. There were only a few words that he could read, although he knew most of the Great Letters. This happened to be one of the words. 'It says GOD.'

'Yes, that's right. Now write it backward and see what you find.'

'Backward?' Peter said doubtfully.

'Yes, that's right.'

Peter did so, his letters staggering childishly across the slate below his mother's neat printing. He was astounded to find another of the few words he could read.

'DOG! Mamma! It says DOG!'

'Yes. It says dog.' The sadness in her voice quenched Peter's excitement at once. His mother pointed from GOD to DOG. 'These are the two natures of man,' she said. 'Never forget them, because someday

you will be King and Kings grow to be great and tall
– as great and tall as dragons in their ninth moultings.'

'Father isn't great and tall,' objected Peter.
Roland was, in fact, short and rather bowlegged.
Also, he carried a great belly in front of him from all
the beer and mead he had consumed.

Sasha smiled.

'He is, though. Kings grow *invisibly*, Peter, and
it happens all at once, as soon as they grasp the sceptre
and the crown is put on their heads in the Plaza of
the Needle?'

'They do?' Peter's eyes grew large and round.
He thought that the subject had wandered far from
his failure to use his napkin at the banquet, but he
was not sorry to see such an embarrassing topic lost
in favour of this tremendously interesting one.
Besides, he had already resolved that he would never
forget to use his napkin again – if it was important
to his mother, then it was important to him.

'Oh yes, they do. Kings grow most *awfully* big,
and that's why they have to be specially careful, for
a very big person could crush smaller ones under his
feet just taking a walk, or turning around, or sitting
down quickly in the wrong place. Bad Kings do such
things often. I think even good Kings cannot avoid
doing them sometimes.'

'I don't think I understand –'

'Then listen a moment longer.' She tapped the
slate again. 'Our preachers say that our natures are
partly of God and partly of Old Man Splitfoot. Do
you know who Old Man Splitfoot is, Peter?'

'He's the devil.'

'Yes. But there are few devils outside of made-up stories, Pete – most bad people are more like dogs than devils. Dogs are friendly but stupid, and that's the way most men and women are when they are drunk. When dogs are excited and confused, they may bite; when men are excited and confused, they may fight. Dogs are great pets because they are loyal, but if a pet is all a man is, he is a bad man, I think. Dogs can be brave, but they may also be cowards that will howl in the dark or run away from danger with their tails between their legs. A dog is just as eager to lick the hand of a bad master as he is to lick the hand of a good one, because dogs don't know the difference between good and bad. A dog will eat slops, vomit up the part his stomach can't stand, and then go back for more.'

She fell silent for a moment, perhaps thinking of what was going on in the banqueting hall right now – men and women roaring with goodnatured drunken laughter, flinging food at each other, and sometimes turning aside to vomit casually on the floor beside their chairs. Roland was much the same, and sometimes this made her sad, but she did not hold it against him, nor did she tax him with it. It was his way. He might promise to reform in order to please her, and he might even do it, but he would not be the same man afterwards.

'Do you understand these things, Peter?'

Peter nodded.

'Fine! Now, tell me.' She leaned toward him. 'Does a dog use a napkin?'

Humbled and ashamed, Peter looked down at the counterpane and shook his head. Apparently the conversation hadn't wandered as far as he had thought. Perhaps because the evening had been very full and because he was now very tired, tears rose in his eyes and spilled down his cheeks. He struggled against the sobs that wanted to come. He locked them in his chest. Sasha saw this and admired it.

'Don't cry over an unused napkin, my love,' said Sasha, 'for that was not my intention.' She rose, her full and pregant belly before her. The delivery of Thomas was now very near. 'Your behaviour was otherwise exemplary. Any mother in the Kingdom would have been proud of a young son who behaved himself half so well, and my heart is full with admiration for you. I am the mother of a prince. That is sometimes hard, but it cannot be changed, and i' truth, I would not change it if I could. But remember that someday lives will depend on your every waking motion; lives may even depend on dreams which come to you in sleep. Lives may not depend on whether or not you use your napkin after the roast chicken . . . but they may. They may. Lives have depended on less, at times. All I ask is that in everything you do, you try to remember the civilized side of your nature. The good side – the God side. Will you promise to do that, Peter?'

'I promise.'

'Then all is well.' She kissed him lightly. 'Luckily, I am young and you are young. We will talk of these things more, when you have more understanding.'

They never did, but Peter never forgot the lesson: he always used his napkin, even when those around him did not.

So Sasha died.

She has little more part in this story, yet there is one further thing about her you should know: she had a doll's house. This doll's house was very large and very fine, almost a castle in miniature. When the time of her marriage came round, Sasha mustered as much cheer as she could, but she was sad to be leaving everyone and everything at the great house in the Western Barony where she had grown up – and she was a little bit nervous, too. She told her mother, 'I have never been married before and do not know if I shall like it.'

But of all the childish things she left behind, the one she regretted most was the doll's house she had had ever since she was a little girl.

Roland, who was a kind man, somehow discovered this, and although he was also nervous about his future life (after all, he had never been married before, either), he found time to commission Quentin Ellender, the greatest craftsman in the land, to build his new wife a new doll's house. 'I want it to be the finest doll's house a young lady ever had,' he told Ellender. 'I want her to look at it once and forget about her old doll's house forever.'

As you'll no doubt realize, if Roland really meant this, it was a foolish thing to say. No one ever forgets a toy that made him or her supremely happy as a child, even if that toy is replaced by one like it that is much nicer. Sasha never forgot her old doll's house, but she was quite impressed with the new one. Anyone who was not a total idiot would have been. Those who saw it declared it was Quentin Ellender's best work, and it may have been.

It was a country house in miniature, very like the one Sasha had lived in with her parents in rolling Western Barony. Everything in it was small, but so cunningly made you would swear it must really work . . . and most things in it did!

The stove, for instance, really got hot and would even cook tiny portions of food. If you put a piece of hard coal no bigger than a matchbox in it, it would burn all day . . . and if you reached into the kitchen with your clumsy big-person's finger and happened to touch the stove while the coal was burning, it would give you a burn for your pains. There were no faucets and no flushing toilets, because the Kingdom of Delain did not know about such things – and doesn't even to this day – but if you were very careful, you could pump water from a hand pump that stood not much taller than your pinkie finger. There was a sewing room with a spinning wheel that really spun and a loom that really wove. The spinet in the parlour would really play, if you touched the keys with a toothpick, and the tone was true. People who saw this said it was a miracle, and surely Flagg must have been involved somehow. When Flagg heard such stories, he only smiled and said nothing. He had not been involved in the doll's house at all – he thought it a silly project, in truth – but he also knew it was not always necessary to make claims and tell people how wonderful you were to achieve greatness. Sometimes all you had to do was look wise and keep your mouth shut.

In Sasha's doll's house were real Kashamin rugs, real velvet curtains, real china plates; the cold cabinet really kept things cold. The wainscoting in the receiving parlour and the front hall was of cherished ironwood. There was glass in all the windows and a many-coloured fanlight over the wide front doors.

All in all it was the jolliest doll's house any child ever dreamed of. Sasha clapped her hands over it with real delight at the wedding party when it was unveiled, and thanked her husband for it. Later she went to Ellender's workshop and not only thanked him but curtsied deeply before him, an act that was almost unheard of – in that day and age, Queens did not curtsy to mere artisans. Roland was pleased and Ellender, whose sight had failed noticeably in the course of the project, was deeply touched.

But it did not make her forget her old dear doll's house at home, as ordinary as it seemed when compared with this one, and she did not spend as many rainy afternoons playing with it – rearranging the furniture, lighting the stove and watching the chimneys smoke, pretending that there was a high tea going on or that there was to be a great dinner party for the Queen – as she had before, even as an older girl of fifteen and sixteen. One of the reasons was very simple. There was no fun making ready for a pretend party at which the Queen would be in attendance when she was the Queen. And maybe that one reason was really all the reasons. She was a grown-up now, and she discovered that being a grown-up was not quite what she had suspected it would be when she was a child. She had thought then that she would make a conscious decision one day to simply put her toys and games and little make-believes away. Now she discovered that was not what happened at all. Instead, she discovered, interest simply faded. It became less and less and less, until a dust of years drew over the bright pleasures of childhood, and they were forgotten.

8

Peter, a little boy who would someday be King, had dozens of toys – no, if I am to tell you the truth, he had *thousands* of toys. He had hundreds of lead soldiers with which he fought great battles, and dozens of play horses. He had games and balls and jacks and marbles. He had stilts that made him five feet high. He had a magical spring-stick on which he could bounce, and all the drawing paper he wanted in a time when paper was extremely hard to make and only wealthy people could afford to have it.

But of all the toys in the castle, the one he loved the best was his mother's doll's house. He had never known the one in the Western Barony, and so to him that was the doll's house of doll's houses. He would sit before it for hours on end when the rain poured down outside, or when the winter wind shrieked out of a blue throat filled with snow. When he fell ill with Children's Tattoo (a disease which we call chicken pox), he had a servant bring it to him on a special table that went over his bed and played with it almost ceaselessly until he was well.

He loved to imagine the tiny people that would fill the house; sometimes they were almost so real he could see them. He talked for them in different voices and invented them all. They were the King family. There was Roger King, who was brave and powerful (if not very tall, and slightly bowlegged), and who had once killed a dragon. There was lovely Sarah King, his wife. And there was their little boy, Petie, who loved and was loved by them. Not to mention, of course, all the servants he invented to make the beds, stoke the stove, fetch the water, cook the meals, and mend the clothes.

Because he was a boy, some of the stories he made up to go with the house were a little more bloodthirsty than the stories Sasha had made up to go with hers as a little girl. In one of them, the Anduan pirates were all around the house, wanting to get in and slaughter the family. There was a famous fight. Dozens of pirates were killed, but in the end they were too many. They made to attack for the final time. But just before they did, the King's Own Guard – this part was played by Peter's lead soldiers – arrived and killed every one of those rotten Anduan sea-dogs. In another story, a nest of dragons burst out of a nearby wood (usually the nearby wood was under Sasha's sofa by the window), meaning to burn up the house with their furious breath. But Roger and Petie rushed out with their bows and killed every one. 'Until the ground was black with their icky old blood,' Peter told his father the King that night at dinner, and this made Roland roar with approval.

After Sasha died, Flagg told Roland that he did not believe it was right for a boy to be playing with doll's houses. It might not make him a sissy, Flagg said, but then again, it might. Certainly it would not sound well, if the tale got out to the general population. And such stories always did. The castle was full of servants. Servants saw everything, and their tongues wagged.

'He's only six,' Roland said, uneasy. Flagg, with his white, hungry face far back in his deep hood and his magical spells, always made him uneasy.

'Six is old enough to train a boy in the way he should go, Sire,' Flagg said. 'Think you well on it. Your judgment will be right in this, as in all things.'

Think you well on it, Flagg said, and that was just what King Roland did. In fact, I should think it fair to say that he never thought on anything so hard during his entire twenty-some-year reign as King of Delain.

That probably sounds strange to you, if you have thought of all the duties a King has – weighty matters such as putting taxes on some things or ending them on others, whether or not to declare war, whether to pardon or condemn. What, you might say, was a decision over whether or not to allow a little boy to play with a doll's house next to those other things?

Maybe nothing, maybe much. I will let you make up your mind on that. I *will* tell you that Roland was not the smartest King who had ever ruled in Delain. Thinking well had always been very hard work for him. It made him feel as if boulders were rolling around in his head. It made his eyes water and his temples throb. When he thought deeply, his nose got stuffed up.

As a boy, his studies in composition and mathematics and history had made his head ache so badly that he had been allowed to give them up at twelve and do what he did best, which was to hunt. He tried very hard to be a good King, but he had a feeling that he could never be good enough, or smart enough, to solve the Kingdom's problems or to make many decisions the right way, and he knew if he made them the wrong way, people would suffer for it. If he had heard Sasha telling Peter about Kings after the banquet, he would have agreed completely. Kings really *were* bigger than other people, and sometimes – a lot of times – he wished he were smaller. If you have ever in your life had serious questions about whether or not you were good enough for some task, then you will know how he felt. What you may not know is that such worries start to feed on themselves after awhile. Even if that feeling that you aren't good enough to get the job done isn't true at first, it can become true in time. This had happened to Roland, and over the years he had come to rely more and more on Flagg. He was sometimes troubled by the idea that Flagg was King in all but name – but these worries came only late at night. In the daytime he was only grateful for Flagg's support.

If not for Sasha, Roland might have been a much worse King than he really was, and that was because the little voice he sometimes heard in the night when he couldn't sleep held much more of the truth than his daytime gratitudes. Flagg really *was* running the Kingdom, and Flagg was a very bad man. We will have to speak more of him later, unfortunately, but we'll let him go for now, and good riddance.

Sasha had broken Flagg's power over Roland a little. Her own advice was good and practical, and it was much more kind and just than the magician's. She never really liked Flagg – few in Delain did, and many shuddered at his very name – but her dislike was mild. Her feelings might have been much different if she had known how carefully Flagg watched her, and with what growing, poisonous hate.

9

Once Flagg really *did* set out to poison Sasha. This was after she asked Roland to pardon a pair of army deserters whom Flagg had wanted beheaded in the Plaza of the Needle. Deserters, he had argued, were a bad example. If one or two were allowed to get away without paying the full penalty, others might try it. The only way to discourage them, he said, was to show them the heads of those who had already tried it. Other would-be deserters would look at those flyblown heads with their staring eyes and think twice about the seriousness of their service to the King.

Sasha, however, had discovered facts about the case from one of her maids that Roland didn't know.

The mother of the older boy had fallen gravely ill. There were three younger brothers and two younger sisters in the family. All might have died in the bitter cold of the Delain winter if the boy hadn't left his encampment, gone home, and chopped wood for his mother. The younger boy had gone because he was the older's best friend, and his sworn blood brother. Without the younger boy, it might have taken two weeks to chop enough wood to keep the family through the winter. With both of them working at top speed, it had taken only six days.

This was putting it in a different light. Roland had loved his own mother very much, and would gladly have died for her. He made inquiries and found out that Sasha had the right of the story. He also found out that the deserters had left only after a sadistic sergeant major had repeatedly refused to relay their requests for compassionate leave to their superior, and that as soon as four cords of wood had been chopped, they had gone back, although both had known they must be court-martialled and face the headsman's axe.

Roland pardoned them. Flagg nodded, smiled, and said only: 'Your will is Delain's will, Sire.' Not for all the gold in the Four Kingdoms would he have allowed Roland to see the sick fury that rose in his heart when his will was balked. Roland's pardon of the boys was greatly praised in Delain, because many of Roland's subjects also knew the true facts and those who didn't know them were quickly informed by the rest. Roland's wise and compassionate pardon of the two was remembered when other, less humane decrees (which were, as a rule, also the magician's

ideas) were imposed. All of this made no difference
to Flagg. He had wanted him killed, and Sasha had
interfered. Why could Roland not have married
another? He had known none of them, and cared for
women not at all. Why not another? Well, it didn'
matter. Flagg smiled at the pardon, but he swore in
his heart then that he would attend Sasha's funeral.

On the night Roland signed the pardon, Flagg
went to his gloomy basement laboratory. There he
donned a heavy glove and took a deathwatch spider
from a cage where he had kept her for twenty years,
feeding her newborn baby mice. Each of the mice he
fed the spider was poisoned and dying; Flagg did this
to increase the potency of the spider's own poison,
which was already potent beyond belief. The spider
was blood red and as big as a rat. Her bloated body
quivered with venom; verom dripped from her
stinger in clear drops that burned smoking holes in
the top of Flagg's worktable.

'Now die, my pretty, and kill a Queen,' Flagg
whispered, and crushed the spider to death in his
glove, which was made of a magical steel mesh
which resisted the poison – yet still that night, when
he went to bed, his hand was swollen and throbbing
and red.

Poison from the spider's crushed, twisted body
gushed into the goblet. Flagg poured brandy over
the deadly stuff, then stirred the two together. When
he took the spoon from the glass, its bowl was
twisted and misshapen. The Queen would take one
sip and fall dying on the floor. Her death would be
quick but extremely painful, Flagg thought with satisfaction.

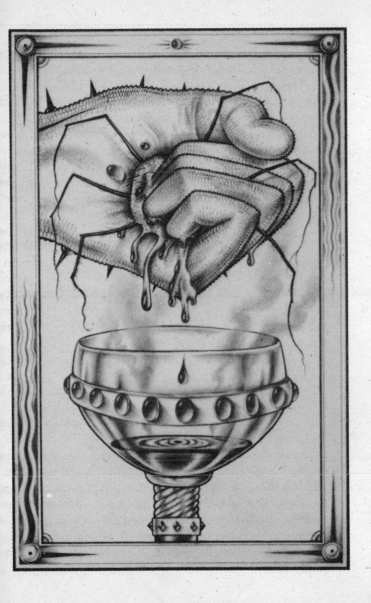

Sasha was in the habit of taking a glass of brandy each night, because she often had trouble falling asleep. Flagg rang for a servant to come and take the drink to her.

Sasha never knew how close she came to death that night.

Moments after brewing the deadly drink, before the servant knocked, Flagg poured it down the drain in the centre of his floor and stood listening to it hiss and bubble away into the pipe. His face was twisted with hate. When the hissing had died away, he flung the crystal goblet into the far corner with all his force. It shattered like a bomb.

The servant knocked and was admitted.

Flagg pointed to where the shards glittered. 'I've broken a goblet,' he said. 'Clean it up. Use a broom, idiot. If you touch the pieces, you'll regret it.'

10

He poured the poison down the drain at the last moment because he realized he might well be caught. If Roland had loved the young Queen just a little less, Flagg would have chanced it. But he was afraid that Roland, in his wounded fury at the loss of his wife, would never rest until he found the killer and saw his head on the spike at the very tip of the Needle. It was the one crime he would see avenged, no matter who had committed it. And would he find the murderer?

Flagg thought he might.

Hunting, after all, was the thing Roland did best.

So Sasha escaped – that time – protected by Flagg's fear and her husband's love. And in the meantime, Flagg still had the King's ear in most matters.

Concerning the doll's house, however – in that matter, you could say Sasha won, even though Flagg had by then succeeded in ridding himself of her.

11

Not long after Flagg made his disparaging comments about doll's houses and royal sissies, Roland crept into the dead Queen's morning room unseen and watched his son at play. The King stood just inside the door, his brow deeply furrowed. He was thinking much harder than he was used to thinking, and that meant the boulders were rolling around in his head and his nose was stuffy.

He saw that Peter was using the doll's house to tell himself stories, to make believe, and that the stories he made up were not sissy stories at all. They were stories of blood and thunder and armies and dragons. They were, in other words, stories after the King's own heart. He discovered in himself a wistful desire to join his son, to help him make up even better tales in which the doll's house and all its fascinating contents and its make-believe family figured. Most of all, he saw that Peter was using Sasha's doll's house to keep Sasha alive in his heart, and Roland approved of this most of all, because he missed his wife sorely. Sometimes he was so lonely he almost cried. Kings, of course, do not cry . . . and if, on one or two occasions after Sasha had died, he awoke with the case on his pillow damp, what of that?

The King left the room as silently as he had come. Peter never saw him. Roland lay awake most of that night, thinking deeply about what he had seen, and although it was hard for him to endure Flagg's disapproval, he saw him the next morning in a private audience, before his resolve could weaken, and told him he had thought the matter over carefully and decided Peter should be allowed to play with the doll's house as long as he wished. He said he believed it was doing the boy no harm.

With that out, he settled back uneasily to wait for Flagg's rebuttal. But no rebuttal came. Flagg only raised his eyebrows – this Roland barely saw in the deep shadow of the hood Flagg always wore – and said, 'Your will, Sire, is the will of the Kingdom.'

Roland knew from the tone that Flagg thought his decision was a bad one, but the tone also told him Flagg would not dispute it further. He was deeply relieved to be let off so cheaply. Later that day, when Flagg suggested that the farmers of the Eastern Barony could stand higher taxes in spite of the drought that had killed most of their crops the year before, Roland agreed eagerly.

In truth, having the old fool (for so Flagg

thought Roland to be in his deeper thoughts) go against his wishes in the matter of the doll's house seemed a very minor thing to the magician. The rise in taxes for the Eastern Barony was the important thing. And Flagg had a deeper secret, one which pleased him well. In the end he had succeeded in murdering Sasha, after all.

12

In those days, when a Queen or any woman of royal birth was taken to bed to deliver a child, a midwife was called in. The doctors were all men, and no man was allowed to be with a woman when she was about to have a child. The midwife who delivered Peter was Anna Crookbrows, of the Third South'ard Alley. She was called again when Sasha's time with Thomas came around. Anna was past fifty at the time when Sasha's second labour began, and a widow. She had one son of her own, and in his twentieth year he contracted the Shaking Disease, which always killed its victims in terrible pain after some years of suffering.

She loved this boy very much, and at last, after every other idea had proved useless, she went to Flagg. This had been ten years before, neither prince yet born and Roland himself still a royal bachelor. He received her in his dank basement rooms, which were near the dungeons – during their interview the uneasy woman could sometimes hear the lost screams of those who had been locked away from the sun's light for years and years. And, she thought with a shudder, if the dungeons were near, then the torture chambers must also be near. Nor did Flagg's apartment itself make her feel any easier. Strange designs were drawn on the floor in many colours of chalk. When she blinked, the designs seemed to change. In a cage hung from a long black manacle, a two-headed parrot cawed and sometimes talked to itself, one head speaking, the other head answering. Musty books frowned down at her. Spiders spun in dark corners. From the laboratory came a mixture of strange chemical smells. Yet she stammered out her story somehow and then waited in an agony of suspense.

'I can cure your son,' he said finally.

Anna Crookbrow's ugly face was transformed into something near beauty by her joy. 'My Lord!' she gasped, and could think of no more, so she said it again. 'Oh, my Lord!'

But in the shadow of his hood, Flagg's white face remained distant and brooding, and she felt afraid again.

'What would you pay for such a miracle?' he asked.

'Anything,' she gasped, and meant it. 'Oh my Lord Flagg, anything!'

'I ask for one favour,' he said. 'Will you give it?'

'Gladly!'

'I don't know what it is yet, but when the time comes, I shall.'

She had fallen on her knees before him, and now

he bent toward her. His hood fell back, and his face was terrible indeed. It was the white face of a corpse with black holes for eyes.

'And if you refuse what I ask, woman . . .'

'I shall not refuse! Oh my Lord, I shall not! I shall not! I swear it on my dear husband's name!'

'Then it is well. Bring your son to me tomorrow night, after dark.'

She led the poor boy in the next night. He trembled and shook, his head nodded foolishly, his eyes rolled. There was a slick of drool on his chin. Flagg gave her a dark, plum-coloured potion in a beaker. 'Have him drink this,' he said. 'It will blister his mouth, but have him drink every drop. Then get the fool out of my sight.'

She murmured to him. The boy's shaking increased for a moment as he tried to nod his head. He drank all of the liquid and then doubled over, screaming.

'Get him out,' Flagg said.

'*Yes, get him out!*' one of the parrot's two heads cried.

'*Get him out, no screaming allowed here!*' the other head screamed.

She got him home, sure that Flagg had murdered him. But the next day the Shaking Disease had left her son completely, and he was well.

Years passed. When Sasha's labour with Thomas began, Flagg called for her and whispered in her ear. They were alone in his deep rooms, but even so, it was better that such a dread command be whispered.

Anna Crookbrows's face went deadly white, but she remembered Flagg's words: *If you refuse . . .*

And would not the King have two children? She had only one. And if the King wanted to remarry and have even more, let him. In Delain, women were plentiful.

So she went to Sasha, and spoke encouragingly, and at a critical moment a little knife glittered in her hand. No one saw the one small cut she made. A moment later, Anna cried: 'Push, my Queen! Push, for the baby comes!'

Sasha pushed. Thomas came from her as effortlessly as a boy zipping down a slide. But Sasha's lifeblood gushed out upon the sheet. Ten minutes after Thomas came into the world, his mother was dead.

And so Flagg was not concerned about the piffling matter of the doll's house. What mattered was that Roland was growing old, there was no meddling Queen to stand in his way, and now he had not one son to choose from but two. Peter was, of course, the elder, but that did not really matter. Peter could be gotten out of the way if time should prove him unsuitable for Flagg's purposes. He was only a child, and could not defend himself.

I have told you that Roland never thought longer or harder on any matter during his entire reign than he did on this one question – whether or not Peter should be allowed access to Sasha's doll's house, cunningly crafted by the great Ellender. I have told you that the result of his thought was a decision that ran against Flagg's wishes. I have *also* told you that Flagg considered this of little importance.

Was it? That you must decide for yourself, after you have heard me to the end.

·n·ow let many long years pass, all in a twinkling – one of the great things about tales is how fast time may pass when not much of note is happening. Real life is never that way, and it is probably a good thing. Time only passes faster in histories, and what is a history except a grand sort of tale where passing centuries are substituted for passing years?

During those years, Flagg watched both boys carefully – he watched them over the ageing King's shoulder as they grew up, calculating which should be King when Roland was no more. It did not take him long to decide it should be Thomas, the younger. By the time Peter was seven, he knew he did not like the boy. When Peter was nine, Flagg made a strange and unpleasant discovery; he feared Peter, as well.

The boy had grown up strong and straight and handsome. His hair was dark, his eyes a dark blue that is common to people of the Western Barony. Sometimes, when Peter looked up quickly, his head cocked a certain way, he resembled his father. Otherwise, he was Sasha's son almost entirely in his looks and ways. Unlike his short father with his bow-legged walk and his clumsy way of moving (Roland was graceful only when he was horsed), Peter was tall and lithe. He enjoyed the hunt and hunted well, but it was not his life. He also enjoyed his lessons – geography and history were his particular favourites.

His father was puzzled and often impatient with jokes; the point of most had to be explained to him, and that took away all the fun. What Roland liked was when the jesters pretended to slip on banana peels, or knocked their heads together, or when they staged pie fights in the Great Hall. Such things were about as far as Roland's idea of good fun extended. Peter's wit was much quicker and more subtle, as Sasha's had been, and his rollicking, boyish laughter often filled the palace, making the servants smile at each other approvingly.

While many boys in Peter's position would have become too conscious of their own grand place in the scheme of things to play with anyone not of their own class, Peter became best friends with a boy named Ben Staad when both children were eight. Ben's family was not royalty, and though Andrew Staad, Ben's father, had some faint claim to the High Blood of the kingdom on his mother's side, they could not even rightly be called nobility. 'Squire' was probably the kindest term one could have applied to Andy Staad, and 'squire's son' to his boy. Even so, the once-prosperous Staad family had fallen upon hard times, and while there could have been queerer choices for a Prince's best friend, there couldn't have been many.

They met at the annual Farmers' Lawn Party when Peter was eight. The Lawn Party was a yearly ritual most Kings and Queens viewed as tiresome at best; they were apt to put in a token appearance, drink the quick traditional toast, and then be away after bidding the farmers enjoy themselves and thanking them for another fruitful year (this was also part of the ritual, even if the crops had been poor). If Roland had been that sort of King, Peter and Ben would never had gotten the chance to know each other. But, as you might have guessed, Roland *loved* the Farmers' Lawn Party, looked forward to it each year, and usually stayed until the very end (and more than once was carried away drunk and snoring loudly).

As it happened, Peter and Ben were paired in the three-legged sack-race, and they won it . . . although it ended up being much closer than at first it seemed it would be. Leading by almost six lengths, they took a bad spill and Peter's arm was cut.

'I'm sorry, my prince!' Ben cried. His face had gone pale, and he may have been visualizing the dungeons (and I know his mother and father, watching anxiously from the sidelines, were; if it weren't for bad luck, Andy Staad was fond of growling, the Staads would have no luck at all); more likely he was just sorry for the hurt he fancied he had caused, or was amazed to see that the blood of the future King was as red as his own.

'Don't be a fool,' Peter said impatiently. 'It was my fault, not yours. I was clumsy. Hurry and get up. They're catching us.'

The two boys, made into a single clumsy three-legged beast by the sack into which Peter's right leg and Ben's left one had been tightly tied, managed to get up and lurch on. Both had been badly winded by the fall, however, and their long lead had been cut to almost nothing. Approaching the finish line, where crowds of farmers (not to mention Roland, standing among them without the slightest feeling of awkwardness, or of being somewhere he shouldn't) were cheering deliriously, two huge, sweating farm boys began to close in. That they would overtake Peter and Ben in the last ten yards of the race seemed almost inevitable.

'*Faster, Peter!*' Roland bellowed, swinging a huge mug of mead with such enthusiasm that he poured most of it onto his own head. In his excitement he never noticed. '*Jackrabbit, son! Be a jackrabbit! Those clod-busters are almost up your butt and over your back!*'

Ben's mother began to moan, cursing the fate that had caused her son to be paired up with the prince.

'If they lose, he'll have our Ben thrown into the deepest dungeon in the castle,' she moaned.

'Hush, woman,' Andy said. 'He'd not. He's a good King.' He believed it, but he was still afraid. Staad luck was, after all, Staad luck.

Ben, meanwhile, had begun to giggle. He couldn't believe he was doing it, but he was. 'Be a jackrabbit, did he say?'

Peter also began to giggle. His legs ached terribly, blood was trickling down his right arm, and sweat was flooding his face, which was starting to

turn an interesting plum colour, but he was also unable to stop. 'Yes, that's what he said.'

'Then let's *hop!*'

They didn't look much like jackrabbits as they crossed the finish line; they looked like a pair of strange crippled crows. It was really a miracle they didn't fall, but somehow they didn't. They managed three ungainly leaps. The third one took them across the finish line, where they collapsed, howling with laughter.

'Jackrabbit!' Ben yelled, pointing at Peter.

'Jackrabbit yourself!' Peter yelled, pointing back.

They slung their arms about each other, still laughing, and were carried on the shoulders of many strong farmers (Andrew Staad was one of them, and bearing the combined weight of his son and the prince was something he never forgot) to where Roland slipped blue ribbands over their necks. Then he kissed each of them roughly on the cheek and poured the remaining contents of his mug over their heads, to the wild cheers and huzzahs of the farmers. Never, even in the memory of the oldest gaffer there that day, had such an extraordinary race been run.

The two boys spent the rest of the day together and, it soon appeared, would be content to spend the rest of their lives together. Because even a boy of eight has certain duties (and if he is to be the King someday he has even more), the two of them could not be together all they wanted to be, but when they could be, they were.

Some sniffed at the friendship, and said it wasn't right for the King in waiting to be friends with a boy who was little better than a common barony clod-buster. Most, however, looked upon it with approval; it was said more than once over deep cups in the meadhouses of Delain that Peter had gotten the best of both worlds – his mother's brains and his father's love of the common folk.

There was apparently no meanness in Peter. He never went through a period when he pulled the wings of flies or singed dogs' tails to see them run. In fact, he intervened in the matter of a horse which was to be destroyed by Yosef, the King's head groom . . . and it was when this tale made its way to Flagg that the magician began to fear the King's oldest son, and to think perhaps he did not have as long to put the boy out of the way as he had once thought. For in the affair of the horse with the broken leg, Peter had displayed courage and a depth of resolve which Flagg did not like at all.

Peter was passing through the stableyard when he saw a horse tethered to the hitching rail just outside the main barn. The horse was holding one of its rear legs off the ground. As Peter watched, Yosef spat on his hands and picked up a heavy maul. What he meant to do was obvious. Peter was both frightened and appalled. He rushed over.

'Who told you to kill this horse?' he asked.

Yosef, a hardy and robust sixty, was a palace fixture. He was not apt to brook the interference of a snot-nosed brat easily, prince or no. He fixed Peter with a thunderous, heavy look that was meant to wilt the boy. Peter, then just nine, reddened, but did not wilt. He seemed to see a look in the horse's mild brown eyes which said, *You're my only hope, whoever you are. Do what you can, please.*

'My father, and his father before him, and his father before *him*,' Yosef said, seeing now that he was going to have to say something, like it or not. '*That's* who told me to kill it. A horse with a broken leg is no good to any living thing, least of all to itself.' He raised the maul a little. 'You see this hammer as a murder weapon, but when you're older, you'll see it for what it really is in cases such as these . . . a mercy. Now stand back, so you don't get splashed.'

He raised the maul in both hands.

'Put it down,' Peter said.

Yosef was thunderstruck. He had *never* been interfered with in such a way.

'Here! Here! What are you a-saying?'

'You heard me. I said *put that hammer down*.' As he said these words Peter's voice deepened. Yosef suddenly realized – really, really realized – that it was the future King standing here in this dusty stable-yard, commanding him. If Peter had actually *said* as much – if he had stood there in the dust squeaking, *Put that down, put it down, I said, I'm going to be King someday, King, do you hear, so you put that down!*, Yosef would have laughed contemptuously, spat, and ended the broken-legged horse's life with one hard swing of his deeply muscled arms. But Peter did not have to say any such thing; the command was clear in his voice and eyes.

'Your father shall hear of this, my princeling,' Yosef said.

'And when he hears it from you, it will be for the second time,' Peter replied. 'I will let you go about your work with no further complaint, Lord High Groom, if I may put a single question to you which you answer yes.'

'Ask your question,' Yosef said. He was impressed with the boy, almost against his will. When he had told Yosef that he, Peter, would tell his father of the incident first, Yosef believed he meant what he said – the simple truth shone in the lad's eyes. Also, he had never been called Lord High Groom before, and he rather liked it.

'Has the horse doctor seen this animal?' Peter asked.

Yosef was thunderstruck. 'That is your question? *That?*'

'Yes.'

'Dear creeping gods, *no!*' he cried, and, seeing Peter flinch, he lowered his voice, squatted before the boy, and attempted to explain. 'A horse with a broken leg is a goner, y'Highness. Always a goner. Leg never mends right. There's apt to be blood poisoning. Turrible pain for the horse. *Turrible* pain. In the end, its poor heart is apt to burst, or it takes a brain fever and goes mad. Now do you understand what I meant when I said this hammer was mercy rather than murder?'

Peter thought long and gravely, with his head down. Yosef was silent, squatting before him in an almost unconscious posture of deference, allowing him the full courtesy of time.

Peter raised his head and asked: 'You say everyone says this?'

'Everyone, y'Highness. Why, my father –'

'Then we'll see if the horse doctor says it, too.'

'*Oh . . . PAH!*' the groom bellowed, and threw the hammer all the way across the courtyard. It sailed into a pigpen and struck head down in the mud. The pigs grunted and squealed and cursed him in their piggy Latin. Yosef, like Flagg, was not used to being balked, and took no notice of them.

He got up and stalked away. Peter watched him, troubled, sure that he must be in the wrong and knowing he was apt to face a severe whipping for this little piece of work. Then, halfway across the yard, the head groom turned, and a reluctant grim little smile hit across his face like a single sunray on a grey morning.

'Go get your horse doctor,' he said. 'Get him yourself, son. You'll find him in his animal surgery at the far end of Third East'rd Alley, I reckon. I'll give you twenty minutes. If you're not back with him by then, I'm putting my maul into yon horse's brains, prince or no prince.'

'Yes, Lord Head Groom!' Peter yelled. 'Thank you!' He raced away.

When he returned with the young horse doctor, puffing and out of breath, Peter was sure that the horse must be dead; the sun told him three times twenty minutes had passed. But Yosef, curious, had waited.

Horse doctoring and veterinary medicine were

then very new things in Delain, and this young man was only the third or fourth who had practised the trade, so Yosef's look of sour distrust was far from surprising. Nor had the horse doctor been happy to be dragged away from his surgery by the sweating, wide-eyed prince, but he became less irritated now that he had a patient. He knelt before the horse and felt the broken leg gently with his hands, humming through his nose as he did so. The horse shifted once as something he did pained her. 'Be steady, nag,' the horse doctor said calmly, 'be oh so steady.' The horse quieted. Peter watched all this in an agony of suspense. Yosef watched with his maul leaning nearby and his arms folded across his chest. His opinion of the horse doctor had gone up a little. The fellow was young, but his hands moved with gentle knowledge.

At last the horse doctor nodded and stood up, dusting stableyard grime from his hands.

'Well?' Peter asked anxiously.

'Kill her,' the horse doctor said briskly to Yosef, ignoring Peter altogether.

Yosef picked up his maul at once, for he had expected no other conclusion to the affair. But he found no satisfaction in being proved correct; the stricken look on the young boy's face went straight to his heart.

'Wait!' Peter cried, and although his small face was full of distress, that deepness was in his voice again, making him sound much, much older than his years.

The horse doctor looked at him, startled.

'You mean she'll die of blood poisoning?' Peter asked.

'What?' the horse doctor asked, eyeing Peter with a new care.

'She'll die of blood poisoning if she's allowed to live? Or her heart will burst? Or she will run mad?'

The horse doctor was clearly puzzled. 'What are you talking about? Blood poisoning? There is no blood poisoning here. The break is healing quite cleanly, in fact.' He looked at Yosef with some disdain. 'I have heard such stories as these before. There is no truth in them.'

'If you think not, you have much to learn, my young friend,' Yosef said.

Peter ignored this. It was now his turn to be bewildered. He asked the young horse doctor, 'Why do you tell the head groom to kill a horse which may heal?'

'Your Highness,' the horse doctor said briskly, 'this horse would need to be poulticed every day and every night for a month or more to keep any infection from settling in. The effort might be made, but to what end? The horse would always limp. A horse that limps can't work. A horse that limps can't run for idlers to bet on. A horse that limps can only eat and eat and never earn its provender. Therefore, it should be killed.'

He smiled, satisfied. He had proved his case.

Then, as Yosef started forward with his hammer again, Peter said; '*I'll* put on the poultices. If a day should come when I can't, then Ben Staad will. And she'll be good because she'll be my horse, and I'll ride her even if she limps so badly she makes me seasick.'

Yosef burst out laughing and clapped the boy on his back so hard his teeth rattled. 'Your heart is kind as well as brave, my boy, but lads promise quick and regret at leisure. You'd not be true to it. I reckon.'

· Peter looked at him calmly. 'I mean what I say.'

Yosef stopped laughing all at once. He looked at Peter closely and saw that the boy did indeed mean it . . . or at least thought he did. There was no doubt in his face.

'Well! I can't tarry here all day,' the horse doctor said, adopting his former brisk and self-important manner. 'I've given you my diagnosis. My bill will be presented to the Treasury in due course . . . Perhaps you'll pay it out of your allowance, Highness. In any case, what you decide to do is not my business. Good day.'

Peter and the head groom watched him walk out of the stableyard, trailing a long afternoon shadow at his heels.

'He's full of dung,' Yosef said when the horse doctor was out the gate, beyond earshot, and thus unable to contradict his words. 'Mark me, y'Highness, and save y'self a lot o' grief. There never was a horse what busted a leg and didn't get blood poisoning. It's God's way.'

'I'll want to talk to my father about this,' Peter said.

'And so I think you must,' Yosef said heavily . . . but as Peter trudged away, he smiled. He thought the boy had done right well for himself. His father would be honour-bound to see the boy was whipped for interfering with his elders, but the head groom knew that Roland set a great store by both of his sons in his old age – Peter perhaps a bit more than

Thomas – and he believed that the boy would get his horse. Of course, he would also get a heartbreak when the horse died, but, as the horse doctor had quite rightly said, that was not his business. He knew about the training of horses; the training of princes was best left in other hands.

Peter *was* whipped for interfering in the head groom's affairs, and although it was no solace to his stinging bottom, Peter's mind understood that his father had afforded him great honour by administering the whipping himself, instead of handing Peter over to an underling who might have tried to curry favour by making it easy on the boy.

Peter could not sleep on his back for three days and was not able to eat sitting down for nearly a week, but the head groom was also right about the horse – Roland allowed Peter to keep her.

'It won't take up your time for long, Peter,' Roland advised him. 'If Yosef says it will die, it will die.' Roland's face was a bit pale and his old hands were trembling. The beating had pained him more than it had pained Peter, who really was his favourite . . . although Roland foolishly fancied no one knew this but himself.

'I don't know,' Peter said. 'I thought that horse-doctoring fellow knew what he was talking about.'

It turned out that the horse-doctoring fellow had. The horse did not take blood poisoning, and it did not die, and in the end its limp was so slight that even Yosef was forced to admit it was hardly noticeable. 'At least, when she's fresh,' he amended. Peter was more than just faithful about putting on the poultices; he was nearly religious. He changed old for new three times a day and did it a fourth time before he went to bed. Ben Staad did stand in for Peter from time to time, but those times were few. Peter named the horse Peony, and they were great friends ever after.

Flagg had most assuredly been right about one thing on the day he advised Roland against letting Peter play with the dollhouse: servants were everywhere, they see everything, and their tongues wag. Several servants had witnessed the scene in the stableyard, but if every servant who later claimed to have been there really had been, there would have been a mob of them crowded around the edges of the stableyard that hot summer day. That had, of course, not been the case, but the fact that so many of them found the event worth lying about was a sign that Peter was regarded as an interesting figure indeed. They talked about it so much that it became something of a nine days' wonder in Delain. Yosef also talked; so, for that matter, did the young horse doctor. Everything that they said spoke well for the young prince – Yosef's word in particular carried much weight, because he was greatly respected. He began to call Peter 'the young King', something he had never done before.

'I believe God spared the nag because the young King stood up for her so brave-like,' he said. 'And he worked at them poultices like a slave. Brave, he is; he's got the heart of a dragon. He'll make a King someday, all right. Ai! You should have heard his voice when he told me to hold the maul!'

It was a great story, all right, and Yosef drank on it for the next seven years – until Peter was arrested for a hideous crime, judged guilty, and sentenced to imprisonment in the cell atop the Needle for the rest of his life.

15

Perhaps you are wondering what Thomas was like, and some of you may already be casting him in a villain's part, as a willing co-schemer in Flagg's plot to snatch the crown away from its rightful owner.

That was not really the case at all, although to some it always seemed so, and of course Thomas did play a part. He did not seem, I admit, to be a really good boy – at least, not at first glance. He was surely not a good boy in the way that Peter was a good boy, but *no* brother would have looked really good beside Peter, and Thomas knew it well by the time he was four – that was the year after the famous sack-race, and the one in which the famous stableyard incident took place. Peter rarely lied and never cheated. Peter was smart and kind, tall and handsome. He looked like their mother, who had been so deeply loved by the King and the people of Delain.

How could Thomas compare with goodness like *that*? A simple question with a simple answer. He couldn't.

Unlike Peter, Thomas was the spitting image of his father. This pleased the old man a little, but it didn't give him the pleasure most men feel when they have a son who carries the clear stamp of their features. Looking at Thomas was too much like looking into a sly mirror. He knew that Thomas's fine blond hair would grey early and then begin to fall out; Thomas would be bald by the time he was forty. He knew that Thomas would never be tall, and if he had his father's appetite for beer and mead, he would be carrying a big belly before him by the time he was twelve five. Already his toes had begun to turn in, and Roland guessed Thomas would walk with his own bowlegged swagger.

Thomas was not exactly a good boy, but you must not think that made him a bad boy. He was sometimes a sad boy, often a confused boy (he took after his father in another way, as well – hard thinking made his nose stuffy and his head feel like boulders were rolling around inside), and often a jealous boy, but he wasn't a bad boy.

Of whom was he jealous? Why, of his brother, of course. He was jealous of Peter. It wasn't enough that Peter would be King, Oh no! It wasn't enough that their father liked Peter best, or that the *servants* liked Peter best, or that their *teachers* liked Peter best because he was always ready at lessons and didn't need to be coaxed. It wasn't enough that *everyone* liked Peter best, or that Peter had a best friend. There was one more thing.

When anyone looked at Thomas, his father the King most of all, Thomas thought he knew they were thinking: *We loved your mother and you killed her in your coming. And what did we get out of the pain and death you caused her? A dull little boy with a round face that has hardly any chin, a dull little boy who couldn't make all fifteen of the Great Letters until he was eight. Your brother Peter was able to make them all when he was six. What did we get? Not much. Why did you come, Thomas? What good are you? Throne insurance? Is that all you are? Throne insurance in case Peter the Precious should fall off his limping nag and crack his head open? Is that all? Well, we don't want you. None of us want you. None of us want you . . .*

The part Thomas played in his brother's imprisonment was dishonourable, but even so he was not a really bad boy. I believe this, and hope that in time you will come to believe it, too.

Once, as a boy of seven, Thomas spent a whole day labouring in his room, carving his father a model sailboat. He did it with no way of knowing that Peter had covered himself with glory that day on the archery range, with his father in attendance. Peter was not, ordinarily, much of a bowman – in that area, at least, Thomas would turn out to be far superior to his older brother – but on that one day, Peter had shot the junior course of targets like one inspired. Thomas was a sad boy, a confused boy, and he was often an unlucky boy.

Thomas had thought of the boat because sometimes, on Sunday afternoons, his father liked to go out to the moat which surrounded the palace and float a variety of model boats. Such simple pleasures made Roland extremely happy, and Thomas had never forgotten one day when his father had taken him – and *just* him – along. In those days, his father had an advisor whose only job was to show Roland how to make paper boats and the King had conceived a great enthusiasm for them. On this day, a hoary old carp had risen out of the mucky water and swallowed one of Roland's paper boats whole. Roland had laughed like a boy and declared it was better than a tale about a sea monster. He hugged Thomas very tight as he said so. Thomas never forgot that day – the bright sunshine, the damp, slightly mouldy odour of the moat water, the warmth of his father's arms, the scratchiness of his beard.

So, feeling particularly lonely one day, he had hit on the idea of making his father a sailboat. It would not be a really great job, and Thomas knew it – he was almost as clumsy with his hands as he was at memorizing his lessons. But he also knew that his father could have any craftsman in Delain – even the great Ellender himself, who was now almost completely blind – make him boats if he so desired. The crucial difference, Thomas thought, would be that Roland's own son had taken *a whole day* to carve him a boat for his Sunday pleasure.

Thomas sat patiently by his window, urging the boat out of a block of wood. He used a sharp knife, nicked himself times without number, and cut himself quite badly once. Yet he kept on, aching hands or no. As he worked he daydreamed of how he and his father would go out on Sunday afternoon and sail the boat, just the two of them all alone, because Peter would be riding Peony in the woods or off playing with Ben. And he wouldn't even mind if that same carp came up and ate his wooden boat, because then his father would laugh and hug him and say it was better than a story of sea monsters eating Anduan clipper ships whole.

But when he got to the King's chamber Peter was there and Thomas had to wait for nearly half an hour with the boat hidden behind his back while his father extolled Peter's bowmanship. Thomas could see that Peter was uncomfortable under the unceasing barrage of praise. He could also see that Peter knew Thomas wanted to talk to their father, and that Peter kept trying to tell their father so. It didn't matter, none of it mattered. Thomas hated him anyway.

At last Peter was allowed to escape. Thomas approached his father, who looked at him kindly enough now that Peter was gone. 'I made you something, Dad,' he said, suddenly shy. He held the boat behind his back with hands that were suddenly wet and clammy with sweat.

'Did you now, Tommy?' Roland said. 'Why, that was kind, wasn't it?'

'Very kind, Sire,' said Flagg, who happened to be idling nearby. He spoke casually but watched Thomas with bright interest.

'What is it, lad? Show me!'

'I remembered how much you liked to have a boat or two out on the moat Sunday afternoons, Dad, and . . .' He wanted desperately to say, *and I wanted you to take me out with you again sometime, so I made this*, but he found he could not utter such a thing. '. . . and so I made you a boat . . . I spent a whole day . . . cut myself . . . and . . . and . . .' Sitting in his window seat, carving the boat, Thomas had made up a long, eloquent speech which he would utter before bringing the boat out from behind his back and presenting it with a flourish to his father, but now he could hardly remember a word of it, and what he could remember didn't seem to make any sense.

Horribly tongue-tied, he took the sailboat with its awkward flapping sail out from behind his back and gave it to Roland. The King turned it over in his big short-fingered hands. Thomas stood and watched him, totally unaware that he had forgotten to breathe.

At last Roland looked up. "Very nice. Very nice, Tommy. Canoe, isn't it?'

'Sailboat.' *Don't you see the sail?* he wanted to cry. *It took me an hour alone just to tie the knots, and it isn't my fault one of them came loose so it flaps!*

The King fingered the striped sail, which Thomas had cut from a pillowcase.

'So it is . . . of course it is. At first I thought it was a canoe and this was some Oranian girl's washing.' He tipped a wink at Flagg, who smiled vaguely at the air and said nothing. Thomas suddenly felt he might vomit quite soon.

Roland looked at his son more seriously, and beckoned for him to come close. Timidly, hoping for the best, Thomas did so.

'It's a good boat, Tommy. Sturdy, like yourself, a bit clumsy like yourself, but good – like yourself.

And if you want to give me a really *fine* present, work hard in your own bowmanship classes so you can take a first-class medal as Pete did today.'

Thomas *had* taken a first in the lower-circle bowmanship courses the year before, but his father seemed to have forgotten this in his joy over Peter's accomplishment. Thomas did not remind him; he merely stood there, looking at the boat in his father's big hands. His cheeks and forehead had flushed to the colour of old brick.

'When it was at last down to just two boys – Peter and Lord Towson's son – the instructor decreed they should draw back another forty koner. Towson's boy looked downcast, but Peter just walked to the mark and nocked an arrow. I saw the look in his eyes, and I said to myself "He's won! By all the gods that are, he hasn't even fired an arrow yet and he's won!" And so he had! I tell you, Tommy, you should have been there! You should have . . .'

The King prattled on, putting aside the boat Thomas had laboured a whole day to make, with barely a second look. Thomas stood and listened, smiling mechanically, that dull, bricklike flush never leaving his face. His father would never bother to take the sailboat he had carved out to the moat – why should he? The sailboat was as pukey as Thomas felt. Peter could probably carve a better one blindfolded, and in half the time. It would look better to their father, at least.

A miserable eternity later, Thomas was allowed to escape.

'I believe the boy worked very hard on that boat,' Flagg remarked carelessly.

'Yes, I suppose he did,' Roland said. 'Wretched-looking thing, isn't it? Looks a little like a dog turd with a handkerchief sticking out of it.' *And like something I would have made when I was his age*, he added in his own mind.

Thomas could not hear *thoughts* . . . but a hellish trick of acoustics brought Roland's *words* to him just as he left the Great Hall. Suddenly the horrible green pressure in his stomach was a thousand times worse. He ran to his bedroom and was sick in a basin.

The next day, while idling behind the outer kitchens, Thomas spied a half-crippled old dog foraging for garbage. He seized a rock and threw it. The stone flew to the mark. The dog yipped and fell down, badly hurt. Thomas knew his brother, although five years older, could not have made such a shot at half the distance – but that was a cold satisfaction, because he also knew that Pete never would have thrown a rock at a poor, hungry dog in the first place, especially one as old and decrepit as this one obviously was.

For a moment, compassion filled Thomas's heart and his eyes filled with tears. Then, for no reason at all, he thought of his father saying, *Looks a little like a dog turd with a handkerchief sticking out of it.* He gathered up a handful of rocks, and went over to where the dog lay on its side, dazed and bleeding from one ear. Part of him wanted to let the dog alone, or perhaps heal it as Peter had healed Peony – to make it his very own dog and love it forever. But part of him wanted to hurt it, as if hurting the dog would ease some of his own hurt. He stood above it, undecided, and then a terrible thought came to him:

Suppose that dog was Peter?

That decided the case. Thomas stood over the old dog and threw stones at it until it was dead. No one saw him, but if someone had, he or she would have thought: *There is a boy who is bad . . . bad, and perhaps even evil.* But the person who saw only the cruel murder of that dog would not have seen what happened the day before – would not have seen Thomas throwing up into a basin and crying bitterly as he did it. He was often a confused boy, often a sadly unlucky boy, but I stick to what I said – he was never a bad boy, not really.

I also said that no one saw the stoning of the mongrel dog behind the outer kitchens, but that was not quite true. Flagg saw it that night, in his magic crystal. He saw it . . . and was well pleased by it.

Roland . . .   Sasha . . .   Peter . . . Thomas. Now there is only one more we must speak of, isn't there? Now there is only the shadowy fifth. The time has come to speak of Flagg, as dreadful as that may be.

Sometimes the people of Delain called him Flagg the Hooded; sometimes simply the dark man – for, in spite of his white corpse's face, he was a dark man indeed. They called him well preserved, but they used the term in a way that was uneasy rather than complimentary. He had come to Delain from Garlan in the time of Roland's grandfather. In those days he had appeared to be a thin and stern-faced man of about forty. Now, in the closing years of Roland's reign, he appeared to be a thin and stern-faced man of about fifty. Yet it had not been ten years, or even twenty, between then and now – it had been seventy-six years in all. Babies who had been sucking toothlessly at their mother's breasts when Flagg first came to Delain had grown up, married, had children, grown old, and died toothlessly in their beds or their chimney corner. But in all that time, Flagg seemed to have aged only ten years. It was magic, they whispered, and of course it was good to have a magician at court, a *real* magician and not just a stage conjurer who knew how to palm coins or hide a sleeping dove up his sleeve. Yet in their hearts, they knew there was *nothing* good about Flagg. When the people of Delain saw him coming, with his eyes peeking redly out from his hood, they quickly found business on the far side of the street.

Did he really come from Garlan, with its far vistas and its purple dreaming mountains? I do not know. It was and is a magical land where carpets sometimes fly, and where holy men sometimes pipe ropes up from wicker baskets, climb them, and disappear at the tops, never to be seen again. A great many seekers of knowledge from more civilized lands like Delain and Andua have gone to Garlan. Most disappear as completely and as permanently as those strange mystics who climb the floating ropes. Those who do return don't always come back changed for the better. Yes, Flagg might well have come to Delain from Garlan, but if he did, it was not in the reign of Roland's grandfather but much, much earlier.

He had, in fact, come to Delain often. He came under a different name each time, but always with the same load of woe and misery and death. This time he was Flagg. The time before he had been known at Bill Hinch, and he had been the King's Lord High Executioner. Although that time was two hundred and fifty years past, his was a name mothers still used to frighten their children when they were bad. 'If you don't shut up that squalling. I reckon Bill Hinch will come and take you away!' they said. Serving as Lord High Executioner under three of the bloodiest Kings in Delain's long history, Bill Hinch had made an end to hundreds – thousands, some said – of prisoners with his heavy axe.

The time before *that*, four hundred years before the time of Roland and his sons, he came as a singer named Browson, who became a close adviser to the King and a Queen. Browson disappeared like smoke after drumming up a great and bloody war between Delain and Andua.

The time before *that* . . .

Ah, but why go on? I'm not sure I could if I wanted to. When times are long enough, even the storytellers forget the tales. Flagg always showed up with a different face and a different bag of tricks, but two things about him were always the same. He always came hooded, a man who seemed almost to have no face, and he never came as a King himself, but always as the whisperer in the shadows, the man who poured poison into the porches of Kings' ears.

Who was he, really, this dark man?

I do not know.

Where did he wander between visits to Delain?

I do not know that, either.

Was he never suspected?

Yes, by a few — by historians and spinners of tales like me, mostly. They suspected that the man who now called himself Flagg had been in Delain before, and never to any good purpose. But they were afraid to speak. A man who could live among them for seventy-six years and appear to age only ten was obviously a magician; a man who had lived for ten times as long, perhaps longer than that . . . such a man might be the devil himself.

What did he want? That question I think I can answer.

He wanted what evil men always want: to have power and use that power to make mischief. Being a King did not interest him because the heads of Kings all too often found their way to spikes on castle walls when things went wrong. But the advisors to Kings . . . the spinners in the shadows . . . such people usually melted away like evening shadows at dawning as soon as the headsman's axe started to fall. Flagg was a sickness, a fever looking for a cool brow to heat up. He hooded his actions just as he hooded his face. And when the great trouble came — as it always did after a span of years — Flagg always disappeared like shadows at dawn.

Later, when the carnage was over and the fever had passed, when the rebuilding was complete and there was again something worth destroying, Flagg would appear once more.

18

This time, Flagg had found the Kingdom of Delain in exasperatingly healthy condition. Landry, Roland's grandfather, was a drunken old fool, easy to influence and twist, but a heart attack had taken him too soon. Flagg knew by then that Lita, Roland's mother, was the last person he wanted holding the sceptre. She was ugly but good-hearted and strong-willed. Such a Queen was not a good growth medium for Flagg's brand of insanity.

If he had come earlier in Landry's reign, there would have been time to put Lita out of the way, as he expected to put Peter out of the way. But he'd had only six years, and that was not long enough.

Still, she had accepted him as an advisor, and that was something. She did not like him much but she accepted him – mostly because he could tell wonderful fortunes with cards. Lita loved hearing bits of gossip and scandal about those in her court and her Cabinet, and the gossip and scandal were doubly good because she got to hear not only what *had* happened but what *would* happen. It was hard to rid yourself of such an amusing diversion, even when you sensed that a person able to do such tricks might be dangerous. Flagg never told the Queen any of the darker news he sometimes saw in the cards. She wanted to know who had taken a lover or who had had words with his wife or her husband. She did not want to know about dark cabals and murderous plans. What she wanted from the cards was relatively innocent.

During the long, long reign of Lita, Flagg was chagrined to find his main accomplishment was to be not turned out. He was able to maintain a foothold but to do little more than that. Oh, there were a few bright spots – the encouragement of bad blood between two powerful squires in the Southern Barony and the descrediting of a doctor who had found a cure for some blood infections (Flagg wanted no cures in the Kingdom that were not magical – which is to say, given or withheld at his own whim) were examples of Flagg's work during that period. It was all pretty small change.

Under Roland – poor bowlegged, insecure Roland – things marched more quickly toward Flagg's goal. Because he did have a goal, you know, in his fuzzy, malevolent sort of way, and this time it was grand indeed. He planned nothing more nor less than the complete overthrow of the monarchy – a bloody revolt that would plunge Delain into a thousand years of darkness and anarchy.

Give or take a year or two, of course.

In Peter's cool gaze he saw the very possible derailment of all his plans and careful work. More and more Flagg came to believe that getting rid of Peter was a necessity. Flagg had overstayed in Delain this time and he knew it. The muttering had begun. The work so well begun under Roland – the steady rises in taxes, the midnight searches of small farmers' barns and silage sheds for unreported crops and foodstuffs, the arming of the Home Guards – must continue to its end under Thomas. He did not have time to wait through the reign of Peter as he had through that of his grandmother.

Peter might not even wait for the mutterings of the people to come to his ears; Peter's first command as King might well be that Flagg should be sent eastward out of the Kingdom and forbidden ever to come again, on pain of death. Flagg might murder an advisor before he could give the young King such advice, but the hell of it was, Peter would *need* no advisor. He would advise himself – and when Flagg saw the cool, unafraid way the boy, now fifteen and very tall, looked at him, he thought that Peter might already have given himself that advice.

The boy liked to read, and he liked history, and in the last two years, as his father grew steadily greyer and frailer, he had been asking a lot of questions of his father's other advisors, and of some of his teachers. Many of these questions – *too* many – had to do either with Flagg or with roads which would lead to Flagg if followed far enough.

That the boy was asking such questions at fourteen and fifteen was bad. That he was getting comparatively honest answers from such timid, watchful men as the Kingdom's historians and Roland's advisors was much worse. It meant that, in the minds of these people, Peter was already almost King – and that they were glad. They welcomed him and rejoiced in him, because he would be an intellectual, like them. And they also welcomed him because, *unlike* them, he was a brave boy who might well grow into a lionhearted King whose tale would be the stuff of legends. In him, they saw again the coming of the White, that ancient, resilient, yet humble force that has redeemed humankind again and again and again.

He had to be put out of the way. *Had* to be.

Flagg told himself this each night when he retired in the blackness of his inner chambers, and it was his first thought when he awoke in that blackness the next morning.

He must be put out of the way, the boy must be put out of the way.

But it was harder than it seemed. Roland loved and would have died for either of his sons, but he loved Peter with a particular fierceness. Smothering the boy in his cradle, making it look as if the Baby Death had taken him, would have once perhaps been possible, but Peter was now a healthy teen-ager.

Any accident would be examined with all the raging scrutiny of Roland's grief, and Flagg had thought more than once that the final irony might be this: Suppose Peter really *did* die an accidental death, and he, Flagg, was somehow blamed for it? A small miscalculation while shinnying up a drainpipe . . . a slip while crawling around on a stable roof playing Dare You with his friend Staad . . . a tumble from his horse. And what would the result be? Might not Roland, wild in his grief and growing senile and confused in his mind, see wilful murder in what was *really* an accident? And might his eye not turn on Flagg? Of course. His eye would turn to Flagg before it turned to anyone else. Roland's mother had mistrusted him, and he knew that, deep down, Roland mistrusted him as well. He had been able to hold that mistrust in check with mingled fear and fascination, but Flagg knew that if Roland ever had reason to think Flagg had caused, or even played a part in, the death of his son –

Flagg could actually imagine situations where he might have to interfere on Peter's behalf to keep the boy safe. It was damnable. Damnable!

He must be put out of the way. Must be put out of the way! Must!

As the days and weeks and months passed, the drumbeat of this thought in Flagg's head grew ever more urgent. Every day Roland grew older and weaker; every day Peter grew older and wiser and thus a more dangerous opponent. What was to be done?

Flagg's thoughts turned and turned and turned on this. He grew morose and irritable. Servants, especially Peter's butler, Brandon, and Brandon's son, Dennis, gave him a wide berth, and spoke to each other in whispers of the terrible smells that sometimes came from his laboratory late at night. Dennis in particular, who would someday take the place of his good old da' as Peter's butler, was terrified of Flagg, and once asked his father if he might say a word about the magician. 'To make him safe, is all I'm thinking,' Dennis said.

'Not a word,' Brandon said, and fixed Dennis,

who was only a boy himself, with a forbidding look. 'Not a word will you say. The man's dangerous.'

'Then is that not all the more reason — ?' Dennis began timidly.

'A dullard may mistake the rattle of a Biter-Snake for the sound of pebbles in a hollow gourd and put out his hand to touch it,' Brandon said, 'but our prince is no dullard, Dennis. Now fetch me another glass of bundle-gin, and say no more on't.'

So Dennis did not speak of it to Peter, but his love of his young master and his fear of the King's hooded adviser both grew after that short exchange. Whenever he saw Flagg sweeping up one of the corridors of the castle in his long hooded robe he would draw aside, trembling, thinking: *Biter-Snake! Biter-Snake! Watch for him, Peter! And listen for him!*

Then, one night when Peter was sixteen, just as Flagg had begun to believe that there really might not be any way to put an end to the boy without unacceptable risk to himself, an answer came. That was a wild night. A terrible autumn storm raged and shrieked around the castle, and the streets of Delain were empty as people sought shelter from the sheets of chilly rain and the battering wind.

Roland had taken a cold in the damp. He took cold more and more easily these days, and Flagg's medicines, potent as they were, were losing their power to cure him. One of these colds — perhaps even the one he was hacking and wheezing with now — would eventually deepen into the Wet Lung Disease, and that would kill him. Magic medicines were not like doctors' medicines, and Flagg knew that one of the reasons the potions he gave the old King were now so slow to work, was that he, Flagg, no longer really *wanted* them to work. The only reason he was keeping Roland alive was that he feared Peter.

I wish you were dead, old man, Flagg thought with childish anger as he sat before a guttering candle, listening to the wind shriek without and his two-headed parrot mutter sleepily to itself within. *For a row of pins — a very short row at that — I'd kill you myself for all the trouble you and your stupid wife and your elder son have caused me. The joy of killing you would almost be worth the ruin of my plans. The joy of killing you —*

Suddenly he froze, sitting upright, staring off into the darkness of his underground rooms, where the shadows moved uneasily. His eyes glittered silver. An idea blazed in his mind like a torch.

The candle flared a brilliant green and then went out.

'*Death!*' one of the parrot's two heads shrieked in the darkness.

'*Murder!*' shrieked the other.

And in that blackness, unseen by anyone, Flagg began to laugh.

20

Of all the weapons ever used to commit regicide – the murder of a King – none has been as frequently used as poison. And no one has greater knowledge of poisons than a magician.

Flagg, one of the greatest magicians who ever lived, knew all the poisons that we know – arsenic; strychnine; the curare, which steals inward, paralyzing all the muscles and the heart last; nicotine; belladonna; nightshade; toadstool. He knew the poison venoms of a hundred snakes and spiders; the clear distillation of the clanah lily which smells like honey but kills its victims in screaming torments; Deadly Clawfoot which grows in the deepest shadows of the Dismal Swamp. Flagg did not know just dozens of poisons but dozens of dozens, each worse than the last. They were all neatly ranked on the shelves of an inner room where no servant ever went. They were in beakers, in phials, in little envelopes. Each deadly item was neatly marked. This was Flagg's chapel of screams-in-waiting – agony's antechamber, foyer of fevers, dressing room for death. Flagg visited it often when he felt out of sorts and wanted to cheer himself up. In this devil's marketplace waited all those things that humans, who are made of flesh and are so weak, dread: hammering headaches, screaming stomach cramps, detonations of diarrhoea, vomiting, collapsing blood vessels, paralysis of the heart, exploding eyeballs, swelling, blackening tongues, madness.

But the worst poison of all Flagg kept separate

from even these. In his study there was a desk. Every drawer of this desk was locked . . . but one was tri-ple-locked. In it was a teak box, carved all over with magical symbols . . . runes and such. The lock on this box was unique. Its plate seemed to be a dull orange steel, but very close inspection showed it was really some sort of vegetable matter. It was, in fact, a kleffa carrot, and once a week Flagg watered this living lock with a tiny spray bottle. The kleffa carrot also seemed to have some dull species of intelligence. If anyone tried to jemmy the kleffa lock open, or even if the wrong someone tried to use the right key, the lock would scream. Inside this box was a smaller box, which opened with a key Flagg wore always around his neck.

Inside this second box was a packet. Inside the packet was a small quantity of green sand. Pretty, you would have said, but nothing spectacular. Nothing to write home to Mother about. Yet this green sand was one of the deadliest poisons in all the worlds, so deadly that even Flagg was afraid of it. It came from the desert of Grenh. This huge poisoned waste lay even beyond Garlan, and was a land unknown in Delain. Grenh could be approached only on a day when the wind was blowing the other way, because a single breath of the fumes which came from the desert of Grenh would cause death.

Not instant death. That was not the way the poison worked. For a day or two – perhaps even three – the person who breathed the poison fumes (or even worse, swallowed the grains of sand) would feel fine – perhaps better than ever before in his life. Then, suddenly, his lungs would grow red-hot, his skin would begin to smoke, and his body would shrivel like the body of a mummy. Then he would drop dead, often with his hair on fire. Someone who breathed or swallowed this deadly stuff would burn from the inside out.

This was Dragon Sand, and there was no antidote, no cure. What fun.

On that wild, rainy night, Flagg determined to give a bit of Dragon Sand to Roland in a glass of wine. It had become Peter's custom to take his father a glass of wine each night, shortly before Roland turned in. Everyone in the palace knew it, and commented on what a loyal son Peter was. Roland enjoyed his son's company as much as the wine he brought, Flagg thought, but a certain maiden had caught Peter's eye and he rarely stayed longer than half an hour with his father these days.

If Flagg came one night after Peter had left, Flagg did not think the old man would turn down a second glass of wine.

A very special glass of wine.

A hot vintage, my lord, Flagg thought, a grin dawning on his narrow face. *A hot vintage indeed, and why not? The vineyard was right next door to hell, I think, and when this stuff starts working in your guts, you'll think hell is where you are.*

Flagg threw back his head and began to laugh.

21

Once his plan was laid – a plan that would rid him of both Roland and Peter forever – Flagg wasted no time. He first used all his wizardry to make the King well again. He was delighted to find that his magic potions worked better than they had for a long, long time. It was another irony. He earnestly wanted to make Roland better, so the potions worked. But he wanted to make the King better so he could kill him and make sure everyone knew it was murder. It was really quite funny, when you stopped to think it over.

On a windy night less than a week after the King's hacking cough had ceased, Flagg unlocked his desk and took out the teak box. He murmured, 'Well done,' to the kleffa carrot, which squeaked mindlessly in reply, and then lifted the heavy lid and took out the smaller box inside. He used the key around his neck to open it, and took out the packet that contained the Dragon Sand. He had bewitched this packet, and it was immune to the Dragon Sand's terrible power. Or so he thought. Flagg took no chances, and removed the packet with a small pair of silver tweezers. He laid it beside one of the King's goblets on his desk. Sweat stood out on his forehead in great round drops, for this was ticklish work indeed. One little mistake and he would pay for it with his life.

Flagg went out into the corridor that led to the dungeons and began to pant. He was hyperventilating. When you breathe rapidly, you fill your whole body with oxygen, and you can hold your breath for a long time. During the critical stage of his preparations, Flagg did not mean to breathe at all. There would be no mistakes, big or little. He was having too much fun to die.

He took a final great gasp of clean air from the barred window just outside the door to his apartment and reentered his rooms. He went to the envelope, took his dagger from his belt, and delicately slit it open. There was a flat piece of obsidian, which the magician used as a paperweight, on his desk – in those days, obsidian was the hardest rock known. Using the tweezers again, he grasped the packet, turned it upside down, and poured out most of the green sand. He saved back a tiny bit – hardly more than a dozen grains, but this bit of extra was extremely important to his plans. Hard as the obsidian was, the rock immediately began to smoke.

Thirty seconds had passed now.

He picked up the obsidian, careful that not a single grain of Dragon Sand should touch his skin – if it did, it would work inward until it reached his heart and set it on fire. He tilted the stone over the goblet and poured it in.

Now, quickly, before the sand could begin to eat into the glass, he poured in some of the King's favourite wine – the same sort of wine Peter would be taking his father about now. The sand dissolved immediately. For a moment the red wine glimmered a sinister green, and then it returned to its usual colour.

Fifty seconds.

Flagg went back to his desk. He picked up the flat rock and took his dagger by its handle. Only a few grains of Dragon Sand had touched the blade when he slit through the paper, but already they were working their way in, and evil little streamers of smoke rose from the pocks in the Anduan steel. He carried both the stone and the dagger out into the hallway.

Seventy seconds, and his chest was beginning to cry for air.

Thirty feet down the hallway, which led to the dungeon if you followed it far enough (a trip no one in Delain wanted to make), there was a grating in the floor. Flagg could hear gurgling water, and if he had not been holding his breath, he would have smelled a foul stench. This was one of the castle's sewers. He dropped both the rock and the blade into it and grinned at the double splash in spite of his pounding chest. Then he hurried back to the window, leaned far out, and took breath after gasping breath.

When he had his wind back, he returned to his study. Now only the tweezers, the packet, and the glass of wine stood on the desk. There was not so much as a grain of sand on the tweezers, and the bit of sand left inside the bewitched packet could not harm him as long as he took reasonable care.

He felt he had done very well indeed so far. His work was by no means done, but it was well begun. He bent over the goblet and inhaled deeply. There was no danger now; when the sand was mixed with a liquid, its fumes became harmless and undetectable. Dragon Sand made deadly vapours only when it touched a solid, such as stone.

Such as flesh.

Flagg held the goblet up to the light, admiring its bloody glow.

'A final glass of wine, my King,' he said, and laughed until the two-headed parrot screamed in fear. 'Something to warm your guts.'

He sat down, turned over his hourglass, and began to read a huge book of spells. Flagg had been reading from this book – which was bound in human skin – for a thousand years and had gotten through only a quarter of it. To read too long of this book, written on the high, distant Plains of Leng by a madman named Alhazred, was to risk madness.

An hour . . . just an hour. When the top half of his hourglass was empty, he could be sure Peter would have come and gone. An hour, and he could take Roland this final glass of wine. For a moment, Flagg looked at the bone-white sand slipping smoothly through the waist of the hourglass, and then he bent calmly over his book.

22

Roland was pleased and touched that Flagg should have brought him a glass of wine that night before he went to bed. He drank it off in two large gulps, and declared that it had warmed him greatly.

Smiling inside his hood, Flagg said: 'I thought it would, your Highness.'

*W*hether it was fate or only luck that caused Thomas to see Flagg with his father that night is another question you must answer for yourself. I only know that he *did* see, and that it happened in large part because Flagg had been at pains over the years to make a special friend of this friendless, miserable boy.

I'll explain in a moment – but first I must correct a wrong idea you may have about magic.

In stories of wizardry, there are three kinds that are usually spoken of almost carelessly, as if any second-class wizard could do them. These are turning lead into gold, changing one's shape, and making oneself invisible. The first thing you should know is that real magic is never easy, and if you think it is, just try making your least favourite aunt disappear the next time she comes to spend a week or two. Real magic is *hard*, and although it is easier to do evil magic than good, even bad magic is tolerably hard.

Turning lead into gold *can* be done, once you know the names to call on, and if you can find someone to show you exactly the right trick of splitting the loaves of lead. Shape changing and invisibility, however, are impossible . . . or so close to it that you might as well use the word.

From time to time Flagg – who was a great eavesdropper – had listened to fools tell tales about young princes who escaped the clutches of evil genies by uttering a simple magic word and popping out of sight, or beautiful young princesses (in the stories they were always beautiful, although Flagg's experience had been that most princesses were spoiled rotten and, as the end products of long, inbred family lines, ugly as sin and stupid in the bargain) who tricked great ogres into becoming flies, which they then quickly swatted. In most stories, the princesses were also good at swatting flies, although most of the princesses Flagg had seen wouldn't have been able to swat a fly dying on a cold windowsill in December. In *stories* it all sounded easy; in *stories* people changed their shapes or turned themselves into walking windowpanes all the time.

In *truth*, Flagg had never seen either trick done. He had once known a great Anduan magician who believed he had mastered the trick of changing his shape, but after six months of meditation and nearly a week of incantations in a series of agonizing body postures, he uttered the last awesome spell and succeeded only in making his nose nearly nine feet long and driving himself insane. And there had been fingernails growing out of his nose. Flagg remembered with a grim little smile. Great magician or not, the man had been a fool.

Invisibility was likewise impossible, at least as far as Flagg himself had been able to determine. Yet it was possible to make oneself . . . *dim.*

Yes, *dim* – that was really the best word for it, although others sometimes came to mind: *ghostly, transparent, unobtrusive.* Invisibility was out of his reach, but by first eating a pizzle and then reciting a number of spells, it was possible to become *dim.* When one was *dim* and a servant approached along a passageway, one simply drew aside and stood still and let the servant pass. In most cases, the servant's eyes would drop to his own feet or suddenly find something interesting to look at on the ceiling. If one passed through a room, conversation would falter, and people would look momentarily distressed, as if all were having gas pains at the same time. Torches and wall sconces grew smoky, Candles sometimes blew out. It was necessary to actually hide when one was *dim* only if one saw someone whom one knew well – for, whether one was *dim* or not, these people almost always saw. *Dimness* was useful, but it was not invisibility.

On the night Flagg took the poisoned wine to Roland, he first made himself *dim*. He did not expect to see anyone he knew. It was after nine o'clock now, the King was old and unwell, the days were short, and the castle went to bed early. *When Thomas is King,* Flagg thought, carrying the wine swiftly through the corridors, *there will be parties every night. He already has his father's taste for drink, although he favours wine rather than beer or mead. It should be easy enough to introduce him to a few stronger drinks . . . After all, am I not his friend? Yes, when Peter is safely out of the way in the Needle and Thomas is King, there will be great parties every night . . . until the people in the alleys and the Baronies are choked enough to rise in bloody revolt. Then there will be one final party, the greatest of all . . . but I don't think Thomas will enjoy it. Like the wine I'm bringing his father tonight, that party will be extremely hot.*

He did not expect to see anyone he knew, and he didn't. Only a few servants passed him, and they drew away from the place where he stood almost absently, as if they felt a cold draught.

All the same, someone saw *him*. Thomas saw him through the eyes of Niner, the dragon his father had killed long ago. Thomas was able to do this because Flagg himself had taught him the trick.

The way his father had rejected the gift of the boat had hurt Thomas deeply, and after that he tended to keep clear of his father. All the same, Thomas loved Roland and badly wanted to make him happy the way Peter made him happy. Even more than that, he wanted to make his father love him the way he loved Peter. In fact, Thomas would have been happy if their father had loved him even half as much.

The trouble was, Peter had all the good ideas first. Sometimes Peter tried to share his ideas with Thomas, but to Thomas the ideas either sounded silly (until they worked) or else he feared he wouldn't be able to do his share of the work, as when Peter had made their father a set of Bendoh men three years ago.

'I'll give Father something better than a bunch of stupid old game pieces,' Thomas had said haughtily, but what he was *really* thinking was that if he couldn't make his father a simple wooden sailboat, he would never be able to help make something as difficult as the twenty-man Bendoh army. So Peter made the game pieces alone over a period of four months – the infantry men, the knights, the archers, the Fusilier, the General, the Monk – and of course Roland had loved them even though they were a bit clumsy. He had immediately put away the jade Bendoh set the great Ellender had carved for him forty years before and put the one Peter had made for him in its place. When Thomas saw this, he crept away to his apartments and went to bed, although it was the middle of the afternoon. He felt as if someone had reached into his chest and cut off a tiny piece of his heart and made him eat it. His heart tasted very bitter to him, and he hated Peter more than ever, although part of him still loved his handsome older brother and always would.

And although the taste had been bitter, he had liked it.

Because it was his heart.

Now there was the business of the nightly glass of wine.

Peter had come to Thomas and said, 'I was thinking it would be nice if we brought Dad a glass of wine every night, Tom. I asked the steward, and he said he couldn't just give us a bottle because he has to make an accounting to the Chief Vintner at the end of each sixmonth, but he said we could pool some of our money and buy a bottle of the Barony Fifth Vat, which is Father's favourite. And it's really not expensive. We'd have lots of our allowances left over. And –'

'I think that's the stupidest idea I ever heard!'

Thomas burst out. '*All* the wine belongs to Father, all the wine in the Kingdom, and he can have as much of it as he wants! Why should we spend *our* money to give Father something he owns anyway? We'll enrich that fat little steward, that's all we'll do!'

Peter said patiently, 'It will please him that we spent our money on him, even if it's something he owns anyway.'

'How do you know *that*?'

Simply, maddeningly, Peter replied: 'I just do.'

Thomas looked at him, scowling. How could he tell Peter that the Chief Vintner had caught him in the wine cellar, stealing a bottle of wine, just the month before? The fat little pig had given him a shaking and threatened to tell his father if Thomas didn't give him a gold piece. Thomas had paid, tears of rage and shame standing in his eyes. *If it had been Peter, you would have turned the other way and pretended not to see, you slug*, he thought. *If it had been Peter, you would have turned your back. Because Peter is going to be King someday soon, and I'll just be a prince forever.* It also occurred to him that Peter never would have tried to steal wine in the first place, but the truth of this thought only made him angrier at his brother.

'I just thought —' Peter began.

' "You just thought, you just thought," ' Thomas mimicked savagely. 'Well, go think somewhere else! When Father finds out you paid the Chief Vintner for his own wine, he'll laugh at you and call you a fool!'

But Roland hadn't laughed at Peter, hadn't called him a fool — he had called him a good son in a voice that was unsteady and almost weepy. Thomas knew, because he had crept after when Peter took their father the wine that first night. He watched through the eyes of the dragon and saw it all.

*I*f you had asked Flagg straight out why he had shown Thomas that place and the secret passageway which led to it, he would have been able to give you no very satisfactory answer. That was because he didn't exactly *know* why he had done it. He had an instinct for mischief in his head, just as some people have a way with numbers or a clear sense of direction. The castle was very old, and there were many secret doors and passages in it. Flagg knew most of them (no one, not even he, knew all of them), but this was the only one he had ever shown Thomas. His instinct for mischief told him that this one might cause trouble, and Flagg simply obeyed his instinct. Mischief, after all was Flagg's cake and pie.

Every now and then he would pop into Thomas's room and cry, 'Tommy, you look glum! I've thought of something you might like to see! Want to go and have a look?' He almost always said *you look glum, Tommy* or *you look a bit in the dumps, Tommy* or *you look like you just sat on a pinchbug, Tommy* because he had a knack of showing up when Thomas was feeling particularly depressed or blue. Flagg knew that Thomas was afraid of him, and Thomas would find an excuse not to go with him unless he particularly needed a friend . . . and felt so low and unhappy he wouldn't be particular about which friend it was. Flagg knew this, but Thomas himself did not – his fear of Flagg ran deep. On the surface of his mind, he thought Flagg was a fine fellow, full of tricks and fun. Sometimes the fun was a bit mean, but that often suited Thomas's disposition.

Do you think it strange that Flagg would know something about Thomas that Thomas didn't know about himself? It really isn't strange at all. People's minds, particularly the minds of children, are like wells – deep wells full of sweet water. And sometimes, when a particular thought is too unpleasant to bear, the person who has that thought will lock it into a heavy box and throw it into that well. He listens for the splash . . . and then the box is gone. Except it is not, of course. Not really. Flagg, being very old and very wise, as well as very wicked, knew that even the deepest well has a bottom, and just because a thing is out of sight doesn't mean it is gone. It is still there, resting at the bottom. And he knew that the caskets those evil, frightening ideas are buried in may rot, and the nastiness inside may leak out after awhile and poison the water . . . and when the well of the mind is badly poisoned, we call the result insanity.

If the magician showed him scary things in the castle sometimes, he did it because he knew that the more frightened of him Thomas was, the more power he would gain over Thomas . . . and he knew he could have that power, because he knew something I've already told you – that Thomas was weak and often neglected by his father. Flagg wanted Thomas to be afraid of him, and he wanted to make sure that, as the years passed, Thomas had to throw many of those locked boxes into the darkness inside him. If Thomas were to go insane at some point after he became King, well, what of that? It would make it easier for Flagg to rule; it would make his power all the greater.

How did Flagg know the right times to visit Thomas, and take him on these strange tours of the castle? Sometimes he saw what had happened to make Thomas sad or angry in his crystal. More often, he simply felt an urge to go to Thomas and heeded it – that instinct for mischief rarely led him wrong.

Once he took Thomas high into the eastern tower – they climbed stairs until Thomas was panting like a dog, but Flagg never seemed to lose his breath. At the top was a door so small that even Thomas had to crawl through it on his hands and knees. Beyond was a dark, rustling room with a single window. Flagg had led him to that window without a word, and when Thomas saw the view – the entire city of Delain, the Near Towns, and then the hills which stood between the Near Towns and the Eastern Barony marching off into a blue haze – he thought that the sight had been worth every stair his aching legs had climbed. His heart swelled with the beauty of it, and he turned to thank Flagg – but something about the white blur of the magician's face inside his hood had frozen the words on his lips.

'Now watch *this*!' Flagg said, and held up his hand. A spurt of blue flame rose from his index

finger, and the rustling sound in the room, which Thomas had first taken for the sound of the wind, turned to a rising whir of leathery wings. A moment later Thomas was screaming and beating the air above his head as he blundered blindly back toward the tiny door. The little round room at the top of the castle's eastern tower had the best view in Delain save for the cell at the top of the Needle, but now he understood why no one visited it. The room was infested with huge bats. Disturbed by the light Flagg had raised, they whirled and swooped. Later, after they were out and Flagg had quieted the boy – Thomas, who hated bats, had been in hysterics – the magician insisted it was just a joke meant to cheer him up. Thomas believed him . . . but for weeks after he awoke screaming with nightmares in which bats flapped around his head, got caught in his hair, and ripped at his face with their sharp claws and ratty teeth.

On another excursion, Flagg took him to the King's treasure room and showed him the mounds of gold coins, tall stacks of gold bars, and the deep bins marked EMERALDS, DIAMONDS, RUBIES, FIREDIMS, and so on.

'Are they really full of jewels?' Thomas asked.

'Look and see,' Flagg said. He opened one of the bins and pulled out a handful of uncut emeralds. They sparkled wildly in his hand.

'My father's *name!*' Thomas gasped.

'Oh, that's nothing! Look over here! Pirate treasure, Tommy!'

He showed Thomas a pile of booty from the encounter with the Anduan pirates some twelve years ago. The Delain Treasury was rich, the few treasure-room clerks old, and this particular heap hadn't been sorted yet. Thomas gasped at heavy swords with jewelled hilts, daggers with blades that had been crusted with serrated diamonds so they would cut deeper, heavy killballs made of rhodo-chrosite.

'All this belongs to the Kingdom?' Thomas asked in an awed voice.

'It all belongs to your *father*,' Flagg replied, although Thomas had actually been correct. 'Some-day it will all belong to Peter.'

'And me,' Thomas said with a ten-year-old's confidence.

'No,' Flagg said, just the right tinge of regret in his voice, 'just to Peter. Because he's the oldest, and he'll be King.'

'He'll share,' Thomas said, but with the slightest tremor of doubt in his vocie. 'Pete *always* shares.'

'Peter's a fine boy, and I'm sure you're right. He'll *probably* share. But no one can *make* a King share, you know. No one can *make* a King do any-thing he doesn't want to do.' He looked at Thomas to guage the effect of this remark, then looked back at the deep, shadowy treasure room. Somewhere, one of the aged clerks was droning out a count of ducats. 'Such a lot of treasure, and all for one man,' Flagg remarked. 'It's really something to think about, isn't it, Tommy?'

Thomas said nothing, but Flagg had been well pleased. He saw that Tommy *was* thinking about it, all right, and he judged that another of those poisoned cas-kets was tumbling down into the well of Thomas's mind – *ker-splash!* And that was indeed so. Later, when

Peter proposed to Thomas that they share the expense of the nightly bottle of wine, Thomas had remembered the great treasure room – and he remembered that all the treasure in it would belong to his brother. *Easy for you to talk so blithely of buying wine! Why not? Someday you'll have all the money in the world!*

Then, about a year before he brought the poisoned wine to the King, on impulse, Flagg had shown Thomas this secret passage . . . and on this one occasion his usually unerring instinct for mischief might have led him astray. Again, I leave it for you to decide.

26

Tommy, you look down in the dumps!' he cried. The hood of his cloak was pushed back on that day, and he looked almost normal.

Almost.

Tommy *felt* down in them. He had suffered through a long luncheon at which his father had praised Peter's scores in geometry and navigation to his advisors with the most lavish superlatives. Roland had never rightly understood either. He knew that a triangle had three sides and a square had four; he knew you could find your way out of the woods when you were lost by following Old Star in the sky; and that was where his knowledge ended. That was where Thomas's knowledge ended, too, so he felt that luncheon would never be done. Worse, the meat was just the way his father liked it – bloody and barely cooked. Bloody meat made Thomas feel almost sick.

'My lunch didn't agree with me, that's all,' he said to Flagg.

'Well, I know just the thing to cheer you up,' Flagg said. 'I'll show you a secret of the castle, Tommy my boy.'

Thomas was playing with a buggerlug bug. He had it on his desk and had set his schoolbooks around it in a series of barriers. If the trundling beetle looked as if he might find a way out, Thomas would shift one of the books to keep him in.

'I'm pretty tired,' Thomas said. This was not a lie. Hearing Peter praised so highly always made him feel tired.

'You'll like it,' Flagg said in a tone that was mostly wheedling . . . but a little threatening, too.

Thomas looked at him apprehensively. 'There aren't any . . . any bats, are there?'

Flagg laughed cheerily – but that laugh raised gooseflesh on Thomas's arms anyway. He clapped Thomas on the back. 'Not a bat! Not a drip! Not a draught! Warm as toast! And you can peek at your father, Tommy!'

Thomas knew that peeking was just another way of saying spying, and that spying was wrong – but this had been a shrewd shot all the same. This next time the buggerlug bug found a way to escape between two of the books, Thomas let it go. 'All right,' he said, 'but there better not be any bats.'

Flagg slipped an arm around the boy's shoulders. 'No bats, I swear – but here's something for you to mull over in your mind, Tommy. You'll not only see your father, you'll see him through the eyes of his greatest trophy.'

Thomas's own eyes widened with interest. Flagg was satisfied. The fish was hooked and landed. 'What do you mean?'

'Come and see for yourself,' was all he would say.

He led Thomas through a maze of corridors. You would have become lost very soon, and I probably would have gotten lost myself before long, but Thomas knew this way as well as you know your way through your own bedroom in the dark – at least he did until Flagg led him aside.

They had almost reached the King's own apartments when Flagg pushed open a recessed wooden door that Thomas had never really noticed before. Of course it had always been there, but in castles there are often doors – whole wings, even – that have mastered the art of being *dim*.

This passage was quite narrow. A chambermaid with an armload of sheets passed them; she was so terrified to have met the King's magician in this slim stone throat that it seemed she would happily have shrunk into the very pores of the stone blocks to avoid touching him. Thomas almost laughed because sometimes he felt a little like that himself when Flagg was around. They met no one else at all.

Faintly, from below them, he could hear dogs barking, and that gave him a rough idea of where he was. The only dogs inside the castle proper were his father's hunting dogs, and they were probably barking because it was time for them to be fed. Most of Roland's dogs were now almost as old as he was, and because he knew how the cold ached in his own bones, Roland had commanded that a kennel be made for them right here in the castle. To reach the dogs from his father's main sitting chamber, one went down a flight of stairs, turned right, and walked ten yards or so up an interior corridor. So Thomas knew they were about thirty feet to the right of his father's private rooms.

Flagg stopped so suddenly that Thomas almost ran into him. The magician looked swiftly around to make sure they had the passageway to themselves. They did.

'Fourth stone up from the one at the bottom with the chip in it,' Flagg said. 'Press it. Quick!'

Ah, there was a secret here, all right, and Thomas loved secrets. Brightening, he counted up four stones from the one with the chip and pressed. He expected some neat little bit of jiggery-pokery – a sliding panel, perhaps – but he was quite unprepared for what did happen.

The stone slid in with perfect ease to a depth of about three inches. There was a click. An entire section of wall suddenly swung inward, revealing a dark vertical crack. This wasn't a wall at all! It was a huge door! Thomas's jaw dropped.

Flagg slapped Thomas's bottom.

'Quick, I said, you little fool!' he cried in a low voice. There was urgency in his voice, and this wasn't simply put on for Thomas's benefit, as many of Flagg's emotions were. He looked right and left to verify that the passage was still empty. 'Go! Now!'

Thomas looked at the dark crack that had been

revealed and thought uneasily about bats again. But one look at Flagg's face showed him that this would be a bad time to attempt a discussion on the subject.

He pushed the door open wider and stepped into the darkness. Flagg followed at once. Thomas heard the low flap of the magician's cloak as he turned and shoved the wall closed again. The darkness was utter and complete, the air still and dry. Before he could open his mouth to say anything, the blue flame at the tip of Flagg's index finger flared alight, throwing a harsh blue-white fan of illumination.

Thomas cringed without even thinking about it, and his hands flew up.

Flagg laughed harshly. 'No bats, Tommy. Didn't I promise?'

Nor were there. The ceiling was quite low, and Thomas could see for himself. No bats, and warm as toast . . . just as the magician had promised. By the light of Flagg's magic finger-flare, he could also see they were in a secret passage which was about twenty-five feet long. Walls, floor, and ceiling were covered with ironwood boards. He couldn't see the far end very well, but it looked perfectly blank.

He could still hear the muffled barking of the dogs.

'When I said be quick, I meant it,' Flagg said. He bent over Thomas, a vague, looming shadow that was, in this darkness, rather batlike itself. Thomas drew back a step, uneasily. As always, there was an unpleasant smell about the magician – a smell of secret powders and bitter herbs. 'You know where the passage is now, and I'll not be the one to tell you not to use it. But if you're ever *caught* using it, you must say you discovered it by accident.'

The shape loomed even closer, forcing Thomas back another step.

'If you say *I* showed it to you, Tommy, I'll make you sorry.'

'I'll never tell,' Thomas said. His words sounded thin and shaky.

'Good. Better yet if no one ever sees you using it. Spying on a King is serious business, prince or not. Now follow me. And be quiet.'

Flagg led him to the end of the passageway. The far wall was also dressed with ironwood, but when Flagg raised the flame that burned from the tip of his finger, Thomas saw two little panels. Flagg pursed his lips and blew out the light.

In utter blackness, he whispered: 'Never open these two panels with a light burning. He might see. He's old, but he still sees well. He might see something, even though the eyeballs are of tinted glass.'

'What —'

'*Shhhh!* There isn't much wrong with his ears, either.'

Thomas fell quiet, his heart pounding in his chest. He felt a great excitement that he didn't understand. Later he thought that he had been excited because he knew in some way what was going to happen.

In the darkness he heard a faint sliding sound, and suddenly a dim ray of light – torchlight – lit the darkness. There was a second sliding sound and a second ray of light appeared. Now he could see Flagg again, very faintly, and his own hands when he held them up before him.

Thomas saw Flagg step up to the wall and bend a little; then most of the light was cut out as he put his eyes to the two holes through which the rays of light fell. He looked for a moment, then grunted and stepped away. He motioned to Thomas. 'Have a look,' he said.

More excited than ever, Thomas cautiously put his eyes to the holes. He saw clearly enough, although everything had an odd greenish-yellow aspect – it was as if he were looking through smoked glass. A sense of perfect, delighted wonder rose in him. He was looking down into his father's sitting room. He saw his father slouched by the fire in his favourite chair – one with high wings which threw shadows across his lined face.

It was very much the room of a huntsman; in our world such a room would often be called a den, although this one was as big as some ordinary houses. Flaring torches lined the long walls. Heads were mounted everywhere: heads of bear, of deer, of elk, of wildebeest, of cormorant. There was even a grand featherex, which is the cousin of our legendary bird the phoenix. Thomas could not see the head of Niner, the dragon his father had killed before he was born, but this did not immediately register on him.

His father was picking morosely at a sweet. A pot of tea steamed near at hand.

That was all that was really happening in that great room that could have (and at times had) held upward of two hundred people – just his father, with a fur robe draped around him, having a solitary after-

noon tea. Yet Thomas watched for a time that seemed endless. His fascination and his excitement with this view of his father cannot be told. His heartbeat, which had been rapid before, doubled. Blood sang and pounded in his head. His hands clenched into fists so tight that he would later discover bloody crescent moons imprinted into his palms where his fingernails had bitten.

Why was he so excited simply to be looking at an old man picking halfheartedly at a piece of cake? Well, first you must remember that the old man wasn't just *any* old man. He was Thomas's father. And spying, sad to say, has its own attraction. When you can see people doing something and they don't see you, even the most trivial actions seem important.

After awhile, Thomas began to feel a little ashamed of what he was doing, and that was not really surprising. Spying on a person is a kind of stealing, after all – it's stealing a look at what people do when they think they are alone. But that is also one of its chief fascinations, and Thomas might have looked for hours if Flagg had not murmured, 'Do you know where you are, Tommy?'

'I –' *don't think so*, he was going to add, but of course he did know. His sense of direction was good, and with a little thought he could imagine the reverse of this angle. He suddenly understood what Flagg meant when he said he, Thomas, would see his father through the eyes of Roland's greatest trophy. He was looking down at his father from a little more than halfway up the west wall . . . and that was where the greatest head of all was hung – that of Niner, his father's dragon.

He might see something, even though the eyeballs are of tinted glass. Now he understood that, too. Thomas had to clap his hands to his mouth to stifle a shrill giggle.

Flagg slid the little panels shut again . . . but he, too, was smiling.

'No!' Thomas whispered. 'No, I want to see more!'

'Not this afternoon,' Flagg said. 'You've seen enough this afternoon. You can come again when you want . . . although if you come too often, you'll surely be caught. Now come on. We're going back.'

Flagg relit the magic flame and led Thomas down the corridor again. At the end, he put the light out and there was another sliding sound as he opened a peephole. He guided Thomas's hand to it so he would know where it was, and then bade him look.

'Notice that you can see the passageway in both directions,' Flagg said. 'Always be careful to look before you open the secret door, or someday you will be surprised.'

Thomas put one eye to the peephole and saw, directly across the corridor, an ornate window with glass sides that angled slightly into the passageway. It was much too fancy for such a small passageway, but Thomas understood without having to be told that it had been put here by whoever had made the secret passageway. Looking into the angled sides, he could indeed see a ghostly reflection of the corridor in both directions.

'Empty?' Flagg whispered.

'Yes,' Thomas whispered back.

Flagg pushed an interior spring (again guiding Thomas's hand to it for future reference), and the door clicked open. 'Quickly now!' Flagg said. They were out and the door was shut behind them in a trice.

Ten minutes later, they were back in Thomas's rooms.

'Enough excitement for one day,' Flagg said. 'Remember what I told you, Tommy: don't use the passageway so often that you'll be caught, and if you *are* caught' – Flagg's eyes glittered grimly – 'remember that you found that place by accident.'

'I will,' Thomas said quickly. His voice was high and it squeaked like a hinge that needed oil. When Flagg looked at him that way, his heart felt like a bird caught in his chest, fluttering in panic.

27

Thomas heeded Flagg's advice not to go often, but he *did* use the passageway from time to time, and peeked at his father through the glass eyes of Niner – peeked into a world where everything became greeny-gold. Going away later with a pounding headache (as he almost always did), he would think: *Your head aches because you were seeing the way dragons must see the world – as if everything was dried out and ready to burn.* And perhaps Flagg's instinct for mischief in this matter was not so bad at all, because, by spying on his father, Thomas learned to feel a new thing for Roland. Before he knew about the secret passage he had felt love for him, and often a sorrow that he could not please him better, and sometimes fear. Now he learned to feel contempt, as well.

Whenever Thomas spied into Roland's sitting room and found his father in company, he left again quickly. He only lingered when his father was alone. In the past, Roland rarely had been, even in such rooms as his den, which was a part of his 'private apartments.' There was always one more urgent matter to be attended to, one more advisor to see, one more petition to hear.

But Roland's time of power was passing. As his importance waned with his good health, he found himself remembering all the times he had cried to either Sasha or Flagg: 'Won't these people ever leave me alone?' The memory brought a rueful smile to his lips. Now that they did, he missed them.

Thomas felt contempt because people are rarely at their best when they are alone. They usually put their masks of politeness, good order, and good breeding aside. What's beneath? Some warty monster? Some disgusting thing that would make people run away, screaming? Sometimes, perhaps, but usually it's nothing bad at all. Usually people would just laugh if they saw us with our masks off – laugh, make a revolted face, or do both at the same time.

Thomas saw that his father, whom he had always loved and feared, who had seemed to him the greatest man in the world, often picked his nose when he was alone. He would root around in first one nostril and then the other until he got a plump green booger. He would regard these with solemn satisfaction, turning each one this way and that in the firelight, the way a jeweller might turn a particularly fine emerald. Most of these he would then rub under the chair in which he was sitting. Others, I regret to say, he popped into his mouth and munched with an expression of reflective enjoyment on his face.

He would have only a single glass of wine at night – the glass which Peter brought him – but after Peter left, he drank what seemed to Thomas huge amounts of beer (it was only years later that Thomas came to realize that his father hadn't wanted Peter to see him drunk), and when he needed to urinate, he rarely used the commode in the corner. Most times he simply stood up and pissed into the fire, often farting as he did so.

He talked to himself. He would sometimes walk around the long room like a man who was not sure where he was, speaking either to the air or to the mounted heads.

'I remember that day we got you, Bonsey,' he would say to one of the elk heads (another of his eccentricities was that he had named every one of the trophies). 'I was with Bill Squathings and that fellow with the great lump on the side of his face. I remember how you come through the trees and Bill let loose, and then that fellow with the lump let loose, then *I* let loose –'

Then his father would demonstrate how he had let loose by raising his leg and farting, even as he mimed drawing back a bowstring and letting fly.

And he would laugh an old man's shrill, unpleasant cackle.

Thomas would slide the little panels back after awhile and slink down the corridor again, his head pounding and an uneasy grin on his face – the head and grin of a boy who has been eating green apples and knows he may be sicker by morning than he is now.

This was the father he had always loved and feared?

He was an old man who farted out stinking clouds of steam.

This was the King his loyal subjects called Roland the Good?

He pissed into the fire, sending up more clouds of steam.

This was the man who made his heart break by not liking his boat?

He talked to the stuffed heads on his walls, calling them silly names like Bonsey and Stag-Pool and Puckerstring; he picked his nose and sometimes ate the boogers.

I don't care for you anymore, Thomas would think, checking the peephole to make sure the corridor was empty and then creeping back to his room like a felon. *You're a filthy, silly old man and you're nothing to me! Nothing at all! No!*

But he *was* something to Thomas. Some part of him went on loving Roland just the same – some part of him wanted to go to his father so his father would have something better to talk to than a bunch of stuffed heads on the walls.

Still, there was that other part of him that liked spying better.

The night that Flagg came to King Roland's private rooms with the glass of poisoned wine was the first occasion in a very long time that Thomas had dared spy. There was a good reason for this.

One night about three months before, Thomas found himself unable to sleep. He tossed and turned until he heard the keep watchman cry eleven. Then he got up, dressed, and left his rooms. Less than ten minutes later, he was looking down into his father's den. He had thought his father might be asleep, but he was not. Roland was awake, and very, very drunk.

Thomas had seen his father drunk many times before, but he had never seen him in anything remotely like his current state. The boy was flabbergasted and badly frightened.

There are people much older than Thomas was then who harbour the idea that old age is always a gentle time – that an old person may exhibit gentle wisdom, gentle crabbiness or craftiness, perhaps the gentle confusion of senility. They will grant these, but find it hard to credit any real fire. They have an illusion that by the seventies, any real fire must have faded to coals. That may be true, but on this night Thomas discovered that coals may sometimes flare up violently.

His father was striding rapidly up and down the length of his sitting room, his fur robe flying out behind him. His nightcap had fallen off; his remaining hair hung down in tangled locks, mostly about his ears. He was not staggering, as he had done on other nights, moving tentatively with one hand out to keep from running into the furniture. He was rolling like a sailor, but he was not staggering. When he did happen to run into one of the high-backed chairs which stood near the walls beneath the snarling head of a lynx, Roland threw the chair aside with a roar that made Thomas cringe. The hairs on his arms prickled. The chair flew across the room and hit the far wall. Its ironwood back splintered down the middle – in this bitter drunkenness, the old King had regained the strength of his middle years.

He looked up at the lynx head with red, glaring eyes.

'*Bite me!*' he roared at it. The raw hoarseness in his voice made Thomas cringe again. '*Bite me, are you afeard? Come down out of that wall, Craker! Jump! Here's my chest, see?*' He tore open the robe, revealing his scrawny chest. He bared his few teeth at Craker's many, and lifted his head. '*Here's my neck! Come on, jump! I'll do you with my bare hands! I'LL RIP YOUR STINKING GUTS OUT!*'

He stood for a moment, chest out and head up, looking like an animal himself – an ancient stag, perhaps, that has been brought to bay and can now hope for nothing better than to die well. Then he whirled away, stopping at a bear's head to shake a fist at it and roar a string of curses at it – curses so terrible that Thomas, cringing in the dark, believed that the bear's outraged spirit might swoop down, reanimate the stuffed head, and tear his father open while he watched.

But Roland was away again. He seized his mug, drained it, then whirled with brew dripping from his chops. He hurled the silver mug across the room, where it struck a stone angle of the fireplace hard enough to leave a dent in the metal.

Now his father came down the room toward him, throwing another chair out of the way, then kicking a table aside with his barefoot. His eyes flicked up . . . and met Thomas's own. Yes – they met his own eyes. Thomas felt their gazes lock, and a grey, swooning terror filled him like frozen breath.

His father stalked toward him, his yellowed teeth bared, his remaining hair hanging over his ears, beer dripping from his chin and the corners of his mouth.

'You,' Roland whispered in a low, terrible voice. 'Why do you stare at me? What do you hope to see?'

Thomas could not move. *Found out*, his mind gibbered, *found out, by all the gods that ever were or shall be, I am found out and I will surely be exiled!*

His father stood there, his eyes fixed on the mounted dragon's head. In his guilt, Thomas was sure his father had spoken to him, but this was not so – Roland had only spoken to Niner as he had spoken to the other heads. Yet if Thomas could see out of the tinted glass eyeballs, then his father could see in, at least to some degree. If Thomas hadn't been utterly paralyzed with fear, he would have run away in a panic – even if he had summoned enough presence of mind to hold his ground, his *eyes* surely would have moved. And if Roland had seen the eyes of the dragon move, what might he have thought? That the dragon was coming to life again? Perhaps. In his drunken state, I even think that likely. If Thomas had so much as blinked his eyes on that occasion, Flagg would have needed no poison later. The King, old and frail in spite of the temporary potency the drink had given him, would almost surely have died of fright.

Roland suddenly leaped forward.

'*WHY DO YOU STARE AT ME?*' he shrieked, and in his drunkenness it was Niner, Delain's last dragon, that he shrieked at, but of course, Thomas did not know that. '*WHY DO YOU STARE AT ME SO? I'VE DONE THE BEST I COULD, ALWAYS THE BEST I COULD! DID I ASK FOR THIS? DID I ASK FOR IT? ANSWER ME, DAMN YOU! I DID THE BEST I COULD AND LOOK AT ME NOW! LOOK AT ME NOW!*'

He pulled his robe wide open, showing his naked body, its grey skin blotchily flushed with drink.

'*LOOK AT ME NOW!*' he shrieked again, and looked down at himself, weeping.

Thomas could take no more. He slammed shut the panels behind the dragon's glass eyes at the same moment his father took his eyes from Niner to look down at his own wasted body. Thomas crashed and blundered down the black corridor and slammed full force into the closed door, braining himself and falling in a heap. He was up in a moment, unaware of the blood pouring down his face from a cut in his forehead, pounding at the secret spring until the door popped open. He rushed out into the corridor, not even thinking to check if anyone was there to see him. All he could see was his father's glaring, bloodshot eyes, all he could hear was his father screaming *Why do you stare at me?*

He had no way of knowing that his father had already fallen into a sleep of deep drunkenness. When Roland woke up the next morning, he was still on the floor, and the first thing he did, in spite of his fiercely aching head and his throbbing, bruised body (Roland was far too old for such strenuous revels), was to look at the dragon's head. He rarely dreamed when he was drunk – there was only an interval of sodden darkness. But last night a terrible dream had come to him: the glass eyes of the dragon's head had moved and Niner came to life. The worm breathed its deadly breath down on him, and although he could not see that fire, he could feel it deep down inside him, hot and getting hotter.

With this dream still lingering fresh in his mind, he dreaded what he might see when he looked up. But all was as it had been for years now. Niner snarled his fearsome snarl, his forked tongue lolled between teeth almost as long as fence pickets, his green-gold eyes stared blankly across the room. Ceremoniously crossed above this fabulous trophy were Roland's great bow and the arrow Foe-Hammer, its tip and shaft still black with dragon blood. He mentioned this terrible dream once to Flagg, who only nodded and looked more thoughtful than usual. Then Roland simply forgot it.

Forgetting was not so easy for Thomas.

He was haunted for weeks by nightmares. In them, his father stared at him and shrieked, '*See what you've done to me!'* and threw his robe open to display his nakedness – old puckered scars, drooping belly, sagging muscles – as if to say this too had all been Thomas's fault, that if he hadn't spied . . .

'Why do you never want to see Father anymore?' Peter asked him one day. 'He thinks you're mad at him.'

'That *I'm* mad at *him*?' Thomas was astounded.

'That's what he said at tea today,' Peter said. He looked at his brother closely, observing the dark circles under Thomas's eyes, the pallor of Thomas's cheeks and forehead. 'Tom, what's wrong?'

'Maybe nothing,' Thomas said slowly.

The next day he took tea with his father and brother. Going took all of his courage, but Thomas *did* have courage, and he sometimes found it – usually when his back was to the wall. His father gave him a kiss and asked him if anything was wrong. Thomas muttered that he hadn't been feeling well, but now he felt fine. His father nodded, gave him a rough hug, then went back to his usual behaviour – which consisted mostly of ignoring Thomas in favour of Peter. For once, Thomas welcomed this – he didn't want his father looking at him any more than necessary, at least for a while. That night, lying awake for a long time in bed and listening to the wind moan outside, he came to the conclusion that he had had a very close shave . . . but that he had somehow gotten away with it.

But never again, he thought. In the weeks after, the nightmares came less and less frequently. Finally they stopped altogether.

Still, the castle's head groom, Yosef, was right

about one thing: boys are sometimes better at pledging vows than they are at keeping them, and Thomas's desire to spy on his father at last grew stronger than both his fears and his good intentions. And that is how it happened that on the night Flagg came to Roland with the poisoned wine, Thomas was watching.

When Thomas got there and slid aside the two little panels, his father and his brother were just finishing *their* nightly glass of wine together. Peter was now almost seventeen, tall and handsome. The two of them sat by the fire, drinking and talking like old friends, and Thomas felt the old hate fill his heart with acid. After some little time, Peter arose and took courteous leave of his father.

'You leave earlier and earlier these nights,' Roland remarked.

Peter made some demurral.

Roland smiled. It was a sweet, sad smile, mostly toothless. 'I hear,' said he, 'that she is lovely.'

Peter looked flustered, which was uncommon with him. He stammered, which was even less common.

'Go,' Roland interrupted. 'Go. Be gentle with her, and be kind . . . but be hot, if there is ardour in you. Later years are cold years, Peter. Be hot while your years are green, and fuel is plentiful, and the fire may burn high.'

Peter smiled. 'You speak as if you are very old, Father, but you still look strong and hale to me.'

Roland embraced Peter. 'I love you,' he said.

Peter smiled with no awkwardness or embarrassment. 'I love you, too, Dad,' he said, and in his lonely darkness (spying is always lonely work, and the spyer almost always does it in the dark), Thomas pulled a horrible face.

Peter left, and for an hour or more not much happened. Roland sat morosely by the fire, drinking glass after glass of beer. He did not roar or bellow or talk to the heads on the walls; there was no destruction of furniture. Thomas had almost made up his mind to leave, when there was a double rap at the door.

Roland had been looking into the fire, almost hypnotized by the flicker-play of the flames. Now he roused himself and called, 'Who comes?'

Thomas heard no response, but his father rose and went to the door as if *he* had. He opened it, and at first Thomas thought his father's habit of talking to the heads on the walls had taken a queer new turn – that his father was now inventing invisible human company to relieve his boredom.

'Strange to see *you* at this hour,' Roland said, apparently walking back toward the fire in the company of no one at all. 'I thought you were always at your spells and conjurations after dark.'

Thomas blinked, rubbed his eyes, and saw that someone was there after all. For a moment he couldn't rightly make out who . . . and then he wondered how he could possibly have thought his father was alone when Flagg was right there beside him. Flagg was carrying two glasses of wine on a silver tray.

'Wives' tale, m'Lord – magicians conjure early as well as late. But of course we have our darksome image to keep up.'

Roland's sense of humour was always improved by beer – so much so that he would often laugh at things that weren't funny in the least. At this remark he threw back his head and bellowed as if it was the greatest joke he had ever heard. Flagg smiled thinly.

When Roland's fit of laughing had passed, he said: 'What's this? Wine?'

'Your son is barely more than a boy, but his deference toward his father and his honour of his King have shamed me, a grown man,' Flagg said. 'I brought you a glass of wine, my King, to show you that I, too, love you.'

He passed it to Roland, who looked absurdly touched.

Don't drink it, Father! Thomas thought suddenly – his mind was full of an alarm he couldn't understand. Roland's head came up suddenly and tilted, almost as if he had heard.

'He's a good boy, my Peter,' Roland said.

'Indeed,' Flagg replied. 'Everyone in the Kingdom says so.'

'Do they?' Roland asked, looking pleased. 'Do they, indeed?'

'Yes – so they do. Shall we toast him?' Flagg raised his glass.

No, Father! Thomas shouted in his mind again,

but if his father had heard his first thought, he didn't hear this one. His face shone with love for Thomas's elder brother.

'To Peter, then!' Roland raised the glass of poisoned wine high.

'To Peter!' Flagg agreed, smiling. 'To the King!'

Thomas cringed in the dark. *Flagg's making two different toasts! I don't know what he means, but . . . Father!*

This time it was Flagg who turned his darkly considering gaze toward the dragon's head for a moment, as if *he* had heard the thought. Thomas froze, and in a moment Flagg's gaze turned back to Roland.

They clinked glasses and drank. As his father quaffed the glass of wine, Thomas felt a splinter of ice push its way into his heart.

Flagg made a half-turn in his chair and threw his glass into the fire. 'Peter!'

'Peter!' Roland echoed, and threw his own. It smashed against the sooty brickwork at the back of the fireplace and fell into the flames, which for a moment seemed to flare an ugly green.

Roland raised the back of his hand to his mouth for a moment, as if to stifle a belch. 'Did you spice it?' he asked. 'It tasted . . . almost mulled.'

'No, my Lord,' Flagg said gravely, but Thomas thought he sensed a smile behind the mask of the magician's gravity, and that splinter of ice slipped further into his heart. Suddenly he wanted no more of spying, not ever. He closed the peepholes and crept back to his room. He felt first hot, then cold, then hot again. By morning he had a fever. Before he was well again, his father was dead, his brother imprisoned in the room at the top of the Needle, and he was a boy King at the age of barely twelve – Thomas the Light-Bringer, he was dubbed at the coronation ceremonies. And who was his closest advisor?

You guess.

When Flagg left Roland (the old man was feeling sprightlier than ever by then, a sure sign the Dragon Sand was at work in him), he went back to his dark basement rooms. He got out the tweezers and the packet containing the remaining few grains of sand and put them on his huge old desk. Then he turned his hourglass over and resumed reading.

Outside, the wind screamed and gobbled – old wives cringed in their beds and slept poorly and told their husbands that Rhiannon, the Dark Witch of the Coos, was riding her hateful broom this night, and wicked work was afoot. The husbands grunted, turned over, told their wives to go back to sleep and leave them alone. They were dull fellows for the most part; when an eye is wanted to see straws flying in the wind, give me an old wife any day.

Once a spider skittered halfway across Flagg's book, touched a spell so terrible not even the magician dared use it, and turned instantly to stone.

Flagg grinned.

When the hourglass was empty, he turned it over again. And again. And again. He turned it over eight times in all, and when the eighth hour's worth of sand was nearly gone, he set about finishing his work. He kept a large number of animals in a dim room down the hall from his study, and he went there first. The little creatures skittered and cringed when Flagg came near. He did not blame them.

In the far corner was a wicker cage containing half a dozen brown mice – such mice were everywhere in the castle, and that was important. Down here there were also huge rats, but it was not a rat Flagg wanted tonight. The Royal Rat upstairs had been poisoned; a simple mouse would be enough to make sure the crime came home to the Royal Ratling. If all went well, Peter would soon be as tightly locked up as these mice.

Flagg reached into the cage and removed one. It trembled wildly in his cupped hand. He could feel the rapid thrumming of its heart, and he knew that if he simply held it, it would soon die of fright.

Flagg pointed the little finger of his left hand at the mouse. The fingernail glowed faintly blue for a moment.

'Sleep,' the magician commanded, and the mouse fell on its side and went to sleep on his open palm.

Flagg took it back into his study and laid it on his desk, where the obsidian paperweight had rested earlier. Now he went into his larder and drew a little mead from an oaken barrel into a saucer. He sweetened it with honey. He put it on his desk, then went out into the corridor and breathed deeply at the window again.

Holding his breath, he came back in and used the tweezers to pour all but the last three or four grains of Dragon Sand into the honey-sweetened mead. Then he opened another drawer of his desk and removed a fresh packet, which was empty. Then, reaching all the way to the back of this drawer, he brought out a very special box.

The fresh packet was bewitched, but its magic was not very strong. It would hold the Dragon Sand safely only for a short while. Then it would begin to work on the paper. It would not set it alight, not inside the box; there would not be air enough for that. But it would smoke and smoulder, and that would be enough. That would be fine.

Flagg's chest was thudding for air, but he still spared a moment to look at this box and congratulate himself. He had stolen it ten years ago. If you had asked him at the time why he took it, he would have known no more than he knew why he had shown Thomas the secret passage that ended behind the dragon's head – that instinct for mischief had told him to take it and that he would find a use for it, so he had. After all those years in his desk, that useful time had come.

PETER was engraved across the top of the box.

Sasha had given it to her boy; he had left it for a moment on a table in a hallway when he had to run down the hallway after something or other; Flagg came along, saw it, and popped it into his pocket. Peter had been grief-stricken, of course, and when a prince is upset – even a prince who is only six years old – people take notice. There had been a search, but the box had never been found.

Using the tweezers, Flagg carefully poured the last few grains of Dragon Sand from the original packet, which had been wholly enchanted, into the packet which had been only incompletely enchanted. Then he went back to the window in the corridor to draw fresh breath. He did not breathe again until the fresh packet had been laid in the antique wooden box, the tweezers laid in there beside it, the top of the box slowly closed, and the original packet disposed of in the sewer.

Flagg was hurrying now, but he felt secure enough. Mouse, sleeping; box, closed; incriminating evidence safely latched inside. It was very well.

Pointing the little finger of his left hand at the mouse lying stretched out on his desk like a fur rug for pixies, Flagg commanded: 'Wake.'

The mouse's feet twitched. Its eyes opened. Its head came up.

Smiling, Flagg wiggled his little finger in a circle and said: 'Run.'

The mouse ran in circles.

Flagg wiggled his finger up and down.

'Jump.'

The mouse began to jump on its hind legs like a dog in a carnival, its eyes rolling wildly.

'Now drink,' Flagg said, and pointed his little finger at the dish holding the honey-sweetened mead.

Outside, the wind gusted to a roar. On the far side of the city, a bitch gave birth to a litter of two-headed pups.

The mouse drank.

'Now,' said Flagg, when the mouse had drunk enough of the poison to serve his purpose, 'sleep again.' And the mouse did.

Flagg hurried to Peter's rooms. The box was in one of his many pockets – magicians have many, many pockets – and the sleeping mouse was in another. He passed several servants and a laughing gaggle of drunken courtiers, but none saw him. He was still *dim*.

Peter's rooms were locked, but that was no problem for one of Flagg's talents. Three passes with his hands and the door was open. The young prince's rooms were empty, of course; the boy was still with his lady friend. Flagg didn't know as much about Peter as he did about Thomas, but he knew enough – he knew, for instance, where Peter kept the few treasures he thought worth hiding away.

Flagg went directly to the bookcase and pulled out three or four boring textbooks. He pushed at a wooden edging and heard a spring click back. He then slid a panel aside, revealing a recess in the back of the case. It was not even locked. In the recess was a silk hair-ribbon his lady had given him, a packet of letters she had written him, a few letters from him to her which burned so brightly he did not dare to send them, and a little locket with his mother's picture inside it.

Flagg opened the engraved box and very carefully shredded one corner of the packet's flap. Now it looked as if a mouse had been chewing at it. Flagg closed the lid again and put the box in the recessed space. 'You cried so when you lost this box, dear

Peter,' he murmured. 'I think you may cry even more when it's found.' He giggled.

He put the sleeping mouse beside the box, closed the compartment, and put the books neatly back in place.

Then he left, and slept well. Great mischief was afoot, and he felt confident that he had moved as as he liked to move – behind the scenes, seen by no one.

31

For the next three days, King Roland seemed healthier, more vigorous, and more decisive than anyone had seen him in years – it was the talk of the court. Visiting his ill and feverish brother in his apartments, Peter remarked to Thomas in awe that what remained of their father's hair actually seemed to be changing colour, from the baby-fine wispy white it had been for the last four years or so to the iron grey it had been in Roland's middle years.

Thomas smiled, but a fresh chill raced through him. He asked Peter for another blanket, but it wasn't really a blanket he needed; he needed to unsee that final strange toast, and that, of course, was impossible.

Then, after dinner on the third day, Roland complained of indigestion. Flagg offered to have the court physician summoned. Roland waved the suggestion away, saying that he felt fine, actually, better than he had in months, in years –

He belched. It was a long, arid, rattling sound. The convivial crowd in the ballroom fell silent with wonder and apprehension as the King doubled over. The musicians in the corner ceased playing. When Roland straightened up, a gasp ran through those present. The King's cheeks were aflame with colour. Smoking tears ran from his eyes. More smoke drifted from his mouth.

There were perhaps seventy people in that great dining hall – rough-dressed Riders (what we would call knights, I suppose), sleek courtiers and their ladies, attendants upon the throne, courtesans, jesters, musicians, a little troupe of actors in one corner who had been going to put on a play later, servants in great numbers. But it was Peter who ran to his father; it was Peter they all saw going to the doomed man, and this did not displease Flagg at all.

Peter. They would remember it had been Peter.

Roland clutched his stomach with one hand and his chest with the other. Smoke suddenly poured out of his mouth in a grey-white plume. It was as if the King had learned some amazing new way of telling the story of his greatest exploit.

But it was no trick, and there were screams as smoke poured not only from his mouth but from his nostrils, ears, and the corners of his eyes. His throat was so red it was nearly purple.

'*Dragon!*' King Roland shrieked as he collapsed into his son's arms. '*Dragon!*'

It was the last word he ever spoke.

32

The old man was tough – incredibly tough. Before he died he was throwing off so much heat that no one, not even his most loyal servants, could approach closer to his bed than four feet. Several times they threw buckets of water on the poor dying King when they saw the bedclothes beginning to smoulder. Each time, the water turned instantly to steam that billowed through his bed-chamber and out into the sitting room where court-iers and Riders stood in numb silence and ladies clustered, weeping and wringing their hands.

Just before midnight, a jet of green flame shot from his mouth and he died.

Flagg went solemnly to the door between the bedchamber and the sitting room and announced the news. There followed an utter silence that stretched out for more than a minute. It was broken by a single word which came from somewhere in the gathered crowd. Flagg did not know who spoke that one word, and he did not care. It was enough that it had been spoken. Indeed, he would have bribed a man to speak it if such could have been done with no danger to him.

'Murder!' this someone said.

There was a universal gasp.

Flagg raised a solemn hand to his mouth to hide a smile.

The court physician amplified one word to three: *Murder by poison.* He did not say *Murder by Dragon Sand*, for the poison was unknown in Delain, except to Flagg.

The King died shortly before midnight, but by dawn the charge was rife in the city and spreading outward toward the far reaches of the Eastern, Western, Southern, and Northern Baronies: *Murder, regicide, Roland the Good dead by poison.*

Even before then, Flagg had organized a search of the castle, from the highest point (the Eastern Tower) to the lowest (the Dungeon of Inquisition, with its racks and manacles and squeezing boots). Any evidence bearing on this terrible crime, he said, must be searched out and reported at once.

The castle rang with the search. Six hundred grimly eager men combed through it. Only two small areas of the castle were exempt; these were the apartments of the two princes, Peter and Thomas.

Thomas was barely aware of this; his fever had worsened to the point where the court physician had become deeply alarmed. He lay in a delirium as dawn's first light fingered its way into his windows. In his dreams, he saw two glasses of wine raised high, heard his father say again and again: *Did you spice it? It tasted mulled.*

Flagg had ordered the search, but by two in the morning, Peter had recovered enough of his wits to take charge of it. Flagg let him. These next few hours would be terribly important, a time when all could be won or lost, and Flagg knew it. The King was dead; the Kingdom was momentarily headless. But not for long; this very day, Peter would be crowned King at the foot of the Needle, unless the crime was brought home to the boy quickly and conclusively.

Under other circumstances, Flagg knew, Peter would have been under suspicion at once. People *always* suspect those who have the most to gain, and Peter had gained a great deal by his father's death. Poison was horrible, but poison might have won him a kingdom.

But in this case, the people of the Kingdom spoke of the boy's loss rather than the boy's gain. Of course, *Thomas* had lost his father, too, they might add after a pause – almost as if they were ashamed of the momentary lapse. But Thomas was a sullen, sulky, awkward boy who had often argued with his father. Peter's affection and respect for Roland, on the other hand, were known far and wide. And why, people would ask – if the monstrous idea was even raised, and so far it had not been – why would Peter kill his father for the crown when he would surely inherit it in a year, or three, or five?

If evidence of the crime were to be found in a secret place that only Peter knew, however – a place in the prince's own rooms – the tide would turn quickly. People would begin to see a murderer's face beneath a mask of affection and respect. They would point out that, to the young, a year may seem like three, three like nine, five like twenty-five. Then they would point out that the King had seemed, in the last few days of his life, to be coming out of a long, dark time – had seemed to be growing hale and vigorous again. perhaps, they would say, Peter had believed his father was entering a long, healthy Indian summer, had panicked and done something as foolish as it was monstrous.

Flagg knew something else; he knew that people have a deep and instinctive distrust of all Kings and princes, for these are people who may order their deaths with a single nod, and for crimes as petty as dropping a handkerchief in their presence. Great Kings are loved, lesser Kings are tolerated; Kings-to-be represent a scary unknown quantity. They might come to love Peter if given a chance, but Flagg knew they would also condemn him quickly if shown enough evidence.

Flagg thought such evidence would be forthcoming soon.

Nothing more than a mouse. Small . . . but big enough in its way to shake a kingdom to its foundations.

In Delain there were only three stages of being: childhood, half-manhood or -womanhood, and adulthood. These 'half-years' lasted from fourteen to eighteen.

When Peter entered half-manhood, the scolding nannies were replaced with Brandon, his butler, and

Dennis, Brandon's son. Brandon would be Peter's butler for years yet, but probably not forever. Peter was very young, and Brandon was nearing fifty. When Brandon was no longer able to buttle, Dennis would take over. Brandon's family had buttled high royalty for nearly eight hundred years, and were justifiably proud of the fact.

Dennis rose each morning at five o'clock, dressed, laid out his father's suit, and shined his father's shoes. Then he wandered blearily into the kitchen and ate breakfast. At quarter to six, he set out from the family's home on the west side of the castle keep and entered the castle proper by the Lesser West Door.

Promptly at six o'clock he would reach Peter's rooms, let himself quietly in, and go about the early chores – building a fire, making half a dozen breakfast muffins, heating water for tea. Then he would quickly circle the three rooms, setting them to rights. This was usually easy, because Peter was not a messy boy. Last of all, he would return to the study and lay out breakfast, for the study was where Peter liked to eat the meals he took in his rooms – usually at his desk by the east windows, with a history book open before him.

Dennis didn't like getting up early, but he liked his job very much, and he liked Peter, who was always patient with him, even when he made a mistake. The only time he had ever raised his voice to Dennis was when Dennis had brought him a light lunch and had neglected to put a napkin on the tray.

'I'm very sorry, y'Highness,' Dennis had said on that occasion. 'I just never thought –'

'Well next time, *do* think!' Peter said. He was not shouting, but it was a close thing. Dennis had never neglected to put a napkin on Peter's tray again – and sometimes, just to be safe, he put on two.

Morning chores done, Dennis faded into the background and his father took over. Brandon was every bit the perfect butler, with his cravat neatly knotted, his hair pulled tightly back and rolled in a bun at the nape of his neck, his coat and breeches without a speck, his shoes shined to a mirror gloss (a mirror gloss Dennis was responsible for). But at night, with his shoes off, his coat hung in the closet, his cravat loosened, and a glass of bundle-gin in his hand, he looked to Dennis a much more natural man.

'Tell you something to always be remembrun, Denny,' he had said to his son on many occasions while in this comfortable state. 'There may be as many's a dozen things in this world which last, but surely no more, and may be less. Passey-o-nut love of a woman don't last, and a runner's wind don't last, nor does a braggart's wind, nor does haytime in the summer or sugartime in spring thaw. But two things that do last is one, royalty, and another, service. If you stick with your young man until he's an old man, and if you take care of him proper, he'll take care of you proper. You serve him an' he'll serve you, if you take the turn o' my mind. Now pour me another glass, and take a drop for yourself, if you like, but no more than a drop or your mother'll skin us both alive.'

Undoubtedly, some sons would quickly have grown bored with this catechism, but Dennis did not. He was the rarest of sons, a boy who had reached twenty and still thought his father wiser than himself.

On the morning after the King's death, Dennis hadn't had to force himself blearily out of bed at five o'clock; he had been awakened at three by his father, with the news of the King's death.

'Flagg's rared up a search party,' his father said, eyes full of bloodshot distress, 'and that's right enough. But my master will be leading it soon enough, I'll warrant, and I'm off to help him hunt for the fiend who done it, if he'll have me.'

'Me, too!' Dennis cried, grabbing for his breeches.

'Not at all, not at all,' his father said with a hard sternness that made Dennis subside at once. 'Things'll go forrad here just as they always have, murder or no – the old ways must be kept to now more than ever. My master and your master will be crowned King at noon, and that's well enough, although he comes to the crown in a bad time. But the death of a King by violence is always an evil thing if it comes not on the field of battle. The old ways will hold, doubt it not, but there may be trouble in the meantime. What's best for you, Dennis, is to go about your work just the same as always.'

He was gone before Dennis could protest.

And when five o'clock came, Dennis told his mother what his father had said and told her he should get about his morning round, even though he knew Peter would be gone. Dennis's mother was more than agreeable. She was dying for news. She told him to go, of course . . . go and then come back to her no later than eight of the clock, and tell her all he heard.

So Dennis went to Peter's rooms, which were utterly deserted. Nevertheless, he observed his regular routine, finishing by setting breakfast in the prince's study. He looked ruefully at the plates and glasses, the jams and jellies, reflecting that surely none of those things would be used that morning. Still, going about his ordered course had made him feel better for the first time since his father had turned him out of bed, for he now understood that, for better or worse, things were never going to be the same again. Times had changed.

He was preparing to leave when he heard a sound. It was so muffled he couldn't rightly tell where it was – only the general area from which it came. He looked toward Peter's bookcase, and his heart leaped in his chest.

Tendrils of smoke were drifting from between the loosely shelved books.

Dennis leaped across the room and began pulling books out by double handfuls. He saw that the smoke was issuing from cracks at one side of the bookcase's back. Also, that sound was clearer with the books gone. It was some sort of animal, squeaking in pained distress.

Dennis clawed and pawed at the bookcase, his fright spiralling toward panic. If there was one thing people were afraid of in that time and place, it was fire.

Soon enough his fingers happened on the secret spring. Flagg had foreseen this, too – after all, the secret panel wasn't really very secret – enough to amuse a boy, but not much more. The back of the bookcase slid to the right a bit, and a puff of grey smoke wafted out. The smell that escaped with the smoke was extremely unpleasant – a mixture of cooking meat, frying fur, and smouldering paper.

Not thinking, Dennis swept the panel all the way open. Of course, when he did that, more air got in. Things which had been only smouldering before now showed the first winks of flame.

This was the crucial point, the one place where Flagg had to be content not with what he was sure would happen but with his best guess of what would *probably* happen. All his efforts of the last seventy-five years now swung upon the fragile hinge of what a butler's son might or might not do in the next five seconds. But the Brandons had been butlers since time out of mind, and Flagg had decided he must depend on their long tradition of impeccable behaviour.

If Dennis had frozen in horror at the sight of those blossoming flames, or if he had turned and run for a pitcher of water, all of Flagg's carefully planted evidence might have burned in greenish tinted flames. The murder of Peter's father would never have been laid at Peter's door and he would have been crowned King at noon.

But Flagg's judgment was right. Instead of freezing or going for water, Dennis reached in and beat the flames out with his bare hands. It took less than five seconds, and Dennis was barely singed. The doleful squeaking went on, and the first thing he saw when he had waved the smoke aside was a mouse, lying on its side. It was in its death agonies. It was only a mouse, and Dennis had killed dozens of them in the line of duty without the slightest feeling of pity. Yet he felt sorry for this poor little bugger. Something terrible, something he could not even begin to understand, had happened to it and was still happening to it. Smoke rose from its fur in fine ribbons. When he touched it, he drew his hand back with a hiss – it was like touching the side of a tiny stove, such as the one in Sasha's doll house.

More smoke drifted lazily from an engraved wooden box with its lid slightly ajar. Dennis lifted the lid a little. He saw the tweezers, the packet. A number of brownish spots had flowered on the packet and it smouldered sluggishly, but had not burst into flame . . . nor did it now. The flames had come from Peter's letters, which were, of course, not enchanted at all. It was the mouse that had set these alight with its fearfully hot body. Now there was only the sullenly smouldering packet, and something warned Dennis not to touch it.

He was afraid. There were things here that he didn't understand, things he was not sure he *wanted* to understand. The one thing he knew for sure was that he badly needed to speak to his father. His father would know what to do.

Dennis took the ash bucket and a small shovel from beside the stove and went back to the secret panel. He used the shovel to pick up the smoking body of the mouse and drop it into the ash bucket. He wet the charred corners of the letters once more, just be be sure. Then he closed the panel, replaced the books, and left Peter's apartments. He took the ash bucket with him, and now he did not feel like

Peter's loyal servant but like a thief – his booty was a poor mouse that died even before Dennis got back out the West Gate of the castle.

And before he had even reached his house on the far side of the castle keep, a horrible suspicion had dawned in his mind – he was the first in Delain to feel this suspicion, but he would not be the last.

He tried to push the thought out of his head, but it kept coming back. What sort of poison, Dennis wondered, had killed King Roland, anyway? Exactly what sort of poison had it been?

By the time he got back to the Brandon house, he was in a bad state indeed, and he would answer none of his mother's questions. Nor would he show her what was in the ash bucket. He told her only that he must see his father the moment he came in – it was dreadfully important. Then he went into his room and wondered exactly what sort of poison it had been. He only knew one thing about it, but that one thing was enough. It had been something hot.

35

Brandon arrived just before ten o'clock, short-tempered, exhausted, and in no mood for foolishness. He was dirty and sweaty, there was a thin cut across his forehead, and cobwebs flew from his hair in long strings. They had found no sign of the assassin at all. His only news was that preparations for Peter's coronation were going full speed ahead in the Plaza of the Needle, under the direction of Anders Peyna, Delain's Judge-General.

His wife told him of Dennis's return. Brandon's brow darkened. He went to the door of his son's room and rapped not with his knuckles but with a closed fist. 'Come 'ee out here, boy, and tell us why you come back with the ash bucket from your master's study.'

'No,' Dennis said. 'You come in here, Dad – I don't want Mother to see what I've got, and I don't want her to hear what we say to each other.'

Brandon barged in. Dennis's mother waited apprehensively by the stove, expecting it was some sort of semi-hysterical foolishness which the boy had thought up, some ill-advised monkeyshine, and that very soon she would hear Dennis's wails as her tired and distraught husband, who must begin today at noon to buttle not a prince but a King, took out all his fears and frustrations on the boy's backside. She hardly blamed Dennis; everyone in the keep seemed hysterical this morning, running around like crazy people just let out of bedlam, repeating a hundred false rumours, then taking them back in order to repeat a hundred new ones.

But there were no raised voices from behind Dennis's door, and neither of them came out for more than an hour. When they did, a single look at her husband's white face made the poor woman feel like fainting dead away. Dennis scurried along at his father's heels like a scared puppy.

Now Brandon was carrying the ash bucket.

'Where are you going?' she asked timidly.

Brandon said nothing. It seemed that Dennis *could* say nothing. He only rolled his eyes at her and then followed his father out the door. She saw neither of them for twenty-four hours, and became convinced that both were dead – or even worse, that they were suffering in the Dungeon of Inquisition below the castle.

Her dire thoughts were not so unlikely, either, for those were a terrible twenty-four hours in Delain. The day mightn't have seemed so terrible in some places, places where revolt and upheaval and alarms and midnight executions are almost a way of life . . . there really are such places, although I wish I didn't have to say so. But Delain had for years – and even centuries – been an ordered and orderly place, so perhaps they were spoiled. That black day really began when Peter was *not* crowned at noon and ended with the stunning news that he was to be tried in the Hall of the Needle for the murder of his father. If Delain had had a stock market, I suppose it would have crashed.

Construction on the dais where the coronation was to take place began at first light. The platform would be a jury-rigged affair of plain boards, Anders Peyna knew, but he also knew that enough flowers and bunting would cover the rude spots. They had had no warning of the King's passing, because murder isn't a thing that can be predicted. If it could be, there would be no murders, and the world would almost certainly be a happier place. Besides, pomp and circumstance wasn't the point – the point was to make the people feel the continuity of the throne. If the citizens got the feeling that everything was still all right in spite of the terrible thing that had happened, Peyna didn't care how many flower girls got splinters.

But at eleven o'clock, construction abruptly ceased. The flower girls were turned away – many of them in tears – by the Home Guards.

At seven that morning, most of the Home Guards had begun dressing in their gorgeous red ceremonial uniforms and their tall grey Wolf-Jaw shakos. They were, of course, to form the ceremonial double line, an aisle down which Peter would walk to be crowned. Then, at eleven, they received new orders; strange unsettling orders. The ceremonial uniforms came off in a blazing hurry and their dull, dun-coloured combat uniforms went on instead. The showy but clumsy ceremonial swords were replaced with the lethal shortswords which were everyday equipment. Impressive but impractical Wolf-Jaw shakos were cast aside in favour of the squat leather helmets that were normal battle dress.

Battle dress – the very term was distressing. *Is* there such a thing as *normal* battle dress? I do not think so. Yet soldiers in battle dress were everywhere, their faces stern and forbidding.

Prince Peter has committed suicide! That was the most common rumour which went flying about the castle keep.

Prince Peter has been murdered! That one ran a close second.

Roland was not dead; it was a mistaken diagnosis, the physician has been beheaded, but the old King is insane and no one knows what to do. That was a third.

There were many others, some even more foolish.

No one slept as darkness stole over the confused, sorrowing castle keep. All the torches in the Plaza of the Needle were lit, the castle blazed with lights, and every house in the keep and on the hills below showed candles and lanterns, as frightened people gathered to talk about the day's events. All agreed wild work was afoot.

The night was even longer than the day. Mrs Brandon kept watch for her men in terrible loneliness. She sat at the window, but for the first time in her life, the air was rife with more gossip than she wanted to hear. Yet for all that, could she stop listening? She could not.

As the small hours of the morning stretched out endlessly toward a dawn that she felt would never come, a new rumour began to supplant all the old ones – it was incredible, unbelievable, and yet it was asserted with more and more assurance until even the guards at their posts were repeating it to one another in undertones. This new rumour terrified Mrs Brandon most of all, because she remembered – too well!

– how white poor Dennis's face had been when he had come in with the prince's ash bucket. There had been something inside, something that smelled sick and burnt, something he wouldn't show her.

Prince Peter's been taken in custody for the murder of his father, this awful rumour went. *He's been taken . . . Prince Peter's been taken . . . the prince has murdered his own father!*

Shortly before dawn, the distracted woman laid her head in her arms and wept. After a bit, her sobbing faded as she fell into a troubled sleep.

·**n**ow tell me what's in that bucket, and be quick about it! We want no fooling, Dennis, d'you understand me?' was the first thing Brandon said when he entered Dennis's room and closed the door behind him.

'I'll show you, Dad,' Dennis said, 'but first, answer me one question: what sort of poison was it that killed the King?'

'No one knows.'

'What were its ways?'

'Show me what's in the bucket, boy. Do it now.' Brandon balled a great hard fist. He did not shake it; he only held it up. That was enough. 'Show me now or be knocked aside.'

Brandon looked at the dead mouse for a long

time, saying nothing. Dennis watched, scared, as his dad's face grew paler, graver, greyer. The mouse's eyes had burned until they were nothing but charred black cinders. Its brown fur had been crisped black. Smoke still rose from its tiny ears, and its teeth, visible in its death grimace, were a sooty black, like the teeth in the grate of a stove.

Brandon made as if to touch it, and then pulled his hand back. He raised his face to his son and spoke in a hoarse whisper. 'Where did you find this?'

Dennis began to stammer out bundles of phrases which didn't mean a thing.

Brandon listened a moment and then squeezed his son's shoulder.

'Draw you a deep breath and put your thoughts all in a row, Denny,' he said. 'I'm on yer side in this, as I am in all else, yer know. Yer did right to keep the sight of this poor thing from yer mom. Now tell me how you found it, and where you found it.'

Eased and reassured, Dennis was able to tell his father the story. His telling was a bit shorter than mine, but it still look several minutes. His father sat in a chair, one knuckle digging into his forehead, shading his eyes. He asked no questions, did not even grunt.

When Dennis had finished. His father muttered four words in an undertone. Just four words – but they froze the boy's heart into a cold blue cake – or so it felt to him at the time. 'Just like the King.'

Brandon's lips were trembling with fright, but he seemed to be trying to smile.

'Do you suppose yonder animal was a King of Mice, Denny?'

'Dad . . . Daddy, I . . . I . . .'

'There was a box, you said.'

'Yes.'

'And a packet.'

'Yes.'

'And the packet was charred, but not burned.'

'Yes.'

'And tweezers.'

'Yes, like Mamma uses to pluck the hairs from out'n her nose –'

'Shh,' Brandon said, and dug his knuckle into his forehead again. 'Let me think.'

Five minutes went by. Brandon sat motionless, almost as if he had gone to sleep, but Dennis knew better. Brandon did not know that Peter's mother had given him the engraved box or that Peter had lost it when he was small; both of those things had happened long before Peter entered his half-man-hood and Brandon came into his service. He did know about the secret panel; he had happened on this in the very first year he had served Peter (and not very far into that year, either). As I may have said, it wasn't really a very secret compartment, as those things went – just enough to satisfy such an open boy as Peter. Brandon knew about it, but had never looked into it after that first time, when it had con-tained nothing more than the glorified junk that any boy calls his treasures – a Tarot deck with a few cards missing, a bag of marbles, a lucky coin, a braided bit of hair from Peony's mane. If a good butler under-stands anything, he understands that quality we call discretion, which is a respect for the borders of other people's lives. He had never looked in that compartment again. It would have been like stealing.

At last Dennis asked: 'Should we go over, Father, so you can look in the box?'

'No. We must go to the Judge-General with this mouse, and you must tell your story to him just as you've told it to me.'

Dennis sat down heavily on his bed. He felt as if he had been punched in the belly. Peyna, the man who ordered jail terms and beheadings! Peyna, with his white, forbidding face and his tall, waxy brow! Peyna, who was, below the King himself, the greatest authority in the Kingdom!

'No,' he whispered at last. 'Dad, I couldn't . . . I . . . I . . .'

'You must,' his father said sternly. 'This is a turrible business – the most turrible business I've ever known of, but it must be reckoned with and set right. You'll tell him just as you've told me, and then it'll be in his hands.'

Dennis looked in his father's eyes and saw that Brandon meant it. If he refused to go, his father would lay hold of the scruff of his neck and drag him to Peyna like a kitten, twenty years old or no.

'Yes, Dad,' he said miserably, thinking that when Peyna's cold, calculating eyes fell on him, he would simply drop dead of a heart attack. Then (with rising panic) he remembered that he had stolen an ash bucket from the prince's rooms. If he didn't die of fright the moment Peyna commanded him to speak, he would probably spend the rest of his life in the castle's deepest dungeon for theft.

'Be easy in your mind, Denny – easy as you

can be, anyway. Peyna's a hard man, but he's fair. You've done nothing to be ashamed of. Just tell him as you've told me.'

'All right,' Dennis whispered. 'Are we going now?'

Brandon got out of the chair and onto his knees. 'First we'll pray. Get here beside me, son.'

Dennis did.

Peter was tried, found guilty of regicide, and ordered imprisoned for life in the cold two rooms at the top of the Needle. All of this was done in only three days. It will not take long to tell you how neatly the jaws of Flagg's cruel trap closed around the boy.

Peyna did not order the preparations for the coronation stopped at once – in fact, he thought that Dennis must be mistaken, that there must be a reasonable explanation for all of this. Just the same, the condition of the mouse, so like the condition of the King, was impossible to ignore, and the Brandon family had a long and valued reputation for honesty and levelheadedness in the Kingdom. That was important, but there was something else of far greater importance: when Peter was crowned, there must not be a single stain on his reputation.

Peyna heard Dennis out and then summoned

Peter. Dennis really might have died of fright at the sight of his master, but he was mercifully allowed to go into another room with his father. Peyna gravely explained to Peter that a charge had been levelled against him . . . a charge that Peter himself might have played a part in the murder of Roland. Anders Peyna was not a man to mince words, no matter how much those words might hurt.

Peter was stunned . . . flabbergasted. You must remember that he was still trying to cope with the idea that his beloved father was dead, killed by a cruel poison that had burned him alive from the inside out. You must remember that he had been leading the search all night, had had no sleep, and was physically exhausted. Most of all, you must remember that, although he had a man's height and breadth of shoulder, he was only sixteen. This stunning news on top of all else caused him to do a very natural thing, but it was a thing he should have avoided at all costs under Peyna's cold and assessing eyes: he burst into tears.

If Peter had hotly denied the charge, or if he had expressed his shock and exhaustion and grief by laughing wildly at such an absurd idea, the whole thing might have ended right there. I'm sure *that* possibility never entered Flagg's mind, but one of Flagg's weaknesses was a tendency to judge others according to what was in his own black and murky heart. Flagg regarded everyone with suspicion, and believed everyone had hidden reasons for the things they did.

His mind was very complex, like a hall of mirrors with everything reflected twice at different sizes.

The track of Peyna's thoughts was not convoluted but very straightforward. He found it very difficult — almost impossible — to believe that Peter could have poisoned his father. If he had raged or laughed out loud, things probably would have ended without even a trip to investigate the supposed box with his name carved on it, or the packet and tweezers it supposedly held. Tears, however, looked very bad. Tears looked like an expression of guilt coming from a boy old enough to commit murder but not old enough to hide what he had done.

Peyna decided he must investigate further. He hated to do this, because it meant taking guards, and that meant some word, some whisper, of these momentary suspicions would leak out, to taint the first weeks of Peter's reign.

Then he reflected that perhaps even this could be avoided. He would take half a dozen Home Guards, no more. He could leave four stationed outside the door. After this ridiculous business had blown over, all of them could be shipped off to the remotest part of the Kingdom. Brandon and his son would also have to be sent away, Peyna thought, and that was a pity, but tongues had a way of wagging, especially when liquor loosened them, and the old man's liking for bundle-gin was well known.

So Peyna ordered work on the coronation platform temporarily suspended. He felt confident that work could begin again in less than half an hour, with the labourers sweating and cursing and hurrying to make up for lost time.

Alas —

The box, the packet, and the tweezers were there, as you know. Peter had sworn on his mother's name he had no such engraved box: his heated denial now looked very foolish. Peyna picked up the charred packet carefully with the tweezers, peered in, and saw three flecks of green sand. They were so small they could barely be seen, but Peyna, mindful of what had befallen both great King and humble mouse, put the packet back in the box and closed the lid. He ordered two of the four Home Guards still in the hall to step in, realizing reluctantly that the matter was steadily growing more serious.

The box was put carefully on Peter's desk, little wisps of smoke escaping from it. One of the guards was sent after the man who knew more about poisons than anyone else in the Kingdom.

That man, of course, was Flagg.

'I had nothing to do with this, Anders,' Peter said. He had recovered himself, but his face was still pale and wretched, his eyes a deeper blue than the old Judge-General had ever seen them.

'The box *is* yours, then?'

'Yes.'

'Why did you deny that you had such a box?'

'I forgot. I haven't seen this box in probably eleven years or more. My mother gave it to me.'

'What happened to it?'

He's not calling me 'm'Lord' or 'your Highness' anymore, Peter thought with a chill. *He's not calling me by any term of respect at all. Can all of this really be happening, I wonder? Father poisoned? Thomas terribly ill? Peyna standing here and doing everything but accusing me of murder? And my box — where in the name of gods did it come from, and who put it in the secret compartment behind the books?*

'I lost it,' Peter said slowly. 'Anders, you don't really believe I murdered my father, do you?'

I did not . . . but now I wonder, Anders Peyna thought.

'I loved him dearly,' Peter said.

I always thought so . . . but now I wonder about that, too, Anders Peyna thought.

40

Flagg bustled in and, without even looking in Peyna's direction, began immediately to bombard the numbed, frightened, outraged prince with questions about the search. Had any trace been found of the poison or the poisoner? Any sign of a plot uncovered? He himself was of the opinion that it might have been a single individual, almost surely insane. He had spent the whole morning before his crystal, Flagg said, but the crystal remained stubbornly dark. He didn't care, though, he could do more than shake bones and peer into crystals. He craved action, not spells. Anything the prince wanted him to do, any dark corner he wanted explored –

'We did not call you here to listen to you babble like your own parrot, with both heads talking at once,' Peyna said coldly. He did not like Flagg. As far as Peyna was concerned, the magician had been demoted to the position of Court Nobody at the moment of Roland's death. He might be able to tell them what those evil green flecks in the packet were, but that was the extent of his usefulness.

Peter'll have no truck with this weasel when he's crowned, Peyna thought. He got just that far, and then his thoughts derailed in dismay, because the chances of Peter's being crowned seemed to be growing slimmer.

'No,' Flagg said, 'I don't suppose you did.' He looked at Peter and said, 'Why am I summoned, my King?'

'*Don't call him that!*' Peyna exploded, deeply shocked in spite of himself. Flagg saw this shock on Peyna's face, and although he affected to look puzzled, he understood perfectly what it meant and was satisfied. A worm of suspicion was working its way toward the centre of the Judge-General's chilly heart. Good.

Peter turned his pale face away from both of them and looked out across the city, once more struggling for control of his emotions. His fingers were laced tightly together. His knuckles were white. He looked much older than sixteen just then.

'Do you see the box on the desk?' Peyna asked.

'Yes, Judge-General,' Flagg said in his stiffest, most formal voice.

'Inside is a packet which appears to be slowly charring. Inside the packet are what look like grains of sand. I would like you to examine them and see if you can tell me what they are. I urge you very strongly not to touch them. I believe that the substance in the packet may have caused King Roland's death.'

Flagg allowed himself to look worried. To tell the truth, he was feeling very fine. Playing a part always made him feel that way. He liked to act.

He picked up the packet, using the tweezers. He peered into it. His gaze sharpened.

'I want a piece of obsidian,' he said. 'I want it right now.'

'I have a piece in my desk,' Peter said dully, and brought it out. It was not as big as the one Flagg had used and then disposed of, but it was thick. He handed it to one of the Home Guards, who handed it to Flagg. The magician held it toward the light, frowning a little . . . but inside his heart, a little man was jumping excitedly up and down, turning cartwheels, and doing somersaults. The obsidian was much like his own, but one side was broken and jagged. Ah, the gods were smiling on him! Indeed, indeed, indeed they were!

'I dropped it a year or two ago,' Peter said, seeing Flagg's interest. He was unaware – as was Peyna, at least for the moment – that he had added another layer of bricks to the wall that was a-building around him. 'The half you're holding landed on my rug, which cushioned its fall. The other half landed on the stones, and shattered into half a hundred pieces. Obsidian is hard, but very brittle.'

'Indeed, my Lord?' Flagg said gravely. 'I've never seen such stone, although I've of course heard of it.'

He put the obsidian on Peter's desk, upended the packet over it, and poured the three grains of sand onto it. In a moment, little tendrils of smoke began to rise from the obsidian. All present could see that each grain was slowly sinking into the pockmark it was creating in the world's hardest known stone. The guards murmured uneasily at the sight.

'*Be silent!*' Peyna roared, whirling on them. The guards drew back, faces long and white with terror. This seemed more and more like witchcraft to them.

'I believe I know what these grains are, and how to test my idea,' Flagg said, rapping the words out. 'But if I'm right, the test must be performed as quickly as possible.'

'Why?' Peyna demanded.

'I believe these are grains of Dragon Sand,' Flagg said. 'I had a very small quantity once, but it disappeared, alas, before I could study it closely. It may well have been stolen.'

Flagg did not miss the way Peyna's eyes flicked toward Peter at this.

'I have been uneasy about it off and on ever since,' he went on, 'because it is reputed to be one of the deadliest substances on earth. I did not have a chance to test its properties and so doubted, but I see much of what I was told proved here, already.'

Flagg pointed at the obsidian. The dimples in which the three specks of green sand rested were each now nearly an inch deep – smoke rose from each like smoke from a tiny campfire. Flagg guessed that each grain had eaten through half the thickness of the stone.

'Those three specks of sand are working their way rapidly through a piece of the hardest rock we know,' he said. 'Dragon Sand is reputed to be so corrosive that it will eat through any solid – any solid at all. And it produces fearsome heat. You! Guard!'

Flagg pointed at one of the Home Guards. He stepped forward, not looking happy to have been chosen.

'Touch the side of the rock,' Flagg said, and as the guard reached a tentative hand forward to touch the paperweight, he added sharply: 'Just the side! Don't get your hand near those holes!'

The guard touched the paperweight and drew his hand back with a gasp. He stuck his fingers in his mouth, but not before Peyna had seen the blisters rising there.

'Obsidian conducts heat very slowly, I've heard,' Flagg said, 'but that piece is as hot as the top of a stove . . . all from three grains of sand that would fit on the moon of your pinkie fingernail, with room left over! Touch the prince's desk, Lord Judge-General!'

Peyna did. He was distressed and amazed by the heat under his hand. Soon the heavy wood must begin to blister and char.

'So we must act quickly,' Flagg said. 'Soon the desk itself will catch fire. If we breathe the fumes – always assuming the stories I've been told are true – all of us will die within days. But, to be sure, another test –'

At this, the Home Guards looked more uneasy than ever.

'All right,' Peyna said. 'What is this test? Be quick, man!' He detested Flagg more than ever now, and if he had ever felt it would not do to underestimate him, he felt that doubly now. Five minutes before, Peyna had been ready to dismiss the man as the Court Nobody. Now it seemed that their lives – and Peyna's case against Peter – depended on him.

'I propose to fill a bucket with water,' Flagg said, speaking more rapidly than ever. His dark eyes gleamed.

The Home Guards and Peyna stared at those small black holes in the obsidian, at those tiny ribbons of steam, with the evil fascination of birds hypnotized by a nest of weaving pythons. How deep into the obsidian now? How close to the wood? Impossible to tell. Even Peter was looking, although the tired mixture of sorrow and confusion had not left his face.

'Water from the prince's pump!' Flagg shouted at one of the guards. 'We want it in a bucket, or a deep pot or pan. Now! Now!'

The guard looked at Peyna.

'Do it,' Peyna said, trying not to sound frightened – but he *was* frightened, and Flagg knew it.

The guard went. In moments, they heard water

being pumped into a bucket he had found in the butler's cupboard.

Flagg was speaking again.

'I propose to dip my finger into this bucket and let a drop of water fall into one of those holes,' he said. 'We'll watch this closely, Lord Judge-General. We must see if the water which goes into the hole turns momentarily green. It's a sure sign.'

'And then?' Peyna asked tautly.

The Home Guard returned. Flagg took the bucket, set it on the desk.

'Then I'll put drops very carefully into the other two holes,' Flagg said. He spoke calmly, but his normally pallid cheeks were flushed. 'Water won't stop Dragon Sand, it's told, but it'll hold it.' This was making things quite a bit worse than they were, but Flagg wanted them frightened.

'Why not just douse it?' one of the guards blurted.

Peyna favoured this upstart with a horrible glare, but Flagg answered the question calmly as he dipped his pinkie finger into the bucket.

'Would you like me to wash those three grains of sand out of the holes they've made in the rock and somewhere onto the lad's desk?' he asked, almost jovially. 'We could leave you in here to put out the fire when the water dried up, sirrah!'

The guard said no more.

Flagg drew his dripping finger out of the bucket.

'Water's warm already,' he said to Peyna, 'just from sitting on the desk.'

He carefully brought his finger, from which a single drop of water hung, over one of the holes.

'Watch closely!' Flagg said sharply, and to Peter he sounded at that moment like a cheap peddler about to perform some monstrously deceiving trick. But Peyna bent close. The Home Guards craned their necks. That single drop of water hung from Flagg's finger, for a moment catching all of Peter's room behind it in perfect curved miniature. It hung . . . elongated . . . and dropped into the hole.

There was a spatting *hisss*, like the sound of grease dropped onto a hot iron skillet. A tiny geyser of steam arose from the hole . . . but before it did, Peyna clearly saw a cat's-eye flash of green. In that moment, Peter's fate was sealed.

'Dragon Sand, by the gods!' Flagg whispered hoarsely. '*Don't, for pity's sake, breathe that steam!*'

Anders Peyna's courage was as hard as his reputation, but he was afraid now. To him that single wink of green light had seemed inexpressibly evil.

'Put out the other two,' he said hoarsely. 'Now!'

'I told you,' Flagg said, calmly dipping his pinkie again and staring at the obsidian. 'They can't be put out – well, there is one way, the tales say, but only one. You wouldn't like it. Yet we can hold them, and then get rid of them. I think.'

He carefully plinked a drop into each of the other two holes. Each time there was a sullen green flash of light, and a plume of steam.

'We're all right for a bit, I think,' Flagg said. One of the Home Guards sighed in gusty relief. 'Bring me gloves . . . or folded cloths . . . anything I can use to pick up this rock. It's as hot as fury, and those drops of water will be boiled away in no time.'

Two hot pads from the butler's closet were

brought quickly. Flagg used them to grasp the obsidian. He lifted it, careful to keep it level, then dropped it into the bucket. As the obsidian sank to the bottom, all of them clearly saw the water turn a momentary light green.

'Now,' Flagg said expansively, 'that is well. One of these guards must take this bucket out of the castle, and to the large pump by the Great Old Tree in the middle of the keep. There you must draw a large basin of water, and put the bucket in the basin. The basin must be taken to the middle of Lake Johanna, and sunk in the middle. The Dragon Sand may heat up the lake in a hundred thousand years, but let those that come in that time – if any do – worry about that, I say.'

Peyna paused for just a moment, biting his lip in uncharacteristic indecision, and then he said: 'You and you and you. Do as he says.'

The bucket was removed. The Home Guards carried it like men carrying a live bomb. Flagg was amused, for all of this was, in large part, magician's foolery, as Peter himself had momentarily suspected. The single drops of water he had allowed to fall into the holes had not been enough to stop the corrosive effect of the sand – at least not for long – but he knew that the water in the bucket would damp it well. Even less liquid would have served for more of the sand . . . a goblet of wine, say. But let them believe what they would; in time they would turn against Peter with that much more fury.

When the guards had gone, Peyna turned to Flagg. 'You said there was one way the effect of Dragon Sand could be neutralized.'

'Yes – the stories say that if it is taken into a living being, that living being will burn in agony until it is dead . . . and when it is over – the dying – the power of the Dragon Sand also dies. I had meant to test it, but before I could do it, my sample disappeared.'

Peyna was staring at him, white around the lips. 'And on what sort of living being did you intend to test this damned stuff, Magician?'

Flagg looked at Peyna with bland innocence. 'Why, on a mouse, my Lord Judge-General, of course.'

41

At three that afternoon, a strange meeting took place in the Royal Court of Delain at the base of the Needle – a great room which, over the years, had become known simply as 'Peyna's Court'.

Meeting – I don't like that word. It's too tame and small to describe the momentous decision that was arrived at that afternoon. I cannot call it a hearing or a trial, because that gathering had no legal meaning at all, but it was very important, as I think you will agree.

The room was large enough to hold five hundred, but there were only seven there that afternoon. Six of them huddled close together, as if it made them nervous to be so few in a place meant for so many.

The royal arms of the Kingdom – a unicorn spearing a dragon – hung on one of the circular stone walls, and Peter found his gaze returning to this again and again. Besides himself, Peyna was there, and Flagg (it was Flagg, of course, who sat slightly apart from the others), and four of the Kingdom's Great Lawyers. There were ten Great Lawyers in all, but the other six were at various farflung places in Delain, hearing cases. Peyna had decided he couldn't wait for them. He knew he had to move fast and decisively, or the Kingdom might bleed. He knew it, but it galled him to know he would need the help of this cool young murderer to avert such bloodshed.

That Peter *was* a murderer was something Anders Peyna had now decided in his own heart. It wasn't the box, the green sand, or even the burning mouse that had decided him. It was Peter's tears. Peter, to do him credit, looked neither guilty nor weak now. He was pale but calm, completely in charge of himself again.

Peyna cleared his throat. The sound echoed dully back from the forbidding stone walls of the court chamber. He pressed a hand to his forehead and was not entirely surprised to find a sheen of cold sweat there. He had heard testimony in hundreds of great and solemn cases; he had sent more men than he cared to remember beneath the headsman's axe. But never had he thought he would have to attend a 'meeting' such as this, or the trial of a prince for the murder of his royal father . . . and such a trial would surely follow if all went as he hoped this afternoon. It was right, he thought, that he be sweating, and right that the sweat should be cold.

Just a meeting. Nothing legal here; nothing official; nothing of the Kingdom. But none of them – not Peyna, not Flagg, not the Great Lawyers, not Peter himself – were fooled. This was the real trial. This meeting. The power was here. That burning mouse had set a great course of events in motion. That course would either be turned here, as a great river may be turned near its source when it is still a brook, or it would be allowed to run onward, gathering power as it went, until no force on earth could turn it or stand before it.

Just a meeting, Anders Peyna thought, and wiped more sweat from his forehead.

Flagg watched the proceedings with a lively eye. Like Peyna, he knew that all would be decided here, and he felt confident.

Peter's head was up, his gaze firm. He met the eyes of each member of this informal jury in turn.

The stone walls frowned down on all seven. The spectators' benches were empty, but Peyna seemed to feel the weight of phantom eyes, eyes that *demanded* justice be rendered in this terrible matter.

'My Lord,' Peyna said at last, 'the sun made you King three hours ago.'

Peter looked at Peyna, surprised but silent.

'Yes,' Peyna said, as if Peter *had* spoken. The

Great Lawyers were nodding, and they looked dreadfully solemn. 'There has been no coronation, but a coronation is only a public event. It is, for all its solemnity, show and not substance. God, the law, and the sun make a King, not the coronation. You are King at this very minute, legally able to command me, all of us here, the entire Kingdom. This puts us in a terrible dilemma. Do you understand what it is?'

'Yes,' Peter said gravely. 'You think your King is a murderer.'

Peyna was a little surprised by this bluntness, but not entirely unhappy with it. Peter had always been a blunt boy; it was a pity that his surface bluntness had concealed such depths of calculation, but the important thing was that such bluntness, probably the result of a boy's stupid bravado, would speed things up.

'What we believe, my Lord, doesn't matter. Guilt or innocence is for a court to determine – so I've always been taught, so I believe with my most sincere heart. There is only one exception to this. Kings are above the law. Do you understand?'

'Yes.'

'*But* –' Peyna raised his finger. '*But* this crime was committed before you were King. So far as I know, this terrible situation has never come before a court of Delain before. The possibilities are terrible. Anarchy, chaos, civil war. To avert all of these things, my Lord, we must have your help.'

Peter looked at him gravely. 'I will help if I can,' he said.

And I think – I pray – you will agree to what I am

about to propose, Peyna thought. He was conscious of fresh sweat on his forehead, but he didn't wipe if off this time. Peter was only a boy, but he was a bright boy – he might take it as a sign of weakness. *You'll say you're agreeing for the good of the Kingdom, but a boy who could have the monstrous, twisted courage to kill his own father is also, I hope, a boy who cannot help believing he will get away with it. You believe we will help you cover this up, but oh my Lord, you are so wrong.*

Flagg, who could almost read these thoughts, raised his hand to his mouth to cover a smile. Peyna hated him, but Peyna had become his number-one helper without even knowing it.

'I want you to put aside the crown,' Peyna said.

Peter looked at him with grave surprise. 'Renounce the throne?' he asked. 'I . . . I don't know, my Lord Judge-General. I should have to think about that before I said yes or no. That might be hurting the Kingdom by trying to help it – as a doctor may kill a sick man by giving him too much medicine.'

The lad's clever, Flagg and Peyna thought together.

'You misunderstand me. It's not a renunciation of the throne I ask for. Only that you put the crown aside until this matter has been decided. If you are found innocent of your father's murder –'

'As I will be,' Peter said. 'If my father had ruled until I was old and toothless, it would have made me perfectly happy. I wanted only to serve him and support him and love him in all I did.'

'Yet your father *is* dead, and you stand accused by circumstance.'

Peter nodded.

'If you are found innocent, you would resume the crown. If you are found guilty –'

The Great Lawyers looked nervous at this, but Peyna did not flinch.

'If you are found guilty, you would be taken to the top of the Needle, where you would spend the rest of your life. None of the royal family may be executed; that law is a thousand years old.'

'And Thomas would become King?' Peter asked thoughtfully. Flagg stiffened slightly.

'Yes.'

Peter frowned, deep in thought. He looked terribly tired, but not confused or afraid, and Flagg felt a faint stirring of fear.

'Suppose I refuse?'

'If you refuse, then you become King in spite of terrible charges which have not been answered. Many of your subjects – most, in light of the evidence – will believe they have come to be ruled by a young man who murdered his own father to gain the throne. I think there will be revolt and civil war, and that those things will come before much time has passed.

'As for myself, I would resign my post and set out toward the west. I am old to begin over, but I should have to try to do so just the same. My life has been the law, and I could not serve a King who has not knelt to the law in such a matter as this.'

There was silence in the chamber, a silence that seemed very long. Peter sat with his head bowed, the heels of his hands planted against his eyes. They all watched and waited. Now even Flagg felt a thin film of sweat on his brow.

Finally Peter raised his head and took his hand from his eyes.

'Very well,' he said. 'Here is my command as King. I will put the crown aside until I am cleared of my father's murder. You, Peyna, will serve Delain as Chancellor during the time it is without a royal head. I would that the trial should take place as soon as may be – tomorrow, even, if that is possible. I will be bound by the decision of the court.

'But you will not try me.'

They all blinked and sat up straighter at this dry note of authority, but Yosef of the stables would not have been surprised by it; he had heard that tone in the boy's voice before, when Peter was only a stripling.

'One of these other four will do that,' Peter continued. 'I'll not be tried by the man who will hold power in my place . . . a man who, by his look and manner, already feels in his heart that I have committed this terrible crime.'

Peyna felt himself flush.

'One of these four,' Peter reiterated, turning to the Great Lawyers. 'Let four stones, three black and one white, be put in a cup. The one who draws the white stone shall preside at my trial. Do you agree?'

'My Lord, I do,' Peyna agreed slowly, hating the flush which even now wouldn't leave his cheeks.

Again, Flagg had to raise a hand to his mouth to cover a small smile. *And that, my little doomed Lord, is the only command you will ever give as King of Delain,* he thought.

43

The meeting which began at three o'clock was over by quarter past the hour. Senates and parliaments may drone on for days and months before deciding a single issue – and often the issue is never decided at all in spite of all the talk – but when great things happen, they usually happen fast. And three hours later, as dark was coming down, something happened which made Peter realize that, mad as it seemed, he was going to be found guilty of this terrible crime.

He was escorted back to his apartments by unsmiling, silent guards. His meals, Peyna said, would be brought to him.

Supper was fetched by a burly Home Guardsman with a heavy stubble of beard on his face. He was holding a tray. On it were a glass of milk and a large, steaming bowl of stew. Peter stood up as the guardsman came in. He reached for the tray.

'Not yet, my Lord,' the guardsman said, the sneer in his voice apparent. 'It needs seasoning, I think.' And with that he spat into the stew. Then, grinning, showing a mouthful of teeth and gaps like an ill-tended picket fence, he held the tray out. 'Here.'

Peter made no motion to take it. He was utterly astonished.

'Why did you do that? Why did you spit in my stew?'

'Does a child who murders his father deserve any better, *my Lord?*'

'No. But one who has not even been tried for the crime does,' Peter said. 'Take that out and bring me a fresh tray. Bring it in fifteen minutes, or you'll sleep tonight below Flagg in the dungeons.'

The guardsman's ugly sneer faltered for a moment and then returned. 'I think not,' he said. He tilted the tray, first just a little, then more, then more. The glass and bowl shattered on the flagstones. Thick stew splattered in ropes.

'Lick it up,' the guardsman said. 'Lick it up like the dog you are.'

He turned to go. Peter, suddenly blazing, leaped forward and slapped the man. The sound of the blow rang in the room like a pistol shot.

With a bellow, the scruffy guardsman pulled out his short-sword.

Smiling humourlessly, Peter lifted his chin and bared his neck. 'Go ahead,' he said. 'A man who would spit in another man's soup is perhaps also the sort of man who would cut an unarmed man's throat. Go ahead. Pigs also do God's bidding, I believe, and my shame and my grief are very great. If God wills me to live, I must, but if God wills me to die and has sent such a pig as you to do the killing, that is very well.'

The Home Guardsman's anger melted into confusion. After a moment he sheathed his sword.

'I'll not dirty my blade,' he said, but his words were almost a mumble, and he was not able to meet Peter's eye.

'Bring me fresh food and drink,' Peter said quietly. 'I don't know who you have been talking to, guardsman, and I don't care. I don't know why you are so eager to condemn me for my father's murder when no testimony has yet been heard, and I don't care about that, either. But you will bring me fresh meat and drink, and a napkin to go with them, and you will do this before the clock strikes half past six, or I will ring for Peyna, and you will sleep below Flagg tonight. My guilt is not proved, Peyna is yet mine to command, and I swear what I say is true.'

During this the Home Guardsman grew paler and paler, because he saw Peter did speak the truth. But this was not the only reason for his pallor. When his mates had told him the prince had been caught red-handed, he had believed them – he had *wanted* to believe them – but now he wondered. Peter did not look or speak like a guilty man.

'Yes, my Lord,' he said.

The soldier went out. A few moments later, the captain of the guard opened the door and looked in.

'I thought I heard some disturbance,' he said. His eye fell on the broken glass and crockery. 'Has there been trouble here?'

'No trouble,' Peter said calmly. 'I dropped the tray. The guardsman has gone to fetch me a fresh meal.'

The captain nodded and left.

Peter sat on his bed for the next ten minutes and thought deeply.

There was a brief knock on the door. 'Come,' Peter said.

The bearded, gap-toothed guard came in with a fresh tray. 'My Lord, I wish to apologize,' he said with awkward stiffness. 'I've never behaved so in my whole life, and I don't know what came over me. For my life I do not. I —'

Peter waved it away. He felt very tired. 'Do the others feel as you do? The other guards?'

'My Lord,' the guardsman said, carefully setting the tray on Peter's desk, 'I'm not sure *I* still feel the way I did.'

'But do the others feel that I am guilty?'

There was a long pause, and the soldier nodded.

'And is there some one reason they tell against me most of all?'

'They speak of a mouse that burned . . . they say you wept when Peyna confronted you . . .'

Peter nodded grimly. Yes. Weeping had been a bad mistake, but he hadn't been able to help it . . . and it was done.

'But most all they only say you were caught, that you wanted to be King, that it must be so.'

'That I wanted to be King and so it must be so,' Peter echoed.

'Yes, my Lord.' The guardsman stood looking at Peter miserably.

'Thank you. Go now, please.'

'My Lord, I apologize —'

'Your apology is accepted. Please go. I need to think.'

Looking as if he wished he had never been born, the Home Guardsman stepped out the door and closed it behind him.

Peter spread his napkin over his knees but didn't eat. Any hunger he might have felt earlier was now gone. He plucked at the napkin and thought of his mother. He was glad — very glad indeed — that she wasn't alive to see this, to see what he had come to. All of his life he had been a lucky boy, a blessed boy, a boy to whom, it sometimes seemed, no bad luck ever came. Now it seemed that all the bad luck which should have been his over the years had only been stored up to be paid at once, and with sixteen years of interest.

But most of all they say you wanted to be King and it must be so.

In some deep way he understood. They wanted a good King they could love. But they also wanted to know they had been saved by only a hair's breadth from a bad one. They wanted blackness and secrets; they wanted their fearful tale of rotten royalty. God only knew why. *They say you wanted to be King, they say it must be so.*

Peyna believes it, Peter thought, *and that guardsman believed it; they will all believe it. This is not a nightmare. I have been accused of my father's murder, and not all my good behaviour and my obvious love for him will dismiss the charge. And part of them* wants *to believe I did it.*

Peter carefully refolded his napkin and laid it over the top of the fresh bowl of stew. He could not eat.

44

There was a trial, and it was a great wonder, and there are histories of the event if you care to read them. But here's the root of the matter: Peter, son of Roland, was brought before the Judge-General of Delain by a burning mouse; tried in a meeting of seven which was not a court; convicted by a Home Guardsman who delivered his verdict by spitting into a bowl of stew. That is the story, and sometimes stories tell more than histories, and more quickly, too.

45

When Ulrich Wicks, who drew the white stone and took Peyna's place on the bench, announced the verdict of the court, the spectators – many of whom had sworn for years that Peter would make the best King in Delain's long history – applauded savagely. They rose to their feet and surged forward, and if a line of Home Guards with their swords drawn had not held them back, they might well have overturned the sentence of lifelong imprisonment and exile at the top of the Needle and lynched the young prince instead. As he was led away, spittle flew in a rain, and Peter was well covered by it. Yet he walked with his head up.

A door to the left of the great courtroom led into a narrow hallway. The hallway stretched perhaps forty paces, and then the stairs began. They wound up and up, around and around, all the way to the top of the Needle, where the two rooms Peter would live in henceforth, until the day he died, awaited him. There were three hundred stairs in all. We will come to Peter at the top, in his rooms, and in good time; his story, as you will see, is not done. But we will not climb with him, because it was a climb of shame, leaving his rightful place as King at the bottom and marching, shoulders back and head erect, toward his place as prisoner of the Kingdom at the top – it would not be kind to follow him or any man on such a walk.

Let us instead think of Thomas for a while, and see what happened when he recovered his wits and discovered that he was King of Delain.

46

'No,' Thomas whispered in a voice that was utterly horrified.

His eyes had grown huge in his pale face. His mouth trembled. Flagg had just told him that he was King of Delain, but Thomas did not look like a boy who has been told he is the King; he looked like a boy who has been told he is to be shot in the morning. 'No,' he said again. 'I don't want to be King.'

It was true. All his life he had been bitterly jealous of Peter, but one thing he had never been jealous of was Peter's coming ascension to the throne. That was a responsibility Thomas had never in his wildest dreams wished for. And now one nightmare was piled on top of another. It seemed it wasn't enough that he had awakened to the news that his brother had been imprisoned in the Needle for the murder of their father, the King. Now here was Flagg, with the appalling news that *he* was King in Peter's place.

'No, I don't want to be King, I *won't be* King. I . . . I refuse! *I UTTERLY REFUSE!*'

'You can't refuse, Thomas,' Flagg said briskly. He had decided this was the best line to take with Thomas: friendly but brisk. Thomas needed Flagg more now than he had ever needed anyone in his whole life. Flagg knew this, but he also knew that he was uniquely at Thomas's mercy. He would be wild and skittish for a time, apt to do anything, and care would have to be taken to establish a firm hold over the boy here at the outset.

You need me, Tommy, but it would be a very bad mistake for me to tell you that. No, you must say it to me. There must be no question about who is in charge. Not now, not ever.

'*Can't* refuse?' Thomas whispered. He had jerked upright on his elbows at Flagg's awful news. Now he fell weakly back on his pillows again. '*Can't?* I feel weak again. I think the fever's coming back. Send for the doctor. I might need to be bled. I –'

'You're fine,' Flagg said, standing up. 'I've filled you full of good medicine, your fever's gone, and all you want is a little fresh air to finish the job. But if you need a doctor to tell you the same thing, Tommy' (Flagg let the smallest note of reproach creep into his voice), 'then you need only to pull the bell.'

Flagg pointed at the bell and smiled a little. It was not a terribly kind smile.

'I understand your urge to hide in your bed, but I wouldn't be your friend unless I told you that any refuge you sense in your bed or in trying to stay sick, is a false refuge.'

'False?'

'I advise you to get up and begin working at getting your strength back. You're to be crowned with royal pomp and ceremony in three days' time. Being carried up the aisle in your bed to the platform where Peyna will stand with the crown and sceptre would be a humiliating way to start a kingly reign, but if it comes to that, I assure you they will do it. Headless kingdoms are uneasy kingdoms. Peyna means to see you crowned as soon as possible.'

Thomas lay on his pillows, trying to absorb this information. He was rabbit-eyed with fear.

Flagg grabbed his red-lined cloak from the bed-post, swirled it over his shoulders, and hooked its gold chain at his neck. Next he took a silver-headed cane from the corner. He flourished it, crossed his waist with it, and made a large bow in Thomas's direction. The cloak . . . the hat . . . the cane . . . these things scared Thomas. Here had come a terrible time when he needed Flagg more than he had ever needed him before, and Flagg looked dressed for . . . for . . .

He looks dressed for travelling.

His panic of a few moments ago was only a minor scare in comparison with the frightful cold hands which seized Thomas's heart now.

'And now, dear Tommy, I wish you a healthy disposition all of your life, all the cheer your heart can stand, a long, prosperous reign . . . and goodbye!'

He started for the door and had actually begun to think the boy was so utterly paralyzed with panic that he, Flagg, would have to think of some stratagem for returning to the little fool's bedside on his own, when Thomas managed a single, strangled word: 'Wait!'

Flagg turned back, an expression of polite concern on his face. 'My Lord King?'

'Where . . . where are you going?'

'Why . . .' Flagg looked surprised, as if it hadn't occurred to him until now to think Thomas would even care. 'Andua to start with. They are great sailors, you know, and there are many lands beyond the Sea of Tomorrow I've never seen. Sometimes a captain will take a magician on board for good luck, to conjure a wind if the ship is becalmed, or to tell the weather. If no one wants a magician – well, I am not as young as I was when I first came here, but I can still run a line and unfurl a sail.' Smiling, Flagg mimed the action, never dropping his cane.

Thomas was up on his elbows again. 'No!' he nearly screamed. 'No!'

'My Lord King –'

'*Don't call me that!*'

Flagg crossed to him, now allowing an expression of deeper concern to fill his face. '*Tommy*, then. Dear old Tommy. Whatever's wrong?'

'What's wrong? *What's wrong?* How can you be so *stupid?* My father's dead by poison, Peter's in the Needle for the crime, I must be King, you are planning to leave, and you want to know *what's wrong?*' Thomas uttered a wild, shrieky little laugh.

'But all these things must be, Tommy,' Flagg said gently.

'I can't be King,' Thomas said. He seized Flagg's arm, and his nails sank deeply into the magician's strange flesh. 'Peter was meant to be King, Peter was always the smart one, I was stupid, I *am* stupid, I can't be King!'

'God makes Kings,' Flagg said. *God . . . and sometimes magicians*, he thought with an inward titter. 'He has made *you* King, and mark me, Tommy, you *will* be King. Either you'll be King or there will be dirt shovelled over you.'

'Let it be dirt, then! I'll kill myself.'

'You'll do no such thing.'

'Better to kill myself than to be laughed at for a thousand years as the prince who died of fright.'

'You'll make a King, Tommy. Never fear. But I must go. These days are cold, but the nights are colder. And I want to be clear of the city before dusk falls.'

'No, stay!' Thomas clutched wildly at Flagg's cloak. 'If I must be King, then stay and advise me, as you advised my father! Don't go! I don't know why you want to go, anyway! You've been here forever!'

Ah, finally, Flagg thought. *This is good – in fact, this is RICH.*

'It *is* hard for me to go,' Flagg said gravely. 'Very hard. I love Delain. And I love *you*, Tommy.'

'Then stay!'

'You don't understand my situation. Anders Peyna is a powerful man – an *extremely* powerful man. And he doesn't like me. I should think it fair to say he probably hates me.'

'Why?'

Partly because he knows how long – how very long – I have been here. More, I think, because he senses exactly what I mean to Delain.

'It's hard to say, Tommy. I suppose it has to do with the fact that he is a very powerful man, and powerful men usually resent other men who are as powerful as themselves. People like a King's closest advisor, perhaps.'

'As you were my father's closest advisor?'

'Yes.' He picked up Thomas's hand and squeezed it for a moment. Then he let go of it and sighed mournfully. 'A King's advisors are much like the deer in a King's private park. Such deer are cosseted and petted and fed by hand. Both advisors and tame deer have pleasant lives, but I've all too often seen a tame park deer end up on the King's table when the King's Preserves wouldn't yield up a wild buck for that night's deer steaks or venison stew. When a ruling King dies, the old advisors have a way of disappearing.'

Thomas looked both angry and alarmed. 'Has Peyna threatened you?'

'No . . . he has been very good,' Flagg said. 'Very patient. I have read his eyes, however, and I know that his patience will not last forever. His eyes tell me that I might find the climate in Andua healthier.' He rose with another swirl of cape. 'So . . . as little as I like to go . . .'

'Wait!' Thomas cried again, and in his pinched, pallid face, Flagg saw all his ambitions about to be fulfilled. 'If you were protected when my father was King, because you were *his* advisor, wouldn't you be protected now that I am King, if you were *my* advisor?'

Flagg appeared to think deeply and gravely. 'Yes . . . I suppose . . . if you made it very clear to Peyna . . . *very* clear indeed . . . that any move made against me would be looked upon with royal disfavour. Very *great* royal disfavour.'

'Oh, I would!' Thomas said eagerly. 'I would! So will you stay? Please? If you go, I really will kill myself! I don't know anything about being a King, and I really will!'

Flagg still stood with his head down, his face deep in shadow, apparently thinking solemnly. He was, in fact, smiling.

But when he raised his head, his face was grave.

'I have served the Kingdom of Delain almost all of my life,' he said, 'and I suppose that if you commanded me to stay . . . to stay and serve you to the best of my abilities . . .'

'I do so command you!' Thomas cried in a quivering, febrile voice.

Flagg sank to one knee. 'My Lord!' he said.

Thomas, sobbing with relief, threw himself into Flagg's arms. Flagg caught him and held him.

'Don't cry, my little Lord King,' he whispered. 'All will be well. Yes, all will be very well for you and me and the Kingdom.' His grin widened, showing very white, very strong teeth.

47

Thomas couldn't sleep a wink the night before he was to be crowned in the Plaza of the Needle, and in the early-morning hours of that dread day he was seized by a terrible fit of vomiting and diarrhoea brought on by nervousness – it was stage fright. Stage fright sounds both silly and comic, but there was nothing either silly or comic about this. Thomas was still only a little boy, and what he felt in the night, when we are all most alone, was an extremity of fear so great that it would not be wrong to call it mortal terror. He rang for a servant and bade him fetch Flagg. The servant, alarmed by Thomas's pallor and the smell of vomit in the room, ran all the way and hardly waited to be given entry before bursting in and telling Flagg that the young prince was very ill indeed, might even be dying.

Flagg, who had an idea of what the trouble was, told the servant to go and tell his master he would be with him shortly, and to fear nothing. He was there in twenty minutes.

'I can't go through with it,' Thomas moaned. He had vomited in his bed, and the sheets stank of it. 'I can't be King, I can't, please, you have to stop it from happening, how can I go through with it when I may vomit in front of Peyna and all of them, vomit or . . . or . . .'

'You'll be fine,' Flagg said calmly. He had mixed a brew which would both soothe Thomas's stomach and temporarily cement his bowels shut. 'Drink this.'

Thomas drank it.

'I'm going to die,' he said, putting the glass aside. 'I won't have to kill myself. My heart will just burst from fear. My father said that sometimes rabbits die that way in snares, even if they aren't badly hurt. And that's what I am. A rabbit in a trap, dying of fear.'

You're partly right, dear Tommy, Flagg thought. *You're not dying of fear as you think, but you are indeed a rabbit in a trap.*

'You will change your mind about that, I think,' Flagg said. He had been mixing a second potion. It was cloudy pink – a restful colour.

'What's that?'

'Something to calm your nerves and let you sleep.'

Thomas drank it. Flagg sat by his bedside. Soon Thomas was sleeping deeply – so deeply that if the servant had seen him at that moment, he might have believed his prediction had come true and Thomas was dead. Flagg took the boy's sleeping hand in his own and patted it with something like love. In his own way he *did* love Thomas, but Sasha would have known Flagg's love for what it was: the love of a master for his pet dog.

He is so much like his father, Flagg thought, *and the old man never knew it. Oh, Tommy, we will have wonderful times, you and I, and before I am done the Kingdom will run with royal blood. I'll be gone, but I won't go far, at least not at first. I'll come back in disguise just long enough to see your flyblown head on a spike . . . and to open your brother's chest with my dagger, and rip his heart from his chest, and eat it raw, as his father ate the heart of his precious dragon.*

Smiling, Flagg left the room.

48

The coronation went off with no trouble or complications at all. Thomas's servants (he had no butler, being too young, but this would be provided for soon) dressed him for the occasion in fine clothes of black velvet which were strewn with jewels (*All mine*, Thomas thought with wonder – and with dawning greed – *These are all mine now*) and high black boots of finest kid leather. When Flagg appeared promptly at eleven-thirty and said, 'It is time, my Lord King,' Thomas was far less nervous than he had expected. The sedative the magician had given him the night before was still working in him.

'Take my arm then,' he said, 'in case I stumble.'

Flagg took Thomas's arm. In the years to come, it was a posture the inhabitants of the court city would become very familiar with – Flagg appearing to bear the boy King up as if he were an old man instead of a healthy youngster.

They walked out together into bright wintry sunshine.

A cheer so great it was like the sound of surf breaking against the long, desolate strands of the

Eastern Barony greeted their coming. Thomas looked around, amazed at the sound, and his first thought was: *Where is Peter? Surely this must be for Peter!* Then he remembered that Peter was in the Needle and realized the cheering was for him. He felt a dawning pleasure . . . and I must tell you that the pleasure was not just in knowing the cheers were for him. He knew that Peter, locked in his lonely tower rooms, must hear the cheering, too.

What does it matter now that you were always best in lessons? Thomas thought with a mean happiness that pricked him even as it warmed him. *What does it matter now? You are locked in the Needle and I . . . I am to be King! What does it matter that you brought him a glass of wine every night and –*

But this last thought caused a strange, greasy sweat to rise on his forehead, and he put it away from him.

The cheers rose again and again as he and Flagg walked first to the Plaza of the Needle and then under the arch formed by the upraised ceremonial swords of the Home Guard, dressed again in their fine red ceremonial uniforms and their tall Wolf-Jaw shakos. Thomas began to positively enjoy himself. He raised a hand in salute, and his subjects' cheers became a storm. Men threw their hats in the air. Women wept for joy. Cries of *The King! The King! Behold the King! Thomas the Light-Bringer! Long live the King!* rose in the air. Thomas, who was only a boy, thought they were for him. Flagg, who had perhaps never been a boy, knew better. The cheers were because the time of unease was past. They were cheering the fact that things could go on as they always had, that the shops

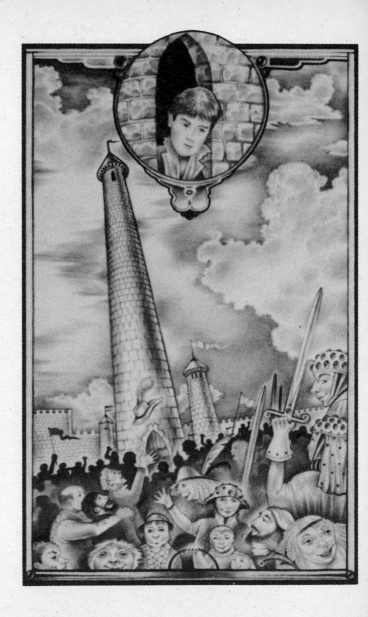

could be reopened, that grim-eyed soldiers in tight leather hats would no longer stand watches around the castle in the night, that everyone could get drunk following this solemn ceremony and not worry about waking to the sounds of confused midnight revolt. No more than that, no less than that. Thomas could have been anyone, anyone at all. He was a figurehead.

But Flagg would see that Thomas never knew that.

Not, at any rate, until it was too late.

The ceremony itself was short. Anders Peyna, looking twenty years older than the week before, officiated. Thomas answered *I will, I shall*, and *I swear* in all the right places, as Flagg had coached him. At the end of the ceremonies, which were conducted in such solemn silence that even those at the farthest edges of the huge crowd could hear them clearly, the crown was placed on Thomas's head. Cheers rose again, louder than ever, and Thomas looked up – up and up the smooth, rounded stone side of the Needle, to the very top, where there was but one window. He couldn't see if Peter was looking down, but he hoped Peter was. He hoped Peter was looking down and biting his lips in frustration until the blood flowed down his chin, as Thomas had often bitten his own lips – bitten them until there was a fine white network of scars there.

Do you hear that, Peter? he shrilled in his mind. *They're cheering for ME! They're cheering for ME! They're finally cheering for ME!*

On his first night as King, Thomas the Light-Bringer awoke straight up and staring in bed, his face stark and horrified, his hands crammed against his mouth as if to stifle a scream. He had just had a terrible nightmare, one even worse than those in which he relived the awful afternoon in the Eastern Tower.

This dream had been a kind of reliving, too. He was in the secret passage again, spying on his father. It was the night his father had been so drunk and furious, striding around the room and shrilling defiance at the heads on the walls. But when his father came to the head of Niner, the things he said were not the same.

Why do you stare at me? his father shrieked in the dream. *He's killed me and I suppose you couldn't stop that, but how could you see your brother imprisoned for it? Answer me, damn you! I did the best I could, and look at me! Look at me!*

His father began to burn. His face turned the dull red of a well-banked fire. Smoke burst from his eyes, his nose, his mouth. He doubled over in agony and Thomas saw that his father's hair was on fire. That was when he woke up.

The wine! he thought now, in horror. *Flagg brought him a glass of wine that night! Everyone knew that Peter brought him wine every night, so everyone thought Peter poisoned the wine! But Flagg brought him wine that night, too, and he never did before! And the poison came from Flagg! He said it was stolen from him years ago, but . . .*

He would not allow himself to think of such things. He would *not*. Because if he *did* think of such things –

'He would kill me,' Thomas whispered, horrified.

You could go to Peyna. Peyna doesn't like him.

Yes, he could do that. But then all his old dislike and jealousy of Peter returned. If he told, Peter would be let out of the Needle and would take *his* place as King. Thomas would be no one again, just a bumbling prince who had been King for one day.

It had taken only one day for Thomas to discover he could *like* being King – he could like it very much, especially with Flagg to help him. Besides, he didn't really *know* anything, did he? He only had an idea. And his ideas had always been wrong.

He's killed me and I suppose you couldn't stop that, but how could you see your brother imprisoned for it?

Never mind, Thomas thought, it must be wrong, it *has* to be wrong, and even if it isn't, it serves him right. He turned over on his side, determined to go back to sleep. And after a long time, sleep came.

In the years ahead, that nightmare sometimes came again – his father accusing his hidden, spying son and then doubling over, smoking, his hair on fire. In those years, Thomas discovered two things: guilt and secrets, like murdered bones, never rest easy; but the knowledge of all three can be lived with.

50

If you had asked him, Flagg would have said with smiling contempt that Thomas could keep a secret from no one except a person who was mentally enfeebled, and perhaps not even from such a one as that. Certainly he could not keep a secret, Flagg would have said, from the man who had engineered his rise to the throne. But men like Flagg are full of pride and confidence in themselves, and although they may see much, they are sometimes strangely blind. Flagg never guessed that Thomas had been behind Niner that night, and that he had seen Flagg given Roland the glass of poisoned wine.

That was a secret Thomas kept.

51

Above the jubilee of the coronation, at the top of the Needle, Peter stood at a small window, looking down. As Thomas had hoped, he had seen and heard everything, from the first cheers when Thomas appeared on Flagg's arm to the last as he disappeared back into the palace itself, also on Flagg's arm.

He stood at the window for nearly three hours after the ceremony was over, watching the crowds.

They were loath to break up and go home. There was much to discuss and much to relive. This-One had to tell That-One just where he had been when he heard the old King was dead, and then they both had to tell T'other-One. The women had a final good cry over Roland and exclaimed over how *fine* Thomas had looked, and how *calm* he had seemed. The children chased each other and pretended *they* were Kings and rolled hoops and fell down and skinned their knees and screamed and then laughed and chased each other again. The men clapped one another on the back and told each other that they guessed all would be well now – it had been a terrible week, but now all would be well. Yet through all of this there ran a dull yellow thread of unease, as if they realized that all was *not* well, that the things which had gone so wrong when the old King had been murdered were not right yet.

Peter, of course, could tell none of this from his high, lonely perch in the Needle, but he sensed something. Yes, something.

At three o'clock, three hours early, the mead-houses opened, supposedly in honour of the new King's coronation, but mostly because there was business to be had. People wanted to drink and celebrate. By seven that night, most of the population of the city was reeling through the streets, drinking the health of Thomas the Light-Bringer (or brawling with each other). It was nearly dark when the revellers finally began to disperse.

Peter left the window, went to the one chair in his 'sitting room' (*that* name was a cruel joke), and simply sat there with his hands folded in his lap. He

saw and watched the room darken. His dinner came
– fatty meat, watery ale, and coarse bread so salty it
would have stung his mouth if he had eaten any. But
Peter did not eat the meat or bread, nor did he drink
the ale.

Around nine o'clock, as the carousing in the
streets began again (this time the crowds were much
more boisterous . . . almost riotous), Peter went
into his prison's second room, stripped to his singlet,
washed with water from the basin, knelt by his bed,
and prayed. Then he got into bed. There was only a
single blanket, although the little bedroom was very
cold. Peter pulled it to his chest, laced his hands
together in back of his head, and looked up into the
darkness.

From outside and below came screams and
cheers and laughter. Now and then there was the
sound of firecrackers, and once, near midnight, there
was an explosive gunpowder flatulence as a drunken
soldier set off a blank charge (the following day, the
unfortunate soldier was sent as far east as the Kingdom of Delain stretched, for his drunken salute to
the new King – gunpowder was rare in Delain, and
jealously hoarded).

Sometime after one in the morning, Peter at
last closed his eyes and slept.

The next morning, he was up at seven. He knelt,
shivering in the cold, his breath puffing white from
his mouth, goosebumps on his bare arms and legs,
and prayed. When his prayers were done, he dressed.
He went into the 'sitting room' and stood by the
window silently for nearly two hours, watching the
city come to life below him. That coming alive was

slower and crankier than usual; most of the adults in Delain woke with drink-swollen heads. They stumbled to their jobs slowly, and in a foul temper. Many of the men went to their tasks blistered by angry wives who had no sympathy with their aching heads (Thomas also had an aching head – he had drunk too much wine the night before – but at least he was spared the lecturing wife).

Peter's breakfast came, Beson, his Chief Warder (who had a hangover of his own), fetched him plain bran cereal with no sugar, watery milk that was rapidly souring, and more of the coarse, salty bread. This was a bitter contrast to the pleasant breakfasts Peter had enjoyed in his study, and he ate none of it.

At eleven, one of the Lesser Warders fetched it silently away.

'Young princeling means to starve, thinks I,' he said to Beson.

'Good,' Beson replied indifferently. 'Spare us the trouble of keeping him.'

'Maybe he fears poison,' the Lesser Warder ventured, and in spite of his aching head, Beson laughed. The jest was a good one.

Peter spent most of his day in the 'sitting-room' chair. In the later part of the afternoon, he stood at the window again. The window was not barred. Unless you were a bird there was nowhere to go but straight down. No one, not Peyna, not Flagg, not Aron Beson, worried that the prisoner might somehow climb down. The Needle's curving stone wall was utterly smooth. A fly might have done it, but not a man.

And if he grew depressed enough to jump,

would anyone care? Not much. It would save the state the expense of feeding and housing a blue-blooded murderer.

As the sun began to move across the floor and up the wall, Peter sat and watched it. His dinner – more fatty meat, watery ale, and salty bread – came. Peter did not touch it.

When the sun was gone, he sat in the dark until nine, and then went into the bedroom. He stripped to his singlet, knelt, and prayed with small white puffs coming from his mouth. He got into bed, laced his hands behind his head, and lay on his back, staring up into the darkness. He lay there thinking about what had become of him. Around one o'clock in the morning, he slept.

So he was on the second day.

And the third.

And the fourth.

For a full week Peter ate nothing, spoke nothing, and did nothing but stand at his sitting-room window or sit in his chair, watching the sun crawl across the floor and then up the wall to the ceiling. Beson was convinced that the boy was in an utter blackness of guilt and despair – he had seen such things before, especially among royalty. The boy would die, he thought, like a wild bird that was never meant to be caged. The boy would die, and good riddance to him.

But on the eighth day, Peter sent for Aron Beson and gave him certain instructions . . . and he did not give them like a prisoner.

He gave them like a King.

Peter *did* feel despair . . . but it was not as deep as Beson believed. He spent that first week in the Needle carefully thinking out his position, and trying to decide what he should do. He had fasted to clear his head. Eventually it *did* clear, but for a while he felt terribly lost, and the weight of his situation pressed down on his head like a blacksmith's anvil. Then he remembered one simple truth: *he* knew he hadn't killed his father, even if everyone else in the Kingdom thought he had.

During the first day or two, he grappled with useless feelings. The childish part of him kept crying out, *Not fair! This is not fair!* And of course it *wasn't*, but that sort of thinking got him no place. As he fasted, he began to regain control of himself. His empty belly peeled the childish part of him away. He began to feel cleaner, husked out, empty . . . like a glass waiting to be filled. After two or three days of eating nothing, the growlings in his stomach subsided, and he began to hear his *real* thoughts more clearly. He prayed, but part of him knew that he was doing more than praying; he was talking to himself, listening to himself, wondering if there was a way out of this prison in the sky where he had been so neatly put.

He had not killed his father. That was the first thing. Someone had blamed it on him. That was the second thing. Who? There was only one person who *could* have, of course; only one person in all of Delain who could have had such an awful poison as Dragon Sand.

Flagg.

It made perfect sense. Flagg knew he would have no place in a kingdom ruled by Peter. Flagg had been careful to make Thomas his friend . . . and to make Thomas fear him. Somehow, Flagg had murdered Roland and then arranged the evidence which had sent Peter here.

He was this far by the third night of Thomas's reign.

Then what was he to do? Simply accept? No, he wouldn't do that. Escape? He *couldn't* do that. No one had ever escaped from the Needle.

Except . . .

A glimmer came to him. This was on the fourth night, as he looked at his dinner tray. Fatty meat, watery ale, salty bread. A plain white plate. No napkin.

Except . . .

The glimmer grew brighter.

There might be a way to escape. There *might*. It would be horribly dangerous, and it would be long. At the end of much work, he might only die in spite of all his efforts. But . . . there might be a way.

And if he did escape, what then? Was there a way to bring the murder home to the magician? Peter did not know. Flagg was a wily old serpent – he would have left no evidence of what he had done to damn him later on. Could Peter worm a confession out of the magician? He *might* be able to, always assuming Peter could lay hands on him in the first place – Peter guessed that Flagg might disappear like smoke if he heard that Peter had escaped the Needle. Would anyone *believe* Flagg's confession, even if Peter could get one out of him? *Oh yes, he confessed to the murder of Roland*, people would say. *Peter, the escaped father-killer, had a sword to his throat. In a fix like that, I might confess to anything, even the murder of God!*

You might be tempted to laugh at Peter, turning such things over in his mind while he was still imprisoned three hundred feet in the sky. You might say he had gotten the cart quite a bit forward of the horse. But Peter had seen a way he might escape. It might, of course, only be a way to die young, but he thought it had a chance of working. Still . . . was there any reason to go through all the work if in the end it could come to nothing? Or, worse still, if it were to cause the Kingdom fresh harm in some way he did not see now?

He thought about these things and prayed over them. The fourth night passed . . . the fifth . . . the sixth. On the seventh night, Peter came to this conclusion: it was better to try than not to try; better to make an effort to right the wrong even if he died trying to do so. An injustice had been done. He discovered a strange thing – the fact that the injustice had been done to *him* didn't seem half so important as the fact that it had been done at all. It ought to be righted.

On the eighth day of Thomas's reign, he sent for Beson.

53

Beson listened to the speech of the imprisoned prince with incredulity and mounting rage. Peter finished and Aron Beson let loose a gutter flood of obscenity that would have made a horse drover blush.

Peter stood before it, impassive.

'You murdering snot-nosed hound!' Beson finished, in a tone that was close to wonder. 'I guess you think yer still livin in the bloody lap o luxury, with yer sairvants to run scurrying every time you lift one o yer perfoomed little fingers. But it ain't like that in here, my young prince. No, *sir*.'

Beson leaned forward from the waist, scruffy chin jutting, and although the stench of the man – sweat and thick cheap wine and great grey scales of dirt – was nearly overpowering, Peter did not give ground. There were no bars between them; Beson had yet to fear a prisoner, and certainly he felt no fear of this young whelp. The Chief Warder was fifty, short, broad of shoulder, deep in the gut. His greasy hair hung in tangles around his cheeks and down the back of his neck. When he had come into Peter's room, one of the Lesser Warders had locked the door behind them.

Beson balled his left hand into a fist and shook it under Peter's nose. His right hand slid into the pouch pocket of his shirt and closed around a smooth cylinder of metal. One hard smash with that loaded fist would break a man's jaw. Beson had done it before.

'You take your *requests*, and you jam them up

your nose with the rest of the boogers, my dear little prince. And the next time you call me in here for any such royal rubbage as *this*, you'll bleed for it.'

Beson started away towards the door, short and hunched over and almost troll-like. He travelled in his own tight little cloud of stink.

'You are in danger of making an extremely bad mistake,' Peter said. His voice was soft but grim, and it carried.

Beson turned back to him, his face incredulous. '*What* did you say?'

'You heard me,' Peter said. 'And when you speak to me next, you stinking little turnip, I think you had better remember you are speaking to royalty, don't you? My lineage did not change when I climbed those steps.'

For a moment Beson could not reply. His mouth opened and closed like the mouth of a fish yanked out of the ocean – although any fisherman catching something as ugly as Beson would surely have thrown it back. Peter's cool requests – requests delivered in a tone which made it clear that they were in reality demands not to be refused – made Beson's head buzz with fury. One of the requests had been that of either an utter sissy or an outright lunatic. That one Beson had dismissed at once as nonsense and tomfoolery. The other, however, had to do with his meals. That, combined with the firm resolute look in Peter's eye, suggested that the young prince had thrown off his despair and meant to live.

The future prospects for idle days and drunken nights had looked bright. Now they had dimmed again. This young boy looked very healthy, very strong. He might live a long time. Beson might very well have to look at the young murderer's face for the rest of his own life – *there* was a thought to set a man's teeth on edge! And –

Stinking turnip? Did he actually call me a stinking turnip?

'Oh, my dear little prince,' Beson said, 'I think you are the one who has made the mistake . . . but I can promise you'll never make it again.' His lips split open in a grin, revealing a few blackened stumps of teeth. Now, about to attack, he moved with surprising grace. His right hand came out of the pouch pocket, wrapped around the bar of metal.

Peter took a step backward, his eyes moving from Beson's fisted hands to Beson's face and then back to his fists. Behind Beson, the tiny barred window in the middle of Peter's door was opened. Two of the Lesser Warders were crammed there cheek to stubbly cheek, grinning and waiting for the fun to start.

'You know that royal prisoners are to be given some consideration in smaller matters,' Peter said, still backtracking and circling. 'That is tradition. And I have asked you for nothing untoward.'

Beson's grin widened. He imagined he heard fear in Peter's voice. He was mistaken. This error would shortly be brought home to him in a way to which he was unaccustomed.

'Such traditions are paid for, even among the royalty, my little prince.' Beson rubbed his left thumb and finger together. His right fist remained tightly balled around the chunk of metal.

'If you mean you wish an odd bit of cash from

time to time, that might be arranged,' Peter said, continuing to circle away. 'But only if you drop this foolish behaviour of yours right now.'

'Afraid, are you?'

'If anyone should be afraid here, I think it is you,' Peter said. 'You apparently mean to attack the brother of the King of Delain.'

This shot struck home, and for a moment Beson faltered. His eyes grew uncertain. Then he glanced towards the open window in the door, saw the faces of his Lesser Warders, and his own face darkened again. If he drew back now, he would have trouble with them – nothing he couldn't handle, of course, but still more annoyance than this little stinker was worth.

He moved forward in a rush and swung the weighted fist. He was grinning. The prince's screams as he fell to the stone floor with his smashed and squirting nose clutched in his hands would be, Beson thought, shrill and babyish.

Peter moved back easily, his feet moving as gracefully as if in a dance. He seized Beson's fist and was not surprised in the least by its weight – he had seen the gleam of metal between Beson's swelled fingers. Peter pulled with a wiry strength that Beson would not have believed five minutes ago. He spun through the air and hit the curving inner wall of Peter's 'sitting room' with a crash that rattled the few teeth remaining in his jaws. Stars exploded in his head. The metal cylinder flew from his fist and rolled across the floor. And before Beson could even begin to recover, Peter had sprung after it and seized it. He moved with the simple, pure liquidity of a cat.

This can't be happening, Beson thought with dawning dismay and stupid surprise. *This absolutely can't be happening.*

He had never feared entering the two-room prison at the top of the Needle, because there had never been a prisoner here, not of noble blood, not of royal blood, who could best him. Oh, there had been some famous fights up here, but he had taught them all who was boss. Perhaps they ruled the roost down below, but up here he was the boss, and they came to respect his dirty, compact power. But now this stripling of a *boy* . . .

Bellowing with rage, Beson came off the wall, shaking his head to clear it, and charged Peter, who had folded the cylinder of metal into his own right hand. The Lesser Warders stood staring at this unexpected development with stupid wonder. Neither thought of interfering; they could believe what was happening no more than Beson himself.

Beson ran at Peter with his arms outstretched. Now that the prince had gotten his fist weight away from him, Beson had no more interest in the sort of free-for-all swinging and hitting he thought of as 'boxing'. He meant to close with Peter, grapple with him, drive him to the floor, land on top of him, and then choke him unconscious.

But the space where Peter had been emptied with magical suddenness as the boy stepped aside and dropped into a crouch. As the squat, troll-like Chief Warder went past, trying to turn, Peter hit him three times with his right fist, which was closed around the metal cylinder. *Hardly fair*, Peter thought, *but, then, it wasn't I that brought this piece of metal into it, was it?* The blows did not look hard at all. If Beson had been watching a fight and had seen those three quick, fluttering punches thrown, he would have laughed and called them 'sissy punches'. Beson's idea of a real man's punch was a roundhouse blow that made the air whistle.

But they weren't sissy punches at all, no matter what the likes of Beson might have thought. Each was driven out from the shoulder, just as Peter's boxing instructor had taught him in their twice-weekly classes over the last six years. The punches were economical, they didn't make the air whistle, but Beson felt as if he had been kicked three times in rapid succession by a very small pony with very big hoofs. There was a flare of agony across the left side of his face as his cheekbone broke. To Beson, it sounded as if a small branch had snapped inside his head. He was driven into the wall again. He hit it like a rag doll and bounced back buckle-kneed. He stared at the prince with obvious dismay.

The Lesser Warders peering through the hole in the door were agog with surprise. Beson, being beaten by a *boy?* It was as unbelievable as rain would have been coming down from a clear blue sky. One of them now looked at the key in his hand, thought briefly of going in there, then thought better of it. A man could get hurt in there. He slipped the key into his pocket, where he could later claim to have forgotten it.

'Are you ready to talk reasonably now?' Peter wasn't even out of breath. 'This is silly. I require only two small favours of you, favours for which you can count on being well and amply repaid. You –'

With a roar, Beson flung himself at Peter again. This time Peter was not expecting an attack, but he managed to pull back anyway, the way a matador pulls back from a bull which charges unexpectedly – the matador may be surprised, perhaps even gored, but he rarely loses his grace. Peter did not lose his, but he *was* wounded. Beson's nails were long, ragged, and filthy – more like animal claws than human nails – and he liked to tell his Lesser Warders (on dark winter's nights when a gruesome tale seemed required) about the time he had slit a prisoner's neck from ear to ear with one of those thumbnails.

Now one drew a bloody line down Peter's left cheek as Beson flailed his way by. The cut zigzagged from temple to jawline, missing Peter's left eye by hardly half an inch. Peter's cheek fell open in a flap, and all his life he would bear the scar of his encounter with Beson there.

Peter grew angry. All the things that had happened to him over the last ten days seemed to slam together in his head, and for a moment he was almost – not quite, but *almost* – angry enough to kill the brutish Chief Warder instead of just teaching him a lesson he would never, never forget.

As Beson turned, he was rocked by left hooks and right jabs. The jabs would ordinarily have done little damage, but the pound and a half of metal in Peter's fist turned them into torpedoes. His knuckles sprung Beson's jaw. Beson roared with pain and again tried to close with Peter. This was a mistake. There was a crunch as his nose broke and blood flooded over his mouth and chin. It dripped on to his filthy jerkin. Then a bright flare of pain as that heavy right hand smashed his lips back. Beson spat a tooth onto the floor and tried to circle away. He had forgotten that his Lesser Warders were watching, afraid to interfere. Beson had forgotten his anger at the young prince's attitude, had lost his former desire to teach the young prince a lesson.

For the first time in his tenure as Chief Warder, he had forgotten everything but a blind desire to survive. For the first time in his tenure as Chief Warder, Beson was afraid.

Nor was it the fact that Peter was now punching him at will that frightened him. He had taken bad beatings before, although never at the hands of a prisoner. No, it was the look in Peter's eyes that had so terrified him. *It is the look of a King. Gods protect me, it is the face of a King – his fury blazes almost with the heat of the sun.*

Peter drove Beson against the wall, measured the distance to Beson's chin, and then drew back his weighted right fist.

'Do you need more convincing, turnip?' Peter asked grimly.

'No more,' Beson replied groggily, through his rapidly puffing lips. 'No more, my King, I cry your mercy, I cry your mercy.'

'What?' Peter asked, flabbergasted. 'What did you call me?'

But Beson was sliding slowly down the curved stone wall. When he had called Peter *my King*, he had done so as unconsciousness stole over him. He would not remember saying it, but Peter never forgot.

Beson was unconscious for over two hours. If not for his thick, snoring breaths, Peter would have been afraid that perhaps he really *had* killed the Chief Warder. The man was a gross, vicious, underhanded pig . . . but for all of that, Peter had no wish to kill him. The Lesser Warders took turns staring in the little window in the oaken door, their eyes wide and round – the eyes of small boys looking at the man-eating Anduan tiger in the King's Menagerie. Neither made any effort to rescue their superior, and their faces told Peter that they expected him to leap on the unconscious Beson at any moment and tear his throat out. Perhaps with his teeth.

Well, why shouldn't they think such things? Peter asked himself bitterly. *They think I killed my own father, and a man who would do such a thing might stoop to any low act, even that of killing an unconscious opponent.*

Finally Beson began to moan and stir. His right eye fluttered and came open – the left *couldn't* open, and wouldn't completely for some days.

The right eye looked at Peter not with hate, but with unmistakable alarm.

'Are you ready to speak reasonably?' Peter asked.

Beson said something Peter couldn't understand. It sounded like mush.

'I don't understand you.'

Beson tried again. 'You could have killed me.'

'I've never killed anyone,' Peter said. 'The time may come when I'll have to, but if it ever does, I hope I don't have to start with unconscious warders.'

Beson sat against the wall, looking at Peter with his one open eye. An expression of deep thought, absurd and a little frightening on his swelled and battered features, settled over his face.

At last he managed another mushy phrase. Peter thought he understood this one, but wanted to be absolutely sure.

'Repeat that, please, Mr Chief Warder Beson.'

Beson looked startled. As Yosef had never been called Lord High Groom before Peter, so Beson had never been called Mr Chief Warder.

'We can do business,' he said.

'That is very well.'

Beson struggled slowly to his feet. He wanted no more to do with Peter, at least not today. He had other problems. His Lesser Warders had just watched him take a bad beating at the hands of a boy who hadn't had anything to eat for a week. Watched – and no more, the cowardly sots. His head ached, and he might well have to whip those poor fools into line before he could slink off to bed.

He had started out when Peter called to him.

Beson turned back. That turning was really all it took. Both of them knew who was in charge here. Beson had been beaten. When his prisoner told him to wait, he waited.

'I have something I want to say to you. It will be good for both of us if I do.'

Beson said nothing. He only stood and watched Peter warily.

'Tell *them*' – Peter jerked his head towards the door – 'to close the spyhole.'

Beson stared at Peter for a moment, then turned towards the staring warders and gave the command.

The Lesser Warders currently jammed cheek to cheek into the opening, stood there staring, not understanding Beson's blurred words . . . or pretending not to. Beson ran his tongue over his blood-flecked teeth and spoke more clearly, obviously with some pain. This time the peephole was swung shut and bolted from the outside . . . but not before Beson had heard the contemptuous laughter of his underlings. He sighed wearily – yes, they would have to be taught some hard lessons before he could go home. Cowards learned quickly, though. This prince, whatever else he might be, was surely no coward. He wondered if he really wanted to do any business at all with Peter.

'I want to give you a note to take to Anders Peyna,' Peter said. 'You'll come back for it tonight, I hope.'

Beson said nothing, but he was trying very hard to think. This was the most unsettling twist yet. Peyna! A note to Peyna! He had had a cold moment when Peter reminded him that he was the brother of the King, but it had been nothing compared with this. Peyna, by the gods!

The more he thought of it the less he liked it.

King Thomas might not much care if his older brother was roughed up in the Needle. The older brother had murdered their father, for one thing; Thomas probably didn't feel much brotherly love right now. And more important, Beson felt little or no fright when the name of King Thomas the Light-Bringer was invoked. Like almost everyone else in Delain, Beson had already begun to view Thomas with a certain contempt. But Peyna, now . . . Peyna was different.

To the likes of Beson, Anders Peyna was more frightening than a whole marching regiment of Kings, anyway. A King was a distant sort of being, bright and mysterious, like the sun. It didn't matter if the sun went behind the clouds and froze you, or came out all hot and white to bake you alive – either way you only accepted, because what the sun did was far beyond the ability of mortal creatures to understand or to change.

Peyna was a more earthly being. The sort of being Beson could understand . . . and fear. Peyna with his narrow face and his ice-blue eyes, Peyna with his high-collared judge's robes, Peyna who decided who would live and who would go under the headsman's axe.

Could this boy really command Peyna from his cell here at the top of the Needle? Or was it only a desperate bluff?

How can it be a bluff if he means to write him a note I shall myself deliver?

'If I were King, Anders Peyna would serve me in any way I commanded,' Peter said. 'I am not a King now, only a prisoner. Still, not long ago I did him a favour for which I think he is very grateful.'

'I see,' Beson replied, as noncommittally as he could.

Peter sighed. Suddenly he felt very weary, and wondered what sort of foolish dream he was pursuing here. Did he really believe he was taking the first few steps on the road to freedom by beating up this stupid warder and then bending him to his will? Did he have any real guarantee that Peyna would do even the smallest thing for him? Perhaps the concept of a favour owed was only in Peter's own mind.

But it had to be tried. Hadn't he decided, on his long, lonely nights of meditation as he grieved for both his father and himself, that the only real sin would be in not trying?

'Peyna is not my friend,' Peter went on. 'I won't even try to tell you that he is. I've been convicted of murdering my father, the King, and I shouldn't think I have a friend left in all of Delain, from north to south. Would you agree, Mr Chief Warder Beson?'

'Yes,' Beson said stonily. 'I would.'

'Nevertheless, I believe that Peyna will undertake to provide you with the bit of cash you are used to receiving from your inmates.'

Beson nodded. When a noble was imprisoned in the Needle for any length of time, Beson would commonly see that the prisoner got a better grade of food than the fatty meat and watery ale, fresh linen once a week, and sometimes a visit from a wife or a sweetheart. He did not do this free, of course. Imprisoned nobles almost always came from rich families, and there was always someone in those families willing to pay Beson for Beson's services, no matter what the crime had been.

This crime was of an exceptionally terrible nature, but here was this boy, saying that no less a one than Anders Peyna might be willing to provide the bribe.

'One other thing,' Peter said softly. 'I believe Peyna will do this because he is a man of honour. And if anything were to happen to me – if you and several of your Lesser Warders were to rush in here tonight, and beat me in revenge for the beating I have given you, for example – I believe that Peyna might take an interest in the matter.'

Peter paused.

'A *personal* interest in the matter.'

He looked closely at Beson.

'Do you understand me?'

'Yes,' Beson said, and then added: 'my Lord.'

'Will you provide me with pen, inkpot, blotter, and paper?'

'Yes.'

'Come here.'

With some trepidation, Beson came.

The Chief Warder's stink was tremendous, but Peter did not draw away – the stink of the crime with which he had been accused had almost inured him to the smell of sweat and dirt, he had discovered. He looked at Beson with a hint of a smile.

'Whisper in my ear,' Peter said.

Beson blinked uneasily. 'What shall I whisper, my Lord?'

'A number,' Peter said.

After a moment, Beson did.

One of the Lesser Warders brought Peter the writing implements he had asked for. He gave Peter the wary look of an alley cat that has been often kicked, and skittered away before he could receive a helping of the anger that had been heaped on Beson's head.

Peter sat down at the rickety table by the window, breath puffing out in the deep cold. He listened to the restless whine of the wind around the tip of the Needle and looked down at the lights of the city.

Dear Judge-General Peyna, he wrote, and then stopped.

Will you see who this is from, crumple it in your hand, and throw it into the fire unread? Will you read it and then laugh contemptuously at the fool who murdered his father and then dared to expect help from the Judge-General of the land? Will you, perhaps, even see through the scheme, and understand what it is I'm up to?

Peter was in a cheerier frame of mind that evening, and thought the answer to all three questions would probably be no. His plan might well fail, but it was unlikely to be foreseen by such an orderly and methodical man as Peyna. The Judge-General would be as apt to imagine himself donning a dress and dancing a hornpipe in the Plaza of the Needle at the full of the moon as he was to guess what Peter was up to. *And what I'm asking is so little*, Peter thought. That ghost of a smile touched his lips again. *At least I hope and believe it will seem so . . . to him.*

Bending forward, he dipped the quill pen in the inkpot and began to write.

56

'**O**n the following evening, shortly after nine had struck, Anders Peyna's butler answered an unaccustomedly late knock and looked down his long nose at the figure of the Chief Warder standing on the doorstep. Arlen – that was the butler's name – had seen Beson before, of course; like Arlen's master, Beson was a part of the Kingdom's legal machinery. But Arlen did not recognize him now. The beating Peter had given Beson had had a day to set, and his face was a sunset of reds and purples and yellows. His left eye had opened a little, but was still little more than a slit. He looked like a dwarvish ghoul, and the butler began to swing the door shut almost at once.

'Wait,' Beson said in a hard growl that made the butler hesitate. 'I come with a message for your master.'

The butler hesitated for a moment and then began to swing the door closed again. The man's sullen, swollen face was frightening. *Could* he actually be a dwarf, down from the north country? Supposedly the last of those wild, fur-clad tribes had either died or been killed off in his grandfather's time, but still . . . one never knew . . .

'It is from Prince Peter,' Beson said. 'If you close this door, you will hear hard things later from your marster, thinks I.'

Arlen hesitated again, torn between closing the door against the ghoul and the power the name of Prince Peter still held. If this man came from Peter, he must be the Needle's Chief Warder. Yet –

'You don't *look* like Beson,' he said.

'You don't look like your father, neither, Arlen, and it's made me wonder more than once where your mother may have been,' the lumpish ghoul retorted rudely, and stuck a smudged envelope through the crack still open in the door. 'Here . . . take it to 'im. I'll wait. Close the door if you want, although it's devilish cold out here.'

Arlen didn't care if it was twenty below. He didn't intend to have the horrible-looking fellow toasting his feet in front of the fire in the servants' kitchen. He snatched the envelope, shut the door, bolted it, started away . . . then returned and double-bolted it.

57

Peyna was in his study, staring into the fire and thinking long thoughts. When Thomas had been crowned the moon had been new; it was not yet at the half, and already he did not like the way things were going. Flagg – that was the worst. Flagg.

The magician already wielded more power than in the days of Roland's reign. Roland had at least been a man, full of years, no matter how slow his thinking might have been. Thomas was only a boy, and Peyna feared that Flagg might soon control all Delain in Thomas's name. That would be bad for the King-dom . . . and bad for Anders Peyna, who had never concealed his dislike of Flagg.

It was pleasant here in the study, before the crackling fire, but Peyna thought he nonetheless felt a cold wind around his ankles. It was a wind which might rise and blow away . . . everything.

Why, Peter? Why, oh why? Why couldn't you wait? And why did you have to seem so perfect on the outside, like a rose-red apple in autumn, and be so rotten below the skin? Why?

Peyna didn't know . . . and would not admit to himself, even now, that doubts as to whether or not Peter really *had* been rotten were beginning to nibble at his heart.

There was a knock at the door.

Peyna roused himself, looked around, and called out impatiently: 'Come! And it better be damned good!'

Arlen came in, looking ruffled and confused. He held an envelope in one hand.

'Well?'

'My Lord . . . there's a man at the door . . . at least, he *looks* like a man . . . that is, his face is most awfully puffed and swelled, as if he had gotten a terrible beating . . . or . . .' Arlen's voice trailed away.

'What's that to do with me? You know I don't

receive this late. Tell him to go away. Tell him to go to the devil!'

'He says he's Beson, my Lord,' Arlen said, more flustered than ever. He raised the smudged envelope, as if to use it as a shield. 'He brought this. He says it's a message from Prince Peter.'

Peyna's heart leaped at that, but he only frowned more strenuously at Arlen.

'Well, is it?'

'From Prince Peter?' Arlen was almost gibbering now. His usual composure was utterly lost, and Peyna found this interesting. He wouldn't have believed Arlen would lose his composure come fire, flood, or invasion of ravaging dragons. 'My Lord, I would have no way of knowing . . . That is, I . . . I . . .'

'Is it *Beson*, you idiot?'

Arlen licked his lips – actually *licked his lips*. This was utterly unheard of. 'Well, it might be, my Lord . . . it looks a bit like him . . . but the fellow on the doorstep is most awfully bruised and lumpy . . . I . . .' Arlen swallowed. 'I thought he looked like a dwarf,' he said, bringing out the worst and then trying to soften it with a lame smile.

It IS Beson, Peyna thought. *It's Beson and if he looks as if he's been beaten it's because Peter administered the beating. That's why he brought the message. Because Peter beat him and he was afraid not to. A beating's the only thing that convinces his sort.*

There came a sudden feeling of exultation in Peyna's heart: he felt as one might feel in a dark cave when a light suddenly shines out.

'Give me the letter,' he said.

Arlen did. He then made as if to scuttle out, and this was also something new, because Arlen did not scuttle. *At least*, Peyna thought, his mind lawyerly as always, *I have never KNOWN him to scuttle*.

He let Arlen get as far as the study door, as a veteran fisherman will let a hooked fish run, and then pulled him up short. 'Arlen.'

Arlen turned back. He looked braced, as if to receive a reprimand.

'There are no more dwarves. Did your mother not tell you so?'

'Yes,' Arlen said reluctantly.

'Good for her. A wise woman. These dreams in your head must have come from your father. Let the Chief Warder in. To the servants' kitchen,' he added hastily. 'I have no wish to have him in here. He stinks. But let him into the servants' kitchen so he may warm himself. The night is cold.' Since the death of Roland, Peyna reflected, all the nights had been cold, as if in reproach for the way the old King had burned, from the inside out.

'Yes, my Lord,' Arlen said with marked reluctance.

'I'll ring for you shortly and tell you what to do with him.'

Arlen went out, a humbled man, and closed the door behind him.

Peyna turned the envelope over in his hands several times without opening it. The dirt was no doubt from Beson's own greasy fingers. He could almost smell the villain's sweat on the envelope. It had been sealed shut with a blot of common candle wax.

He thought, *I would do better, perhaps, to throw*

this directly into the fire, and think of it no more. Yes, throw it into the fire, then ring Arlen and tell him to give the little hunched-over Chief Warder – he really DOES look like a dwarf, now that I think of it – a hot toddy and send him away. Yes, that is what I should do.

But he knew that he wouldn't. That absurd feeling – that feeling that here was a ray of light in hopeless darkness – would not leave him. He put his thumb under the flap of the envelope, broke the seal, took out a brief letter, and read it by firelight.

Peyna,

I have decided to live.

I had read only a little about the Needle before I actually found myself in the place, and although I had heard a bit more, most of it was only gossip. One of the things I heard was that certain small favours might be purchased. It seems this really is so. I of course have no money, but I thought you might perhaps defray my expenses in this matter. I did you a favour not long ago, and if you were to pay the Chief Warder a sum of eight guilders – such sum to be paid anew at the beginning of each year I spend in this unhappy place – I would consider the favour repaid. This sum, you will notice, is very small. That is because I require only two things. If you will arrange for Beson to 'wet his beak' so that I may have them, I'll trouble you no more.

I am aware that you would be put in a bad light if it

came out that you have helped me, even in a small way. I suggest that you make my friend Ben your go-between, if you decide to do as I ask. I have not spoken to Ben since my arrest, but I think and hope he remains true to me. I would ask him rather than you, but the Staads are not well off, and Ben has no money of his own. It shames me to ask money from anyone, but there is no other to whom I may turn. If you feel you cannot do as I request, I will understand.

I did not murder my father.

Peter

*P*eyna looked at this amazing letter for quite some time. His eyes kept returning to the first line, and the last.

I have decided to live.

I did not murder my father.

It did not surprise him that the boy continued to protest – he had known criminals to go on for years and years protesting their innocence of crimes of which they were patently guilty. But it was not like a guilty man to be so bald in his own defence. So . . . so commanding.

Yes, that was what bothered him most about the letter – its tone of command. A true King, Peyna felt, would not be changed by exile; not by prison; not even by torture. A true King would not waste time justifying or explaining. He would simply state his will.

I have decided to live.

Peyna sighed. After a long time, he drew his inkpot to him, took a sheet of fine parchment from his drawer, and wrote upon it. His note was even shorter than Peter's had been. It took him less than five minutes to write it, blot it, sand it, fold it, and seal it shut. With that done, he rang for Arlen.

Arlen, looking much chastened, appeared almost at once.

'Is Beson still here?' Peyna asked.

'I think so, sir,' Arlen said. In fact he *knew* Beson was still there, because he had been peeking through the keyhole at the man, watching him lurch back and forth restlessly from one end of the servants' kitchen to the other with a cold chicken leg clutched like a club in one hand. When the meat on the leg was all gone, Beson had crunched the bones – horrible splintering sounds they made – and sucked contentedly at the marrow.

Arlen was still not utterly convinced the man was not a dwarf . . . perhaps even a troll.

'Give him this,' Peyna said, handing Arlen the note, 'and this for his trouble.' Two guilders clinked into Arlen's other hand. 'Tell him there may be a reply. If so, he's to bring it at night, as he did this one.'

'Yes, my Lord.'

'Don't linger and chat with him, either,' Peyna said. It was as close as he was able to come to making a joke.

'No, my Lord,' Arlen said glumly, and went

out. He was still thinking of the crunching sounds the chicken bones had made when Beson bit through them.

'Here,' Beson said grumpily when he came into Peter's cell the next day, thrusting the envelope at Peter. In truth, he *felt* grumpy. The two guilders handed to him by Arlen had been an unexpected windfall, and Beson had spent most of the night drinking it up. Two guilders bought a great lot of mead, and today his head felt large and very painful. 'Damned messenger boy is what I'm turning into.'

'Thank you,' Peter said, holding the envelope.

'Well? Ain'tcher going to open it?'

'Yes. When you leave.'

Beson bared his teeth and clenched his fists. Peter simply stood there, looking at him. After a moment, Beson lowered his fists. 'Damned messenger boy, is all!' he repeated, and went out, slamming the heavy door behind him. There was the thud of iron locks being turned, followed by the sliding sound of bolts – three of them, each as thick as Peter's wrist – being slid into place.

When the sounds had stopped, Peter opened the note. It was only three sentences long.

I am aware of the long-standing customs of which you speak. The sum you mentioned could be arranged. I will do so, but not until I know what favours you expect to buy from our mutual friend.

Peter smiled. Judge-General Peyna was not a sly man – slyness was not at all in his nature, as it was in Flagg's – but he was exceedingly careful. This note was the proof of that. Peter had expected Peyna's condition. He would have felt wary if Peyna had not asked what he wanted. Ben would be the go-between, Peyna would cease to actually be a part of the bribe very shortly, but still he walked carefully, as a man might walk on loose stones which might slide out from under his feet at any moment.

Peter went to the door of his cell, rapped, and after some conversation with Beson, was given the inkpot and dirty quill pen again. Beson did more muttering about being nothing but a damned mess-enger boy, but he was not really unhappy about the situation. There might be another two guilders in this for him.

'If them two write back and forth long enough, I guess I could get rich arter it,' he said to no one at all, and roared laughter in spite of his aching head.

61

Peyna unfolded Peter's second note and saw that this time the prince had left off both of their names. That was very well. The boy learned fast. As he read the note itself, his eyebrows shot up.

Perhaps your request to know my business is presumptuous, perhaps not. It matters little, since I am at your mercy. Here are the two things your eight guilders per year are to purchase:

1. I want to have my mother's doll's house. It always took me to pleasant places and pleasant adventures, and I loved it much as a boy.

2. I would like to have a napkin brought with my meals – a proper royal napkin. The crest may be removed, if you like.

These are my requests.

Peyna read this note over and over again before throwing it into the fire. He was troubled by it because he did not understand it. The boy was up to something . . . or was he? What could he want with his mother's doll's house? So far as Peyna knew, it was still in storage somewhere in the castle, gathering dust under a sheet, and there could be no reason not to give it to him – not, that was, if a good man was charged with going through it carefully first, to make sure all the sharp things – tiny knives and such – were removed from it. He remembered quite well how enchanted Peter had been with Sasha's doll's house as a very young boy. He also remembered – vaguely, very vaguely – that Flagg had protested that it was hardly fitting for a boy who would someday be King to be playing with dolls. Roland had gone against Flagg's advice that time . . . wisely, Peyna thought, for Peter had given the doll's house up, all in good time.

Until now.

Has he gone mad, then?

Peyna did not think so.

The napkin, now . . . that he could understand. Peter had always insisted upon a napkin at every meal, always spread it neatly on his lap like a small tablecloth. Even when on camping trips with his father, Peter had insisted on a napkin. So oddly like Peter not to ask for better food than the normal poor prison rations, as almost any other noble or royal prisoner would have done before asking for anything else. No, he had asked for a napkin instead.

That insistence on always being neat . . . on always having a napkin . . . that was his mother's doing. I'm sure of it. Do the two go together, somehow? But how? Napkins . . . and Sasha's doll's house. What do they mean?

Peyna did not know, but that absurd feeling of hope remained. He kept remembering that Flagg had not wanted Peter to have the doll house as a little boy. Now, years later, here was Peter asking to have it again.

There was another thought wrapped up inside this, as neatly as filling is wrapped up in a tart. It was a thought Peyna hardly dared to entertain. If – just *if* – Peter had not murdered his father, who did that leave? Why, the person who had originally owned that hideous poison, of course. A person who would have been nothing in the Kingdom if Peter had followed his father . . . a person who was nearly *everything* now that Thomas sat on the throne in Peter's place.

Flagg.

But this thought was hideous to Peyna. It suggested that justice had somehow gone wrong, and that was bad. But it also suggested that the simple logic in which he had always prided himself had been washed away in the revulsion he had felt at the sight of Peter's tears, and this idea – the idea that he had made the single most important decision of his career on the basis of emotion rather than fact – was much worse.

What harm can there be in his having the doll's house, as long as the sharp things are removed?

Peyna drew his writing materials to him and wrote briefly. Beson had another two guilders to drink up – already he had been paid half the sum he would receive for the prince's little favours each year. He looked forward to more correspondence, but there was no more.

Peter had what he wanted.

62

As a child Ben Staad had been a slim, blue-eyed boy with curly blond hair. The girls had been sighing and giggling over him since he was nine years old. 'That'll stop soon enough,' Ben's father said. 'All the Staads make handsome enough lads, but he'll be like the rest of us when he gets his growth, I reckon – his hair'll darken to brown and he'll go around squintin' at everything and he'll have all the luck of a fat pig in the King's slaughtering pen.'

But neither of the first two predictions came true. Ben was the first Staad male in several generations to remain as blond at seventeen as he had been at seven, and who could tell a brown hawk from an auger hawk at four hundred yards. Far from developing a nearsighted squint, his eyes were amazingly keen . . . and the girls still sighed and giggled over him as much now, at seventeen, as they had when he was nine.

As for his luck . . . well, that was another matter. That most of the Staad men had been unlucky, at least for the last hundred years or so, was beyond argument. Ben's family thought that Ben might be the one to redeem them from their genteel poverty. After all, his hair hadn't darkened and his eyes hadn't grown dim, so why should he not escape the curse of bad luck as well? And after all, Prince Peter was his friend, and Peter would someday be King.

Then Peter was tried and convicted of his father's murder. He was in the Needle before any of the bewildered Staad family could get their minds around what had happened. Ben's father, Andrew, went to Thomas's coronation, and he came home with a bruise on his cheek – a bruise his wife thought it might be prudent not to speak of.

'I'm *sure* Peter's innocent,' Ben said that night at supper. 'I simply refuse to believe –'

The next moment he was sprawling on the floor, his ear ringing. His father was towering over him, pea soup dripping from his moustache, his face so red it was almost purple, and Ben's baby sister, Emmaline, was crying in her high chair.

'Don't mention the murdering whelp's name again in this house,' his father said.

'Andrew!' his mother cried. 'Andrew, he doesn't understand –'

His father, normally the kindest of men, turned his head and stared at Ben's mother. 'Be quiet, woman,' he said, and something in his voice made her sit down again. Even Emmaline stopped crying.

'Father,' Ben said quietly, 'I can't even remember the last time you struck me. It's been ten years, I think, maybe longer. And I don't think you ever struck me in anger, until now. But it doesn't change my mind. I don't believe –'

Andrew Staad raised one warning finger. 'I told you not to mention his name,' he said, 'and I meant it, Ben. I love you, but if you say his name, you'll be leaving my house.'

'I'll not say it,' Ben replied, getting up, 'but because I love you, Da'. Not because I'm scared of you.'

'Leave off!' Mrs Staad cried, more frightened than ever. 'I won't have the two of you bickering this way! Do you want to drive me insane?'

'No, Mother, don't worry, it's over,' Ben said. 'Isn't it, Da'?'

'It's over,' his father said. 'You're a good son in all things, Ben, and always have been, but mention him not.'

There were things Andy Staad felt he couldn't tell his son – although Ben was seventeen, Andy still saw him as a boy. He would have been surprised if he'd known that Ben understood his reasons for striking out quite well.

Before the unfortunate turn of events of which you now know, Ben's friendship with the prince had already begun changing things for the Staads. Their Inner Baronies farm had once been very large. Over the last hundred years, they had been forced to sell the land off, a piece at a time. Now fewer than sixty reels remained, most of that mortgaged.

But over the last ten years or so, things had gradually improved. Bankers who had been threatening first became willing to extend the outstanding mortgages, and to even offer new loans at interest rates so cheap they were unheard of. It had hurt Andrew Staad bitterly to see the land of his ancestors whittled away reel by reel, and it had been a happy day for him when he was able to go to Halvay, the owner of the next farm over, and tell him that he had changed his mind about selling him the three reels Halvay had wanted to buy for the last nine years. And he knew who he had to thank for these wonderful changes, too. His son . . . his son who was a close friend of the prince who also happened to be the King-in-waiting.

Now they were only the unlucky Staads again. If that had been all, only a case of things going back to the way they had been, he could have stood up under it without striking his son at the dinner table . . . an act of which he was already ashamed. But things *weren't* going to go back to the way they had been. Their position had worsened.

He had been lulled when the bankers had started behaving like sheep instead of wolves. He had borrowed a great deal of money, some to buy back land which he had already sold, some to install things like the new windmill. Now, he felt sure, the bankers would take off their sheepskins, and instead of losing the farm a piece at a time, he might lose it all at once.

Nor was that all. Some instinct had told him to forbid any of his family members to go to Thomas's coronation and he had listened to that inner voice. Tonight he was glad.

It had happened after the coronation, and he supposed he should have expected it. He went into a meadhouse to have a drink before starting home. He was very depressed by the whole sorry business of the King's murder and Peter's imprisonment; he felt that he needed a drink. He had been recognized as Ben's father.

'Did yer son help his friend do the deed, Staad?' one of the drunks had called, and there had been nasty laughter.

'Did he hold the old man while the prince poured the burnin' pizen down his thrut?' one of the others called out in turn.

Andrew had put his mug down half empty. This was not a good place to be. He would leave. Quickly.

But before he could get out, a third drunk – a giant of a man who smelled like a pile of mouldy cabbages – pulled him back.

'And how much did *you* know?' this giant had asked in a low, rumbling voice.

'Nothing,' Andrew said. 'I know nothing about this business, and neither does my son. Let me pass.'

'You'll pass when – and *if* – we decide to *let* yer pass,' the giant said, and shoved him backward into the waiting arms of the other drunks.

The pummelling then began. Andy Staad was pushed from one to the next, sometimes slapped, sometimes elbowed, sometimes tripped. No one quite dared to go as far as punching him, but they came close; he had seen in their eyes how badly they had wanted to. If the hour had been later and they had been drunker, he might have found himself in very serious trouble indeed.

Andrew was not tall, but he was broad-shouldered and well muscled. He calculated that he might be able to dust off any two of these idlers in a fair fight – with the exception of the giant, and he thought that perhaps he could give even *that* fellow a run for his money. One or two, possibly even three . . . but there were eight or ten there in all. If he had been Ben's age, full of pride and hot blood, he still might have had a go at them. But he was forty-five, and did not relish the thought of creeping home to his family beaten within an inch of his life. It would hurt him and frighten them, and both things would be to no purpose – it was just the Staad luck come home with a vengeance, and there was nothing to do but endure it. The barkeeper stood watching it all, doing nothing, not attempting to put a stop to it.

At last they had let him escape.

Now he feared for his wife . . . his daughter . . . and most of all for his son Ben, who would be the prime target for bullies such as those. *If it'd been Ben in there instead of me*, he thought, *they would have used their fists, all right. They would have used their fists and beaten him unconscious . . . or worse.*

So, because he loved his son and was afraid for him, he had struck him and threatened to drive him from the house if Ben ever mentioned the prince by name again.

People are funny, sometimes.

What Ben Staad didn't already understand abstractly about this strange new state of affairs he discovered very concretely the next day.

He had driven six cows to market and sold them for a good price (to a stockman who didn't know him, or the price mightn't have been so good). He was walking toward the city gates, when a bunch of loitering men set upon him, calling him murderer and accomplice and names even less pleasant.

Ben did well against them. They beat him quite badly in the end – there were seven of them – but they paid for the privilege with bloody noses, black eyes, and lost teeth. Ben picked himself up and went home, arriving after dark. He ached all over, but he was, all things considered, rather pleased with himself.

His father took one look at him and knew exactly what had happened. 'Tell your mother you fell down,' he said.

'Aye, Da',' Ben said, knowing his mother would not believe any such story.

'And after this, I'll take the cows to market, or the corn, or whatever we have to take to market . . . at least until the bankers come an' take the place out from under us.'

'No, Da',' Ben said, just as calmly as he had said *Aye*. For a young man who had taken a bad beating, he was in a very strange mood indeed – almost cheerful, in fact.

'What do you mean, telling me no?' his father asked, thunderstruck.

'If I run or hide, they'll come after me. If I stand my ground, they'll grow tired soon enough and look for easier sport.'

'If someone draws a knife from his boot,' Andrew said, voicing his greatest fear, 'you'll never live to see them grow tired of it, Benny.'

Ben put his arms around his father and hugged him tight.

'A man can't outsmart the gods,' Ben said, quoting one of Delain's oldest proverbs. 'You know that, Da'. And I'll fight for P . . . for him you'd not have me mention.'

His father looked at him sadly and said, 'You'll never believe it of him, will you?'

'No,' Ben said steadfastly. 'Never.'

'I think you've become a man while I wasn't looking,' his father said. 'It's a sad way to have to become a man, scuffling in the streets of the market with gutter louts. And these are sad times that have come to Delain.'

'Yes,' Ben said. 'They are sad times.'

'Gods help you,' Andrew said, 'and gods help this unlucky family.'

Thomas had been crowned near the end of a long, bitter winter. On the fifteenth day of his reign, the last of that season's great storms fell on Delain. Snow fell fast and thick, and long after dark the wind continued to scream, building drifts like sand dunes.

At nine o'clock on that bitter night, long after anyone sensible should have been out, there was a fist began to fall on the front door of the Staad house. It was not light or timid, that fist; it hammered rapidly and heavily on the stout oak. *Answer me and be quick*, it said. *I haven't all night.*

Andrew and Ben sat before the fire, reading. Susan Staad, wife of Andrew and mother of Ben, sat between them, working at a sampler which would read GOD BLESS OUR KING when finished. Emma-line had long since been put to bed. The three of them looked up at the knock, then around at each other. There was only curiosity in Ben's eyes, but both Andrew and Susan were instantly, instinctively afraid.

Andrew rose, putting his reading glasses in his pocket.

'Da'?' Ben asked.

'I'll go,' Andrew said.

Let it only be some traveller, lost in the dark and seeking shelter, he hoped, but when he opened the door a soldier of the King stood there on the stoop, stolid and broad-shouldered. A leather helmet – the helmet of a fighting man – clung to his head. There was a shortsword in his belt, near to hand.

'Your son,' he said, and Andrew felt his knees buckle.

'Why do you want him?'

'I come from Peyna,' the soldier said, and Andrew understood that this was all the answer he was to have.

'Da'?' Ben asked from behind him.

No, Andrew thought miserably, *please, this is too much bad luck, not my son, not my son –*

'Is that the boy?'

Before Andrew could say no – useless as that would have been – Ben had stepped forward.

'I am Ben Staad,' he said. 'What do you want with me?'

'You must come with me,' the soldier said.

'Where?'

'To the house of Anders Peyna.'

'*No!*' his mother cried from the doorway of their small living room. 'No, it's late, it's cold, the roads are full of snow –'

'I have a sleigh,' the soldier said inexorably, and Andrew Staad saw the man's hand drop to the shaft of his shortsword.

'I'll come,' Ben said, getting his coat.

'Ben –' Andrew began, thinking: *We'll never see him again, he's to be taken away from us because he knew the prince.*

'It will be all right, Da',' Ben said, and hugged him. And when Andrew felt that young strength embracing him, he could almost believe it. But, he thought, his son had not learned fear yet. He had not learned how cruel the world could be.

Andrew Staad held his wife. The two of them stood in the doorway and watched Ben and the soldier break their way through the drifts toward the sleigh, which was only a shadow in the dark with lanterns glowing eerily on either side. Neither of them spoke as Ben climbed up on one side, the soldier on the other.

Only one soldier, Andrew thought, *that's something. Maybe it's only for questioning that they want him. Pray it's only for questioning that they want my son!*

The Staads stood in silence, membranes of snow blowing around their ankles, as the sleigh pulled away from the house, the flames in the lanterns jiggling, the sleigh bells jingling.

When they were gone, Susan burst into tears.

'We'll never see him again,' she sobbed. 'Never, never! They've taken him! Damn Peter! Damn him for what he's brought my son to! Damn him! Damn him!'

'Shh, mother,' Andrew said, holding her tightly. 'Shh. Shh. We'll see him before morning. By noon at the latest.'

But she heard the quiver in his voice and cried all the harder. She cried so hard she woke little Emmaline up (or maybe it was the draught from the open door), and it was a very long time before Emmaline would go back to sleep. At last Susan slept with her, the two of them in the big bed.

Andy Staad did not sleep all that night.

He sat up by the fire, hoping against hope, but in his heart he believed he would never see his son again.

Ben Staad stood in Anders Peyna's study an hour later. He was curious, even a little awed, but not afraid. He had listened closely to everything Peyna said, and there had been a muted chink as money changed hands.

'You understand all of this, lad?' Peyna asked in his dry courtroom voice.

'Yes, my Lord.'

'I would be sure. This is no child's business I send you on. Tell me again what you are to do.'

'I am to go to the castle and speak to Dennis, son of Brandon.'

'And if Brandon interferes?' Peyna asked sharply.

'I am to tell him he must speak to you.'

'Aye,' Peyna said, settling back in his chair.

'I am not to say "Tell no one of this arrangement." '

'Yes,' Peyna said. 'Do you know why?'

Ben stood thoughtfully for a moment, head down. Peyna let him think. He liked this boy; he seemed coolheaded and unafraid. Many others brought before him in the middle of the night would have been gibbering with terror.

'Because if I said such a thing, he would be quicker to tell than if I said nothing,' Ben said finally.

A smile touched Peyna's lips. 'Good,' he said. 'Go on.'

'You've given me ten guilders. I'm to give two to Dennis, one for himself and one for whoever finds the doll house that belonged to Peter's mother. The other eight are for Beson, the Chief Warder. Whoever finds the doll's house will deliver it to Dennis. Dennis will deliver it to me. I will deliver it to Beson. As for the napkins, Dennis himself will take them to Beson.'

'How many?'

'Twenty-one each week,' Ben replied promptly. 'Napkins of the royal house, but with the crest removed. Your man will engage a woman to remove the royal crests. From time to time you will send someone to me with more money, either for Dennis or for Beson.'

'But none for yourself?' Peyna asked. He had already offered; Ben had refused.

'No. I believe that's everything.'

'You are quick.'

'I only wish I could do more.'

Peyna sat up, his face suddenly harsh and forbidding. 'You must not and you shall not,' he said. 'This is dangerous enough. You are procuring favours for a young man who has been convicted of committing a foul murder – the second-foulest murder a man may do.'

'Peter is my friend,' Ben said, and he spoke with a dignity that was impressive in its simplicity.

Anders Peyna smiled faintly, and raised one finger to point at the fading bruises on Ben's face. 'I would guess,' he said, 'that you are already paying for that friendship.'

'I would pay such a price a hundred times

over,' Ben said. He hesitated just a moment and then went on boldly: 'I don't believe he killed his father. He loved King Roland as much as I love my own da'.'

'Did he?' Peyna asked, apparently without interest.

'He did!' Ben cried. 'Do *you* believe he murdered his father? Do you *really* believe he did it?'

Peyna smiled such a dry and ferocious smile then that even Ben's hot blood was cooled.

'If I didn't, I should be careful who I said it to,' he said. 'Very, very careful. Or I should soon feel the headsman's blade go through my neck.'

Ben stared at Peyna silently.

'You say you are his friend, and I believe you.' Peyna sat up straighter in his chair and levelled a finger at Ben. 'If you would be a true friend, do just the things I have asked, and no more. If you see any hope for Peter's eventual release in your mysterious summons here – and I see by your face that you do – you must give that hope up.'

Rather than ring for Arlen, Peyna saw the boy out himself – out the back way. The soldier who had brought him tonight would be on his way to the Western Barony tomorrow.

At the door, Peyna said, 'Once more: do not stray from the things we've agreed upon *so much as one solitary bit*. The friends of Peter are not much cared for in Delain now, as your bruises prove.'

'I'd fight them all!' Ben said hotly. 'One at a time or all at once!'

'Aye,' Anders Peyna said with that dry,

ferocious smile. 'And would you ask your mother to do the same? Or your baby sister?'

Ben gaped at the old man. Fear opened in his heart like a small and delicate rose.

'It will come to that, if you do not exercise all your care,' Peyna said. 'The storms are not over in Delain yet, but only beginning.' He opened the door; snow swirled in, driven by a black gust of wind. 'Go home now, Ben. I think your parents will be happy to see you so soon.'

This was an understatement of some size. Ben's parents were waiting at the door in their nightclothes when Ben let himself in. They had heard the jingle of the approaching sleigh. His mother hugged him close, weeping. His father, red-faced, unaccustomed tears standing in his eyes, wrung Ben's hand until it ached. Ben remembered Peyna saying *The storms are not over but only beginning*.

And still later, lying in bed with his hands behind his head, staring up into the darkness and listening to the wind whistle outside, Ben realized that Peyna had never answered his question – had never said whether or not he believed Peter to be guilty.

66

'O'n the seventeenth day of Thomas's reign, Brandon's son, Dennis, brought the first lot of twenty-one napkins to the Needle. He brought them from a storeroom that neither Peter nor Thomas nor Ben Staad nor Peyna himself knew about – although all would become aware of it before the grim business of Peter's imprisonment was done. Dennis knew because he was a butler's son from a long line of butlers, but familiarity breeds contempt, so they say, and he thought nothing much about the storeroom from which he fetched the napkins. We'll speak more of this room later; let me tell you now only that all would have been struck with wonder at the sight of it, and Peter in particular. For had he known of this room which Dennis took completely for granted, he might have attempted his escape as much as three years sooner . . . and much, for better or for worse, might have been changed.

The royal crest was removed from each napkin by a woman Peyna had hired for the quickness of her needle and the tightness of her lips. Each day she sat in a rocker just outside the doorway of the storeroom, picking out stitches that were very old indeed. When she did this her lips were tight for more reasons than one; to unmake such lovely needlework seemed to her almost a desecration, but her family was poor, and the money from Peyna was like a gift from heaven. So there she sat, and would sit, for years to come, rocking and plying her needle like one of those weird sisters of whom you may have heard in another tale. She spoke to no one, not even her husband, about her days of unmaking.

The napkins had a strange, faint smell — not of mildew but of must, as if from long disuse — but they were otherwise without fault, each of them twenty rondels by twenty, big enough to cover the lap of even the most dedicated eater.

There was a bit of comedy attached to the first napkin delivery. Dennis hung about Beson, expecting a tip. Beson let him hang about a while because he expected that sooner or later the dimwitted lad would remember to tip *him*. They both came to the conclusion that neither was going to be tipped at the same time. Dennis started for the door, and Beson helped him along with a kick in the seat of the pants. This caused a pair of Lesser Warders to laugh heartily. Then Beson pretended to wipe his bottom with the handful of napkins for the Lesser Warders' further amusement, but he was careful only to pretend — after all, Peyna was in this business somewhere, and it was best to tread lightly.

Perhaps Peyna would not be around a great deal longer, however. In the meadhouses and wineshops, Beson had begun to hear whispers that Flagg's shadow had fallen on the Judge-General, and that if Peyna was not very, very careful, he might soon be watching the proceedings at court from an even more commanding angle than the bench upon which he now sat — he might be looking in the window, these wags said behind their hands, from one of the spikes atop the castle walls.

On the eighteenth day of Thomas's reign, the first napkin was on Peter's breakfast tray when it was delivered in the morning. It was so large and the breakfast so small that it actually covered the meal completely. Peter smiled for the first time since he had come to this cold, high place. His cheeks and chin were shadowed with the beginnings of a beard which would grow full and long in these two draughty rooms, and he looked quite a desperate character . . . until he smiled. The smile lit his face with magical power, and made it strong and radiant, a beacon to which one could imagine soldiers rallying in battle.

'Ben,' he muttered, picking the napkin up by one corner. His hand shook a bit. 'I knew you'd do it. Thank you, my friend. Thank you.'

The first thing Peter did with his first napkin was to wipe away the tears that now ran freely down his cheeks.

The peephole in the stout wooden door popped open. Two Lesser Warders appeared again like the two heads of Flagg's parrot, packed into the tiny space cheek to scruffy cheek.

'Hope that baby won't forget to wipe his chin-ny-chin!' one cried in a cracked, warbling voice.

'Hope that baby won't forget to wipe the eggy off his shirty!' the other cried, and then both screamed with derisive laughter. But Peter did not look at them, and his smile did not fade.

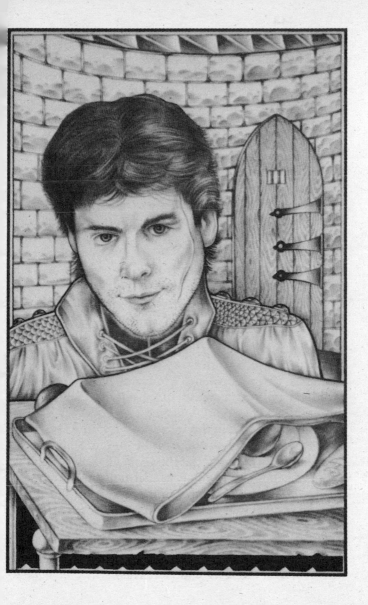

The warders saw that smile and made no more jokes. There was something about it which forbade joking.

Eventually they closed the peephole and left Peter alone.

A napkin came with his lunch that day.

With his dinner that night.

The napkins came to Peter in his lonely cell in the sky for the next five years.

The doll's house arrived on the thirtieth day of Thomas the Light-Bringer's reign. By then modils, those first harbingers of Spring (which we call bluets) were coming up in pretty little roadside bunches. Also by then Thomas the Light-Bringer had signed into Law the Farmers' Tax Increase, which quickly became known as Tom's Black Tax. The new joke told in the meadhouses and wineshops was that the King would soon be changing his royal name to Thomas the Tax-Bringer. The increase was not eight per cent, which might have been fair, or eighteen per sent, which might have been bearable, but eighty per cent. Thomas had had some doubts about it at first, but it hadn't taken Flagg long to convince him.

'We must tax them more on what they admit they own, so we can collect at least some of what's due us on all they hide from the tax collector,' Flagg said. Thomas, his head fuddled by the wine that now flowed constantly in the court chambers of the castle, had nodded with what he hoped was a wise expression on his face.

For his part, Peter had begun to fear that the doll's house had been lost after all these years – and that was almost the truth. Ben Staad had commissioned Dennis to find it. After several days of fruitless searching, Dennis had confided in his good old da' – the only person he dared trust with such a serious matter. It had taken Brandon another five days to find the doll's house in one of the minor storage rooms on the ninth floor, west turret, where its cheerful pretend lawns and long, rambling wings were hidden under an ancient (and slightly moth-eaten) dustcloth that was grey with the years. All of the original furnishings were still in the house, and it had taken Brandon and Dennis and a soldier handpicked by Peyna three more days to make sure all the sharp things were removed. Then, at last, the doll's house was delivered by two squire boys, who toiled up the three hundred stairs with the heavy, awkward thing spiked to a board between them. Beson followed closely behind, cursing and threatening terrible reprisals if they should drop it. Sweat rolled down the boys' faces in rivers, but they made no reply.

When the door of Peter's prison opened and the doll's house was brought in, Peter gasped with surprise – not just because the doll's house was finally here, but because one of the two boys carrying it was Ben Staad.

Give not a sign! Ben's eyes flashed.

Don't look at me too long! Peter's flashed back.

After the advice he had given, Peyna would have been stunned to see Ben here. He had forgotten that the logic of all the wise old men in the world cannot often stand against the logic of a boy's heart, if the boy's heart is large and kind and loyal. Ben Staad's was all three.

It had been the easiest thing in the world to exchange places with one of the squires meant to carry the doll's house to the top of the Needle. For a guilder – all the money Ben had in the world, as a matter of fact – Dennis had arranged it.

'Don't tell your father of this,' Ben cautioned Dennis.

'Why not?' Dennis had asked. 'I tell my old da' almost everything . . . don't you?'

'I *did*,' Ben said, remembering how his father had forbidden him to mention Peter's name any more in the house. 'But when boys grow up, I think that sometimes changes. However that may be, you mustn't tell him this, Dennis. He might tell Peyna, and then I'd be in a hot pot on a high fire.'

'All right,' Dennis promised. It was a promise he kept. Dennis had been cruelly hurt when his master, whom he had loved, had been first accused and then convicted of murder. In the last few days, Ben had gone a long way towards filling the empty place in Dennis's heart.

'That's good,' Ben said, and punched Dennis playfully on the shoulder. 'I only want to see him a minute, and refresh my heart.'

'He was your best friend, wasn't he?'

'Still is.'

Dennis had stared at him, amazed. 'How can you claim a man who murdered his own father as your best friend?'

'Because I don't believe he did it,' Ben said. 'Do you?'

To Ben's utter amazement, Dennis burst into wretched tears. 'All my heart says the same, and yet –'

'Listen to it, then,' Ben said, and gave Dennis a large rough hug. 'And dry off your mug before someone sees you bawling like a kid.'

'Put it in the other room,' Peter said now, distressed at the slight tremble in his voice. Beson didn't notice; he was too busy cursing the two boys for their slowness, their stupidity, their very existence. They carried the doll's house into the bedroom and set it down. The other boy, who had a very stupid face, dropped his end too quickly and too hard. There was the tiny sound of something breaking inside. Peter winced. Beson cuffed the boy – but he smiled as he did it. It was the first good thing that had happened to him since these two lads had appeared with the accursed thing.

The stupid boy stood up, wiping the side of his face, which was already starting to swell, and staring at Peter with frank wonder and fear, his mouth wide open; Ben remained on his knees a moment longer. There was a small rattan mat in front of the house's front door – what we would call a welcome mat, I suppose. For just a moment Ben allowed his thumb to move over the top of this, and his eyes met Peter's.

'Now get out!' Beson cried. 'Get out, both of you! Go home and curse your mothers for ever bringing such slow, clumsy fools as yourselves into the world!'

The boys passed Peter, the loutish one shrinking away as if the prince might have a disease he could catch. Ben's eyes met Peter's once more, and Peter trembled at the love he saw in his old friend's gaze. Then they were gone.

'Well, you have it now, my good little princeling,' Beson said. 'What shall we be bringing you next? Little ruffly dresses? Silk underpants?'

Peter turned slowly and looked at Beson. After a moment, Beson dropped his eyes. There was something frightening in Peter's gaze, and Beson was forced to remember again that, sissy or not, Peter had beaten him so badly that his ribs had ached for two days and he had had dizzy spells for a week.

'Well, it's your business,' he muttered. 'But now that you have it, I could find a table for you to put it on. And a chair to sit in while you . . .' He grimaced. 'While you play with it.'

'And how much would this cost?'

'A mere three guilders, I should think.'

'I have no money.'

'Ah, but you know powerful people.'

'No more,' Peter said. 'I traded a favour for a favour, that's all.'

'Sit on the floor, then, and get chilblains on your arse, and be damned to you!' Beson said, and strode from the room. The little flood of guilders he had enjoyed since Peter came to the Needle had apparently dried up. It put Beson in a foul mood for days.

Peter waited until he had heard all the locks and bolts go rattling home before lifting the rattan mat

Ben had rubbed with his thumb. Beneath he found a square of paper no larger than the stamp on a letter. Both sides had been written on, and there were no spaces between the words. The letters were tiny indeed – Peter had to squint to read them, and guessed that Ben must have made them with the aid of a magnifying glass.

Peter – Destroy this after you have read it. I don't believe you did it. Others feel the same I am sure. I am still your friend. I love you as I always did. Dennis does not believe it, either. If I can ever help get to me through Peyna. Let your heart be steadfast.

As he read this, Peter's eyes filled with warm tears of gratitude. I think that real friendship always makes us feel such sweet gratitude, because the world almost always seems like a very hard desert, and the flowers that grow there seem to grow against such high odds. 'Good old Ben!' he whispered over and over again. In the fullness of his heart, he couldn't think to say anything else. 'Good old Ben! Good old Ben!'

For the first time he began to think that his plan, wild and dangerous as it was, might have a chance of succeeding.

Next he thought of the note. Ben had put his life on the line to write it. Ben was noble – barely – but not royal; thus not immune from the headsman's axe. If Beson or one of his jackals found this note, they would guess that one or the other of the boys who had brought the doll's house must have written it. The loutish one looked as if he couldn't read even the large letters in a child's book, let alone write such tiny ones as these. So they would look for the other boy, and from there to the chopping block might be a short trip for good old Ben.

He could think of only one sure way to get rid of it, and he didn't hesitate; he crumpled the little note up between the thumb and forefinger of his right hand and ate it.

By now I am sure you have guessed Peter's plan of escape, because you know a good deal more than Peyna did when he read Peter's requests. But in any case, the time has come to tell you straight out. He planned to use linen threads to make a rope. The threads would come, of course, from the edges of the napkins. He would descend this rope to the ground and so escape. Some of you may be laughing very hard at this idea. *Threads from napkins to escape a tower three hundred feet high?* you could be saying. *Either you are mad, Storyteller, or Peter was!*

Nothing of the sort. Peter knew how high the Needle was, and he believed he must never be greedy about how many threads he took from each napkin. If he unravelled too much, someone might become very curious. It didn't have to be the Chief Warder; the laundress who washed the napkins might be the one to notice rather a lot of each one was gone. She might mention it to a friend . . . who could mention it to another friend . . . and so the story would

spread . . . and it wasn't really Beson Peter was
worried about, you know. Beson was, all things
said, a fairly stupid fellow.

Flagg was not.

Flagg had murdered his father –

– and Flagg kept his ear to the ground.

It was a shame Peter never stopped to wonder
about that vague smell of must about the napkins, or
to ask if the person hired to remove the royal crests
had been let go after removing a certain number, or
if that person was still at work – but, of course, his
mind was on other things. He could not help noticing
that they were very old, and this was certainly a good
thing – he was able to take a great many more threads
from each than he ever would have guessed in even
his most optimistic moments. How many more than
that he could have taken he came to know only in
time.

Still, I can hear some of you saying, *threads from
napkins to make a rope long enough to reach from the
window of the Needle's topmost cell to the courtyard?
Threads from napkins to make a rope strong enough to
support one hundred and seventy pounds? I still think you
are joking!*

Those of you who think so are forgetting the
doll's house . . . and the loom within, a loom so tiny
that the threads of napkins were perfect for its tiny
shuttle. Those of you who think so are forgetting
that everything in the doll's house was tiny, but
worked perfectly. The sharp things had been
removed, and that included the loom's cutting
blade . . . but otherwise it was intact.

It was the doll's house about which Flagg had had vague misgivings so long ago which was now Peter's only real hope of escape.

71

I would have to be a much better story-teller than I am, I think, to tell you how it was for Peter during the five years he spent at the top of the Needle. He ate; he slept; he looked out the window, which gave him a view to the west of the city; he exercised morning, noon, and evening; he dreamed his dreams of freedom. In the summer his apartment sweltered. In the winter it froze.

During the second winter he caught a bad case of the grippe which almost killed him.

Peter lay feverish and coughing under the thin blanket on his bed. At first, he was only afraid he would lapse into delirium and rave about the rope that was hidden in a neat coil under two of the stone blocks on the east side of his bedroom. As his fever grew worse, the rope he had woven with the tiny doll house loom came to seem less important, because he began to think he would die.

Beson and his Lesser Warders were convinced of it. They had, in fact, begun to wager on when it would happen. One night, about a week after the onset of his fever, while the wind raged blackly out-side and the temperature dropped down to zero,

Roland appeared to Peter in a dream. Peter was convinced that Roland had come to take him to the Far Fields.

'I'm ready, Da'!' he cried. In his delirium he didn't know if he had spoken aloud or only in his mind. 'I'm ready to go!'

Ye'll not be dying yet, his father said in this dream . . . or vision . . . or whatever it was. *Ye've much to do, Peter.*

'*Father!*' Peter shrieked. His voice was powerful, and below him, the warders — Beson included — quailed, thinking that Peter must be seeing the smoking, murdered ghost of King Roland, come to take Peter's soul to hell. They made no more wagers that night, and in fact one of them went to the Church of the Great Gods the very next day and embraced his religion again, and eventually became a priest. This man's name was Curran, and I may tell you of him in another story.

Peter really *was* seeing a ghost in a way — although whether it was the actual shade of his father or only a ghost born in his fever-struck brain, I cannot say.

His voice lapsed into a mutter; the warders did not hear the rest.

'It's so cold . . . and I am so hot.'

My poor boy, his glimmering father said. *You've had hard trials, and there are more of them ahead, I think. But Dennis will know . . .*

'Know what?' Peter gasped. His cheeks were red, but his forehead was as pale as a wax candle.

Dennis will know where the sleepwalker goes, his father whispered, and was gone.

Peter lapsed into a faint that quickly became a deep, sound sleep. In that sleep, his fever broke. The boy who had made it his practice over the last year to do sixty push-ups and a hundred sit-ups each day awoke the next morning too weak to even get out of bed . . . but he was lucid again.

Beson and the Lesser Warders were disappointed. But after that night, they always treated Peter with a kind of awe, and took care never to go too close to him.

Which, of course, made his job that much easier.

All that is an easy enough tale to tell, though it would no doubt be better if I could say for sure that the ghost was there or that it was not. But like other matters in the larger tale, you'll have to make up your own mind about it, I suppose.

But how am I to tell you about Peter's endless, drudging work at that tiny loom? That tale is beyond me. All the hours spent, sometimes with frosty breath pluming from his mouth and nose, sometimes with sweat running down his face, always in fear of discovery; all those long hours alone, with nothing but long thoughts and almost absurd hopes to fill them. I can tell you some things, and will, but to convey such hours and days of slow time is impossible for me, and might be impossible for anyone except one of the great storytellers whose race is long vanished. Perhaps the only thing that even vaguely suggests how much time Peter spent in those two rooms was his beard. When he came in, it was only a shadow on his cheeks and a smudge under his nose – a boy's beard. In the 1,825 days which followed, it grew long and luxuriant; by the end it reached the middle of his chest, and although he was only twenty-one, it was shot with grey. The only place it did not grow was along the length of the jagged scar left by Beson's thumbnail.

Peter dared pluck only five threads from each napkin the first year – fifteen threads each day. He kept them under his mattress, and at the end of each week, he had one hundred and five. In our measure, each thread was about twenty inches long.

He wove the first batch a week after he received the doll's house, working carefully with the loom. Using it was not as easy at seventeen as it had been at five. His fingers had grown; the loom had not. Also, he was horribly nervous. If one of the warders caught him at his work, he could tell them he was using the loom to weave errant threads from the old napkins for his own amusement . . . *if* they believed it. And *if* the loom worked. He wasn't sure that it would until he saw the first slim cable, perfectly woven, emerging from the loom's far end. When Peter saw this, his nervousness abated somewhat and he was able to weave a little faster, feeding the threads in, tugging them to keep them straight, operating the foot pedal with his thumb. The loom squeaked a little at first, but the old grease soon limbered up and it ran as perfectly as it had in his childhood.

But the cable was terribly thin, not even a quarter of an inch through the centre. Peter tied off the ends and tugged experimentally. It held. He was a little encouraged. It was stronger than it looked, and he thought it *should* be strong. They were royal napkins, after all, woven from the finest cotton thread in the land, and he had woven tightly. He pulled

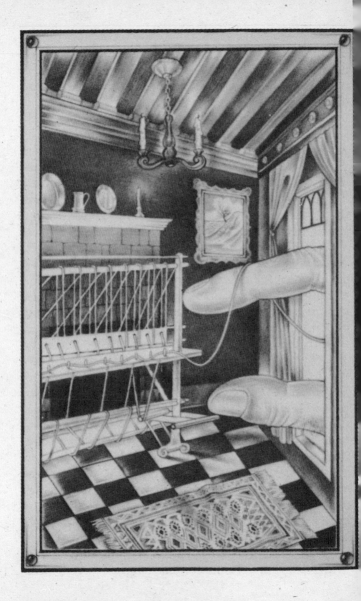

harder, trying to guess how many pounds of strain he was putting on the slim cotton cable.

He pulled even harder, the rope still held, and he felt more hope come stealing into his heart. He found himself thinking about Yosef.

It had been Yosef, head of the stables, who told him about that mysterious and terrible thing called 'breaking strain'. It was high summer, and they had been watching huge Anduan oxen pull stone blocks for the plaza of the new market. A sweating, cursing drover sat astride each ox's neck. Peter had then been no more than eleven, and he thought it better than a circus. Yosef pointed out that each ox wore a heavy leather harness. The chains that pulled the dressed blocks of stone were attached to the harness, one on each side of the animal's neck. Yosef told him the cutters had to make a careful estimate of just how much each block of stone weighed.

'Because if the blocks are too heavy, the oxen might hurt themselves trying to pull them,' Peter said. This wasn't even a question, because it seemed obvious to him. He felt sorry for the oxen, dragging those great blocks of rock.

'Nay,' Yosef said. He lit a cigarette made of cornshuck, almost burning off the end of his nose, and drew deeply and contentedly. He always liked the young prince's company. 'Nay! Oxen aren't stupid – people only think them so because they are large and tame and helpful. Says more about the people than about the oxen, if you ask me, but leave that b'hind, leave that b'hind.

'If an ox can pull a block, he'll pull it; if he can't, why, he'll try twice and then stand with 'is head down. And he'll stand so, even if a bad master whups his hide to ribbons. Oxen look stupid, but they ain't. Not a bit.'

'Then why do the cutters have to guess at the weight of the blocks they cut, if the ox knows what he can pull and what he can't?'

'T'ain't the blocks; it's the *chains*.' Yosef pointed to one of the oxen, which was dragging a block that looked to Peter almost as big as a small house. The ox's head was down, its eyes fixed patiently ahead, as its drover sat astride it and guided it with little taps of his stick. At the end of the double length of chain, the block moved slowly along, goring a furrow in the earth. It was so deep that a small child would need to work to climb out of it. 'If an ox can pull a block, he will, but an ox don't know nothing about chains, or about the breaking strain.'

'What's that?'

'Put a thing under enough of a tug, and it'll snap,' Yosef said. 'If yonder chains were to snap, they'd fly around something turrible. You wouldn't want to be a witness to what can happen if a heavy chain lets go when it's under such a tug as those oxen can put on. It's apt to fly anywhere. Back'rds, mostly. Apt to hit the drover and tear him apart, or cut the legs from under the beast itself.'

Yosef took another drag at his makeshift cigarette and then tossed it in the dirt. He fixed Peter with a shrewd, friendly glare.

'Breaking strain,' he said, 'is a good thing for a prince to know about, Peter. Chains break if you put on enough of a tug, and people do, too. Keep it in mind.'

He kept it in mind now, as he pulled at his first cable. How much of a 'tug' was he putting on? Five rull? At least. Ten? Perhaps. But maybe that was only wishful thinking. He would say eight. No, seven. Better to make a mistake on the pessimistic side, if a mistake was to be made. If he miscalculated . . . well, the cobblestones in the Plaza of the Needle were very, very hard.

He tugged harder still, the muscles on his arms now beginning to stand out a little. When the first cable finally snapped, Peter guessed he might be applying as much as fifteen rull – almost sixty-four pounds – of tug.

He was not unhappy with this result.

Later that night, he threw the broken cable out of his window, where the men who cleaned the Plaza of the Needle daily would sweep it up with the rest of the rubbish the following day.

Peter's mother, seeing his interest in the dollhouse and the little furnishings inside, had taught him how to weave cables and braid them into tiny rugs. When we have not done a thing for a long period, we are apt to forget exactly how that thing was done, but Peter had nothing but time, and after some experimentation, the trick of braiding came back to him.

'Braiding' was what his mother had called it and so that was how he thought of it, but braiding was not really the right word for it; a braid, precisely speaking, is the hand-weaving of two cables. *Wrapping*, which is how rugs are made, is the hand-weaving of three or more cables. In wrapping, two cables are placed apart, but with their tops and bottoms even. The third is placed between them, but lower, so its end sticks out. This pattern is carried on as length after length is added. The result looks a little bit like Chinese finger-pullers . . . or the braided rugs in your favourite grandmother's house.

It took Peter three weeks to save enough threads to try this technique, and most of a fourth to remember exactly how the over-and-under pattern of wrapping had gone. But when he was done, he had a real rope. It was thin, and you would have thought him mad to entrust his weight to it, but it was much stronger than it looked. He found he could break it, but only by wrapping its ends firmly around his hands and pulling until the muscles bulged on his arms and chest and the cords stood out on his neck.

Overhead in his sleeping chamber were a number of stout oak beams. He would have to test his weight from one of these, when he had a rope long enough. If it snapped, he would have to start all over again . . . but such thoughts were useless and Peter knew it – so he just got to work.

Each thread he pulled was about twenty inches long, but Peter lost roughly two inches in the weaving and wrapping. It took him three months to make a rope of three strands, each strand consisting of a hundred and five cotton threads, into a cable three feet long. One night, after he was sure all of the warders were drunk and at cards below, he tied this pigtail to a rope over one of the beams. When it had been looped over and tied in a slipknot, less than a foot and a half hung down.

It looked woefully thin.

Nevertheless, Peter seized it and hung from it,

mouth tightened to a grim white line, expecting the threads to let go at any moment and spill him to the floor. But they held.

They held.

Hardly daring to believe it was happening, Peter hung there from a rope almost too thin to see. He hung there for almost a full minute, and then he stood on his bed to pull the slipknot free. His hands trembled as he did it, and he had to fumble at the knot twice, because his eyes kept blurring with tears. He didn't believe his heart had been so full since reading Ben's tiny note.

72

He had been keeping the rope under his mattress, but Peter realized this would not do much longer. The Needle was three hundred and forty feet high at the peak of its conical roof; his window was just about three hundred feet above the cobblestones. He was six feet tall and believed he would dare to drop as much as twenty feet from the end of his rope. But even at best, he would eventually have to hide two hundred and seventy feet of rope.

He discovered a loose stone on the east side of the bedroom floor, and cautiously pried it up. He was surprised and pleased to find a little space beneath. He couldn't see into it properly so he reached in and felt around in the darkness, his whole body stiff and tense as he waited for something down there in the dark to crawl over his hand . . . or bite it.

Nothing did, and he was just about to withdraw it, when one of his fingers brushed something – cold metal. Peter brought it out. It was, he saw, a heart-shaped locket on a fine chain. Both locket and chain looked to be made of gold. Nor did he think, by its weight, that the locket was false gold. After some poking and feeling, he found a delicate catch. He pushed it and the locket sprang open. Inside were two pictures, one on each side – they were as fine as any of the tiny paintings in Sasha's doll house; even finer, perhaps. Peter stared at their faces with a boy's frank wonder. The man was very handsome, the woman very beautiful. There was a faint smile on the man's lips and a devil-may-care look in his eyes. The woman's eyes were grave and dark. Part of Peter's wonder came from the fact that this locket must be very old, judging by what he could make out of their dress, but only part of it. Most came from the fact that these two faces looked eerily familiar. He had *seen* them before.

He closed the locket and looked on the back. He thought there were initials entwined there, but they were too flounced and curlicued for him to read.

On impulse, he delved into the hold again. This time he touched paper. The single sheet of foolscap he brought out was ancient and crumbling, but the writing was clear and the signature unmistakable. The name was Leven Valera, the infamous Black Duke of the Southern Barony. Valera, who might someday have been King, had instead spent the last twenty-five years of his life in the room at the top of the Needle for the murder of his wife. No wonder the pictures in the locket looked familiar! The man was Valera; the woman was Valera's murdered wife, Eleanor, about whose beauty ballads were still sung.

The ink Valera had used was a strange rusty black, and the first line of his note chilled Peter's heart. The note *entire* chilled his heart, and not only because the similarity between Valera's position and his own seemed too great for coincidence.

> *To the Finder of the Note —*
> *I write with my own Blood, drawn from a vayne I have opened in my left Forearm, my pen the Shaft of a Spune which I have sharpened long and long upon the stones of my Bedchamber. Nearly a quarter of a Centurie I have spent here in the skie; I came here a Young Man and now am I Old. The Coughing Spells and Fayver have come on me again, and this time I think I shall not survive.*
>
> *I did not kill my Wyfe. Nay, though all the Evidence say otherwise, I did not kill my Wyfe. I did love her and love her still, although her dear Face has grown misty in my treacherous Mind.*
>
> *I believe 'twas the King's Magician who killed Eleanor, and arranged Matters to see me put asyde, for I stood in his Way. It seems his Plans have worked and he has prospered; yet I believe there are Gods who punish Wickedness in the end. His Day shall come, and I have come to feel more and more strongly as my own Death approaches that he shall be brought down by One who comes to this Place of Dispair, One who finds and reads this Letter written in my Blood.*
>
> *If 'tis so, I cry out to you; Avenge, Avenge, Avenge! Ignore me and my lost Years if you must, but never, never,*

never ignore my dear Eleanor, murdered as she slept in her Bed! It was not I who poisoned her Wine; I write the name of the Murderer here in Blood: Flagg! 'Twas Flagg! Flagg! Flagg!

Take the Locket, and show it to him the instant before you relieve this the World of Its greatest Scoundrel – show him so that he may know in that Instant that I have been a part of his Downfall, even from beyond my unjust Murderer's Grayve.

Leven Valera

Perhaps now you can understand the true source of Peter's chill; perhaps not. Perhaps you will understand it better if I remind you that, although he looked to be a man in a hale and hearty middle age, Flagg was really very old.

Peter had read about the supposed crime of Leven Valera, yes. But the books in which he had read of it were histories. *Ancient* histories. This crumbling, yellowed parchment first spoke of the King's magician, and then spoke of Flagg by name. *Spoke* his name? Cried it, shrieked it – in blood.

But Valera's supposed crime had happened in the reign of Alan II –

– and Alan II had ruled Delain four hundred and fifty years ago.

'God, oh great God,' Peter whispered. He staggered back to his bed and sat down on it heavily, just before his knees would have unhinged and spilled him to the floor. 'He's done it all before! He's done it all before, and in exactly the same way, *but he did it over four centuries ago!*'

Peter's face was deadly white; his hair was standing on end. For the first time he realized that Flagg, the King's magician, was in reality Flagg the monster, loose in Delain again now, serving a new King – serving his own young, confused, easily led brother.

Peter at first entertained giddy thoughts of promising Beson another bribe to take the locket and the crumbling sheet of foolscap to Anders Peyna. In his initial flush of excitement, it seemed to him that this note must point the finger of guilt at Flagg and set him, Peter, free. A little reflection convinced him that while that might happen in a storybook, it would not happen in real life. Peyna would laugh and call it a forgery. And if he took it seriously? That might mean the end of both the Judge-General and the imprisoned prince. Peter's ears were sharp, and he listened closely to the gossip of the meadhouses and the wineshops as it was passed back and forth between Beson and the Lesser Warders. He had heard of the Farmers' Tax Increase, had heard the bitter joke which suggested that Thomas the Light-Bringer should be renamed Thomas the Tax-Bringer. He had even heard that some few daring wags had renamed his brother Foggy Tom the Constantly Bombed. The headsman's axe had swung with the regularity of a clock's pendulum since Thomas had ascended Delain's throne, only *this* clock called out *treason-*

sedition, treason-sedition, treason-sedition with a regularity that would have been monotonous, had it not been so frightening.

By now Peter had begun to suspect Flagg's goal: to bring the ordered monarchy of Delain to an utter smash. Showing the locket and the note would only get him laughed at or cause Peyna to take some sort of action. And that would undoubtedly get them both killed.

In the end Peter put the locket and foolscap back where they had come from. And with them he put the little three-foot pigtail it had taken him a month to weave. On the whole, he did not feel too bitter about the evening's work – the rope had held, and the finding of the locket and foolscap after more than four hundred years proved at least one thing – the hiding place was not apt to be discovered.

Still, he had much food for thought, and he lay long awake that night.

When he slept, he seemed to hear Leven Valera's dry, stony voice whispering in one ear: *Avenge! Avenge! Avenge!*

74

Time, yes, time – Peter spent a great deal of time at the top of the Needle. His beard grew long, save for where that white scar streaked his cheek like a lightning bolt. He saw many changes from his window, as it grew. He heard of more terrible changes yet. The headsman's pendulum had not slowed down but actually speeded up: *treason-sedition, treason-sedition*, it sang, and sometimes half a dozen heads rolled in the course of but a single day.

During Peter's third year of imprisonment, the year in which Peter was first able to do thirty chin-ups in a single effort from his bedchamber's central beam, Peyna resigned his post as Judge-General in disgust. It was the talk of the meadhouses and wine-shops for a week, and the talk of Peter's keepers for a week and a day. The warders believed that Flagg would have Peyna jailed almost before the heat of the old man's bum had left the judge's bench, and that soon after the citizens of Delain would find out once and for all if there was blood or ice water in the Judge-General's veins. But when Peyna remained free, the talk died down. Peter was glad Peyna had not been arrested. He bore him no ill will, in spite of Peyna's willingness to believe that he had murdered his father; and he knew that the arrangement of the evidence had been Flagg's doing.

Also during Peter's third year in the Needle, Dennis's good old da', Brandon, died. His passing was simple but dignified. He had finished his day's work in spite of a terrible pain in his chest and side and came slowly home. He sat down in the little living room, hoping the pain would pass. Instead it grew worse. He called his wife and son to his side, kissed them both, and asked if he might have a glass of bundle-gin. This was provided. He drank it off, kissed his wife again, and then sent her from the room.

'You must serve your master well now, Dennis,' he said. 'Ye're a man now, with a man's tasks set before you.'

'I'll serve the King as well as I may, Da',' Dennis said, although the thought of taking over his father's responsibilities terrified him. His good, homely face was shiny with tears. For the last three years, Brandon and Dennis had battled for Thomas, and Dennis's responsibilities had been much the same as before, with Peter; but it had never been the same, somehow – never even *close* to the same.

'Thomas, aye,' Brandon said, and then whispered: 'But if the time comes to do yer first master a service, Dennis, you mustn't hesitate. I have never –'

At that moment, Brandon clutched the left side of his chest, stiffened, and died. He died where he would have wanted to die, in his own chair, in front of his own fire.

In Peter's fourth year of imprisonment – his rope below the stones growing steadily longer and longer – the Staad family disappeared. The throne possessed itself of what little there remained of their lands, as it had done when other noble families disappeared. And as Thomas's reign progressed, there were more and more disappearances.

The Staads were only one item of meadhouse gossip in a busy week that included four beheadings, an increased levy against shopkeepers, and the imprisonment of an old woman who had for three days walked back and forth in front of the palace, screaming that her grandson had been taken and tortured for speaking against the previous year's Cattle Levies. But when Peter heard the Staad name in the warders' conversation, his heart had stopped for a moment.

The chain of events leading to the disappearance of the Staads was one familiar to everyone in Delain by now. The tick-tocking pendulum of the headsman's axe had thinned the numbers of the nobility terribly. Many of these nobles died because their families had served the Kingdom for hundreds – or thousands – of years, and they could not believe such an unjust fate would or could fall on them. Others, seeing bloody handwriting on the wall, fled. The Staads were among these.

And the whispering began.

Tales were told behind cupped hands, tales suggesting that these nobles had not simply scattered to the four winds but had gathered together some-where, perhaps in the deep woods at the northern end of the Kingdom, to plan an overthrow of the throne.

These stories passed to Peter like the wind through his window, the draughts beneath his door . . . They were dreams of a wider world. Mostly he worked on his rope. During the first year, the rope grew longer by eighteen inches every three weeks. At the end of that year, he had a slim cable that was twenty-five feet long – a cable that was, theoretically at least, strong enough to bear his weight. But there was a difference between dangling from a beam in his bedroom and dangling above a drop of three hundred feet, and Peter knew it. He was, quite literally, stak-ing his life on that slim cord.

And twenty-five feet a year was perhaps not enough; it would take more than eight years before he could even try, and the rumblings he heard at second hand had grown loud enough to be disturbing. Above all else, the Kingdom must endure – there must be no revolt, no chaos. Wrongs must be put right, but by law, not by bows and slings and maces and clubs. Thomas, Leven Valera, Roland, he himself, even Flagg paled into insignificance next to that. There must be law.

How Anders Peyna, growing old and bitter by his fire, would have loved him for that!

Peter determined that he must make his effort to escape as soon as possible. Accordingly he made long calculations, doing the figures in his head so as to leave no trace. He did them again and again and again, proving to himself that he had made no mistake.

In his second year in the Needle, he began to pluck ten threads from each napkin: in his third year fifteen; in his fourth year, twenty. The rope grew. Fifty-eight feet long after the second year; a hundred and four after the third; a hundred and sixty after the fourth.

The rope at that time would still have fetched up a hundred and forty feet from the ground.

During his last year, Peter began to take thirty threads from each napkin, and for the first time his robberies showed clearly – each napkin looked frayed on all four sides, as if mice had been at it. Peter waited in agony for his thefts to be discovered.

75

But they were not discovered then, or ever. There was not so much as a question ever raised. Peter had spent endless nights (or so they seemed to him) wondering and worrying when Flagg would hear some wrong thing, some wrong note, and so get wind of what he was up to. He would send some underling, Peter supposed, and the questions would begin. Peter had thought things out with agonizing care, and he had made only one wrong assumption – but that one led to a second (as wrong assumptions so often do) and that second was a dilly. He had assumed that there was some finite number of napkins – perhaps a thousand or so in all – and that they were being used over and over again. His thinking on the subject of the napkin supply never went much further than that. Dennis could have told him differently and saved him perhaps two years of work, but Dennis was never asked. The truth was simple but staggering. Peter's napkins were not coming from a supply of a thousand, or two thousand, or twenty thousand; there were nearly *half a million of these old, musty napkins in all.*

On one of the deep levels below the castle was a storeroom as big as a ballroom. And it was filled with napkins . . . napkins . . . nothing but napkins. They smelled musty to Peter and that wasn't surprising – most of them coincidentally or not, dated from a time not long after the imprisonment and death of Leven Valera, and the existence of all those napkins

– coincidentally or not – was, indirectly at least, the work of Flagg. In a queer sort of way, he had created them.

Those had been dark times indeed for Delain. The chaos Flagg so earnestly wished had almost come upon the land. Valera had been removed; mad King Alan had ascended the throne in his place. If he had lived another ten years, the Kingdom surely would have drowned in blood . . . but Alan was struck down by lightning while playing cubits on the back lawn in the pouring rain one day (as I told you, he was mad). It was lightning, some said, sent by the gods themselves. He was followed by his niece, Kyla, who became known as Kyla the Good . . . and from Kyla, the line of succession had run straight and true down through the generations to Roland, and the brothers to whose tale you have been listening. It was Kyla, the Good Queen, who brought the land out of its darkness and poverty. She had nearly bankrupted the Royal Treasury to do it, but she knew that currency – hard currency – is the life's blood of a kingdom. Much of Delain's hard currency had been drained away during the wild, weird reign of Alan II, a King who had sometimes drunk blood from the notched ears of his servants and who had insisted that he could fly; a King more interested in magic and necromancy than profit and loss and the welfare of his people. Kyla knew it would take a massive flow of both love and guilders to set the wrongs of Alan's reign right, and she began by trying to put every able-bodied person in Delain back to work, from eldest to youngest.

Many of the older citizens of the castle keep had

been set to making napkins – not because napkins were needed (I think I have already told you how most of Delain's royalty and nobility felt about them), but because *work* was needed. These were hands that had been idle for twenty years or more in some cases, and they worked with a will, weaving on looms exactly like the one in Sasha's doll's house . . . except in the matter of size, of course!

For ten years these old people, over a thousand of them, made napkins and drew hard coin from Kyla's Treasury for their work. For ten years people only slightly younger and a little more able to get about had taken them down to the cool, dry store-room below the castle. Peter had noticed that some of the napkins brought to him were moth-eaten as well as musty-smelling. The wonder, although he didn't know it, was that so many of them were still in such fine condition.

Dennis could have told him that the napkins were brought, used once, removed (minus the few threads Peter plucked from each), and then simply thrown away. After all, why not? There were enough of them, all told, to last five hundred princes five hundred years . . . and longer. If Anders Peyna had not been a merciful man as well as a hard one, there really might have been a finite number of napkins. But he knew how badly that nameless woman in the rocking chair needed the work and the pittance it brought in (Kyla the Good had known the same, in her time), and so he kept her on, as he continued to see that Beson's guilders went on flowing after the Staads were forced to flee. She became a fixture outside the room of the napkins, that old woman with her needle for unmaking rather than making. There she sat in her rocker, year after year, removing tens of thousands of royal crests, and so it was really not surprising that no word of Peter's petty thievery ever reached Flagg's ears.

So you see that, except for that one mistaken assumption and that one unasked question, Peter could have gotten about his work much faster. It *did* sometimes seem to him that the napkins were not shrinking as rapidly as they ought to have done, but it never occurred to him to question his basic (if vague) idea that the napkins he used were being regularly returned to him. If he had asked himself that one simple question – !

But perhaps, in the end, all things worked for the best.

Or perhaps not. That is another thing you must decide for yourself.

76

Eventually Dennis got over his fright of being Thomas's butler. After all, Thomas ignored him almost completely, except to sometimes berate him for forgetting to put out his shoes (usually Thomas himself had left his shoes somewhere else, then forgotten where) or to insist Dennis have a glass of wine with him. The wine always made Dennis feel sick to his stomach, although he had come to enjoy a wee drop of bundle-gin in the evenings. He drank it nonetheless. He did not need his good old da' around to tell him one did not refuse to drink with the King when asked. And sometimes, usually when he was drunk, Thomas would forbid Dennis to go home but insist that he spend the night in Thomas's apartments instead. Dennis supposed – and rightly – that these were nights on which Thomas simply felt too lonely to bear his own solitary company. He would give long, besotted, rambling sermons on how difficult it was to be King, how he was trying to do the best job he could and be fair, and how everyone hated him for some reason or other just the same. Thomas often wept during these sermons, or laughed wildly at nothing, but usually he just fell asleep halfway through some mangled defence of one tax or another. Sometimes he staggered off to his bed, and Dennis could sleep on the couch. More often, Thomas fell asleep – or passed out – on the couch, and Dennis made his uncomfortable bed on the cooling hearth. It was perhaps the strangest existence any King's butler had ever known, but, of course, it seemed normal enough to Dennis because it was all he had ever known.

Thomas mostly ignoring him was one thing. *Flagg* ignoring him was another, even more important thing. Flagg had, in fact, entirely dismissed Dennis's part in his scheme to send Peter to the Needle. Dennis had been no more than a tool to him – a tool which had served its purpose and could be put aside. If he *had* thought of Dennis, it would have seemed to him that the tool had been well rewarded: Dennis was the King's butler, after all.

But on an early winter's night in the year when Peter was twenty-one and Thomas sixteen, a night when Peter's thin rope was finally nearing completion, Dennis saw something which changed everything – and it is with the thing Dennis saw that cold night that I must begin to narrate the final events in my tale.

77

It was a night much like those during the terrible time just before and after Roland's death. The wind shrieked out of a black sky and moaned in the alleys of Delain. Frost lay thick in the pastures of the Inner Baronies and on cobbles of the castle city. At first, a three-quarters moon chased in and out of the rushing clouds, but by midnight the clouds had thickened enough to obscure the moon completely, and by two in the morning, when Thomas awoke Dennis by rattling the latch of the door between his sitting room and the corridor outside, it had begun to snow.

Dennis heard the rattling and sat up, grimacing at the stiffness in his back and the pins and needles in his legs. Tonight Thomas had fallen asleep on the couch instead of lurching his way to bed, so it had been the hearth for the young butler: Now the fire was almost out. The side of him which had been lying closer to it felt baked; the other side of him felt frozen.

He looked towards the rattling sound . . . and

for a moment terror froze his heart and vitals. For that one moment he thought there was a ghost at the door, and he almost screamed. Then he saw it was only Thomas in his white nightshirt.

'M-My Lord King?'

Thomas took no notice. His eyes were open, but they were not looking at the latch; they were wide and dreaming and they looked straight ahead at nothing. Dennis suddenly guessed that the young King was sleepwalking.

Even as Dennis decided this, Thomas seemed to realize that the reason the latch wouldn't work was that the bolt was still on. He drew it and then passed out into the hall, looking more ghostlike than ever in the guttering light of the corridor sconces. There was a swirl of nightshirt hem, and then he was gone on bare feet.

Dennis sat stock-still on the hearth for a moment, cross-legged, his pins and needles forgotten, his heart thumping. Outside, the wind hurled snow against the diamond-shaped panes of the sitting-room window and uttered a long banshee howl. What should he do?

There was only one thing, of course – the young King was his master. He must follow.

Perhaps it was the wild night which had brought Roland so vividly to Thomas's mind, but not necessarily – in fact, Thomas thought of his father a great deal. Guilt is like a sore, endlessly fascinating, and the guilty party feels compelled to examine it and pick at it, so that it never really heals. Thomas had drunk far less than usual but, strangely, had seemed drunker than ever to Dennis. His sentences had been

broken and garbled, his eyes wide and staring, showing too much of the whites.

This was, to a large extent, because Flagg was
gone. There had been rumours that the renegade
nobility – Staads among them – had been seen gathered together in the Far Forests at the northern
reaches of the Kindom. Flagg had led a regiment of
tough, battle-hardened soldiers in search of them.
Thomas was always more skittish when Flagg was
gone. He knew it was because he had come to depend
completely on the dark magician . . . but he had
come to depend on Flagg in ways he did not fully
understand. Too much wine was no longer
Thomas's only vice. Sleep is often denied to those
with secrets, and Thomas was afflicted with severe
insomnia. Without knowing it, he had become
addicted to Flagg's sleeping potions. Flagg had left a
supply of the drug with Thomas when he led the
soldiers north, but Flagg had expected to be gone
only three days – four at the most. For the last three
days, Thomas had slept badly, or not at all. He felt
strange, never quite awake, never quite asleep.
Thoughts of his father haunted him. He seemed to
hear his father's voice in the wind, crying out *Why
do you stare at me? Why do you stare at me so?* Visions of
wine . . . visions of Flagg's darkly cheerful face . . .
visions of his father's hair catching fire . . . these
things drove sleep away and left him wide-eyed in
the long watches of the night while the rest of the
castle slept.

When Flagg had still not returned on the eighth
night (he and his soldiers were even then camped
fifty miles from the castle and Flagg was in a foul

mood; the only trace of the nobles they found had been frozen hoofprints that might have been days or weeks old), Thomas sent for Dennis. It was later that night, that eighth night, that Thomas arose from his couch and began to walk.

So Dennis followed his lord and master the King down those long, draughty stone corridors, and if you have come this far, I think you must know where Thomas the Light-Bringer finished up.

Late stormy night had passed into early stormy morning. No one was abroad in the corridors – at least, Dennis saw no one. If anyone *had* been abroad, he or she might well have fled in the other direction, perhaps screaming, believing he or she had seen two ghosts walking, the one leading in a long white nightshirt that could easily have been mistaken for a shroud, the other following in a plain jerkin, but with bare feet and a face pale enough to have been mistaken for the face of a corpse. Yes, I believe anyone who saw them would have fled, and told long prayers before sleeping . . . and even many prayers might not have kept the nightmares at bay.

Thomas stopped in the middle of a corridor that Dennis had seldom been down, and he opened a recessed door which Dennis had never really noticed at all. The boy King stepped into another corridor (no chambermaid passed them with an armload of sheets, as one had once passed Thomas and Flagg when Flagg had brought the prince this way some years before; all good chambermaids were long since in their beds), and partway down it, Thomas stopped so suddenly that Dennis almost ran into him.

Thomas looked around, as if to see if he had been followed, and his dreaming eyes passed directly over Dennis. Dennis's skin crawled, and it was all he could do to keep from crying out. The sconces in this almost forgotten hallway guttered and stank foully of *das* oil; the light was faint and gruesome. The young butler could feel his hair trying to clump up and push out in spikes as those empty eyes – eyes like dead lamps lit only by the moon – passed over him.

He was there, standing right there, but Thomas did not see him; to Thomas, his butler was *dim*.

Oh, I must run, part of Dennis's mind whispered distractedly – but inside his head, that distracted little whisper was like a scream. *Oh, I must run, he has died, he has died in his sleep and I am following a walking corpse!* But then he heard the voice of his da', his own dear, dead da', whispering: *If the time ever comes to do yer first master a service, Dennis, you mustn't hesitate.*

A voice deeper than either told him that the time for that service had come. And Dennis, a lowly servant boy who had changed a kingdom once by discovering a burning mouse, perhaps changed it again by holding his place, in spite of the terror which froze his bones and pushed his heart into his throat.

In a strange, deep voice that was nothing at all like his usual voice (but to Dennis that voice sounded weirdly familiar), Thomas said: 'Fourth stone up from the one at the bottom with the chip in it. Press it Quick!'

The habit of obedience was so ingrained in Dennis that he had actually begun to move forward before realizing that Thomas, in his dream, had commanded himself in the voice of another. Thomas pushed the stone before Dennis could move more than a single step. It slid in perhaps three inches. There was a click. Dennis's jaw dropped, as part of the wall swung inward. Thomas pushed it farther, and Dennis saw there was a huge secret door here. Secret doors made him think of secret panels, and secret panels made him think of burning mice. Again he felt an urge to run and fought it down.

Thomas went in. For a moment he was only a glimmering nightshirt in the dark, a nightshirt with no one inside it. Then the stone wall closed again. The illusion was perfect.

Dennis stood there, shifting from one cold bare foot to the other cold bare foot. What should he do now?

Again, it was his da's voice he seemed to hear, impatient now, brooking no refusal. *Follow, you paltry boy! Follow, and be quick! This is the moment! Follow!*

But Da', the dark —

He seemed to feel a stinging slap, and Dennis thought hysterically: *Even when you're dead you got a strong right hand, Da'! All right, all right, I'm going!*

He counted up four from the chipped stone and pushed. The door swung about four inches inward on darkness.

There was a tiny clittering sound in the awesome silence of the corridor – a sound like mice made of stone. After a moment Dennis realized that sound was his own teeth, chattering together.

Oh Da;, I'm so scared, he mourned . . . and then followed King Thomas into the darkness.

79

Fifty miles away, rolled into five blankets against the bitter cold and the roaring wind, Flagg cried out in his sleep at the precise moment Dennis followed the King into the secret passageway. On a knoll not far distant, wolves howled in unison with that cry. The soldier sleeping nearest Flagg on the left died instantly of a heart attack, dreaming that a great lion had come to gobble him up. The soldier sleeping on Flagg's right woke up in the morning to discover he was blind. Worlds sometimes shudder and turn *inside* their axes, and this was such a time. Flagg felt it, but did not grasp it. The salvation of all that is good is only this – at times of great import, evil beings sometimes fall strangely blind. When the King's magician awoke in the morning, he knew that he had had a bad dream, probably from his own long-forgotten past, but he did not remember what it had been.

The darkness inside the secret passage was utter and complete, the air still and dry. In it, coming from somewhere ahead, Dennis heard a terrible, desolate sound.

The King was weeping.

At that sound, some of Dennis's fear left him. He felt a great wonder, and a great pity for Thomas, who always seemed so unhappy, and who had grown fat and pimply as King – often he was pallid and shaky-handed from too much wine the night before, and his breath was usually bad. Already Thomas's legs were beginning to bow, and unless Flagg was with him, he had a tendency to walk with his head down and his hair hanging in his face.

Dennis felt his way forward, his hands held out in front of him. The sound of weeping grew closer in the dark . . . and then, suddenly, the dark was no longer complete. He heard a faint sliding noise and then he could see Thomas faintly. He was standing at the end of the corridor, and faint amber light was coming in from two small holes in the dark. To Dennis, those holes looked strangely like floating eyes.

Just as Dennis began to believe that he would be all right, that he would probably survive this strange night walk, Thomas shrieked. He shrieked so loudly it seemed that his vocal cords must split open. The strength ran out of Dennis's legs and he fell to his knees, hands clapped over his mouth to stop his own screams, and now it seemed to him that this secret way was filled with ghosts, ghosts like strange flapping bats that might at any moment snare themselves in his hair; oh yes, the place seemed filled with the unquiet dead to Dennis, and perhaps it was; perhaps it was.

He almost swooned . . . almost . . . but not quite.

Somewhere below him, he heard barking dogs and realized they were above the old King's kennels. The few of Roland's dogs still alive had never been moved outside again. They were the only living beings — besides Dennis himself — that had heard those wild shrieks. But the dogs were real, not ghosts, and Dennis held on to that thought the way a drowning man might hold on to a floating mast.

A moment or two later, he realized that Thomas was not *just* shrieking – he was crying out words. At first Dennis could make out only a single phrase, howled out again and again: '*Don't drink the wine! Don't drink the wine! Don't drink the wine!*'

81

Three nights later, a light knock came at the closed sitting-room door of a farm in one of the Inner Baronies, a farm quite close to where the Staad family had lived not so long ago.

'Come!' Anders Peyna growled. 'And it better be damned good, Arlen!'

Arlen had aged in the years since Beson had appeared at Peyna's door with Peter's note. The changes in him, however, were slight when compared with the changes in Peyna. The former Judge-General's hair was almost all gone. His spareness of frame had become gauntness. The loss of hair and weight were very little, however, when compared with the changes in his face. Formerly he had been stern. Now he was grim. Dark-brown hollows floated below his eyes. The stamp of despair was clear on his face, and there was a good reason for this. He had seen the things he had spent his life defending brought to ruin . . . and this ruin had been accomplished with shocking ease, and in a shockingly brief period of time. Oh, I suppose all men of intelligence know how fragile such things as Law and Justice and Civilization really are, but it's not a thing they think of willingly, because it disturbs one's rest and plays hob with one's appetite.

Seeing his life's work knocked casually apart like a child's tower of blocks was bad enough, but there was another thing which haunted Peyna these last four years, something that was even worse. This was the knowledge that Flagg had not achieved all the dark changes in Delain alone. Peyna had helped him. For who else had seen Peter brought to a trial which was perhaps *too* speedy? Who else had been so convinced of Peter's guilt . . . and not so much by the evidence as by a young boy's shocked tears?

Since the day Peter had been led to the top of the Needle, the chopping block in the Plaza of the Needle had been stained a sinister rusty colour. Not even the hardest rain could wash it clean. And Peyna thought he could detect that sinister red stain spreading out from the block – spreading out to cover the Plaza, the market streets, the alleys. In his troubled dreams Peyna saw rills of fresh blood washing in bright, accusing threads between the cobblestones and running down the gutters in streamlets. He saw the redans of Castle Delain gleaming bloody in the sun. He saw the carp in the moat floating belly-up, poisoned by the blood which poured out of the sewers in floods and which rose from the springs in the earth itself. He saw the blood rising everywhere, staining the fields and forests. In these unhappy dreams even the sun began to look like a bloodshot, dying eye.

Flagg had let him live. In the meadhouses, people whispered behind their hands that he had reached an agreement with the magician – that he had perhaps given Flagg the names of certain traitors, or that perhaps Peyna 'had something' on Flagg, some secret that would come out if Peyna died suddenly. This was of course, ridiculous. Flagg was not a man to be threatened – not by Peyna, not by anyone. There were no secrets. There had been no agreements or deals. Flagg had simply let him live . . . and Peyna knew why. Dead, he would perhaps have been at peace. Alive, he was left to twist on the rack of his own bad conscience. He was left to watch the terrible changes Flagg had wrought on Delain.

'Well?' he asked irritably. 'What is it, Arlen?'

'A boy has come, my Lord. He says he must see you.'

'Send him away,' Peyna said moodily. He reflected that, even a year ago, he would have heard a knock at the front door, but it seemed that he became more deaf with every passing day. 'I see no one after nine, you know that. Much has changed, but not that.'

Arlen cleared his throat. 'I know the boy. It is Dennis, son of Brandon. It is the King's butler who calls.'

Peyna stared at Arlen, hardly believing what he had heard. Perhaps he was growing deaf even faster than he had thought. He asked Arlen to repeat, and it came out sounding just the same.

'I'll see him. Send him in.'

'Very good, my Lord.' Arlen turned to leave.

The similarity to the night Beson had come with Peter's note – even down to the cold wind screaming outside – came strongly to Peyna now. 'Arlen,' he called.

Arlen turned back. 'My Lord?'

The right corner of Peyna's mouth quirked the smallest bit. 'Are you quite sure it's not a dwarf-boy?'

'Quite sure, my Lord,' Arlen replied, and the *left* corner of his own mouth twitched the tiniest bit. 'There are no dwarves left in the known world. Or so my mother told me.'

'Obviously she was a woman of good sense and clear discernment, dedicated to raising her son properly and not to be held responsible for any inherent flaws in the material she had to work with. Bring the boy here directly.'

'Yes, my Lord.' The door closed.

Peyna looked into his fire again and rubbed his old, arthritis-crippled hands together in a gesture of unaccustomed agitation. Thomas's butler. Here. Now. Why?

But there was no sense in speculating; the door would open in a moment and the answer would come walking through it in the form of a man-boy who would be shaking with the cold, perhaps even frostbitten.

Dennis would have found it a good deal easier to reach Peyna if Peyna had still been at his fine house in the castle city, but his house had been sold from beneath him for 'unpaid taxes' following his resignation. Only the few hundred guilders he had put away over the course of forty years had allowed him to buy this small, draughty farmhouse and continue to pay Beson. It was technically in the Inner Baronies, but he was still many miles west of the castle . . . and the weather had been very cold.

In the hallway beyond the door, he heard the murmur of approaching voices. Now. Now the answer would come through the door. Suddenly that absurd feeling – that feeling of hope, like a ray of strong light shining in a dark cave – came back to him. *Now the answer will come through the door*, he thought, and for a moment he found himself believing that was really true.

As he drew his favourite pipe from the rack beside him. Anders Peyna saw that his hands were trembling.

82

The boy was really a man, but Arlen's use of the word was not unjustified – at least not on this night. He was cold, Peyna saw, but he also knew that the cold alone does not make anyone shudder as Dennis was shuddering.

'Dennis!' Peyna said, sitting forward sharply (and ignoring the twinge in his back the sudden movement caused). 'Has something happened to the King?' Dreadful images, awful possibilities suddenly filled Peyna's old head – the King dead, either from too much wine, or possibly by his own hand. Everyone in Delain knew that the young King was deeply moody.

'No . . . that is . . . yes . . . but no . . . not the way you mean . . . the way I think you mean . . .'

'Come in here close to the fire,' Peyna snapped. 'Arlen, don't just stand there gawking! Get a blanket! Get two! Wrap this boy up before he shakes himself to death like a buggerlug bug!'

'Yes, my Lord,' Arlen said. He had never gawked in his life – he knew it, and Peyna did, too. But he recognized the gravity of this situation and left quickly. He stripped the two blankets from his own bed – the only other two in this glorified peasant's hut were the ones on Peyna's – and brought them back. He took them to where Dennis crouched as close to the fire as he could without bursting into flames. The deep frost which had covered his hair had begun to melt and to run down his cheeks like tears. Dennis wrapped himself in the blankets.

'Now, tea. Strong tea. A cup for me, a pot for the boy.'

'My Lord, we only have half a canister left in the whole – '

'Bugger how much we have left! A cup for me, a pot for the boy.' He considered. 'And make a cup for yourself, Arlen, and then come in here and listen.'

'My Lord?' Even all of his breeding could not keep Arlen from looking frankly astounded at this.

'Damn!' Peyna roared. 'Would you have me believe you're as deaf as I've become? Get about it!'

'Yes, my Lord,' Arlen said, and went to brew the last tea in the house.

Peyna had not forgotten everything he had ever known about the fine art of questioning; in point of fact, he had forgotten damned little of that, or anything else. He had had long sleepless nights when he wished that he *could* forget some things.

While Arlen made the tea, Peyna went about the task of putting this frightened – no; this *terrified* – young man at his ease. He asked after Dennis's mum. He asked if the drainage problems which had so plagued the castle of late had improved. He asked Dennis's opinion on the spring plantings. He steered clear of any and all subjects which might be dangerous . . . and little by little, as he warmed, Dennis calmed.

When Arlen served the tea, hot and strong and steaming, Dennis slurped half the cup at a gulp, grimaced, then slurped the rest. Impassive as ever, Arlen poured more.

'Easy, my lad,' Peyna said, lighting his pipe at last. 'Easy's the word for hot tea and skittish horses.'

'Cold. Thought I was going to freeze coming out here.'

'You *walked*?' Peyna was unable to conceal his surprise.

'Yes. Had my mother leave word with the lesser servants that I was home with the grippe. That'll hold all for a few days, it being so catching this time of year . . . or should do. Walked. Whole way. Didn't dare ask a ride. Didn't want to be remembered. Didn't know it was quite this far. If I'd known, I might have taken a ride after all. I left at three of the clock.' He struggled, his throat working, and then burst out: 'And I'm not going back, not ever! I seen the way *he* looks at me since he come back! Narrow and on the side, his eyes all dark! *He* never used to look at me that way – never used to look at me at all! *He* knows I seen something! Knows I heard something! *He* don't know what, but *he* knows there's something! He hears it in my head, like I'd hear the bell ringin' out from the Church of the Great Gods! If I stay, *he'll* get it out of me! I know he will!'

Peyna stared at the boy under furrowed brows, trying to sort out this amazing flood of declaration.

Tears were standing in Dennis's eyes. 'I mean F–'

'Softly, Dennis,' Peyna said. His voice was mild, but his eyes were not. 'I know who you mean. Best not to speak his name aloud.'

Dennis looked at him with dumb, simple gratitude.

'You'd better tell me what you came to say,' Peyna told him.

'Yes. Yes, all right.'

Dennis hesitated for a moment, trying to get himself under control and to arrange his thoughts. Peyna waited impassively, trying to control his rising excitement.

'You see,' Dennis began at last, 'three nights ago Thomas called me to come and stay with him, as he sometimes does. And at midnight, or sometime thereabouts –'

'**D**ennis told what you have already heard, and to his credit, he did not try to lie about his own terror, or gloss it over. As he spoke, the wind whined outside and as the fire burned low Peyna's eyes burned hotter and hotter. Here, he thought, were worse things than he ever could have imagined. Not only had Peter poisoned the King, *Thomas had seen it happen.*

No wonder the boy King was so often moody

and depressed. Perhaps the rumours that passed in the meadhouses, rumours that had Thomas more than half mad already, were not so far-fetched as Peyna had thought.

But as Dennis paused to drink tea (Arlen refilled his cup from the bitter lees of the pot), Peyna drew back from that idea. If Thomas had witnessed *Peter* poisoning Roland, why was Dennis here now . . . and in such deadly terror of *Flagg?*

'You heard more,' Peyna said.

'Aye, my Lord Judge-General,' Dennis said. 'Thomas . . . he raved quite some time. We were closed up in the dark together long.'

Dennis struggled to be clearer, but found no words to convey the horror of that closed-in passage-way, with Thomas shrieking in the darkness before him and the dead King's few surviving dogs barking below them. No words to describe the *smell* of the place – a smell of secrets which had gone rancid like milk spilled in the dark. No words to tell of his grow-ing fear that Thomas had gone mad while in the grip of his dream.

He had screamed the name of the King's magician over and over again; had begged the King to look deep into the goblet and see the mouse that simultaneously burned and drowned in the wine. *Why do you stare at me so?* he had shrieked. And then: *I brought you a glass of wine, my King, to show you that I, too, love you.* And finally he had shrieked out words that Peter himself would have recognized, words better than four hundred years old: *'Twas Flagg! Flagg! 'Twas Flagg!*

Dennis reached for his cup, got it halfway to his

mouth, and then dropped it. The cup shattered on the hearthstones.

The three of them looked at the shards of crockery.

'And then?' Peyna asked, in a deceptively gentle voice.

'Nothing for a long, long time,' Dennis said in a halting voice. 'My eyes had . . . had gotten used to the darkness, and I could see him a little. He was asleep . . . asleep at those two little holes, with his chin on his breast and his eyes closed.'

'And he remained so for how long?'

'My Lord, I know not. The dogs had all quietened again. And perhaps I . . . I . . .'

'Dozed a bit yourself? I think it is likely, Dennis.'

'Then, later, he seemed to wake. His eyes opened, at any rate. He closed the little panels and all was dark again. I heard him moving and I drew my legs back so he would not trip over them . . . his nightshirt . . . it brushed my face . . .'

Dennis grimaced as he remembered a feeling like cobwebs drawn in a whisper over his left cheek.

'I followed him. He let himself out . . . I followed still. He closed the door so that it looked like only plain stone wall again. He went back to his apartments and I followed him.'

'Did you meet anyone?' Peyna rapped so sharply that Dennis jumped. 'Anyone at all?'

'No. No, my Lord Judge-General. No one at all.'

'Ah.' Peyna relaxed. 'That is very well. And did anything else happen that night?'

'No, my Lord. He went to bed and slept like a dead man.' Dennis hesitated and then added, 'I didn't sleep a wink, meself, and haven't slept many since, either.'

'And in the morning he —?'

'Remembered nothing.'

Peyna grunted. He steepled his fingers and looked at the dying fire through the little finger-building he had built.

'And did you go back to that passageway?'

Curiously, Dennis asked: 'Would you have gone back, my Lord?'

'Yes,' Peyna said dryly. 'The question is, did *you*?'

'I did,'

'Of course you did. Were you seen?'

'No. A chambermaid passed me in the hallway. The laundry is down that way, I think. I smelled lye soap, like my mum uses. When she was gone, I counted up four from the chipped stone and went in.'

'To see what Thomas had seen.'

'Aye, my Lord.'

'And did you?'

'Aye, my Lord.'

'And what was it?' Peyna asked, knowing. 'When you slid aside those panels, what did you see?'

'My Lord, I saw King Roland's sitting room,' Dennis said. 'With all them heads on the walls. And . . . my Lord . . .' In spite of the heat of the dying fire, Dennis shuddered. 'All of them heads . . . they seemed to be *looking* at me.'

'But there was one head you *didn't* see,' Peyna said.

'No, my Lord, I saw them a —' Dennis stopped,

eyes widening. 'Niner!' He gasped. 'The peepholes –'
He stopped his eyes now almost as big as saucers.

Silence fell again inside. Outside, the winter wind
moaned and whined. And miles away, Peter, rightful
King of Delain, hunched over a tiny loom high in the
sky and wove a rope almost too fine to see.

At last, Peyna fetched a deep sigh. Dennis was
looking up at him from his place on the hearth plead-
ingly . . . hopefully . . . fearfully. Peyna bent forward slowly and touched his shoulder.

'You did well to come here, Dennis, son of
Brandon. You did well to make a reason for your
absence – quite a plausible one, I think. You'll sleep
here with us tonight, in the attic, under the eaves.
It'll be cold, but I think you'll sleep better than you
have of late. Am I wrong?'

Dennis shook his head slowly once, and a tear
spilled from his right eye and ran slowly down his
cheek.

'And your mum knows naught of your reason
for needing to be away?'

'No.'

'Then the chances are very good she'll not be
touched by it. Arlen will take you up. Those are his
blankets, I think, and you'll have to return them. But
there's straw above, and it's clean.'

'I'll sleep just as well with only one blanket, my
Lord,' Arlen said.

'Hush! Young blood runs hot even in its sleep,
Arlen. Your blood has cooled. And you may want
your blankets . . . in case dwarves and trolls come
in your dreams.'

Arlen smiled a little.

'In the morning, we'll talk more, Dennis – but you may not see your mum for a bit now; I must tell you that, although I suspect you already know it might not be healthy for you to go back to Delain, by the look of you.'

Dennis tried to smile, but his eyes were shiny with fear. 'I had thoughts of more than the grippe when I came here, and that's the honest truth. But now I've put your own health in danger as well, haven't I?'

Peyna smiled dryly. 'I'm old, and Arlen is old. The health of the old is never very strong. Sometimes that makes them more careful than they should be . . . but sometimes it makes them dare much.' *Especially*, he thought, *if they have much to atone for.* 'We'll speak more in the morning. In the meantime, you deserve your rest. Will you light his way upstairs, Arlen?'

'Yes, my Lord.'

'And then come back to me.'

'Yes, my Lord.'

Arlen led the exhausted Dennis from the room, leaving Anders Peyna to brood before his dying fire.

85

When Arlen came back, Peyna said quietly: 'We have plans to make, Arlen, but perhaps you'll draw us a drop of wine. It would be well to wait until the boy is asleep.'

'My Lord, he was asleep before his head touched the hay he had gathered for his pillow.'

'Very well. But draw us a drop of wine anyway.'

'A drop is all there is to draw,' Arlen said.

'Good. Then we'll not have to set out with big heads tomorrow, will we?'

'My Lord?'

'Arlen, we leave here tomorrow, the three of us, for the north. I know it, you know it. Dennis says there's grippe in Delain – and so there is; one who would grip us if he could, anyway. We go for our *health*.'

Arlen nodded slowly.

'It would be a crime to leave that good wine behind us for the tax man. So we'll drink it . . . and then take ourselves off to bed.'

'As you say, my Lord.'

Peyna's eyes glinted. 'But before *you* go to bed, you'll mount to the attic and get the blanket you left with the boy, against my strict and specific instructions.'

Arlen gaped at Peyna. Peyna mocked his gape with uncanny aptness. And for the first and last time in his service as Peyna's butler, Arlen laughed out loud.

86

Peyna went to bed but could not sleep. It wasn't the sound of the wind that kept him awake, but the sound of cold laughter coming from inside his own head.

When he could stand that laughter no longer, he got up, went back into the sitting room, and sat before the cooling fireplace ashes, his white hair floating in small clouds over his skull. Unaware of his comic look (and if he *had* been aware of it, he would have been unmindful), he sat wrapped in his blankets like the oldest Indian in the universe and looked into the dead fire.

Pride goes before a fall, his mother had told him when he was a child, and Peyna had understood that. *Pride's a joke that'll make the stranger inside you laugh sooner or later*, she had also told him, and he hadn't understood that . . . but he did now. Tonight the stranger inside was laughing very hard indeed. Too hard for him to be able to sleep, even though the next day was apt to be long and difficult.

Peyna was fully able to appreciate the irony of his position. All his life, he had served the idea of the law. Ideas like 'prison break' and 'armed rebellion' horrified him. They still did, but certain truths had to be faced. That the machinery of revolt had come to exist in Delain, for instance. Peyna knew that the nobles who had fled to the north called themselves 'exiles', but he also knew that they were edging ever closer to calling themselves 'rebels'. And if he were to keep that revolt from happening, he might well have to use the machinery of rebellion to help a prisoner break out of the Needle. *That* was the joke the stranger inside was laughing at, laughing too loudly for sleep to be even a remote possibility.

Such actions as the ones he was now thinking about went against the grain of his whole life, but he would go ahead anyway, even if it killed him (which it just might). Peter had been falsely imprisoned. Delain's true King was not on the throne, but locked in a cold two-room cell at the top of the Needle. And if it took lawless forces to put things right again, so it must be. But . . .

'The napkins,' Peyna muttered. His mind circled back to them and back to them. 'Before we resort to force of arms to free the rightful King and see him enthroned, the business of the napkins should be investigated. He'll have to be asked. Dennis . . . and the Staad boy, perhaps . . . aye . . .'

'My Lord?' Arlen asked from behind him. 'Are you unwell?'

Arlen had heard his master rise, as butlers almost always do.

'I am unwell,' Peyna agreed gloomily. 'But it's nothing my physician can fix, Arlen.'

'I'm sorry, my Lord.'

Peyna turned to Arlen, and fixed his bright, sunken eyes upon the butler.

'Before we become outlaws, I want to know why he asked for his mother's doll's house . . . and for napkins with his meals.'

87

'Go back to the castle?' Dennis asked the next morning, in a hoarse voice that was almost a whisper. 'Go back to where *he* is?'

'If you feel you can't, I'll not press you,' Peyna said. 'But you know the castle well enough, I think, to stay out of *his* way. If, that is, you know a way to get in unnoticed. To be noticed would be bad. You look much too lively for a boy who is supposed to be home sick.'

The day was cold and bright. The snow on the long, rolling hills of the Inner Baronies threw back a diamond dazzle which made the eyes water before long. *I'll probably be snowblind by noon, and it'll serve me right*, Peyna thought grumpily. The stranger inside seemed to find this prospect hilarious indeed.

Castle Delain itself could be seen in the distance, blue and dreaming on the horizon, its walls and towers looking like an illustration in a book of fairy stories. Dennis, however, did not look like a young hero in search of adventure. His eyes were full of fear, and his face bore the expression of a man who has escaped from a den of lions . . . only to be told he's forgotten his lunch, and must go back in and get it, even though he's lost his appetite.

'There might be a way to get in,' he said. 'But if *he* smells me, how I get in or where I hide won't matter. If he smells me, he'll run me down.'

Peyna nodded. He did not want to add to the boy's fear, but in this situation, nothing less than the truth could serve them. 'What you say is true.'

'But you still ask me to go?'

'If you can, I still ask it.'

Over a meagre breakfast, Peyna had told Dennis what he wanted to know, and had suggested some ways Dennis might go about getting the information. Now Dennis shook his head, not in refusal but in bewilderment.

'Napkins,' he said.

Peyna nodded. 'Napkins.'

Dennis's fearful eyes went back to that distant fairy-tale castle dreaming on the horizon. 'When he was dying, my da' said if I ever saw a chance to do a service for my first master, I must do it. I thought I'd done it coming here. But if I must go back . . .'

Arlen, who had been busy, closing up the house, now joined them.

'Your house key, please, Arlen,' Peyna said.

Arlen handed it to him, and Peyna handed it to Dennis.

'Arlen and I go north to join the' – Peyna hesitated and cleared his throat – 'the exiles,' he finished. 'I've given you Arlen's key to this house. When we reach their camp, I'll give mine to a fellow you know, if he be there. I think he will be.'

'Who's that?' Dennis asked.

'Ben Staad.'

Sunshine broke on Dennis's gloomy face. 'Ben? Ben's with them?'

'I think he may be,' Peyna said. In truth, he knew perfectly well that the entire Staad family was with the exiles. He kept his ear firmly to the earth, and his ears had not grown so deaf that he was not able to hear many movements in the Kingdom.

'And you'd send him down here?'

'If he'll come, aye, I mean to,' Peyna replied.

'To do what? My Lord, I'm still not clear about that.'

'Nor am I,' Peyna said, looking cross. He felt

more than cross; he felt bewildered. 'I've spent my whole life doing some things because they were logical and not doing others because they were not. I've seen what happens when people act on intuition, or for illogical reasons. Sometimes the results are ludicrous and embarrassing; more often they are simply horrible. But here I am, just the same, behaving like a crackbrained crystal gazer.'

'I don't understand you, my Lord.'

'Neither do I, Dennis. Neither do I. Do you know what day this is?'

Dennis blinked at this sudden change in direction, but answered readily enough. 'Yes – Tuesday.'

'Tuesday. Good. Now I'm going to ask you a question that my cursed intuition tells me is very important. If you don't know the answer – even if you are not sure – for the gods' sake, say so! Are you ready for the question?'

'Yes, my Lord,' Dennis said, but he wasn't sure that he really was. Peyna's piercing blue eyes under the wild tangle of his white brows had made him very nervous. The question was apt to be very difficult indeed. 'That is, I think so.'

Peyna asked his question, and Dennis relaxed. It didn't make much sense to him – it was only more nonsense about the napkins, as far as he could see – but at least he knew the answer, and gave it.

'You're sure?' Peyna persisted.

'Yes, my Lord.'

'Good. Then here is what I want you to do.'

Peyna spoke to Dennis for some time, as the three of them stood in the chilly sunshine in front of the 'retirement cottage' where the old judge would never come again. Dennis listened earnestly, and when Peyna demanded that he repeat the instructions back, Dennis was able to do it quite neatly.

'Good,' Peyna said. 'Very, very good.'

'I'm glad I've pleased you, sir.'

'Nothing about this business pleases me, Dennis. Nothing at all. If Ben Staad is with those unfortunate outcasts in the Far Forests, I mean to send him away from relative safety and into danger because he *may* be of some use to King Peter. I'm sending you back to the castle because my heart tells me there's something about those napkins he asked for . . . and the doll's house . . . *something*. Sometimes I think I almost have it, and then it dances out of my grasp again. He did not ask for those things idly, Dennis. I'd wager my life on that. But I don't *know*.' Peyna abruptly slammed his fist down on his leg in frustration. 'I am putting two fine young men into terrible danger, and my heart tells me I am doing the right thing, but I . . . don't . . . know . . . *WHY!*'

And inside the man who had in his heart once condemned a boy because of that boy's tears, the stranger laughed and laughed and laughed.

88

The two old men parted from Dennis. They shook hands all around; then Dennis kissed the Judge's ring, which bore the Great Seal of Delain on its face. Peyna had given up his Judge-General's bench, but had not been able to part with the ring, which to him summed up all the goodness of the law. He knew he had made mistakes from time to time, but he had not allowed them to break his heart. Even over this last and greatest of mistakes, his heart did not break. He knew as well as we in our own world do that the road to hell is paved with good intentions – but he also knew that, for human beings, good intentions are sometimes all there are. Angels may be safe from damnation, but human beings are less fortunate things, and for them hell is always close.

He protested Dennis's act of kissing his ring, but Dennis insisted. Then Arlen shook Dennis's hand and wished him speed o' the gods. Smiling (but Peyna could still see the fear lurking in Dennis's eyes), Dennis wished them the same. Then the young butler turned east, toward the castle, and the two old men headed west, toward the farmstead of one Charles Reechul. Reechul, who raised Anduan huskies for a living, paid the grinding taxes the King had imposed without complaint, and was thus considered loyal . . . but Peyna knew that Reechul was sympathetic to the exiles encamped in the Far Forests, and had helped others reach them. Peyna had never expected to need Reechul's services himself, but the time had come.

The farmer's eldest daughter, Naomi, drove Peyna and Arlen north on a sled pulled by twelve of the dogger's strongest huskies. By Wednesday night, they reached the edge of the Far Forests.

'How long to the camp of the exiles?' Peyna asked Naomi that night.

Naomi cast the thin, evil-smelling cigar she had been smoking into the fire. 'Two more days if the skies keep fair. Four more days if it snows. Maybe never, if it blizzards.'

Peyna turned in. He drifted off to sleep almost at once. Logic or illogic, he was sleeping better than he had in years.

The weather kept clear the next day, and on Friday as well. At dusk of that day – the fourth since Peyna and Arlen had parted from Dennis – they reached the small huddle of tents and makeshift wooden huts for which Flagg had searched in vain.

'Ho! Who comes, and can you say the password?' a voice called. It was strong, sturdy, cheerful, and unafraid. Peyna recognized it.

'It's Naomi Reechul,' the girl called, 'and the password two weeks ago was "tripos". If it's not that now, Ben Staad, then put an arrow through me and I'll come back and haunt you!'

Ben appeared from behind a rock, laughing. 'I'd not dare meet you as a ghost, Naomi – you're fearsome enough alive!'

Ignoring this, she turned to Peyna. 'We've come,' she said.

'Yes,' Peyna said. 'So I see.'

And I believe it's well that we have . . . because something tells me that time has grown short . . . very short indeed.

Peter had the same feeling.

By Sunday, two days after Peyna and Arlen reached the camp of the exiles, his rope would still, by his calculations, finish up thirty feet short of the ground. This meant that when he dangled from the end of it with his arms fully extended, he would face a drop of at least twenty-one feet. He knew that he would be wiser by far to go on with his rope for another four months – even another two. If he dropped from the rope, fell badly, and broke both of his legs so that the Plaza guards found him groaning on the cobbles when they made their round-o'-the-clock, he would have wasted more than four years, simply because he did not have the patience to pursue his labour another four months.

This was logic Peyna could have appreciated, but Peter's feeling that he must now hurry was much stronger. Once Peyna would have snorted at the idea that feelings could be more trustworthy than logic . . . but now he might have been less sure.

Peter had been having a dream – for almost a week running now it had played over and over, gradually becoming more distinct. In it, he saw Flagg, bent over some bright and glowing object – it lit the magician's face a sickly greenish-yellow. In this dream, there always came a point when Flagg's eyes first widened, as if in surprise, and then narrowed to cruel slits. His brows pulled down; his forehead darkened; a grimace as bitter as a crescent moon twisted his mouth. In this expression, the dreaming Peter read one thing and one thing only: death. Flagg said only one word as he leaned forward and blew upon the brightly glowing object, which whiffed out like a candle when the magician's breath touched it. Only one word, but one was enough. The word from Flagg's mouth was Peter's own name, uttered in tones of angry discovery.

The night before, Saturday night, there had been a fairy-ring around the moon. The Lesser Warders thought it would soon snow. Examining the sky this afternoon, Peter knew they were right. It was his father who had taught Peter to read the weather and, standing at the window, Peter felt a pang of sadness . . . and a renewed spark of cold, quiet anger . . . the need to make things right again.

I'll make my try under cover of darkness and under cover of storm, he thought. *There'll even be a bit of snow to cushion my fall.* He had to grin at that idea – three inches of light, powdery snow between him and the cobbles would do precious little one way or the other. Either his perilously thin rope would hold . . . or it would break. Assuming it held, he would take the drop. And his legs would either take the impact . . . or they wouldn't.

And if they do take it, where will you go on them? a little voice whispered. *Any who might have shielded you or helped you . . . Ben Staad, for instance . . . have long since been driven from the castle keep . . . from the very Kingdom itself, for all you know.*

He would trust to luck, then. King's luck. It was a thing his father had often talked about. *There are lucky Kings and unlucky. But you'll be your own King and you'll have your own luck. M'self, I think you'll be very lucky.*

He had been King of Delain – at least in his own heart – for five years now, and he thought his luck had been the kind which the Staad family, with its famous bad luck, would have understood. But perhaps tonight would make up for all.

His rope, his legs, his luck. Either all would hold or all would break, quite possibly at the same time. No matter. Poor as it had been, he would trust to his luck.

'Tonight,' he murmured, turning from the window . . . but something happened at supper which changed his mind.

90

It took Peyna and Arlen all day Tuesday to make the ten miles to the Reechul farm, and they were nearly done in when they arrived. Castle Delain was twice as far, but Dennis probably could have been knocking at the West Gate – if he had actually been mad enough to do such a thing – by two that afternoon, in spite of his long walk the day before. Such is the difference, of course, between young men and old men. But what he *could* have done really didn't matter, because Peyna had been very clear in his instructions (especially for a man who claimed not to have the slightest idea of what he was doing), and Dennis meant to follow them to the letter. As a result, it would be some time yet before he entered the castle.

After covering not quite half the distance, he began to look for a place where he could hole up for the next few days. So far he had met no one on the road, but noon had passed and soon there would be people returning from the castle market. Dennis wanted no one to see him and mark him. He was, after all, supposed to be home, sick in bed. He did not have to look long before he found a place that suited him well enough. It was a deserted farmstead, once well kept but now beginning to fall into ruin. Thanks to Thomas the Tax-Bringer, there were many such places on the roads leading to the castle keep.

Dennis remained there until late Saturday afternoon – four days in all. Ben Staad and Naomi were already on their way back from the Far Forests to Peyna's farm by then, Naomi pushing her team of huskies for all they were worth. The knowledge would have eased Dennis a bit if he had known – but of course he did not, and he was lonely.

There was no food at all upstairs, but in the cellar he found a few potatoes and handful of turnips. He ate the potatoes (Dennis hated turnips, always had, and always would), using his knife to cut out the rotten places – which meant he cut away three-fourths of every potato. He was left with a handful of white globes the size of pigeons' eggs. He ate a few, looked toward the turnips in the vegetable bin, and sighed. Like them (he didn't) or hate them (he did), he supposed he would be reduced to eating them by Friday or so.

If I'm hungry enough, Dennis thought hopefully, *maybe they'll taste good. Maybe I'll just gobble those old turnips up and beg for more!*

He finally did have to eat a number of them, although he managed to hold out until Saturday noon. By then, they actually had begun to *look* good, but as hungry as he was, they still *tasted* terrible.

Dennis, who suspected the days ahead might be very hard, ate them anyway.

91

Dennis also found an old pair of snowshoes in the basement. The straps were far too large, but he had plenty of time to shorten them. The lacings had begun to rot, and there was nothing Dennis could do about that, but he thought they would serve the purpose. He wouldn't need them for long.

He slept in the cellar, fearing surprise, but during the daylight hours of those four long days, Dennis spent most of his time in the parlour of the deserted farmstead, watching the traffic pass to and fro – what little there was began around three o' the clock and had mostly ceased by five, when early-winter shadows began to cover the land. The parlour was a sad, empty place. Once it had been a cheery spot in which the family had gathered to discuss the day just done. Now it belonged only to the mice . . . and to Dennis, of course.

Peyna, after hearing Dennis declare that he could read and write 'pretty well for a fellow in service' and seeing him draw his Great Letters (this had been over breakfast on Tuesday – the last real meal Dennis had had since his own lunch on Monday, a meal he looked back on with understandable nostalgia), had provided him with several sheets of paper and a lead pencil. And during most of the hours he spent in the deserted house, Dennis laboured earnestly over a note. He wrote, scratched out, rewrote, frowned horribly as he reread, scratched his head, resharpened his pencil with his knife, and wrote again. He was ashamed of his spelling, and terrified he would forget some crucial thing Peyna had told him to put in. There were several times, times when his poor frazzled brain could make no more progress, when he wished Peyna had stayed up an hour longer on the night Dennis had come and written his own damned note, or called it aloud to Arlen. Most times, however, he was glad of the job. He had worked hard his whole life, and idleness made him nervous and uneasy. He would rather have worked his sturdy young man's body than his not-so-sturdy young man's brains, but work was work, and he was glad to have it.

By Saturday noon, he had a letter he was pretty well satisfied with (which was good, since he had worked his way down to the final two sheets of notepaper). He looked at it with some admiration. It covered both sides of the paper, and was by far the longest thing he had ever written. He folded it to the size of a medicine tablet, and then peeked out the sitting-room window, waiting impatiently for it to be dark enough to leave. Peter saw the gathering clouds from his own poor sitting room atop the Needle, Dennis from the sitting room of this deserted house; but both had been taught by their fathers – one a King and the other a butler to that King – to read the sky, and Dennis also thought there would be snow tomorrow.

By four, the long, blue shadow of the house had begun to creep out from the foundations, and Dennis no longer felt so eager to go. It was danger ahead . . . deadly danger. He was to go where Flagg was perhaps even now brooding long over his infernal magics, perhaps even now checking upon a certain sick butler. But how he felt did not really matter, and he knew it – the time had come to do his duty, and as every butler in his family line had done for centuries and centuries, Dennis would do his best.

He left the house in the bleak sunset hour, donned the snowshoes, and struck off across the field on a direct line toward the castle keep. The idea of wolves occurred to his uneasy mind, and he could only hope there would be none, and if there were, that they would leave him alone. He hadn't the slightest idea that Peter had decided to make his dangerous escape attempt the following night, but like Peyna – and Peter himself – he felt a need to hurry; it seemed to him that there were mackerel-scale clouds laid across his heart as well as the sky.

As he trudged through the snow-desolate fields, Dennis's thoughts turned to how he might enter the castle without being seen and challenged. He thought he knew how it could be done . . . if, that was, Flagg did not smell him.

He had no more than thought the magician's name when a wolf howled somewhere out in the still white wastes. In a dark room below the castle, Flagg's own sitting room, the magician sat bolt upright suddenly in his chair, where he had fallen asleep with a book of arcane lore open on his stomach.

'Who speaks the name of Flagg?' the magician whispered, and the two-headed parrot shrieked.

Standing in the centre of a long and desolate field of white, Dennis heard that voice, as dry and scabrous as a spider's scuttle, in his own head. He paused, his breath indrawn and held. When he finally let it go, it plumed frosty from his mouth. He was cold all over, but hot drops of sweat stood out on his forehead.

From his feet he heard dry snapping noises – *Pouck! Pouck! Pouck!* – as several of the snowshoes' rotted cross-lacings let go.

The wolf howled in the silence. It was a hungry, heartless sound.

'No one,' Flagg muttered in the sitting room of his dark apartments. He was rarely sick – could remember being sick only three or four times in all of his long life – but he had caught a bad cold in the north, sleeping on the frozen ground, and although he was improving, he was still not well.

'No one. A dream. That's all.'

He took the book from his lap, closed it, and set it on a side table – the surface of this table had been handsomely dressed in human skin – and settled back in his chair. Soon he slept again.

In the snowy fields west of the castle, Dennis slowly relaxed. A single drop of stinging sweat ran into his eye and he wiped it away absently. He had thought of Flagg . . . and somehow Flagg had *heard* him. But now the dark shadow of the magician's thought had passed over him, as the shadow of a hawk may pass over a crouching rabbit. Dennis let out a long, shaky sigh. His legs felt weak. He would try – oh, with all his heart he would try – to think of the magician no more. But as the night came on and the moon with its ghostly fairy-ring rose in the sky, that was a thing easier resolved upon than done.

92

At eight of the clock, Dennis left the fields and entered the King's Preserves. He knew them well enough. He had been a squireen for Brandon when his da' buttled the old King in the fields of the hunt, and Roland had come here often, even in his old age. Thomas came less often, but on the few occasions when the boy King did come, Dennis had, of course, been required to come with him. Soon he struck on a trail he knew, and just before midnight he reached the verge of this toy forest.

He stood behind a tree, looking out at the castle wall. It was half a mile away over open, snow-covered ground. The moon was still shining, and Dennis was all too aware of the sentries who walked the castle parapet. He would have to wait until Prince Ailon had driven his silvery chariot over the edge of the world before crossing that open space. Even then he would be horribly exposed. He had known from the first that this would be the riskiest part of the whole adventure. Parting from Peyna and Arlen, with the good sun shining down, the risk had seemed acceptable. Now it seemed utterly mad.

Go back, a cowardly voice inside him begged, but Dennis knew he couldn't. His father had laid a charge on him, and if the gods meant him to die trying to fulfil it, then he would die.

Faint and yet clear, like a voice heard in a dream, came the call of the Crier, drifting out to him from the castle's central tower: '*Twelve o'clock and all's well . . .*'

Nothing's well, Dennis thought miserably. *Not one single thing*. He drew his thin coat more tightly around him and began the long job of waiting down the moon.

Eventually it left the sky, and Dennis knew he had to move. Time had grown short. He stood, said a brief prayer to his gods, and began to walk across the open space as rapidly as he could, expecting a hail of *Who goes there?* from the castle walls at every moment. The hail did not come. The clouds had thickened across the night sky. All below the castle wall was one dark shadow. In less than ten minutes, Dennis had reached the edge of the moat. He sat on its low bank, the snow crunching under his bottom, and took the snowshoes off. He slid down onto the moat itself, which was frozen and covered with more snow.

Dennis's thundering heart slowed down. He was in the shadow of the bulking castle wall now, and would not be seen unless a sentry happened to look straight down, and most probably not even then.

Dennis was careful not to go all the way across the moat – not yet – because the ice close to the castle wall would be rotted and thin. He knew why this was so; the reason for the thin ice and the unpleasant smell here and the mossy wetness on the huge stones of the outer wall was his hope of entering the castle secretly. He moved carefully to the left, ears listening for the noise of running water.

At last he heard it, and looked up. There, at eye

height, was a round black hole in the solid castle wall. Fluid ran from it in listless streams. It was a sewer outflow pipe.

'Now for it,' Dennis muttered. He drew back five paces, ran, and leaped. As he did, he felt the ice, rotted by the constant outflow of warm waste from the pipe, give under his feet. Then he was clinging to the mossy lip of the pipe. It was slick, and he had to clutch hard to keep from falling. He pulled himself up, digging for purchase with his feet, and finally yanked himself inside. He paused for a moment, trying to get his breath back, then began to crawl along the pipe, which slanted steadily upward. He and several of his playmates had found these pipes when they were children, and had been quickly warned off by their parents, partly because they might become lost, mostly because of the sewer rats. Still, Dennis thought he knew where he would come out.

An hour hater, in a deserted corridor of the castle's east wing, a sewer grating moved – was still – then moved again. It was shoved partway aside, and a few moments later a very dirty (and very smelly) butler named Dennis pulled himself out of a hole in the floor and lay panting on the cold cobbles. He could have used a longer rest, but someone might come along, even at this unearthly hour. So he replaced the grating and looked around.

He did not recognize the hallway at once, but this in no way upset him. He started down it toward the T-intersection at the far end. At least, he reflected, there had been no rats in the warren of sewer pipes below the castle. That had been a great relief. He had been prepared for them, not just because of the gruesome tales his da' had told him, but because there *had* been rats on a few occasions when he and his mates had ventured with fearful screeches of laughter down into the pipes as children – the rats had been part of the scary, dare-you adventure of it.

Probably there were just a few mice, and your memory's exaggerated them into rats, Dennis thought now. This was not the truth, but Dennis would never know it. His memory of the rats in the sewers was a true one. The pipes had been infested with great, disease-bearing rodents since time out of mind. It had only been for the last five years that they had ceased to teem in the sewers. They had been wiped out by Flagg. The magician had rid himself of both a piece of stone and his own dagger by means of a sewer grating similar to the one from which Dennis had emerged on this early Sunday morning. He had rid himself of them, of course, because there were a few flecks of the deadly green Dragon Sand on each. The fumes from those few grains had killed the rats, burning many of them alive even as they paddled through the scummy water in the pipes, suffocating all the others before they could flee. Five years later, the rats had still not come back, although most of the poisonous fumes had dissipated. Most, but not all. If Dennis had entered one of the sewer pipes a bit closer to Flagg's apartments, he might well have died himself. Perhaps it was luck that saved him, or fate, or those gods he prayed to; I'll not take a stand on the matter. I tell tales, not tea leaves, and on the subject of Dennis's survival, I leave you to your own conclusions.

He reached the junction, peered around the corner, and saw a sleepy young Guard o' the Watch passing farther up the way. Dennis pulled back. His heart was thumping hard again, but he was satisfied – he knew where he was. When he looked back, the guard was gone.

Dennis moved quickly, up this corridor, down that flight of stairs, across t'other gallery. He moved with speedy sure-footedness, for he had spent his whole life in the castle. He knew it well enough, certainly, to find his way from the east wing, where he had come out of the sewers, to the lower west wing, where the napkins were stored.

But because he dared not be seen – not by anyone – Dennis went by the most obscure corridors he knew, and at the sound of every footfall (either real or imagined, and I do think quite a few of them were imagined), he withdrew into the nearest cranny or niche. In the end, it took him over an hour.

He thought he had never been so hungry in his life.

Never mind your cussed belly now, Dennis – take care of your master first, your belly later.

He was standing far back in a shadowy doorway. Faintly, he heard the Crier call four o'clock. He was about to move forward when slow, echoing footfalls came down the hallway . . . a clank of steel-and-scabbard – a creak of leather leggings.

Dennis pushed himself farther back into the shadows, sweating.

A Guard o' the Watch paused just in front of the thinly shadowed doorway where Dennis hid. The fellow stood for a moment rooting in his nose with his little finger, and then leaned over to blow a stream of snot between his knuckles. Dennis could have reached out and touched him, and felt certain that any moment the guard would turn . . . his eyes would widen . . . he would draw his shortsword . . . and that would be the end of Dennis, son of Brandon.

Please, Dennis's frozen mind whispered. *Please, oh, please* –

He could smell the guard, could smell the old wine and burned meat on his breath, and the sour sweat coming out of his skin.

The guard started to move on . . . Dennis began to relax . . . then the guard stopped and began rooting in his nose again. Dennis could have screamed.

'I have a girrul name of Marchy-Marchy-Melda,' the guard began to sing in a low-pitched, droning voice, rooting in his nose all the while. He produced a large green something, examined it thoughtfully, and flicked it onto the wall. *Splat.* 'She's got a sister named Es-a-merelda . . . I would sail the seven seas . . . Just to kiss her dimply knees! Tootie-sing-tay, sing-tiy, and pass me a bucket-da wine.'

Something exceedingly horrible was now happening to Dennis. His nose had begun to itch and tickle in a way which was unmistakable. Very soon he would sneeze.

Go! he screamed in his mind. *Oh, why don't you go, you stupid fool?*

But the guard seemed to have no intentions of going. He had apparently struck a rich lode up in the left nostril, and he meant to mine it.

'I have a girrul name of Darchy-Darchy-Darla. . . . She's got a sister named Red Headed Carla. . . . I would take a thousand sips . . . From her pretty pretty lips. . . . Tootie-sing-tay, sing-tiy, and pass me a bucket-da wine.'

I'll hit you over the HEAD *with a bucket of wine, you fool!* Dennis thought. *Move* ON*!!* The itch in his nose grew steadily worse, but he did not dare even touch it, for fear the guard would see the movement from the corner of his eye.

The guard frowned, bent over, blew his nose between his knuckles again, and finally moved on, still singing his droning song. He was barely out of sight before Dennis threw his arm over his own nose and mouth and sneezed into the crook of his elbow. He waited for the clash of metal as the guard drew his sword and whirled back, but the fellow was half asleep, and still half drunk from whatever party he had been at before his tour of duty commenced. Once, Dennis knew, such a slovenly creature would have been quickly discovered and sent to the farthest reaches of the Kingdom, but times had changed. There was a click of a latch, the *scree-eeee* of hinges as a door was drawn open, and then it boomed closed, cutting off the guard's song just as he reached the chorus again. Dennis sagged back in his niche for a moment, eyes closed, cheeks and forehead on fire, his feet twin blocks of ice.

For a few minutes there I didn't think of my belly at all! he thought, and then had to slam both hands over his mouth to stifle a giggle.

He peeked out of his hiding place, saw no one about, and moved to a doorway down the corridor and on his right. He knew this doorway very well, although the empty rocker and the needlework case outside it were new to him. The door led to the room where all of those napkins had been stored since the time of Kyla the Good. It had never been locked before, and was not now. Old napkins were apparently not considered worth locking up. He peered inside, hoping that his answer to Peyna's key question still held true.

Standing there in the road on that bright morning five days ago, Peyna had asked him this: *Do you know when they take fresh stores of napkins to the Needle, Dennis?*

This seemed like a simple question indeed to Dennis, but you may have noticed that all questions seem simple if you know the answers, and most horribly difficult if you don't. That Dennis knew the answer to this one was a testament to his honesty and honour, although those traits were so deeply ingrained in his character that he would have been surprised if someone had told him this. He had taken money – Anders Peyna's money, in fact – from Ben Staad to make sure those napkins were delivered. Only a guilder, true, but money was money and pay was pay. He had felt honour-bound to make sure, from time to time, that the service was continuing.

He told Peyna about the big storeroom (Peyna was flabbergasted to hear of it) and how each Saturday night around seven o'clock, a maid took twenty-one napkins, shook then, ironed them, folded them, and set them in a stack on a small wheeled cart. This cart stood just inside the room's doorway. Early on Sunday morning – at six o'clock, less than two hours from right now – a servant boy would pull the cart to the Plaza of the Needle. He would rap at the bolted door at the base of the ugly stone tower, and one of the Lesser Warders would pull the cart inside and place the napkins on a table, where they would be doled out, meal by meal, through the week.

Peyna had been satisfied.

Dennis now hurried forward, feeling inside his shirt for the note he had written at the farmhouse. He had a bad moment or two when he couldn't find it, but then his fingers closed over it and he sighed with relief. It had only slipped a little to one side.

He lifted the Sunday breakfast napkin. Sunday lunch. For a moment he almost passed over Sunday supper as well, and if he had done that, my tale would have had a very different ending – better or worse I cannot say, but surely different. In the end, however, Dennis decided three napkins deep was safe enough. He had found a pin in a crack between two boards in the farmhouse living room and had nipped it into one shoulder strap of the rough linsey camisole he wore as underwear (and if he had been thinking a little better, he would have nipped the note to his underwear with it in the bargain, and spared himself that bad moment, but as I may have told you, Dennis's brains were sometimes a little lacking). Now he retrieved the pin and carefully attached the note to an inner fold of the napkin.

'Let it find you, Peter,' he murmured in the ghostly silence of that storeroom, piled high with napkins made in another age. 'Let it find you, my King.'

Dennis knew he must lie low now. The castle would be waking up soon; stableboys would be stumbling out to the barns, washerwomen would be moving to the laundries, cook's apprentices would be stumbling puffy-eyed and sleepy to their fires (thinking of the kitchens made Dennis's belly rumble anew – by now even the hateful turnips would have tasted quite nice – but food, he reckoned, would have to wait).

He worked his way farther back into the big room. The stacks were so high, the ways so zigzagging and irregular, that it was like working his way into a maze. The napkins gave off a sweet, dry, cottony smell. He finally reached one of the far corners, and here he reckoned he could be safe. He overspilled a stack of the napkins, spread them out, and took another handful for a pillow.

It was by far the most luxurious mattress he had ever lain upon and, hungry as he was, he needed sleep much more than food after his long walk and the frights of the night. He was asleep in no time at all, and he was troubled by no dreams. We leave him now, with the first part of his job well and bravely accomplished. We will leave him turned upon his side, right hand curled under his right cheek, sleeping on a bed of royal napkins. And I would like to make a wish for you, Reader – that your sleep this night be as sweet and as blameless as his was all that day.

94

'**O**n Saturday night, as Dennis was standing in the horror of that wolf's howl and feeling the
shade of Flagg's thought pass over him, Ben Staad and
Naomi Reechul were encamped in a snowy hollow
thirty miles north of Peyna's farm . . . or what had
been Peyna's farm before Dennis showed up with his
story of a King who walked and talked in his sleep.

They had made the sort of rough camp people
make when they mean to spend only a few hours and
then push on. Naomi had seen to her beloved huskies
while Ben put up a small tent and built a roaring fire.

Shortly, Naomi joined him at the fire and
cooked deer meat. They ate in silence, and then
Naomi went to check the dogs again. All were sleeping except for Frisky, her favourite. Frisky looked at
her with almost human eyes, and licked her hand.

'A good pull today, m'dear,' Naomi said.
'Sleep, now. Catch a moon rabbit.'

Frisky obediently put her head down on her
paws. Naomi smiled and went back to the fire. Ben sat
before it, his knees pulled up to his chest and his arms
around them. His face was sombre and thoughtful.

'Snow's coming.'

'I can read the clouds as well as you, Ben Staad.
And the fairies have made a ring around Prince
Ailon's head.'

Ben glanced at the moon and nodded. Then he
looked back at the fire. 'I'm worried. I've had dreams
of . . . well, dreams of one it's better not to name.'

She lit a cigar. She offered the little package, which was wrapped in muslin to prevent drying, to Ben, who shook his head.

'I've had the same dreams, I think,' she said. She tried to make her voice casual, but was betrayed by a slight tremor.

He stared around at her, eyes wide.

'Aye,' she said, as if he had asked. 'In them, he looks into some bright glowing thing and speaks Peter's name. I've never been one of your skittish little girls who screeches at the sight of a mouse or a spider in its web, but I wake from that dream wanting to scream aloud.'

She looked both ashamed and defiant.

'How many nights have you had it?'

'Two.'

'I've had it four a-running. Mine's just the same as yours. And you needn't look like I'm going to laugh at you or call you Little Nell Weeping at the Well. I also wake up wanting to scream.'

'This bright thing . . . at the end of my dreams, he seems to blow it out. Is it a candle, do you think?'

'No. You know it's not.'

She nodded.

Ben considered. 'Something far more dangerous than a candle, I think . . . I'll take that cigar you offered, if I may.'

She gave him one. He lit it from the fire. They sat a while in silence, watching the sparks rise toward the dark wind which trawled nets of powdery field snow through the sky. Like the light in the dream they'd shared, the sparks blew out. The night seemed very black. Ben could smell snow in that wind. A great deal of snow, he thought.

Naomi seemed to read his thought. 'I think such a storm as the old folks tell about may be on the way. What do you think?'

'The same.'

With a hesitation utterly unlike her usual forth-right manner, Naomi asked: 'What does the dream mean, Ben?'

He shook his head. 'I can't tell. Danger to Peter, that much is clear. If it means anything else – anything I can ken – it's that we must hurry.' He looked at her with an urgent directness that made her heart speed up. 'Can we reach Peyna's farm tomorrow, do you think?'

'We should be able to. No one but the gods can say that a dog won't break a leg or that a killer bear who can't sleep his winter sleep won't come out of the woods and kill us all, but aye . . . we *should* be able to. I exchanged all the dogs I used on the run up, except for Frisky, and Frisky's almost tireless. If the snow comes early it'll slow us down, but I think it will hold off . . . and off . . . and for every hour it does, it'll be that much worse when it finally comes. Or so I think. But if it *does* hold off, and if we take turns jumping off the sledge and running alongside, I think we can make it. But what can we do except sit there, unless your friend the butler returns?'

'I don't know.' Ben sighed and rubbed a hand over his face. What good, indeed? Whatever it was the dreams foretold, it would happen at the castle, not at the farm. Peyna had sent Dennis to the castle, but how did Dennis mean to get in? Ben didn't know, because

Dennis hadn't told Peyna. And if Dennis did gain entry undetected, where would he hide? There were a thousand possible places. Except . . .

'Ben!'

'What?' Jerked out of his thoughts, he turned to her.

'What did you think of just now?'

'Nothing.'

'Yes, *something*. Your eyes gleamed.'

'Did they? I must have been thinking of pies. It's time you and I turned in. We'll want to be off at first light.'

But in the tent, Ben Staad lay awake long after Naomi had gone to sleep. There were a thousand places in the castle to hide, yes. But he could think of two rather special ones. He thought he might well find Dennis in one . . . or the other.

At last he fell asleep . . .

. . . and dreamed of Flagg.

95

Peter began that Sunday as he always did, with his exercises and a prayer.

He had awakened feeling fresh and ready. After a quick look at the sky to gauge the progress of the coming storm, he ate his breakfast.

And, of course, he used his napkin.

96

By Sunday noon, everyone in Delain had come out of his or her house at least once to look worriedly toward the north. Everyone agreed that the storm, when it came, would be one to tell stories about in later years. The clouds rolling in were a dull grey, the colour of wolf pelts. Temperatures rose until the icicles hanging beneath the eaves of the alleys began to drip for the first time in weeks, but the old-timers told each other (and anyone else who would listen) that they were not fooled. The temperature would plummet quickly, and hours later – perhaps two, perhaps four – the snow would begin. And, they said, it might fall for days.

By three o'clock that afternoon, those farmers of the Inner Baronies fortunate enough to still have livestock to watch out for had gotten their animals into the barns. The cows went mooing their displeasure; the snow had melted enough for them to crop last fall's dry grasses for the first time in months. Yosef, older, greyer, but still lively enough at seventy-two, saw that all the King's horses were stabled. Presumably there was someone else to take care of all the King's men. Wives took advantage of the mild temperatures to attempt to dry sheets which otherwise simply would have frozen on the lines, and then took them in as the daylight lowered toward an early, storm-coloured dark. They were disappointed; their washing had not dried. There was too much moisture in the air.

Animals were skittish. People were nervous. Wise meadhouse keepers would not open their doors. They had observed the falling mercury in their barometric glasses, and long experience had taught them that low air pressure makes men quick to fight.

Delain battened down for the coming storm, and everyone waited.

97

Ben and Naomi took turns running beside the sledge. They reached the Peyna farm at two o'clock that Sunday afternoon – at about the same time Dennis was stirring awake on his mattress of royal napkins and Peter was beginning his meagre lunch.

Naomi looked beautiful indeed – the flush of her exercise had coloured her tanned cheeks the pretty dusky red of autumn roses. As the sledge pulled into Peyna's yard, the dogs barking wildly, she turned her laughing face to Ben.

'A record run, by the gods!' she cried. 'We've made it three – no, *four!* – hours earlier than I would have believed when we left! And not one dog has burst its heart! *Aiy,* Frisky! *Aiy!* Good dog!'

Frisky, a huge black-and-white Anduan husky with grey-green eyes, was at the head of the tether. She was jumping in the air, straining against the traces. Naomi unhooked her and danced with her in the snow. It was a curious waltz, both graceful and barbaric. Dog and mistress seemed to laugh at each other in a powerful shared affection. Some of the other dogs were lying down on their sides now, panting hard, obviously exhausted, but neither Frisky nor Naomi seemed even slightly winded.

'*Aiy*, Frisky! *Aiy*, my love! Good dog! You've led a famous chase!'

'But for what?' Ben asked glumly.

She released Frisky's paws and turned to him, angry . . . but the dejection on his face robbed her of her anger. He was looking toward the house. She followed his gaze and understood. They were here, yes, but where was *here*? An empty farmhouse, that was all. What in the world had they come so far and so fast *for*? The house would have been just as empty an hour . . . two hours . . . four hours from now. Peyna and Arlen were in the north, Dennis somewhere in the depths of the castle. Or in a prison cell or a coffin awaiting burial, if he had been caught.

She went to Ben and put a hesitant hand on his shoulder. 'Don't feel so bad,' she said. 'We've done all we could do.'

'Have we?' he asked. 'I wonder.' He paused, and sighed deeply. He had taken off his knitted cap and his golden hair gleamed mellowly in the dull afternoon light. 'I'm sorry, Naomi. I don't mean to snap at you. You and your dogs have done wonders. It's just that I feel we're very far from where we could give any real aid. I feel helpless.'

She looked at him, sighed, and nodded.

'Well,' he said, 'let's go in. Maybe there'll be

some sign of what we're to do next. We'll at least be out of the blow when it comes.'

There were no clues inside. It was just a big, draughty, empty farmhouse that had been quit in a hurry. Ben prowled restlessly from room to room and found nothing at all. After an hour, he collapsed unhappily beside Naomi in the sitting room . . . in the very chair where Anders Peyna had sat when he listened to Dennis's incredible story.

'If only there was a way to track him,' Ben said.

He looked up to see her staring at him, her eyes bright and round and full of excitement.

'There might be!' she said. 'If the snow holds off –'

'What are you talking about?'

'*Frisky!*' she cried. 'Don't you see? *Frisky* can track him! She has the keenest nose of any dog I've ever known!'

'The scent would be days old,' he said, shaking his head. 'Even the greatest tracking dog that ever lived could not . . .'

'Frisky may *be* the greatest tracking dog that ever lived,' Naomi replied, laughing. 'And tracking in winter's not like tracking in summer, Ben Staad. In summer, trace dies quickly . . . it rots, my da' says, and there are a hundred other traces to cover the one the dog seeks. Not just of other people and other animals, but of grasses and warm winds, even the smells that come on running water. But in the winter, trace *lasts*. If we had something that belonged to this Dennis . . . something that carried his scent . . .'

'What about the rest of your team?' Ben asked.

'I should open the shed over there' – she pointed at it – 'and leave my bedroll in it. If I show them where it is and then free them, they'll be able to forage for their own food – rabbits and such – and they'll also know where to come for shelter.'

'They won't follow us?'

'Not if they're told not to.'

'You can do that?' He looked at her with some awe.

'No,' Naomi said matter-of-factly. 'I don't speak Dog. Nor does Frisky speak Human, but she understands it. If I tell Frisky, she'll tell the others. They'll hunt what they need, but they won't range far enough to lose the scent of my bedroll, not with the storm coming. And when it starts, they'll go to shelter. It won't matter if their bellies are hungry or full.'

'And if we had something that belonged to this boy Dennis, you really believe Frisky could track him?'

'Aye.'

Ben looked at her long and thoughtfully. Dennis had left this farm on Tuesday; it was now Sunday. He didn't believe any scent could last that long. But there *was* something in the house which would bear Dennis's scent, and perhaps even a fool's errand would be better than only sitting here. It was the pointless *sitting* more than anything else that grated on him, the hours ahead when things of grave importance might be happening elsewhere, while they sat and twiddled their thumbs here. Under other circumstances, the possibility of being snowbound with a girl as beautiful as Naomi would have delighted him, but not while a kingdom might be won and lost twenty miles to the east . . . and his best friend might be living or dying with only that confounded butler to help him.

'Well?' she asked eagerly 'What do you think?'

'I think it's crazy,' he said, 'but worth a try.'

She grinned. 'Do we have something with his scent strong upon it?'

'We do,' he said, getting up. 'Bring your dog in, Naomi, and lead her upstairs. To the attic.'

Although most humans don't know it, scents are like colours to dogs. Faint scents have faint colours, like pastels washed out by time. Clear scents have clear colours. Some dogs have weak noses, and they read scents the way humans with poor eyes see colours, believing this delicate blue may actually be a grey, or that dark brown may actually be a black. Frisky's nose, on the other hand, was like the eye-sight of a man with the gaze of a hawk, and the scent in the attic where Dennis had slept was very strong and very clear (it may have helped that Dennis had been some days without a bath). Frisky sniffed the hay, then sniffed the blanket THE GIRL held for her. She scented Arlen upon it, but disregarded the scent; it was weaker, and not at all the scent she had found on the hay. Arlen's smell was lemony and tired, and

Frisky knew at once that it was the smell of an old man. Dennis's smell was more exciting and vital. To Frisky's nose, it was the electric blue of a summer lightning stroke.

She barked to show that she knew this smell and had put it safely away in her library of scents.

'All right, good girl,' THE TALL-BOY said. 'Can you follow it?'

'She'll follow it,' THE GIRL said confidently. 'Let's go.'

'It'll be dark in an hour.'

'That's so,' THE GIRL said, and then grinned. When THE GIRL grinned that way, Frisky thought her heart might just burst with love of her. 'But it isn't her *eyes* that we want, is it?'

THE TALL-BOY smiled. 'I guess not,' he said. 'You know, I must be crazy, but I think we're going to pick up these cards and play them.'

'Course we are,' she said. 'Come on, Ben. Let's use what little daylight's left – it'll be dark soon enough.'

Frisky, her nose full of that bright-blue scent, barked eagerly.

99

Peter's supper came promptly at six o'clock that Sunday night. The storm clouds hung heavy over Delain and the temperature had begun to drop, but the winds hadn't yet begun to blow and not a snowflake had fallen. On the far side of the Plaza, shivering in stolen cook-boy's whites, Dennis stood anxiously, drawn back into the deepest shadow he could find, staring at the single square of pale-yellow light at the top of the Needle – Peter's candle.

Peter, of course, knew nothing of Dennis's vigil – he was filled with the wonder of the idea that, live or die, this would be the last meal he would ever eat in this damned prison cell. It was just more tough, salty meat, half-rotted potatoes, and watery ale, but he would eat it all. For the last three weeks he had eaten little and spent all the waking time he did not spend working at the tiny loom exercising, readying his body. Today, however, he had eaten everything brought to him. He would need all his strength tonight.

What will happen to me? he wondered again, sitting down at the little table and grasping the napkin that lay over his meal. *Where exactly will I go? Who will take me in? Anyone? All men, it's said, must trust in the gods . . . but Peter, you are trusting so much it's ridiculous.*

Stop. What'll be is what'll be. Now eat, and think no more of –

But that was where his restless thoughts broke off, because as he shook the napkin out, he felt a small stab, like the prick of a nettle.

Frowning, he looked down and saw that a tiny bead of blood had seeped up on the ball of his right forefinger. Peter's first thought was of Flagg. In the fairy tales, it was always a needle that bore the poison. Perhaps he had been poisoned now, by

Flagg. That was his first thought, and not such a silly one, at that. After all, Flagg had used poison before.

Peter picked the napkin up, saw a tiny folded object with black, smudgy marks on it . . . and flipped the napkin back down at once. His face remained calm and peaceful, giving away none of the wild excitement that had burst up inside him at the sight of the note pinned inside the napkin.

He glanced casually towards the door, suddenly afraid he would see one of the Lesser Warders – or Beson himself – staring suspiciously in at him. But there was no one. The prince had been a great object of curiosity when he first came to the Needle, stared at as avidly as a rare fish is stared at in a collector's tank – some of them had even smuggled their lady-loves up to look at the murdering monster (and they would have been imprisoned for it themselves, if they had been caught). But Peter was a model pris-oner, and he had palled quickly. No one was looking at him now.

Peter forced himself to eat his entire meal, although he no longer wanted it. He wanted to take not the slightest chance of rousing suspicions – now more than ever. He had no idea who the note might be from, or what it might say, or why it had aroused such a fever in him. But for a note to come now, only hours before he planned to make his try to escape, seemed an omen. But of what?

When his meal was finally eaten, he glanced towards the door again, made sure the spyhole was closed, and walked to his bedrom with his napkin still held casually in one hand, almost as if he had forgotten that he held it at all. In the bedroom, he unpinned the note (his hands were trembling so badly he pricked himself again) and unfolded it. It was written closely on both sides in letters which were rusty and a bit childish, but readable enough. His glance went first to the signature . . . and his eyes widened. The note was signed *Dennis – your Friend and Servant For-Ever*.

'Dennis?' Peter muttered, so flabbergasted he was unaware that he had whispered aloud. '*Dennis?*'

He turned back then, and the letter's opening was enough to shock his heartbeat into a fast drum-roll. The salutation was *My King*.

100

My King,
As you may Noe, for the last 5 Yeres I have Buttled in Service to your Brother, Thomas. In just this last Week I have found out that You did not Murther you Father Roland the Good. I Noe who Did, and Thomas Noes as Well. You would Noe the name of this Black Killer if I dared to Rite it, but I do Not. I went to Peyna. Peyna has gone to join the Exiles with his Butler, Orlon. He has commanded I come to the Castle, and Rite to you this note. Peyna says that the Exiles may soon become Rebels and this must not Be. He thinks you may have some sort of Plan, but what he Noes Not. He commands that I be of Service to You, and my Da commanded it too, before He Dyed, and my Heart commands it, for our Famly has

always served the King and you are the Right King. If you have a Plan, I will aid you in Any Way I can, even if it means my Death. As you read this, I am across the Platza in the shadows looking at the Needle where you are Pent Up. If you have a Plan, come I pray You and stand at the Window. If You have something on which You can rite, then throe down a Note and I will try to retreeve It late this Night. Wave twyce if you will try this idea.

Your friend Ben is with the Exiles. Peyna said He would send Him. I Noe were He (Ben) will be. If You say I should fetch Him (Ben) I can, in a Day. Or perhaps Two if there is Snoe. I Noe that throwing down a Note might be Riskee, but I feel Time is short. Peyna feels the Same Way. I will be Watching and Praying.

Dennis

Your Friend and Servant For-Ever

101

It was a long time before Peter would put his whirling thoughts in order. His mind kept circling back to one question: What had Dennis seen to change his mind so radically and completely? What, in the names of all the gods, could it have been?

Little by little he came to realize that it didn't matter – Dennis had seen *something*, and that was enough.

Peyna. Dennis had gone to Peyna, and Peyna

had sensed . . . well, the old fox had sensed *some-thing. He thinks you may have some sort of Plan, but what he Noes Not.* Old fox indeed. He had not forgotten Peter's request for the doll's house, and the napkins. He hadn't known exactly what those things meant, but he had sensed something in the wind. Aye, well and truly.

Then what was Peter to do?

Part of him – a very large part – wanted to go ahead just as he had planned. He had worked his courage up to this desperate adventure; now it was hard to let it go for nothing but more waiting. And there were the dreams, urging him on, as well.

You would Noe the name of this Black Killer if I dared to rite It, but I do Not. Peter knew just the same, of course, and it was that more than anything else that convinced him Dennis really had stumbled on to something. Peter felt that Flagg might soon awake to this new development – and he wanted to be gone before that happened.

Was a day too long to wait?

Perhaps. Perhaps not.

Peter was torn in an agony of indecision. Ben . . . Thomas . . . Flagg . . . Peyna . . . Dennis . . . they whirled in his brain like figures seen in a dream. What should he do?

In the end, it was the appearance of the note itself – not what was in it – that persuaded him. For it to come this way, pinned to a napkin on the very night he meant to try his rope made of napkins . . . it meant he should wait. But only for a night. Ben would not be able to help.

Could *Dennis* help him, though? What could he do?

And suddenly, in a flash of light, an idea came to him.

Peter had been sitting on his bed, hunched over the note, his brows furrowed. Now he straightened up, his eyes alight.

His eyes fell on the note again.

If You have something on which You can rite, then throe down a Note and I will try to retreeve It late this Night.

Yes, of course, he had something to write on. Not the napkin itself, because it might be missed. Not Dennis's note, either, because it was written on both sides, from side to side and top to bottom.

But Valera's parchment was not.

Peter went back into his sitting room. He glanced at the door and saw that the spyhole was closed. Dimly he could hear the warders at cards below. He crossed to the window and waved twice, hoping that Dennis was really out there somewhere, and could see him. He would just have to hope so.

Peter went back to the bedroom, pulled up the loose stone, and after some reaching and fumbling, retrieved the locket and the parchment. He turned the parchment over to the blank side . . . but what was he to do for ink?

After a moment the answer came to him. The same thing Valera had done, of course.

Peter worked at his thin straw mattress, and after some tugging opened a seam. The stuffing was of straw, and before long, he had found a number of good long stalks that would serve as pens. Then he opened the locket. It was in the shape of a heart, and the point at the bottom was sharp. Peter closed his eyes for a moment and said a brief prayer. Then he opened them and drew the point of the locket across his wrist. Blood welled up at once – much more than had come from the pinprick earlier. He dipped the first straw in his blood and began to write.

102

Standing in the cold darkness across the Plaza, Dennis saw Peter's shape come to the small window at the top of the Needle. He saw Peter raise his arms over his head and cross them twice. There would be a message, then. It doubled – no, trebled – his risk, but he was glad.

He settled in to wait, feeling numbness slowly creep over his feet and kill the feeling in them. The wait seemed very long. The Crier called ten . . . then eleven . . . finally twelve o' the clock. The clouds had hidden the moon, but the air seemed strangely light – another sign of a coming storm.

He was beginning to think that Peter must have forgotten him, or changed his mind, when that shape came to the window again. Dennis straightened up, wincing at a pain in his neck, which had been cocked upward for the last four hours. He thought he saw something arc out . . . and then Peter's shape left the high window. A moment later, the light up there was extinguished.

Dennis looked left and right, saw no one, took all of his courage in his hands, and ran out into the Plaza. He knew perfectly well that there might be someone – a more alert Guard o' the Watch than last night's tuneless singer, for instance – whom he *hadn't* seen, but there was nothing to be done about that. He was also gruesomely aware of all the men and women who had been beheaded not far from here. What if their ghosts were still around, lurking –?

But thinking about such things did no good, and so he tried to put them from his mind. Of more immediate concern was just finding the thing that Peter had thrown. The area at the foot of the Needle below Peter's window was a featureless white snow-field.

Feeling horribly exposed, Dennis began to cast about like an inept hunting dog. He wasn't sure what he had seen glimmering in the air – it had been there only for a second – but it had looked solid. That made sense; Peter would not have thrown a piece of paper, which might have fluttered anywhere. But what, and where was it?

As the seconds ticked by, turning into minutes, Dennis began to feel more and more frantic. He dropped to his hands and knees and began to crawl about, peering into footprints which had melted to the size of dragon prints earlier that day and which were now refreezing, hard and blue and shiny. Sweat coursed down his face. And he began to be devilled by a recurring idea – that a hand would fall on his shoulder, and when he turned he would see the grinning face of the King's magician inside his dark cowl.

A little late for hide and seek, isn't it, Dennis? Flagg would say, and although his grin would widen, his eyes would burn a baleful, hellish red. *What have you lost? Can I help you find it?*

Don't think his name! For the gods' sake, don't think his name!

But it was hard to stop. Where was it? Oh, where was it?

Back and forth Dennis crawled, his hands now as numb as his feet. Back and forth, back and forth. Where was it? Bad enough if *he* was unable to find it. Worse still if the snow held off until morning light and someone else did. Gods knew what it might say.

Dimly, he heard the Crier call one o' the clock. He was now covering ground he had already covered before, becoming more and more panicky.

Stop, Dennis. Stop, boy.

His da's voice, too clear in his head to be mistaken. Dennis had been on his hands and knees, his nose almost on the ground. Now he straightened up a little.

You're not SEEING anything anymore, boy. Stop and close your eyes for a moment. And when you open 'em, look around. Really look around.

Dennis closed his eyes tight and then opened them wide. This time, he looked around almost casually, scanning the whole snowy, tracked area around the foot of the Needle.

Nothing. Nothing at –

Wait! There! Over there!

Something glimmered.

Dennis saw a curve of metal, barely poking half an inch out of the snow. Beside it, he could see a round track made by one of his knees – he had almost crawled over the thing during his frantic hunt.

He tried to pluck it from the snow and on his first try only pushed it farther in. His hand was almost too numb to close. Digging in the snow for the metal object, Dennis realized that if his knee had come down on it instead of beside it, he would have driven it more deeply into the snow without even feeling it – his knees were as numb as the rest of him. And then he never would have seen it at all. It would have remained buried until the spring thaws.

He touched it, forced his fingers to close, and brought it out. He looked at it wonderingly. It was a locket – a locket which might be gold, in the shape of a heart. There was a fine chain attached to it. The locket was shut – but caught in its jaws was a folded piece of paper. Very old paper.

Dennis pulled the note free, closed his hand gently over the old paper, and slipped the locket's chain over his head. He got creakily to his feet and ran back towards the shadows. That run was, in a way, the worst part of the whole business for him. He had never felt so exposed in his whole life. For every step he ran, the comforting shadows of the buildings on the far side of the Plaza seemed to recede a step.

At last he reached comparative safety and stood in the shadows for a while, panting and shuddering. When he had gotten his breath, he returned to the castle, slinking along the Fourth Alley in the shadows and entering by Cook's Way. There was a Guard of the Watch at the doorway leading into the castle proper, but he was as sloppy about his duties as his mate had been the night before. Dennis waited, and eventually the guard wandered off. Dennis darted inside.

Twenty minutes later, he was safely back in the storeroom of the napkins. Here he unfolded the note and looked at it.

One side was closely writ in an archaic hand. The writer had used a strange rust-coloured ink and Dennis could make nothing of it. He turned the note over and his eyes widened. He recognized the 'ink' that had been used to write the short message on *this* side easily enough.

'Oh, King Peter,' he moaned.

The message was smeared and blurry – the 'ink' had not been blotted – but he could read it.

Meant to try Escape tonight. Will wait I night. Dare wait no longer. Don't go for Ben. No time. Too dangerous. I have a Rope. Thin. May break. Too short. Will be a drop in any case. 20 feet. Midnight tomorrow. Help me away if you can. Safe place. May be hurt. In the hands of the gods. I love you my good Dennis. King Peter.

Dennis read this note three times and then burst into tears – tears of joy. That light Peyna had sensed was now shining brightly in Dennis's own heart. That was well, and soon all would be well.

His eyes returned again and again to the line *I*

love you my good Dennis, written in the King's own blood. He had not needed to add that for the message to make sense . . . and yet, he had.

Peter, I would die a thousand deaths for you, Dennis thought. He put the note inside his jerkin, and lay down with the locket still around his neck. It was a very long time before sleep found him this time. And he had not slept long before he snapped wide awake. The door of the storeroom was opening – the low creak of its hinges seemed an inhuman shriek to Dennis. Before his sleep-fuddled mind even had time to realize he had been found, a dark shadow with burning eyes swept down on him.

103

The snow began at around three o' the clock that Monday morning – Ben Staad saw the first flakes go skating past his eyes as he and Naomi stood at the edge of the King's Preserves, looking out towards the castle. Frisky sat on her haunches, panting. The humans were tired, and Frisky was tired as well, but she was eager to go – the scent had grown steadily fresher.

She had led them easily from Peyna's farm to the deserted house where Dennis had spent some four days, eating raw potatoes and thinking sour thoughts about turnips which turned out to be as sour as the thoughts themselves. In that empty Inner

Baronies farmstead, the bright-blue scent she had followed this far had been everywhere – she had barked excitedly, running from room to room, nose down, tail wagging cheerfully.

'Look,' Naomi said. 'Our Dennis burnt something here.' She was pointing at the fireplace.

Ben came and looked, but he could make out nothing – there were only bundles of ash which fell apart when he poked at them. Of course, they were Dennis's early tries at his note.

'Now what?' Naomi asked. 'He went to the castle from here, that's clear. The question is, do we follow or spend the night here?'

It had then been six o'clock. Outside it was already dark.

'I think we had better go on,' Ben said slowly. 'After all, it was you who said we wanted Frisky's nose, not her eyes . . . and I, for one, would testify before the throne of any King in creation that Frisky has a noble nose.'

Frisky, sitting in the doorway, barked as if to say she knew it.

'All right,' Naomi said.

He looked at her closely. It had been a long run from the camp of the exiles, with little rest for either of them. He knew they should stay . . . but he was nearly frantic with urgency.

'*Can* you go on?' he asked. 'Don't say you can if you can't, Naomi Reechul.'

She put her hands on her hips and looked at him haughtily. 'I could go on a hundred koner from the place where you dropped dead, Ben Staad.'

Ben grinned. 'You may get your chance to

prove it, too,' he said. 'But first we'll have a bite to eat.'

They ate quickly. When the meal was finished, Naomi knelt by Frisky and quietly told her that she must take up the scent again. Frisky didn't have to be asked twice. The three of them quit the farmhouse, Ben with a large pack on his back, Naomi with one only slightly smaller.

To Frisky, Dennis's scent was a blue mark in the night, as bright as a wire glowing with an electric charge. She began to follow at once, and was confused when THE GIRL called her back. Then it came to her; if Frisky had been human, she would have slapped her forehead and groaned. In her impatience to be off, she had started sniffing up Dennis's back-trail. By midnight she would have had them back at Peyna's farmhouse.

'That's all right, Frisky,' Naomi said. 'Take your time.'

'Sure,' Ben said. 'Take a week or two, Frisky. Take a month, if you want.'

Naomi cast a sour glance Ben's way. Ben shut up – prudently, perhaps. The two of them watched Frisky nose back and forth, first across the dooryard of the deserted farm, then across the road.

'Has she lost it?' Ben asked.

'No, she'll pick it up in a minute or two.' *I think*, Naomi didn't say aloud. 'It's just that she's found a whole tangle of scents in the road and she has to sort them out.'

'Look!' Ben said doubtfully. "She's off into the field there. That can't be right, can it?'

'I don't know. Would he have taken the road to the castle?'

Ben Staad *was* human, and he *did* slap his forehead. 'No, of course not. I'm a dolt.'

Naomi smiled sweetly and said nothing.

In the field, Frisky had paused. She turned towards THE GIRL and THE TALL-BOY and barked impatiently for them to follow. Anduan huskies were the tame descendants of the great white wolves the residents of the Northern Barony had feared in earlier times, but tame or not, they were hunters and trackers before they were anything else. Frisky had isolated that bright-blue thread of scent again, and was in a fever to be off.

'Come on,' Ben said. 'I just hope she's found the right scent.'

'Of course she has! Look!'

She pointed, and Ben was just able to make out long, shallow tracks in the snow. Even in the dark Ben and Naomi knew the tracks for what they were – snowshoes.

Frisky barked again.

'Let's hurry,' Ben said.

By midnight, as they began to draw close to the King's Preserves, Naomi began to regret the crack she'd made about how she could go on a hundred koner from the place where Ben dropped dead, because she had begun to feel as if that might soon happen to her.

Dennis had made the trip in better time, but Dennis had set out after four days of rest, Dennis had had snowshoes, and Dennis had not been following a dog who sometimes lost the scent and had to cast

about for it again. Naomi's legs felt hot and rubbery.
Her lungs burned. There was a stitch in her left side.
She had taken a few mouthfuls of snow, but they
could not slake her raging thirst.

Frisky, who was not burdened by a pack and
who could run lightly along the snow crust, was not
tired at all. Naomi was able to walk on the crust for
short distances, but then she would strike a rotten
spot and plunge through the crust into soft snow up
to her knees . . . and on several occasions, up to her
hips. Once she plunged in waist-deep and floundered
about in a tired fury until Ben worked his way over
and pulled her out.

'Wish . . . sled,' she panted now.

'. . . wishes . . . horses . . . beggars'd ride,' he
panted back, grinning in spite of his own weariness.

'Funny,' she gasped. 'Ha-ha. Ought to be a
court jester, Ben Staad.'

'King's Preserves up there. Less snow . . . easier.'

He bent over, hands on his knees, and gasped
for breath. Naomi suddenly felt that she had been
selfish and unkind, thinking about how she herself
felt, when Ben must be even closer to the point of
exhaustion – he was much heavier than she,
especially with the weight of the larger pack he
carried added into the bargain. He had been breaking
through the snow crust on almost every step, leaping
through the long fields like a man running in deep
water, and yet he had not complained or slowed.

'Ben, are you all right?'

'No,' he wheezed and grinned. 'But I'll make it,
pretty child.'

'I am not a child!' she said angrily.

'But you *are* pretty,' he said, and put his thumb to the tip of his nose. He wiggled his fingers at her.

'Oh, I'll get you for that –'

'Later,' he panted. 'Race you to the woods. Come on.'

So they raced, with Frisky chasing along the scent ahead of them, and he beat her, and that made her madder than ever . . . but she admired him, too.

now they stood looking across the seventy koner of open ground between the edge of the forest where King Roland had once slain a dragon and the walls of the castle where he had been slain himself. A few more snowflakes skirled down from the sky . . . and a few more . . . and suddenly, magically, the air was filled with snow.

In spite of his weariness, Ben felt a moment of peace and joy. He looked at Naomi and smiled. She tried a scowl but it wouldn't fit her face and so she smiled, too. A moment later, she ran her tongue out and tried to catch a flake of snow. Ben laughed quietly.

'How did he get inside, if he did?' Naomi asked.

'I don't know,' Ben said. He had grown up on a farm, and knew nothing of the castle's sewer system. Probably every bit as well for him, you might say, and you would be right. 'Perhaps your champion dog can show us how he did it.'

'You really think he did, don't you, Ben?'

'Oh, aye,' Ben said. 'What do you think, Frisky?'

At the sound of her name, Frisky got up, ranged along the scent for a few feet, and looked back at them.

Naomi looked at Ben. Ben shook his head.

'Not yet,' he said.

Naomi called Frisky softly, and she came back, whining.

'If she could talk, she'd tell you she's afraid of losing the scent. The snow will cover it.'

'We'll not wait long. Dennis had the snowshoes, but we're going to have something he didn't, Naomi.'

'What's that?'

'Cover.'

105

In spite of Frisky's growing restlessness at being checked on the scent, Ben made them wait fifteen minutes. By then the air had become a shifting cloud of white. Snow frosted Naomi's brown hair and his own blond hair; Frisky wore a cold ermine stole. They could no longer see the castle walls ahead of them.

'All right,' Ben said softly, 'let's go.'

They crossed the open ground behind Frisky. The big husky moved slowly now, her nose constantly at the snow, puffing it up every now and again in cold little bursts. The bright-blue runner of scent was dimming, being covered by the white no-smell stuff from the sky.

'We may have waited too long,' Naomi said quietly beside him.

Ben said nothing. He knew it, and the knowledge gnawed at his heart like a rat.

Now a dark bulk loomed out of the whiteness – the castle wall. Naomi had moved slightly ahead. Ben reached out and grabbed her arm. 'The moat,' he said. Don't forget that. It's up here somewhere. You'll go over the side and land on the ice and break your ne–'

He got just so far and then Naomi's eyes blazed with alarm. She pulled out of his grip. 'Frisky!' she hissed. 'Hai! Frisky! Danger! Drop-off!' She darted after the dog.

That girl is absolutely giddy bonkers, Ben thought with a certain admiration. Then *he* darted after *her*.

Naomi needn't have worried. Frisky had stopped at the edge of the moat. Her nose was buried in the snow and her tail was wagging happily. Now she bit down on something and dragged it out of the loose powder. She turned to Naomi, eyes asking:- *Now am I a good dog, or what? What do you think?*

Naomi laughed and hugged her dog.

Ben glanced towards the castle wall. 'Hush!' he whispered at her. 'If the guards hear you, we're in the slate-cracker for sure! Where do you think we are? Your back garden?'

'Pooh! If they heard anything, they'd think it was snow sprites and run for their mommies.' But she whispered, too. Then she buried her face in Frisky's fur and told her again what a good dog she was.

Ben scratched Frisky's head. Because of the snow, neither of them had the horribly exposed sense Dennis had had when he had sat in the same place, taking off the snowshoes Frisky had now found.

'Nose of the gods, all right,' Ben said. 'But what happened after he took off the snowshoes, Frisky? Did he grow wings and fly over the West'rd Redan? Where did he go from here?'

As if in answer, Frisky broke away from both of them and went floundering and slipping down the steep bank to the frozen moat.

'Frisky!' Naomi called, her voice low but alarmed.

Frisky only stood on the ice looking up at them, hock-deep in new snow. Her tail was wagging slightly, and her eyes begged them to come. She did not bark; somehow she knew better, even though Naomi had not thought to warn her to silence. But she barked in her *mind*. The scent was still here, and she wanted to follow it before it disappeared completely, as it now would within minutes.

Naomi looked questioningly at Ben.

'Yes,' he said. 'Of course. We have to. Come on. But keep her to heel – don't let her range ahead. There's danger here. I feel it.'

He held out his hand. Naomi grasped it, and they slid down to the moat together.

Frisky led them slowly across the ice towards the castle wall. She was now actually *digging* for the scent, her nose furrowing the snow. It had begun to be overlaid with a thick, unpleasant smell – dirty, warm water, garbage, ordure.

Dennis had known that the ice would begin to grow dangerously rotten as he got closer to the outflow pipe. Even if he hadn't known, he was able to see the three feet or so of open water next to the wall.

Things weren't so easy for Ben, Naomi, and Frisky. They had simply assumed that if the ice was thick along the moat's outer bank, it must be thick all the way across. And their eyes were of little use to them in the thickly falling snow.

Frisky's eyes were the weakest of the three, and she was in the lead. Her ears were sharp enough, and she had heard the ice groaning beneath the new snow . . . but the scent was too much on her mind for her to take much notice of the faint creaks . . . until the ice gave way beneath her and she plunged into the moat with a splash.

'Frisky! Fr–'

Ben clapped a hand over her mouth. She struggled to get away from him. Ben had now seen the danger, however, and held her fast.

Naomi needn't have worried. Of course all dogs can swim, and with her thick, oily coat, Frisky was safer in the water than either of the humans would have been. She paddled almost to the castle wall amid chunks of rotted ice and whipped-cream globs of snow that quickly turned into dark slush and disappeared. She raised her head, smelling, searching for the scent . . . and when she knew where it went, she turned and paddled back towards Ben and Naomi. She found the edge of the ice. Her paws broke it off, and she tried again. Naomi cried out.

'Be still, Naomi, or you'll have us in the dungeons by dawn,' Ben said. 'Hold my ankles.' He let her go and then sprawled on his belly. Naomi crouched behind him and seized his boots. This close to the ice, Ben could hear it groaning and muttering. *It could have been one of us*, he thought, *and that would have been trouble indeed*.

He spread his legs out a bit to distribute his weight better, and then grabbed Frisky by the forepaws just below her wide, strong chest. 'Here you come, girl,' Ben grunted. 'I hope.' Then he pulled.

For a moment, Ben thought that the ice would just go on breaking under Frisky's weight as he dragged her forward – first he and then Naomi would follow Frisky into the moat. Crossing that moat on his way into the castle to play with his friend Peter on a summer's day, with blue sky and white clouds reflecting off its surface, Ben had always thought it beautiful, like a painting. He had never once suspected that he might die in it one black night during a snowstorm. And it smelled very bad.

'Pull me backward!' he grunted. 'Your damn dog weighs a ton!'

'Don't you say mean things about my dog, Ben Staad!'

Ben's eyes were slitted shut with strain, his lips split open over clenched teeth. 'A million pardons. And if you don't start pulling me, I'm going to be taking a bath, I think.'

Somehow she managed to do it, although Ben

and Frisky together must have been three times her own weight. Ben's prone, splayed body dug a channel in the new powder; a snow pyramid built up in his crotch, the way it will build up in the angle of a wooden plough.

At last – it seemed like 'at last' to Ben and Naomi, although in truth it was probably only a matter of seconds – Frisky's chest stopped breaking the ice and slid on to it. A moment later, her rear paws were digging for purchase. Then she was up and shaking herself vigorously. Dirty moat water sprayed into Ben's face.

'Pah!' he grimaced, wiping it off. 'Thanks a lot, Frisky!'

But Frisky paid no attention. She was looking towards the wall of the castle again. Although the ice was already freezing to her pelt in dirty spicules, the scent was what interested her. She had smelled it clearly, above her but not *far* above her. There was a darkness there. No cold white no-smell stuff there.

Ben was getting to his feet, brushing the snow off.

'I'm sorry I yelled like that,' Naomi whispered. 'If it had been any other dog but Frisky . . . do you think I was heard?'

'If you'd been heard, we'd have been challenged,' Ben whispered back. 'Gods, that was close.' Now they could see the open water just in front of the ancient stone wall of Castle Delain's outer redan, because they were looking for it.

'What do we do?'

'We can't go on,' Ben whispered, 'that's obvious. But what did he *do*, Naomi? Where did he *go* from here? Maybe he *did* fly.'

'If we –'

But Naomi never finished the thought, because that was when Frisky took matters into her own paws. All of her ancestors had been famous hunters, and it was in her blood. She had been set upon this exciting, enticing electric-blue scent, and she found she could not leave it. So she screwed her haunches down to the ice, tensed her sled-toughened muscles, and leaped into the dark. Her eyes, as I've said, were the least of her sensory equipment, and her leap really *was* blind; she could not see the dark hole of the sewer pipe from the edge of the ice.

But she had seen it from the water, and even if she hadn't, she had her nose, and she *knew* it was there.

I*t's Flagg*, Dennis's sleep-fuddled mind thought as that dark shape with the burning eyes swept down on him. *It's Flagg, he's found me, and now he'll rip my throat out with his teeth –*

He tried to scream, but no sound came out.

The mouth of the intruder *did* open; Dennis saw huge white teeth . . . and then a big warm tongue was lapping his face.

'Ulf!' Dennis said, trying to push the thing

away. Paws came up on either shoulder, and Dennis fell back on his mattress of napkins like a pinned wrestler. Lap-lap, lick-lick. '*Ulf!*' Dennis said again, and the dark, shaggy shape uttered a low, companionable woof, as if to say *I know it, I'm glad to see you, too.*

'Frisky!' a low voice called from the darkness. 'Stand down, Frisky! No sounds!'

The dark shape was not Flagg at all; it was an extremely large dog – a dog which looked too much like a wolf for comfort, Dennis thought. When the girl spoke, it drew away and sat down. It looked happily at Dennis; its tail thumped mutedly on Dennis's bed of napkins.

Two more shapes in the darkness, one taller than the other. Not Flagg, that much was clear. Castle guards, then. Dennis grabbed his dagger. If the gods were good, he might be able to get rid of both of them. If not, then he would try to die well in the service of his King.

The two figures had stopped a little short of him.

'Come on,' Dennis said, and raised his dagger (it was really not much more than a pocketknife, and was rather rusty and quite dull) in a brave gesture. 'First you two and then your devil-dog!'

'Dennis?' The voice was eerily familiar. 'Dennis, have we really found you?'

Dennis started to lower his dagger, then brought it up again. It had to be a trick. *Had* to be. But the voice sounded so much like –

'Ben?' he whispered. 'Is it Ben Staad?'

'It's Ben,' the taller shape confirmed, and gladness filled Dennis's heart. The shape began to come forward. Alarmed, Dennis raised his dagger again.

'Wait! Do you have a light?'

'Flint and steel, yes.'

'Strike it.'

'Aye.'

A moment later, a big yellow spark, surely dangerous in that room filled with dry cotton napkins, flared in the gloom.

'Come forward, Ben,' Dennis said, reseating his poor excuse for a dagger in its sheath. He got to his feet, trembling with gladness and relief. Ben was here. By what magic Dennis did not know – only that he had somehow happened. His feet caught in the napkins and he stumbled forward, but there was no danger that he might fall, because Ben's arms swept him up in a strong embrace. Ben was here and all would be well, Dennis thought, and it was all he could do to keep from bursting into unmanly tears.

107

There followed a great exchange of stories – I think you have heard most of them, and the parts you haven't can be told quickly enough.

Frisky's leap was a bull's-eye. She carried straight into the pipe and then turned around to see if Naomi and Ben would follow her.

If they hadn't done so, Frisky would have

eventually leaped back to the ice – she should have been greatly disappointed to do it, but she would not have left her mistress for the most exciting scent in the world. *Frisky* knew that; Naomi was less sure. She didn't even dare call Frisky back, for fear of a guard's overhearing. She therefore intended to go after the dog. She would not leave Frisky, and if Ben tried to make her, she would deck him with a right hook.

She needn't have worried. The minute he spotted the pipe, Ben understood where Dennis had gone.

'Noble nose, Frisky,' he said again. He turned to Naomi 'Can you make it?'

'If I draw back and run, I can make it.'

'Don't misjudge where the ice goes rotten or you'll take a dunking. And your heavy clothes will drag you down very quickly.'

'I won't misjudge.'

'Let me go first,' Ben said. 'If I have to, maybe I can catch you.'

He drew back a few paces and jumped so strongly that he almost took off the top of his head on the upper curve of the pipe. Frisky barked once, excitedly. 'Shut up, dog!' Ben said.

Naomi drew back to the edge of the moat, stood there for a moment (the snow had by then been coming down so heavily that Ben couldn't see her), and then ran forward. Ben held his breath, hoping she wouldn't misjudge the edge of the good ice. If she ran too far before trying to make her leap, the longest arms in the world wouldn't catch her.

But she timed it perfectly. Ben didn't need to

catch her; all he had to do was to get out of her way as she carried into the pipe. She didn't even bump her head, as Ben had done.

'The worst part of it was the smell,' Naomi said as they told their story to a wondering Dennis. 'How did you stand it?'

'Well, I just kept reminding myself of what would happen to me if I got caught,' Dennis said. 'Every time I did that, the air seemed to smell a little better.'

Ben laughed at this and nodded, and Dennis looked at him with shining eyes for a moment. Then he looked back at Naomi. 'It *did* smell awfully bad, though,' he agreed. 'I remember that it smelled bad when I was a kid, but not *that* bad. Maybe a kid doesn't really know how bad a smell is. Or something.'

'I guess that could be,' Naomi said.

Frisky was lying on a pile of royal napkins with her muzzle on her paws, her eyes moving from one person to the next as each spoke. She knew very little of what they were saying, but if she had, and if she could have spoken, she would have told Dennis that his perceptions of what made a really bad smell hadn't changed at all since he was a boy. It had been the last dying remainder of the Dragon Sand they had smelled, of course. The odour had been much stronger to Frisky than to THE GIRL and THE TALL-BOY. Dennis's scent had still been there, now mostly in splashes and blobs on the curved walls (these were the places Dennis had touched with his hands; the floor of the pipes was covered with a foul warm water that had washed away all scent). It was the same bright electric blue. The other scent was a dull leathery green – Frisky was afraid of it. She knew that some scents could kill, and she knew that, not so long ago, this had been just such a scent. But it was losing its potency now, and in any case, Dennis's scent led away from the greater concentrations of it. Not too long before they reached the grating Dennis had used to get out of the sewer system, she began to lose the green smell altogether – and Frisky was never in her whole life so happy to lose a smell.

'You met no one? No one at all?' Dennis asked anxiously.

'No one,' Ben said. 'I ranged a little bit ahead to keep an eye out. I saw guards several times, but we always had plenty of time to get to some cover before they could see us. In truth, I think we could have come directly here and passed twenty guards and only have been challenged once or twice. Most of them were drunk.'

Naomi nodded. 'Guards o' the Watch,' she said. 'Drunk. And not drunk out on picket along the northern borders of some pissy little barony no one ever heard of; drunk in the castle. *Right in the castle!*'

Dennis, remembering the toneless, nose-blowing singer, nodded gloomily. 'I suppose we should be glad. If the Guard o' the Watch was now what it was in Roland's day, we'd all be in the Needle along wi' Peter. But I can't be glad, somehow.'

'I'll tell you this,' Ben said in a soft voice, 'if I were Thomas, I'd quake in my boots every time I looked north, if such as we saw tonight are all he has around him.'

Naomi looked very troubled at this. 'Pray the gods it never comes to that,' she said.

Ben nodded.

Dennis reached out and stroked Frisky's head. 'Followed me all the way from Peyna's, did you? What a smart dog you are, aye!'

Frisky thumped her tail happily.

Naomi said: 'I would hear this story of the sleep-walking King, Dennis, if you would tell it again.'

So Dennis told his story, much as he told it to Peyna and as I have told it to you, and they listened as spellbound as children hearing the tale of the talking wolf in the gammer's nightcap.

By the time he had finished, it was seven o'clock. Outside, a dim glow had come over Delain – that clotted storm-light was as bright at seven as it would be at noon, for the greatest storm of that winter – and perhaps the greatest in history – had come to Delain. The wind howled around the eaves of the castle like a tribe of banshees. Even down here, the fugtives could hear it. Frisky raised her head and whined uneasily.

'What do we do now?' Dennis asked.

Ben, who had gone over Peter's brief note again and again, said: 'Until tonight, nothing. The castle's awake by now, and there's no way we could get out of here without being seen under any circumstances. We sleep. Get our strength back. And tonight, before midnight –'

Ben spoke briefly. Naomi grinned; Dennis's eyes grew bright with excitement. 'Yes!' Dennis said. 'By the gods! You're a genius, Ben!'

'Please, I wouldn't go *that* far,' Naomi said, but by then her grin was so broad it seemed in danger of splitting her head in two. She reached over, put her arms around Ben, and kissed him soundly.

Ben turned an absolutely alarming shade of red (he looked as if he might be on the verge of 'bursting his brains,' as they said in Delain in those long-ago days) – I must tell you, though, that he also looked delighted.

'Will Frisky help us?' Ben asked when he got his breath back.

At the sound of her name, Frisky looked up again.

'Of course she will. But we'll need . . .'

They discussed this new plan for some time longer, and then Ben's lower face seemed to almost disappear in a great yawn. Naomi also looked tired out. They had been awake for over twenty-four hours by then, you will remember, and had come a great distance.

'Enough,' Ben said. 'It's time for sleep.'

'Hooray!' Naomi said, beginning to arrange more napkins in a mattress for herself beside Frisky. 'My legs feel as if –'

Dennis cleared his throat politely.

'What is it?' Ben asked.

Dennis looked at their packs – Ben's big one,

Naomi's slightly smaller one. 'I don't suppose you've got . . . um, anything to eat in there, do you?'

Impatiently, Naomi said: 'Of course we do! What do you think –' Then she remembered that Dennis had left Peyna's farmhouse six days ago, and that the butler had been skulking and hiding ever since. He had a pallid, undernourished look, and his face was too narrow and too bony. 'Oh, Dennis, I'm sorry, we're idiots! When did you eat last?'

Dennis thought about this. 'I can't remember exactly,' he said. 'But the last sit-down meal I had was my lunch, a week ago.'

'Why didn't you say so first thing, you dolt?' Ben exclaimed.

'I guess because I was so excited to see you,' Dennis said, and grinned. As he watched the two of them open their packs and begin rooting through the remainder of their supplies, his stomach gurgled noisily. Saliva squirted into his mouth. Then a thought struck him.

'You didn't bring any turnips, did you?'

Naomi turned to look at him, puzzled. 'Turnips? *I* don't have any. Do you, Ben?'

'No.'

A gentle and supremely happy smile spread across Dennis's face. 'Good,' he said.

109

That was a mighty storm indeed, and it's still told of in Delain today. Five feet of new snow had fallen by the time an early, howling dark came down on the castle keep. Five feet of new snow in one day is mighty enough, but the wind made drifts that were much, much bigger. By the time dark fell, the wind was no longer blowing a force-gale; it was blowing a hurricane. In places along the castle walls, snow was piled twenty-five feet deep, and covered the windows of not just first and second floors, but the third-floor windows as well.

You might think this would have been good for Peter's escape plans, and it might have been if the Needle hadn't stood all alone in the Plaza. But it did, and here the wind blew its hardest. A strong man couldn't have stood against that wind; he would have been sent rolling, head over heels, until he crashed against the first stone wall on the far side of the Plaza. And the wind had another effect, as well – it was like a giant broom. As fast as the snow fell, the wind blew it out of the Plaza. By dark there were huge drifts piled against the castle and clogging most of the alleys on the west side of the castle keep, but the Plaza itself was clean as a whistle. There were only the frozen cobbles, waiting to break Peter's bones if his rope should break.

And I must tell you now that Peter's rope was *bound* to break. When he tested it, it had held his weight . . . but there was one fact about that mystic

thing called 'breaking strain' that Peter didn't know.
Yosef hadn't known, either. The ox drivers knew it,
though, and if Peter had asked them, they would have
told him an old axiom, one known to sailors, loggers,
seamstresses, and anyone else who works with thread
or rope: *The longer the cord, the sooner the break*.

Peter's short test rope had held him.

The rope to which he meant to entrust his life –
the very *thin* rope – was about two hundred and
sixty-five feet long.

It was bound to break, I tell you, and the cobbles
below waited to catch him, and break his bones, and
bleed away his life.

110

There were many disasters and near-
disasters on that long, stormy day, just as there were
many acts of heroism, some successful and some
doomed to failure. Some farmhouses in the Inner
Baronies blew over, as the houses of the indolent pigs
were blown over by the wolf's hungry breath in the
old story. Some of those who were thus rendered
homeless managed to work their way across the
white wastes to the castle keep, roped together for
safety; others wandered off the Delain Great Road
and into the whiteness, where they were lost – their
frozen, wolf-gnawed bodies wouldn't be found until
the spring.

But by seven that evening, the snow had finally begun to abate a little, and the wind to fall The excitement was ending, and the castle went to bed early. There was little else to do. Fires were banked, children tucked in, last cups of field-tea drunk, prayers said.

One by one, the lights went out. The Crier called in his loudest voice, but the wind still tore his voice out of his mouth at eight o' the clock and again at nine; it was not until ten that he could be heard again, and by then, most people were asleep.

Thomas was also asleep – but his sleep was not easy. There was no Dennis to stay with him and comfort him this night; Dennis was still home ill. Thomas had thought several times of sending a page to check on him (or even to go himself; he liked Dennis very much), but something always seemed to come up – papers to sign . . . petitions to hear . . . and, of course, bottles of wine to be drunk. Thomas hoped Flagg would come and give him a powder to help him sleep . . . but ever since Flagg's useless trip into the north, the magician had been strange and distant. It was as if Flagg knew there was something wrong, but could not quite tell what it was. Thomas hoped the magician would come, but hadn't dared to summon him.

As always, the shrieking wind reminded Thomas of the night his father died, and he feared he would have a hard time getting to sleep . . . and that, once he was asleep, horrible nightmares might come, dreams in which his father would scream and rant and finally burst into flames. So Thomas did what he had grown accustomed to doing; he spent the day with a glass of wine always in his hand, and if I told

you how many bottles of wine this mere boy consumed before he finally went to bed at ten o' the
clock, you probably wouldn't believe me – so I won't
say. But it was a lot.

Lying there miserably on his sofa, wishing that
Dennis was in his accustomed place on the hearth,
Thomas thought: *my head aches and my stomach feels
sick . . . Is being King worth all this? I wonder.* You
might wonder, too . . . but before Thomas himself
could wonder anymore, he fell heavily asleep.

He slept for almost an hour . . . and then he rose
and walked. Out the door he went and down the
halls, ghostly in his long white nightshirt. This night
a late-going maid with an armload of sheets saw him,
and he looked so much like old King Roland that the
maid dropped her sheets and fled, screaming.

Thomas's darkly dreaming mind heard her
screams and thought they were his father's.

He walked on, turning into the less used corridor. He paused halfway down and pushed the
secret stone. He went into the passageway, closed
the door behind him, and walked to the end of the
corridor. He pushed aside the panels which were
behind Niner's glass eyes, and though he was still
asleep, he pushed his face up to the holes, as if looking
into his dead father's sitting room. And here we will
leave the unfortunate boy for a while, with the smell
of wine surrounding him and tears of regret running
from his sleeping eyes and down his cheeks.

He was sometimes a cruel boy, often a sad boy,
this pretend King, and he had almost always been a
weak boy . . . but even now I must tell you that I do
not believe he was ever really a *bad* boy. If you hate

him because of the things he did – and the things he
allowed to be done – I will understand; but if you do
not pity him a little as well, I will be surprised.

111

At quarter past eleven on that momentous night, the storm breathed its last gasp. A
tremendous cold gust of wind swept down on the
castle. It ran in excess of a hundred miles an hour. It
tore the thinning clouds overhead apart like the swipe
of a great hand. Cold, watery moonlight shone
through.

In the Third East'ard Alley was a squat stone
tower called the Church of the Great Gods; it had
stood there since time out of mind. Many people
worshipped there, but it was empty now. A good
thing, too. The tower was not very tall – nowhere
near the height of the Needle – but it nevertheless
stood high above the neighbouring buildings in the
Third East'ard Alley, and all day long it had been
punished by the unbroken force of the storm wind.
This final gust was too much for it. The top thirty
feet – all stone – simply blew off, as a hat might fly
off a scarecrow in a high gale. Part landed in the alley;
part hit the neighbouring buildings. There was a
tremendous crash.

Most of the populace of the castle keep, wearied

by the excitement of the storm and already sleeping deeply, took no mind of the fall of the Church of the Great Gods (although they would wonder greatly over the snow-covered wreckage in the morning). Most simply muttered, turned over, and went back to sleep.

Some Guards of the Watch – those not too drunk to care – heard it, of course, and ran to see what had happened. Other than by these few, the fall of the tower went mostly unremarked when it happened . . . but there were a few others who heard it, and by now you know them all.

Ben, Dennis, and Naomi, who were getting ready for their attempt to rescue the rightful King, heard it in the napkin storeroom, and looked around at each other with wide eyes. 'Never mind,' Ben said, after a moment. 'I don't know what it was, but it doesn't matter. Let's get on with it.'

Beson and the Lesser Warders, all of them drunk, didn't hear the Church of the Great Gods fall down, but Peter did. He was sitting on the floor of his bedroom, carefully pulling his woven rope through his fingers, looking anxiously for weak points. He raised his head at the snow-muted thunder of falling stones, and went rapidly to the window. He could see nothing; whatever had fallen was on the Needle's far side. After considering for several moments, he went back to his rope. Midnight was close now, and he had come to much the same conclusion as his friend Ben. It didn't matter. The dice had been thrown. Now he must go on.

Deep in the darkness of the secret passage, Thomas heard the muffled thunder-thud of the falling tower and woke up. He heard the muffled barking of dogs below him and realized in horror where he was.

And one other who had been sleeping lightly and dreaming troubled dreams awoke at the fall of the tower. He woke even though he was deep in the bowels of the castle.

'*Disaster!*' one of the parrot's two heads screamed.

'*Fire, flood, and escape!*' the other screamed.

Flagg had awakened. I have told you that evil is sometimes strangely blind, and so it is. Sometimes evil is lulled with no reason, and sleeps.

But now Flagg had awakened.

112

Flagg had come back from his trip into the north with a bit of a fever, a heavy cold, and a troubled mind.

Something wrong, something wrong. The very stones of the castle seemed to whisper it to him . . . but Flagg was damned if he knew what it was. All he knew for sure was that unknown 'something wrong' had sharp teeth. It felt like a ferret running around in his brain, taking a bite here and a bite there. He knew exactly when that animal had begun to run and gnaw: while he was coming back from the fruitless expedition in search of the rebels. Because . . . because . . .

Because the rebels should have been there!

They hadn't been, and Flagg hated to be fooled. Worse, he hated feeling that he might have made a mistake. If he had made a mistake about where the rebels were to be found, then perhaps he had made mistakes about other things. What other things? He didn't know. But his dreams were bad. That small, bad-tempered animal ran around in his head, worrying him, insisting that he had forgotten things, that other things were going on behind his back. It raced, it gnawed, it ruined his sleep. Flagg had medicines that would rid him of his cold, but none that would touch that growing ferret in his brain.

What could possibly be wrong?

He asked himself this question over and over again, and in truth it seemed – on the surface, at least – that *nothing* could be. For many centuries, the old dark chaos inside him had hated the love and light and order of Delain, and he had worked hard to destroy all that – to knock it down as that last cold gust of storm had knocked down the Church of the Great Gods. Always, something had interfered with his plans – a Kyla the Good, a Sasha, some*one*, some-*thing*. But now he saw no possible interference, no matter where he looked. Thomas was totally his creature; if Flagg told him to step off the highest parapet of the castle, the fool would want to know only at which o'clock he should do it. The farmers were groaning under the weight of the killing taxes Flagg had persuaded Thomas to impose.

Yosef had told Peter there was a breaking strain on people as well as on ropes and chains, and so there is – the farmers and the merchants of Delain had nearly reached theirs. The rope by which the great blocks of taxes are attached to any citizenry is simple loyalty – loyalty to King, to country, to government. Flagg knew that if he made the tax-blocks big enough, all the ropes would snap, and the stupid oxen – for that was really how he saw the people of Delain – would stampede, knocking down everything in their path. The first of the oxen had already broken free and had gathered in the north. They called themselves exiles now, but Flagg knew they would call themselves rebels soon enough. Peyna had been driven away and Peter was locked in the Needle.

So what could be wrong?

Nothing! Damn it, *nothing!*

But the ferret ran and squirmed and gnawed and twisted. Many times over the last three or four weeks he had awakened in a cold sweat, not because of his recurring fever but because he had had some horrible dream. What was the substance of this dream? He could never remember. He only knew that he woke from it and with his left hand pressed to his left eye, as if he had been wounded there – and that eye would burn, although he could find nothing wrong with it.

113

On this night, Flagg awoke with his dream fresh in his mind, because he was awakened before it was over. It was, of course, the fall of the Church of the Great Gods which woke him.

'*Huh!*' Flagg cried, sitting bolt upright in his chair. His eyes were wide and staring, his white cheeks damp and shiny with sweat.

'*Disaster!*' one of the parrot's heads screamed.

'*Fire, flood, and escape!*' the other screamed.

Escape, Flagg thought. *Yes – that's what's been on my mind all this time, that's what's been gnawing at me.*

He looked down at his hands and saw that they were trembling. This infuriated him, and he sprang out of his chair.

'He means to escape,' he muttered, running his hands through his hair. 'He means to *try*, anyway. But how? *How?* What's his plan? Who helped him? They'll pay with their heads, I promise that . . . and they won't come off all in a chop, no! They'll come off an inch . . . a half-inch . . . a *quarter*-inch . . . at a time. They'll be driven insane with the agony long before they die . . .'

'*Insane!*' one of the parrot heads shrieked.

'*Agony!*' the other shrieked back.

'*Will you shut up and let me think!*' Flagg howled. He seized a jar filled with murky brown fluid from a nearby table and threw it at the parrot's cage. It struck and shattered; there was a flash of bright, heatless light. The parrot's two heads squawked in terror; it fell off its perch and lay stunned at the bottom of its cage until morning.

Flagg began to pace rapidly back and forth. His teeth were bared. His hands worked together restlessly, the fingers of one warring with the fingers of the other. His boots struck up greenish sparks from the nitre-caked stones of his laboratory floor; these sparks smelled like summer lightning.

How? When? Who helped?

He could not remember. Already the dream was fading. But . . .

'I *have* to know!' he whispered. 'I *have* to know!'

Because it would be soon; he sensed that much. It would be very, very soon.

He found his key ring and opened the bottom drawer of his desk. He took out a box made of finely carved ironwood, opened it, and drew out a leather bag. He opened the bag's drawstring top and carefully took out a chunk of rock that seemed to glow with its own inner light. This rock was as milky as an old man's blind eye. It looked like a piece of soapstone, but was in fact a crystal – Flagg's magic crystal.

He circled his room, turning down the lamps and capping the candles. Soon his apartment was in absolute darkness. Dark or not, Flagg returned to his desk with quick confidence, passing easily around objects that you or I would have barked our shins on or fallen over. The dark was nothing to the King's magician; he liked the dark, and he could see in it like a cat.

He sat down and touched the stone. He slipped his palms down its sides, feeling its ragged edges and angles.

'Show me,' he murmured. 'This is my command.'

At first, nothing. Then, little by little, the crystal began to glow from within. There was only a tiny light at first, diffuse and pallid. Flagg touched the crystal again, this time with the tips of his fingers. It had grown warm.

'Show me Peter. This is my command. Show me the whelp that dares put himself in my way, and show me what he plans to do.'

The light grew brighter . . . brighter . . . brighter. Eyes glittering, cruel thin lips parted to show his teeth, Flagg bent over his crystal. Now Peter, Ben, Dennis, and Naomi would have recognized their dream – and they would have recognized the glow which lit the magician's face, the glow which was not a candle.

The crystal's milky cast suddenly disappeared, drawing into the brightening glow. Now Flagg could see into its heart. His eyes widened . . . then narrowed in bewilderment.

It was Sasha, very pregnant, sitting at a little boy's bed. The little boy was holding a slate. On it were written two words: GOD *and* DOG.

Impatiently, Flagg passed his hands over the crystal, which now gave off waves of heat

'Show me what I need to know! This is my command!'

The crystal cleared again.

It was Peter, playing with his dead mother's doll's house, pretending the house and the family inside were being attacked by Indians . . . or dragons . . . or some foolish thing. The old King stood in the corner, watching his son, wanting to join in . . .

'Bah!' Flagg cried, waving his hands over the crystal again. 'Why do you show me these old, meaningless stories? I need to know how he plans to escape . . . and when! Now show me! *This is my command!*'

The crystal had grown hotter and hotter. If he

did not allow it to go dark soon, it would split apart forever, Flagg knew, and magic crystals were not easy to come by – it had taken thirty years of searching to find this one. But he would see it broken into a billion pieces before he gave up.

'This is my command!' he repeated again, and for the third time, the milkiness of the crystal drew inward. Flagg bent over it until its heat made his eyes water and gush tears. He slitted them . . . and then, in spite of the heat, they flew open wide in shock and fury.

It was Peter. Peter was slowly descending the side of the Needle. Surely this was some treacherous magic, because, although he was making hand-over-hand motions, there was no rope to be seen –

Or . . . *was* there?

Flagg waved a hand in front of his face, dissipating the heat for a moment. A rope? Not exactly. But there was something . . . something as gossamer as a strand of spiderweb . . . and yet it bore his weight.

'*Peter*,' Flagg breathed, and at the sound of his voice, the tiny figure looked around.

Flagg blew on the crystal and its bright, wavering light went out. He saw its afterglow in front of his eyes as he sat in the dark.

Peter. Escaping. When? It had been night in the crystal, and Flagg had seen errant, gritty sheaves of snow blowing past the tiny figure working its way down the rounded wall. Was it to be later tonight? Tomorrow night? Sometime next week? Or –

Flagg pushed back from his desk and stood up with a lurch. His eyes filled with fire as he looked around his dark and stinking basement rooms.

– or had it happened already?

'Enough,' he breathed. 'By all the gods that ever were and ever will be, this is *enough.*'

He strode across the darkened room and seized a huge weapon that hung on the wall. It was clumsy, but he held it with ease and familiarity. Familiar with it? Yes, of course he was! He had swung it many times when he had lived here and done business as Bill Hinch, the most feared executioner Delain had ever known. This terrible blade had bitten through hundreds of necks. Above the blades, which were of twice-forged Anduan steel, was Flagg's own modification – a spiked iron ball. Each spike had been tipped with poison.

'*ENOUGH!*' Flagg screamed again in a fury of rage and frustration and fear. The two-headed parrot even in the depths of its unconsciousness, moaned at that sound.

Flagg pulled his cloak from the hook by the door, swept it over his shoulders, and fastened the clasp – a hammered-silver scarab beetle – at his throat.

It was enough. This time his plans would not be thwarted, certainly not by one hateful boy. Roland was dead, Peyna unbenched, the nobles driven into exile. There was no one to raise an outcry over one dead prince . . . especially one who had murdered his own father.

If you have not escaped, my fine prince, you never will – and something tells me you're still in the coop. But part of you WILL leave tonight, I promise you that – that part I intend to carry out by the hair.

As he strode down the corridor toward the Dungeon Gate, Flagg began to laugh . . . a sound which would have given a stone statue bad dreams.

Flagg's intuition was right. Peter had finished going over his rope of twisted linen fibres, but
he was still in his tower room, awaiting the Crier's
announcement of midnight, when Flagg burst out of
the Dungeon Gate and began to cross the Plaza of the
Needle. The Church of the Great Gods had fallen at
quarter past eleven; it was quarter of twelve when
the crystal showed Flagg what he wanted to know
(and perhaps you'll agree with my idea that it tried
to show him the truth in two other ways at first),
and when Flagg started across the Plaza, it was still
lacking ten minutes of midnight.

The Dungeon Gate was on the northeast side of
the Needle. On the southwest side was a little castle
entrance known as the Peddlers' Gate. A straight
diagonal line could have been drawn between the
Dungeon Gate and the Peddlers' Gate. At the exact
midpoint of that line was the Needle itself, of course.

At almost the same time that Flagg came out of
the Dungeon Gate, Ben, Naomi, Dennis, and Frisky
came out of the Peddlers' Gate. They approached
each other without knowing it. The Needle was
between them, but the wind had dropped, and Ben's
party should have heard the clang-rasp of Flagg's
boot heels against the cobbles; Flagg should have
heard the faint squeak of an ungreased wheel. But all
of them, including Frisky (who was back to her old
job of pulling again), were lost in their own
thoughts.

Ben and his party reached the Needle first.

'Now –' Ben began, and at that moment, from the *other* side, less than forty paces around the outside perimeter from where they now stood, Flagg began to hammer on the triple-bolted Warders' Door.

'*Open!*' Flagg screamed. '*Open in the name of the King!*'

'What –' Dennis began, and then Naomi clamped a hand like steel over his mouth and looked at Ben with frightened eyes.

The voice came spiralling up to Peter on the cold post-storm air. It was faint, that voice, but perfectly clear.

'*Open in the name of the King!*'

Open in the name of hell, you mean, Peter thought.

The good brave boy had become a good brave man, but when he heard that hoarse voice and remembered that narrow white face and those reddish eyes, always shadowed by the hood of his robe, Peter's bones turned to ice and his stomach to fire. His mouth went as dry as a wood chip. His tongue stuck to the roof of his mouth. His hair stood on end. If someone has ever told you that being good and being brave means you will never be afraid, what that someone told you is not so. At that moment, Peter had never been so afraid in his whole life.

It's Flagg, and he's come for me.

Peter got up and, for a moment, he thought he was going to simply fall over as his legs buckled under him. Doom was down there, hammering at the Warders' Door to be let in.

'Open up! *On your feet, you licey drunken buggers! Beson, you son of a sot!*'

Don't hurry, Peter told himself. *If you hurry you'll make a mistake and do his work for him. No one's come to let him in yet. Beson's drunk — he was tiddly at supper and probably paralyzed by the time he got to bed. Flagg hasn't a key or he wouldn't be wasting time knocking. So . . . one step at a time. Just as you planned it. He's got to get in, and then climb those stairs — all three hundred of them. You may beat him yet.*

He went into his bedroom and pulled out the rough iron cotter pins that held the crude bedframe together. The bed collapsed. Peter grabbed one of the iron side-bars and carried it back into the sitting room. He had measured this bar carefully and knew it was wider than his window, and while its outer surface was rusted, he thought it was strong yet through the middle. *It had better be,* he thought. *It would be a bitter joke indeed if my rope held but my anchor broke.*

He looked out briefly. He could see no one now, but he had observed three figures crossing the Plaza toward the Needle shortly before Flagg's wild pounding had begun. Dennis had recruited friends, then. Had one of them been Ben? Peter hoped so, but did not dare to really believe it. Who was the third? And why the wagon? They were questions he had no time for now.

'*Oh, you dogs! Open this door! Open it in the King's name! Open it in the name of* FLAGG! *Open the door! Open* –'

In the stillness of almost midnight, Peter heard the rattle-thud of the wrist-thick iron bolts far below being drawn back. He supposed the door opened, but he didn't hear that. Silence . . .

. . . and then a gurgling, choked scream.

The unfortunate Lesser Warder who finally answered Flagg's summons lived less than four seconds after drawing the third bolt on the Warders' Door. He caught a nightmare glimpse of a white face, glaring red eyes, and a black cloak that blew backward in the dying breeze like the wings of a raven. he screamed. Then the air was filled with a dry whooshing sound. The Lesser Warder, who was still half drunk, looked up just as Flagg's battle-axe split his head in two.

'Next time someone knocks in the name of the King, bestir yourselves and you won't have a mess to clean up in the morning!' Flagg bellowed. Then, laughing wildly, he kicked aside the body and strode up the corridor toward the stairs. Things were still all right. He had awakened to the danger in time. He knew it.

He *felt* it.

He opened a door on the right and stepped into the main corridor leading away from the courtroom where Anders Peyna had once dispensed justice. At the end of that corridor, the stairs began. He looked up, grinning his dreadful, sharklike grin.

'*Here I come, Peter!*' he cried happily, his voice echoing and rebounding, spiralling up and up and up to where Peter stood preparing to tie his thin rope to the bar he had taken from the bed. '*Here I come, dear Peter, to do what I should have done a long, long time ago!*'

Flagg's grin broadened and now he looked terrible indeed – he looked like a demon which might have climbed lately from some reeking pit in the earth. He raised the executioner's axe; drops of the slain warder's blood fell onto his face and ran down his cheeks like tears.

'*Here I come, dear Peter, to chop off your head!*' Flagg screamed and began to run up the stairs.

One. Three. Six. Ten.

Peter's shaking hands went wrong somehow. A knot he had made easily a thousand times before now fell apart and he had to start over again.

Don't let him scare you.

That was idiotic. He was scared, all right: scared green. Thomas would have been astounded to know that Peter had *always* been frightened of Flagg; Peter had just hid it better.

If he's going to kill you, make HIM *do it! Don't do it for him!*

The thought came from inside his own head . . . but it sounded like his mother's voice. Peter's hands steadied a bit, and he began to knot the end of his rope to his anchor again.

118

'**I**'ll *carry your head on my saddle horn for a thousand years!*' Flagg screamed. Up and up, around and around. '*Oh, what a pretty trophy you'll make!*'

Twenty. Thirty. Forty.

His boot heels struck green fire from the stones. His eyes glared. His grin was poison.

'*HERE I COME, PETER!*'

Seventy – two hundred and thirty steps to go.

119

'**I**f you have ever awakened in a strange place in the middle of the night, you'll know that just to be alone in the dark can be frightening enough;

now try to imagine waking in a secret passage, looking through concealed eyeholes into the room where you saw your own father murdered!

Thomas shrieked. No one heard him (unless the dogs below did, and I doubt that – they were old, deaf, and making too much noise themselves).

Now, there was an idea about sleepwalking in Delain – one that has also been commonly held as the truth in our world. This idea is that if a sleepwalker wakes up before returning to his or her bed, he or she will go mad.

Thomas might have heard this tale. If so, he could attest that it wasn't true at all. He'd had a bad scare, and he had screamed, but he did not come even *close* to going mad.

In fact, his initial fright passed rather quickly – more quickly than some of you might think – and he looked back into the peepholes again. This may strike some of you as strange, but you have to remember that, before the terrible night when Flagg had come with his own glass of wine after Peter left, Thomas had spent some pleasant times in this dark passageway. The pleasantness had a sour undertone of guilt, but he had also felt close to his father. Now, being back here, he felt a queer sense of nostalgia.

He saw that the room had hardly changed at all. The stuffed heads were still there – Bonsey the elk, Craker the lynx, Snapper the great white bear from the north. And, of course, Niner the dragon, which he now looked through, with Roland's bow and the arrow Foe-Hammer mounted above it.

Bonsey . . . Craker . . . Snapper . . . Niner.

I remember all their names, Thomas thought with

some wonder. And I remember you. Dad. I wish you were alive now and that Peter was free, even if it meant no one even knew I was alive. At least I could sleep at night.

Some of the furniture had been covered with white dust-sheets, but most had not. The fireplace was cold and dark, but a fire had been laid. Thomas saw with mounting wonder that even his father's old robe was still there, hung in its accustomed place on the hook by the bathroom door. The fireplace was cold, but it wanted only a match struck and held to the kindling to bring it alive, roaring and warm; the room wanted only his father to do the same for *it.*

Suddenly Thomas became aware of a strange, almost eerie desire in himself; he wanted to go into that room. He wanted to light the fire. He wanted to put on his father's robe. He wanted to drink a glass of his father's mead. He would drink it even if it had gone bad and bitter. He thought . . . he thought he might be able to sleep in there.

A wan, tired smile dawned on the boy's face, and he decided to do it. He wasn't even afraid of his father's ghost. He almost hoped it would come. If it did, he could tell his father something.

He could tell his father he was sorry.

120

'**C**OMING, *PETER!*' Flagg shrieked, grinning. He smelled like blood and doom; his eyes were deadly fire. The headsman's axe swished and whickered, and a last few drops of blood flew from the blade and splashed on the walls. 'COMING NOW! COMING FOR YOUR HEAD!'

Up and around, up and around, higher and higher. He was a devil with murder on his mind.

A hundred. A hundred and twenty-five.

'**E**aster,' Ben Staad panted to Dennis and Naomi. The temperature had begun to fall again, but all three of them were sweating. Some of the sweat came from exertion – they were working very hard. But much of their sweat had been caused by fear. They could hear Flagg shrieking. Even Frisky, with her brave heart, felt afraid. She had withdrawn a little and huddled on her haunches, whimpering.

'**C**OMING, YOU LITTLE WHELP!'

Closer now – his voice was flatter, with less echo.

'*COMING TO DO WHAT I SHOULD HAVE DONE A LONG TIME AGO!*'

The twin blades swished and whickered.

123

This time the knot held.

Gods help me, Peter thought, and looked back once more toward the sound of Flagg's rising, shrieking voice. *Gods help me now*.

Peter threw one leg out the window. Now he sat astride the sill as if it were Peony's saddle, one leg on the stone floor of his sitting room, the other dangling over the drop. He held the heap of his rope and the iron bar from his bed in his lap. He tossed the rope out the window, watching as it fell. It tangled and bound up halfway down, and he had to spend more time shaking the rope like a fishline before it would drop free again.

Then, uttering one final prayer, he grasped the iron bar and pulled it against the window. His rope hung down from the middle. Peter slipped the leg that was inside over the sill, twisted around at the waist, holding on to the bar for dear life. Now only his bottom was on the sill. He made a half-turn so that the cold outer edge of the sill was pressed against his belly instead of his butt. His legs hung down. The iron bar was seated firmly across the window.

Peter let go of it with his left hand and caught

hold of his narrow napkin rope. For a moment he paused, battling his fear.

Then he closed his eyes and let go of the bar with his right hand. His whole weight was on the rope now. He was committed. For better or worse, his life now depended on the napkins. Peter began to lower himself.

'**C**OMING –'

Two hundred.

'*FOR YOUR HEAD* —'

Two hundred and fifty.

'*MY DEAR PRINCE!*'

Two hundred and seventy-five.

'**B**en, Dennis, and Naomi could see Peter, a dark man-shape against the curved wall of the Needle, high above their heads – higher than even the bravest acrobat would dare to go.

'Faster,' Ben panted – almost moaned. 'For your lives . . . for *his* life!'

They went about emptying the cart even fas-
er . . . but in truth, all they could do was almost
lone.

Flagg raced up the stairs, his hood falling
back, his lank dark hair flying off his waxy brow.
Almost there now – almost there.

The wind was light now, but very cold.
It blew against Peter's bare cheeks and bare hands,
numbing them. Slowly, slowly, he descended, moving with careful deliberation. He knew that if he let
his descent get out of hand, he would fall. In front of
him, the great mortared stone blocks rolled steadily
upward – very soon he came to feel that he was
remaining still and it was the Needle itself which was
moving. His breath came in tight gasps. Cold dry
snow rattled on his face. The rope was thin – if his
hands grew much number, he wouldn't be able to
feel it at all.

How far had he come?

He didn't dare look down and see.

Above him, individual strands of thread, cun‑
ningly woven together as a woman might braid a
rug, had begun to pop threads. Peter did not know
this, which was probably just as well. The breaking
strain had nearly been reached.

128

'**F**aster, King Peter?' Dennis whispered.
The three of them had finished emptying the cart;
now they could only watch. Peter had descended
perhaps half of the distance.

'He's so high,' Naomi moaned. 'If he falls –'

'If he falls, he'll be killed,' Ben said with a flat
and toneless finality that silenced them all.

129

'**F**lagg reached the top of the stairs and ran
down the corridor, his chest heaving as he gasped for
breath. Sweat stood out all over his face. His grin
was huge, horrible.

He put his great axe down and pulled the first
of the three bolts on the door to Peter's quarters. He

ulled the second . . . and paused. It would not be
mart to simply go rushing in, oh no, not smart at
ll. The caged bird might be trying to fly the coop
ight this moment, but he might also be standing
o one side of the door, ready to brain Flagg with
omething the moment he rushed in.

When he opened the spyhole in the middle of
he door and saw the bar from Peter's bed placed
across the window, he understood everything and
roared with rage.

'*Not so easy as that, my young bird!*' howled Flagg.
'*Let's see how you fly with your rope cut, shall we?*'

Flagg yanked the third bolt and charged into
Peter's room with his axe held high over his head.
After one quick look out the window, his grin resur-
faced. He decided not to cut the rope after all.

·D·own and down Peter went. His arm
muscles trembled with exhaustion. His mouth was
dry; he couldn't remember ever wanting a drink as
badly as he did right now. It seemed that he had been
on this rope for a very, very long time, and a queer
certainty had stolen into his heart – he would never
get the drink of water he wanted. He was meant to
die after all, and that wasn't even the worst of it. He
was going to die thirsty. Right now *that* seemed the
worst of it.

He still did not dare look *down,* but he felt a queer compulsion – every bit as strong as his brother's compulsion to go into their father's sitting room – to look *up.* He obeyed it – and some two hundred feet above, he saw Flagg's white, murderous face grinning down at him.

'Hello, my little bird,' Flagg called down cheerfully. 'I've an axe, but I really don't think I'll need to use it after all. I've put it aside, see?' And the magician held out his bare hands.

All the strength was trying to run out of Peter's arms and hands – just the sight of Flagg's hateful face had done that. He concentrated on holding on. He couldn't feel the thin rope at all anymore – he knew he still had it because he could see it coming out of his fists, but that was all. His breath rasped in and out of his throat in hot gasps.

Now he looked down . . . and saw the white, upturned circles of three faces. Those circles were very, very small – he was not twenty feet above the frozen cobbles, or even forty feet; he was still a *hundred* feet up, as high as the fourth floor of one of our buildings.

He tried to move and found he could not – if he moved, he would fall. So he hung there against the side of the building. Cold, gritty snow blew in his face, and from the prison above, Flagg began to laugh.

131

Why doesn't he *move*?' Naomi cried, digging one mittened hand into Ben's shoulder. Her eyes were fixed on Peter's twisting form. The way he hung there, slowly turning, made it look dreadfully like the body of a man who had been hanged. 'What's *wrong* with him?'

'I don't –'

Above them, Flagg's chilly laughter abruptly stopped.

'Who goes there?' he called. His voice was like thunder, like doom. 'Answer me, if you want to keep your heads! *Who goes there?*'

Frisky whined and shrank against Naomi's side.

'Oh gods, now you've done it,' Dennis said. 'What do we do, Ben?'

'Wait,' Ben said grimly. 'And if the magician comes down, fight. We wait for what happens next. We –'

But that was all the waiting any of them had to do, for in the next few seconds, much – not all, but a great deal – was resolved.

132

Flagg had seen the thinness of Peter's rope, its whiteness – and in a trice he understood everything, from beginning to end – the napkins and the doll's house as well. Peter's means of escape had been under his nose the whole time, and he had very nearly missed it. But . . . he saw something else as well. Little pops of fibre where the strands were giving way, some fifteen feet down the taut length of rope.

Flagg could have turned the iron bar he was resting his hand on and sent Peter plummeting that way, with the anchor trailing after to perhaps bash his head in when he struck bottom. He could have swung the battle-axe and parted the fragile rope.

But he preferred to let matters take their course, and a moment after he had challenged the voices, matters *did* take their course.

The rope's breaking strain was reached. It parted with a twang like a lute string that has been wound too far on its peg.

'Goodbye, birdie,' Flagg cried happily, leaning far out to watch Peter's fall. He was laughing. 'Goodb–'

Then his voice ceased and his eyes widened as they had when he looked into the crystal and saw the tiny figure descending the side of the Needle. He opened his mouth and screamed with rage. That awful cry woke up more people in Delain than the fall of the Tower.

Peter heard that twanging sound, felt th
rope part.

Cold wind rushed up past his face. He tried t
steel himself for the crash, knowing it would come i
less than a second. The pain if he didn't die instantl
would be the worst.

And that was when Peter struck the thick, dee
drift of royal napkins which Frisky had hauled out o
the castle and across the Plaza in a stolen cart – th
royal napkins which Ben, Dennis, and Naomi ha
worked so feverishly to pile up. The size of that pil
– it looked like a whitewashed haystack – was neve
really known, because Ben, Dennis, and Naomi al
had different estimates on the subject. Perhap
Peter's own idea was the best, since he was the one
who fell squarely into the middle of it – he believe
that messy, lovely, lifesaving pile of napkins mus
have been at least twenty feet high, and for all I
know, he may have been right.

He fell squarely into the middle, as I have
said, making a crater. Then he fell over on his back
and lay still. Far above, Ben heard Flagg howl with

rage and he thought: *You don't need to do that, everything's going to be just fine for you, magician. He has died anyway, in spite of all we could do.*

Then Peter sat up. He looked dazed but very much alive. In spite of Flagg, in spite of the fact that there might be Guards of the Watch racing toward them at that moment, Ben Staad whooped. It was a sound of pure triumph. He grabbed Naomi and kissed her.

'*Hoorah!*' Dennis cried, grinning dizzily. '*Hoorah for the King!*'

Then Flagg screeched again far above them – the sound of a devil-bird cheated of its prey. The whooping, the kissing and the hoorahing all stopped right then.

'*You'll pay with your heads!*' Flagg shrieked. He was insane with rage. '*You'll pay with your heads, all of you! Guards of the Watch, to the Needle! To the Needle! The regicide has escaped! To the Needle! Kill the murdering prince! Kill his gang! Kill them all!*'

And in the castle that surrounded the Plaza of the Needle on all four sides, windows began to be lit . . . and from two sides came the sound of running feet and the clash of metal as swords were drawn.

'*Kill the prince!*' Flagg shrieked hellishly from the top of the Needle. '*Kill his gang! KILL THEM ALL!*'

Peter tried to get up, floundered, and fell over again. Part of his mind was crying out urgently that he *must* get on his feet, that they *must* be away or they would be killed . . . but another part insisted that he was already dead, or severely wounded, and all of this was only a dream of his perishing mind. He seemed to have landed in a bed of the very napkins which had occupied so much of his mind over the last five years . . . and how could that be anything *but* a dream?

Ben's strong hand gripped his upper arm, and he knew it was all real, all happening.

'Peter, are you all right? Are you really all right?'

'Not hurt a bit,' Peter said. 'We have to get away from here.'

'*My King!*' Dennis cried, falling on his knees before the dazed Peter and grinning the same dizzy, foolish grin. '*My oath of fealty forever! I swear my –*'

'Swear later!' Peter cried, laughing in spite of himself. As Ben had pulled him to his feet, so Peter now pulled Dennis to his. 'Let's get out of here!'

'Which gate?' Ben asked. He knew – as Peter did himself – that Flagg would already be on his way back down. 'They come from all sides, by the sound.'

In truth, Ben thought any direction would do for the battle which would surely come, and result in their eventual slaughter. But dazed or not, Peter knew perfectly well where he wanted to go.

'The West Gate,' he said, 'and quickly! *Run!*'

The four of them ran, Frisky at their heels.

135

Still fifty yards from the West Gate, Peter's band met a party of seven sleepy, confused guards. Most of them had sheltered from the storm n one of the warm Lower Kitchens of the castle, drinking mead and exclaiming to one another that they would have something to tell their grandchildren about. They did not know the half of what they would have to tell their grandchildren about, as it happened. Their 'leader' was a man-boy of just twenty, and only a goshawk . . . what we would call a corporal, I suppose. Still, he hadn't had anything to drink and was reasonably alert. And he was determined to do his duty.

'Halt in the name of the King!' he called out as Peter's group closed with his slightly larger one. He tried to thunder this command, but a storyteller should tell as much of the truth as he can, and I must tell you that the goshawk's voice was more squeak than thunder.

Peter was unarmed, of course, but Ben and Naomi both carried shortswords, and Dennis had his rusty dagger. All three of them at once pushed in front of Peter. Ben's and Naomi's hands went to their hilts. Dennis had already pulled his dagger.

'*Stop!*' Peter cried; his voice *was* thunder. 'You must not draw!'

Surprised – shocked, even – Ben threw a glance at Peter.

Peter stepped to the fore. He stood with his eyes flashing moonlight and his beard riffling in the light, chill-edged wind. He was dressed in the rough clothes of a prisoner, but his face was commanding and regal.

'Halt in the name of the King, you say,' Peter said. He stepped calmly toward the terrified goshawk until the two of them were almost chest to

chest – less than six inches separated them. The guard
fell back a step in spite of his own drawn sword and
the fact that Peter's hands were empty. 'And yet I tell
you, goshawk: *I am the King*.'

The guard licked his lips. He looked around at
his men.

'But . . .' he began. 'You . . .'

'What is your name?' Peter asked quietly.

The goshawk gaped. He could have run Peter
through in a second, but he only gaped helplessly,
like a fish drawn from water.

'Your name, goshawk?'

'My Lord . . . I mean . . . prisoner . . .
you . . . I . . .' The young soldier fumbled once
more and then said helplessly, 'My name is Galen.'

'And do you know who I am?'

'Yes,' one of the others growled. 'We know
you, *murderer*.'

'I did not murder my father,' Peter said quietly.
'It was the King's magician who did that. He is hot
behind us now, and I advise you – very strongly, I
advise you – to 'ware of him. Soon he will trouble
Delain no more; I promise this on my father's name.
But for now you must let me pass.'

There was a long moment of silence. Galen held
his sword up again as if to run Peter through. Peter did
not flinch. He owed the gods a death; it was a debt he
had owed ever since he had come a shrieking, naked
baby from his mother's belly. It was a debt every man
and woman in creation owed. If he was to pay that
debt now, let it be so . . . but he was the rightful King,
not a rebel, not a usurper, and he would not run, or
stand aside, or let his friends hurt this lad.

The sword wavered. Then Galen let it fall until the tip of the blade touched the frozen cobbles.

'Let 'em pass,' he muttered. 'Mayhap he murdered, mayhap he didn't – all I know is that it's royal muck and I'll not step into it, lest I drown in a quicksand of Kings and princes.'

'You had a wise mother, goshawk,' Ben Staad said grimly.

'Yes, let 'im pass,' a second voice said unexpectedly. 'By gods, I'll not strike my blade at such – from the look of 'im, it would burn off my hand when it went in.'

'You will be remembered,' Peter said. He looked around at his friends. 'Follow me now,' he said 'and be quick. I know what I must have, and I know where to get it.'

At that moment Flagg burst from the base of the Needle, and such a howl of rage and fury rose in the night that the young guards quailed before it. They backed up, turned, and ran, scattering to the four pegs of the compass.

'Come on,' Peter said. 'Follow me. The West Gate!'

136

Flagg ran as he had never run before. He sensed the oncoming ruin of all his plans now, at what was practically the last moment. It must not happen! And he knew as well as Peter where all of this must end.

He passed the cowering guards without looking around. They sighed with relief, thinking he must not have seen them . . . but Flagg did. He saw them all, and marked each; after Peter died, their heads would decorate the tower walls for a year and a day, he thought. As for the brat in charge of their patrol – he would die a thousand deaths in the dungeon first.

He ran under the arch of the West Gate, and down the Main Western Gallery into the castle itself. Sleepy folk, who had come out in their nightclothes to see what all this row was about, cowered before his whitely burning face and fell aside, forking their first and last fingers at him to ward off evil . . . for now Flagg looked like what Flagg really was; a demon. He vaulted over the banister of the first staircase he came to, landed on his feet (the iron on his heels flashed green fire like the eyes of lynxes), and ran on.

On toward Roland's apartments.

137

'The locket,' Peter panted to Dennis as they ran. 'Do you still have the locket I threw down?'

Dennis clutched at his throat, and found the golden heart – Peter's own blood dried on the tip – and nodded.

'Give it to me.'

Dennis passed it to him as they ran. Peter did not put the chain over his neck, but looped it in his fist so that the heart bounced and spun as he ran, flashing red-gold in the light of the wall sconces.

'Soon, my friends,' Peter panted.

They turned a corner. Ahead Peter saw the door to his father's apartments. It was here that he had last seen Roland. He had been a King, responsible for the lives and welfare of thousands; he had also been an old man grateful for a warming glass of wine and a few minutes of talk with his son. It was here that it would end.

Once upon a time, his father had slain a dragon with an arrow called Foe-Hammer.

Now, Peter thought, as blood pounded in his temples and his heart raced hotly in his chest, *I must try to slay another dragon – a much greater one – with that same arrow*.

138

Thomas lit the fire, donned his dead father's robe, and drew Roland's chair close to the hearth. He felt that he would soon fall soundly asleep, and that was very good. But as he sat there, owlishly nodding, looking around at the trophies mounted on the walls with their glassy eyes sparkling eerily in the flames, it occurred to him that he wanted two more things – things that were almost sacred, things he would certainly never have dared touch when his father was alive. But Roland was dead, so Thomas had taken another chair to stand on, and from the wall he had taken down his father's bow and his father's great arrow, Foe-Hammer, from their places on the wall above Niner's head. For a moment he stared directly into one of the dragon's green-amber eyes. He had seen much through those eyes, but now, looking into them, he saw nothing but his own pallid face, like the face of a prisoner looking out of a cell.

Although everything in the room had been numbingly cold (the fire would warm things up, at least around the fireplace, but it would take a while), he thought that the arrow was strangely warm. He vaguely remembered an old tale he had heard as a small child – according to this tale, a weapon used to slay a dragon never lost the dragon's heat. *It seems that tale was true*, Thomas thought sleepily. But there was nothing scary about the arrow's heat; in fact, it seemed comforting. Thomas sat down with the bow clutched loosely in one hand and Foe-Hammer with its strange, sleeping warmth clutched in the other, never realizing that his brother was now coming in search of this very weapon, and that Flagg – the author of his birth and the Chief Warder of his life – was hot on Peter's heels.

139

Thomas hadn't stopped to consider what he would do if the door to his father's rooms had been locked, and Peter never did, either – in the old days it never had been, and as things turned out, the door wasn't locked now.

Peter had to do no more than lift the latch. He burst in, the others hot on his heels. Frisky was barking wildly, all of her fur standing on end. Frisky understood the true nature of things better, I'll warrant. Something was coming, something with a black scent like the poison fumes that sometimes killed the coal miners of the Eastern Barony when their tunnels went too deep. Frisky would fight the owner of that scent if she had to; fight and even die. But if she could have spoken, Frisky would have told them that the black scent approaching them from behind did not belong to a man; it was a monster chasing them, some horrible It.

'Peter, what –' Ben began, but Peter ignored him. He knew what he must have. He rushed across the room on his exhausted, trembling legs, looked up at the head of Niner, and reached for the bow and the arrow that had always hung above that head. Then his hand faltered.

Both were gone.

Dennis, the last one in, had closed the door behind him and shot the bolt. Now a single great blow fell on that door. The stout hardwood panels, reinforced with bands of iron, boomed.

Peter looked over his shoulder, eyes widening. Dennis and Naomi cringed backward. Frisky stood before her mistress snarling. Her grey-green eyes showed the whites all around.

'*Let me pass!*' Flagg roared. '*Let me pass the door!*'

'Peter!' Ben shouted, and drew his sword.

'*Stand away!*' Peter shouted back. '*If you value your lives stand away! All of you, stand away!*'

They scattered back just as Flagg's fist, now glowing with blue fire, slammed down against the door again. Hinges, bolt, and iron bands all burst at the same time with the noise of an exploding cannon. Blue fire spoked through the cracks between the boards in narrow rays. Then the stout planks burst apart. Shattered chunks of wood flew in a spray. The ragged remains of the door stood for a moment longer and then fell inward with a handclap sound.

Flagg stood in the corridor, his hood fallen back. His face was waxen white. His lips were strips of liver drawn back to show his teeth. His eyes flared with furnace fire.

In his hand he grasped his heavy executioner's axe.

He stood there a moment longer and then stepped inside. He looked left and saw Dennis. He looked right, and saw Ben and Naomi, with Frisky hunched, snarling, at her feet. His eyes marked them . . . catalogued them for future reference . . . and dismissed them. He strode through the remains of the door, now looking only at Peter.

'You fell but you did not die,' he said. 'You may think your God was kind. But I tell you, my own gods were saving you for me. Pray to your God now that your heart should burst apart in your chest. Fall on your knees and pray for that, because I tell you that *my* death will be much worse than any you can imagine.'

Peter stood where he was, between Flagg and his father's chair, where Thomas sat, as yet unseen by all the others. Peter met Flagg's infernal gaze, unafraid. For a moment Flagg seemed to flinch under that firm gaze, and then his unhuman grin blazed forth.

'You and your friends have cause me great trouble, my prince,' Flagg whispered. '*Great* trouble. I should have ended your miserable life long ago. But now all troubles will end.'

'I know you,' Peter replied. Although he was unarmed, his voice was steady and unafraid. 'I think my father knew you, too, although he was weak. Now I assume my kingship, *and I command you, demon!*'

Peter drew himself up to his full height. The flames in the fireplace reflected from his eyes, making them blaze. In that moment, Peter was every inch Delain's King.

'*Get you gone from here. Leave Delain behind, now and forever. You are cast out. GET YOU GONE!*'

Peter thundered this last in a voice which was greater than his own; he thundered in a voice that was *many* voices – all the Kings and Queens there had ever been in Delain, stretching back to the time when the castle had been little more than a collection of mud huts and people had drawn together in terror around their fires during the darks of winter as the wolves howled and the trolls gobbled and screamed in the Great Forests of Yestertime.

Flagg seemed to flinch again . . . almost to

cringe. Then he came forward – slowly, very slowly. His huge axe swung in his left hand.

'You may command in the next world,' he whispered. 'By escaping, you've played into my hands. If I'd thought of it – and in time I should have – I would have engineered a trumped-up escape myself! Oh, Peter, your head will roll into the fire and you'll smell your hair burning before your brain knows you're dead. You'll burn as your father burned . . . and they'll give me a *medal* for it in the Plaza! For did you not murder your own father for the crown?'

'*You* murdered him,' Peter said.

Flagg laughed. 'I? *I?* You've gone insane in the Needle, my boy.' Flagg sobered. His eyes glittered. 'But suppose – just for an instant – suppose I did? Who would believe it?'

Peter still held the chain of the locket looped over his right hand. Now he held that hand out and the locket hung below it, swinging hypnotically, raying flashes of ruddy light on the wall. At the sight of it, Flagg's eyes widened and Peter thought: *He recognizes it! By all the Gods, he recognizes it!*

'You killed my father, and it wasn't the first time you'd arranged things in the same way. You had forgotten, hadn't you? I see it in your eyes. When Leven Valera stood in your way during the evil days of Alan II, his wife was found poisoned. Circumstances made Valera's guilt seem without question . . . as they made *my* guilt seem without question.'

'Where did you find that, you little *bastard?*' Flagg whispered, and Naomi gasped.

'Yes, you forgot,' Peter repeated. 'I think that, sooner or later, things like you always begin to repeat themselves, because things like you know only a very few simple tricks. After a while, someone always sees through them. I think that is all that saves us, ever.'

The locket hung and swung in the firelight.

'Who would care now?' Peter asked. 'Who would believe? Many. If they believed nothing else, they would believe you are as old as their hearts tell them you are, monster.'

'Give it to me!'

'You killed Eleanor Valera, and you killed my father.'

'Yes, I brought him the wine,' Flagg said, his eyes blazing, 'and I *laughed* when his guts burned, and I laughed harder when you were taken up the stairs to the top of the Needle. But those who hear me say so in this room will all soon be dead, and no one saw me bring wine to these rooms! They only saw you?'

And then, from behind Peter, a new voice spoke. It was not strong, that voice; it was so low it could scarcely be heard, and it trembled. But it struck all of them – Flagg included – dumb with wonder.

'There was one other who saw,' Peter's brother, Thomas, said from the shadowed depths of his father's chair. '*I* saw you, magician.'

140

Peter drew aside and made a half-turn, the hand with the locket hanging from it still outstretched.

Thomas! he tried to say, but he could not speak, so struck was he by wonder and horror at the changes in his brother. He had grown fat and somehow old. He had always looked more like Roland than Peter had, and now the resemblance was so great it was eerie.

Thomas! he tried to say again, and realized why the bow and arrow were no longer in their places above the head of Niner. The bow was in Thomas's lap, and the arrow was nocked in the gut string.

It was then that Flagg shrieked and threw himself forward, raising the great executioner's axe over his head.

141

It was not a shriek of rage but of terror. Flagg's white face was drawn; his hair stood on end. His mouth trembled loosely. Peter had been surprised by the resemblance but knew his brother; Flagg was fooled completely by the flickering fire and the deep shadows cast by the wings of the chair in which Thomas sat.

He forgot Peter. It was the figure in the chair he charged with the axe. He had killed the old man once by poison, and yet here he was again, sitting in his smelly mead-soaked robe, sitting with his bow and arrow in his hands, looking at Flagg with haggard, accusing eyes.

'*Ghost!*' Flagg shrieked. '*Ghost or demon from hell, I care not! I killed you once! I can kill you again! Aiiiiyyyyyyyyyeeeeee—!*'

Thomas had always excelled at archery. Although he rarely hunted, he had gone often to the archery ranges during the years of Peter's imprisonment, and, drunk or sober, he had his father's eye. He had a fine yew bow, but he had never drawn one like this. It was light and limber, and yet he felt an amazing strength in its lancewood bolt. It was a huge but graceful weapon, eight feet from end to end, and he did not have room to draw fully while sitting down; yet he pulled its ninety-pound draw with no strain at all.

Foe-Hammer was perhaps the greatest arrow ever made, its bolt of sandalwood, its three feathers honed from the wing of an Anduan peregrine, its tip of flashed steel. It grew hot at the draw; he felt its heat bake his face like an open furnace.

'You told me only lies, magician,' Thomas said softly. He released.

The arrow flew from the bow. As it crossed the room, it passed directly through the centre of Leven Valera's locket, which still dangled from the stunned

Peter's outstretched fist. The gold chain parted with a tiny *chink!* sound.

As I have told you, ever since that night in the north forests when he and the troop he had commanded had camped following their fruitless expedition in search of the exiles, Flagg had been plagued by a dream he couldn't remember. He always awoke from it with his hand pressed to his left eye, as if he had been wounded there. The eye would burn for minutes after he awoke, although he could find nothing wrong with it.

Now the arrow of Roland, bearing the heart-shaped locket of Valera on its tip, flew across Roland's sitting room and plunged into that eye.

Flagg screamed. The two-bladed axe dropped from his hands, and the haft of that blood-soaked weapon shattered apart once and for all when it struck the floor. He staggered backward, one eye glaring at Thomas. The other had been replaced by a golden heart with Peter's blood drying at the tip. From around the edges of that heart, some stinking black fluid – it was most assuredly not blood – dribbled out.

Flagg shrieked again, dropped to his knees –

– and suddenly he was gone.

Peter's eyes widened. Ben Staad cried out. For a moment Flagg's clothes held his shape; for a moment the arrow hung in empty air with the pierced heart dangling from it. Then the clothes crumpled and Foe-Hammer clattered to the cobbles. Its steel tip was smoking. So it had smoked, long ago, when Roland pulled it from the dragon's throat. The heart glowed a dull red for a moment, and forever after its shape was branded into the stones where it fell when the magician disappeared.

Peter turned to his brother.

Thomas's unearthly calm broke apart. No longer did he look like Roland: he looked like a scared and horribly tired little boy.

'Peter, I'm sorry,' he said, and he began to cry. 'I am sorrier than you will ever know. You'll kill me now, I guess, and I deserve to be killed – yes, I know I do – but before you do, I'll tell you something: I've paid. Yes, I have. Paid and paid and paid. Now kill me, if such is your pleasure.'

Thomas raised his throat and closed his eyes. Peter walked toward him. The others held their breaths, their eyes wide and round.

Gently, then, Peter pulled his brother from his father's chair and embraced him.

Peter held his brother until the storm of his weeping had passed, and told him that he loved him and would always love him; then both wept, there below the dragon's head with their father's bow at their feet; and at some point, the others stole from the room and left the two brothers alone.

142

'**D**id they all live happily ever after?

They did not. No one ever does, in spite of what the stories may say. They had their good days, as you do, and they had their bad days, and you know about those. They had their victories, as you do, and they had their defeats, and you know about those, too. There were times when they felt ashamed of themselves, knowing that they had not done their best, and there were times when they knew they had stood where God had meant them to stand. All I'm trying to say is that they lived as well as they could, each and every one of them; some lived longer than others, but all lived well, and bravely, and I love them all, and am not ashamed of my love.

Thomas and Peter went to Delain's new Judge-General together, and Peter was taken back into custody. His second stint as a prisoner of the Kingdom was much shorter than the first – only two hours. It took Thomas fifteen minutes to tell his tale, and the Judge-General, who had been appointed with Flagg's approval and who was a timid little creature, took another hour and three-quarters to verify that the terrible magician was really gone.

Then all charges were overturned.

That evening all of them – Peter, Thomas, Ben, Naomi, Dennis, and even Frisky – met in Peter's old rooms. Peter poured wine all around, even giving Frisky some in a little dish. Only Thomas declined the vintage.

Peter wanted Thomas to stay with him, but Thomas insisted – rightly, I think – that if he stayed, the citizens would tear him apart for what he had allowed to happen.

'You were only a child,' Peter said, 'controlled by a powerful creature who terrified you.'

With a sad grin, Thomas replied: 'That is partly

true, but people would not remember that, Pete. They'd remember Tommy Tax-Bringer, and come for me. They'd tear through stone to get to me, I think. Flagg's gone, but I'm here. My head is a silly thing, but I've decided I'd like to keep it on my shoulders a while longer.' He paused, seemed to debate, and then went on. 'And I'm best away. My hate and jealousy were like a fever. It's now gone, but after a few years of being in your shadow as you ruled, I might relapse. I've come to know myself a little bit, you see. Yes – a little bit. No; I must leave, Peter, and tonight. The sooner the better.'

'But . . . where will you go?'

'On a quest,' Thomas said simply. 'To the south, I think. You may see me again, but you may not. I'll go south on a quest . . . I have many things on my conscience, and much to atone for.'

'What quest?' Ben asked.

'To find Flagg,' Thomas replied. 'He's out there, somewhere. In this world or in some other, he's out there. I know it; I feel his poison in the wind. He got away from us at the last second. You all know it, and I do, too. I would find him and kill him. I would avenge our father and make up for my own great sin. And I would go into the south first, for I sense him there.'

Peter said, 'But who'll go with you? I can't – there's too much to do here. But I won't just allow you to go alone!' He looked very concerned, and if you had seen a map of those days, you would have understood his expression, for the south was nothing but a great white space on the maps.

Surprising all of them, Dennis said: 'I would go, my Lord King.'

Both brothers looked toward him, surprised. Ben and Naomi also turned, and Frisky looked up from her wine, which she was lapping with cheerful enthusiasm (she liked the smell, which was a cool, velvety purple; not as good as the taste, but almost).

Dennis blushed mightily, but he didn't sit down.

'You were always a good master, Thomas, and – beggin' your pardon, King Peter – something inside me says you're my master still. And since I was the one to find that mouse and send you to the Needle, my King –'

'Bosh!' Peter said. 'That's all forgotten.'

'Not by me, it ain't,' Dennis said stubbornly. 'You could say I was too young, too, and didn't know no better, but maybe I've my own mistakes to atone for.'

He looked at Thomas, shyly.

'I would come with you, Lord Thomas, if you would have me; I would be at your side in your quest.'

On the verge of tears, Thomas said: 'I will have you and welcome, good old Dennis. I only hope you can cook better than I can.'

They left that very night, under cover of darkness – two figures on foot, their packs heavy with supplies, wending their way into the night. They looked back once and waved.

All three of them waved back. Peter was weeping as if his heart would break; indeed, he thought it might.

I'll never see him again, Peter thought.

Ah, well – perhaps he did, and perhaps he didn't; but I rather think he did, you know. All I can tell you is that Ben and Naomi were eventually married, that Peter ruled long and well, and that Thomas and Dennis had many strange adventures, and that they did see Flagg again, and confronted him.

But now the hour is late, and all of that is another tale, for another day.

FIRESTARTER

Stephen King

From the author of THE SHINING, CARRIE and THE DEAD ZONE, Stephen King's most mesmerizing and menacing novel yet . . .

The story of a sinister government agency, a fateful drug experiment, and a pigtailed girl named Charlie, who has an unimaginably terrifying gift.

'Stephen King's finest novel yet . . . the most tightly plotted of King's chillers, it is also the most terrifying.'
Cosmopolitan

'Goes beyond the frightening'
Publishers Weekly

'King does this better than anyone else. We finished the book about three non-stop hours after we picked it up'
Playboy

FICTION
0 7515 0439 4

THE DEAD ZONE

Stephen King

Awake in the dead zone and awake ... into a nightmare.

Recoil in horror as you are touched by a young man cursed with the power to perceive the evil in men's souls. And whose ability to see into the future forces him into a terrifying confrontation with a charismatic, power-hungry and infinitely dangerous man.

'Ominous and nerve-wracking'
New York Times

'Read this stunning novel and you will feel the hairs on the nape of your neck rise'
Time Out

'One of the most topical and suspenseful thrillers of the year'
John Barkham Reviews

'Truly frightening ... will scare you witless'
Cosmopolitan

Stephen King is the master of the psychic suspense novel. With THE DEAD ZONE he has surpassed himself.

FICTION
0 7515 0432 7

DIFFERENT SEASONS

Stephen King

Four spine-chilling stories from the grand master of the supernatural, stories with an interlacing of horror that capture the ever-growing dark corners of our century.

RITA HAYWORTH AND SHAWSHANK REDEMPTION: a compulsive and bizarre story of unjust imprisonment and escape.

APT PUPIL: a golden schoolboy and an old man with a hideous past join in a dreadful union.

THE BODY: four young boys journey into the woods and find life, death and the end of innocence.

THE BREATHING METHOD: a macabre story told in a strange club of a woman determined to give birth – no matter what.

'A dazzling display'
Time

'Some of his best work'
Publishers Weekly

'Each is vintage King, that is to say, storytelling of a high order'
John Barkham Reviews

FICTION
0 7515 0433 5

☐	Firestarter	Stephen King	£5.9
☐	The Dead Zone	Stephen King	£6.9
☐	Different Seasons	Stephen King	£6.9
☐	Danse Macabre	Stephen King	£5.9
☐	Skeleton Crew	Stephen King	£6.9
☐	Cujo	Stephen King	£4.9

Warner Books now offers an exciting range of quality titles by both established and new authors. All of the books in this series are available from:

Little, Brown and Company (UK),
P.O. Box 11,
Falmouth,
Cornwall TR10 9EN.

Fax No: 01326 317444.
Telephone No: 01326 317200
E-mail: books@barni.avel.co.uk

Payments can be made as follows: cheque, postal order (payable to Little, Brown and Company) or by credit cards, Visa/Access. Do not send cash or currency. UK customers and B.F.P.O. please allow £1.00 for postage and packing for the first book, plus 50p for the second book, plus 30p for each additional book up to a maximum charge of £3.00 (7 books plus).

Overseas customers including Ireland, please allow £2.00 for the first book plus £1.00 for the second book, plus 50p for each additional book.

NAME (Block Letters) ....

....

ADDRESS ....

....

....

☐ I enclose my remittance for ....

☐ I wish to pay by Access/Visa Card

Number ☐☐☐☐☐☐☐☐☐☐☐☐☐☐☐☐☐

Card Expiry Date ☐☐☐☐